The Celibate Mouse

by Diana Hockley

The Celibate Mouse
Published by
Diana Hockley 2011
www.dianahockley.webs.com

Book layout and cover design
by Publicious Pty Ltd
www.publicious.com.au

Printed in Australia by
SOS Print+Media
www.sos.com.au

International printing by
Lightning Source
www.lightningsource.com

ISBN: 978-0-9870612-9-4

All characters and events in this publication are fictitious, any resemblance to real persons, living or dead, or any events past or present are purely coincidental.

For Lara, my daughter, of whom I am very proud.

Also by Diana Hockley

The Naked Room

ACKNOWLEDGEMENTS

The Celibate Mouse has been a product in the making since 2008. During that time I have had the help, support and encouragement of many people on the Next Big Writer, worldwide workshop site extraordinaire. There are so many to thank on there and here are the main suspects!

Many hugs for my long-suffering husband, Andrew, for his patience and perseverance in coping while I am in a daze.

My gratitude to my writing friends and colleagues for all your assistance in getting this novel off the drawing board: Joy Campbell, Jessica Chambers, Caroline Kellems, Wayne Zurl, sonny, kyla, Verity Farrell, Nathan B Childs, R M Keegan, Carolyn Kuczek, Susan Ethridge, Susan Stec, Isobel IV, James, Sue (slho906), Jeni Decker, Sibyl Nelson, Skeptikoi, Stefanie Dubois, Greg Crites, glenmore, eskay, Sean Walsh, Kydd Dustin, C L Withers, Tina Hayes, Jeanne Bannon, Caminara, Ceridwen, Keith Campell, Ann Elle Altman. Thank you to my mate, Pam, for your support and encouragement on the many occasions when I was a wreck and ready to hit the bottle, and to Margaret, who encouraged me and stored many CDs of this novel when I was paranoid about losing the original manuscript to fire, floods and aliens.

A special thank you and hugs to Melanie Mather, who was so patient and kind when I rang or emailed begging hysterically for police procedural information, and to Rachel Kriel for her nursing advice on the art of murdering.

To Andy from Publicious, thank you for your patience and as a fellow author, your understanding of paranoia!

Contents

Control was everything.

CHAPTER 1

A Little Unpleasantness at the Sheepdog Trials

Susan

Saturday: noon.

There is no mistaking the crack of a high-powered rifle. Jack Harlow, competitor in the sheepdog championship, was shot in front of an audience of twenty-five hundred people, two judges, three sheep and his border collie, Stephen. He went down like a pole-axed steer, slamming into the gate at the last holding pen, a moment frozen in time before pandemonium erupted. The sheep, seizing the opportunity to escape, leaped over the dog and took to their trotters.

Perspiration prickled up my spine and then spread over my body. My daughter, Marli, buried her face in the front of my sweater.

At first, people believed that a vehicle had back-fired behind the grandstand. Rumours circled the arena at lightning speed. A wave of conflicting information, punctuated by cries of disbelief, spread around the grandstand. A young woman seated a couple of levels below shouted, 'I thought he had a heart attack, but someone said Jack's been shot!'

The people in our immediate vicinity, gasped. White-faced, Marli pulled away and wiped her eyes. 'Aren't you going to go down there, mum?'

'Certainly not! I'm on stress leave, remember? The local police will handle it.' *I can't cope with this, it's too soon.* Officiating over another crime scene, even temporarily, would shatter my hard won fragile composure.

The overcast, sullen day got worse. A woman whom I later discovered to be Harlow's wife, Penelope, was walking back from the food kiosk when a group of agitated people encircled her. A moment later she dropped her takeaway meal and attempted to scramble, screaming, over the fence into the arena. She got stuck. Bystanders pushed and pulled until she landed in a heap on the other side. Clouds of dust rose as she got to her feet and staggered across the grass to be met by a flustered official waving a clipboard. The mob of people around the victim parted for a moment and I glimpsed someone folding a coat to put under Harlow's head. *No, you mustn't do that!*

As Jack Harlow's dog was hauled away from his inert body, its heartrending howls reached the stand. Distressed, I fumbled for a tissue. A man jumped the fence, rushed over, picked the animal up and headed for the exit gate. A judge removed the coat from under the victim's head and commenced CPR. People sat, white-faced with shock. Denial seemed to be the initial reaction; fear had yet to set in. 'Did you hear that, Fran? Who on earth would want to shoot Jack?' called a woman sitting on the seat below us.

'Half the fucking town, I'd say,' a man sitting nearby muttered. Sniggers of agreement rippled through the surrounding spectators.

Shocked by their callous response, I watched as the

woman named Fran glanced around the stand, presumably hoping to pass on the information to anyone who might be appreciative. We made eye contact. She hesitated a moment, and then asked, 'Do *you* know the Harlows?'

'No, we're visitors here.' I took a couple of deep breaths to quell an imminent threat of nausea. Disappointed, the woman turned away to join a nearby huddle of frightened onlookers.

The action in the ring stepped up as someone with common sense began to manage the situation. The mob of people around the victim parted; a coat was placed over Harlow's head. His widow flapped around in the centre of the group, while a woman tried to comfort her. Men circled, staring at the ground, speaking into mobile phones. An official from the sheepdog association organised another dog to round up the three sheep cavorting across the trial bridge.

'How they're going to get this lot organised I don't know, but I'm damned sure not going to be amongst them,' I muttered, watching the children caught up in the drama. Several small boys had taken advantage of the lull in proceedings to kick a soccer ball back and forth on the far side of the arena. A patch of sunlight suddenly pierced the clouds, lighting the scene in the centre of the arena like a surreal theatrical production.

When the report and inevitable phone video footage aired on the early evening television newscast, many would kick themselves for not making an effort to attend. The final of the championship sheep dog trials had never been so exciting.

I cast my eyes around the surrounding area. The victim had dropped like a stone, so it had been most likely a direct hit to the head or heart. He'd fallen to his right, so the shooter needed to be somewhere in the vicinity of the announcer's box to my right. The tower at the side of the arena, about five metres high, looked like an excellent place to pick off a target, but was a risky proposition which would take a lot of nerve. Heads bobbed inside the box, as I weighed up the likelihood of it being the source of the shot. A man leaned out of the window and shouted to someone on the ground. *Not up there, unless it is a conspiracy.*

Unlikely. Cars lined the fence on both sides of the pillars which supported the small announcer's box. The sniper could have fired from inside one, or crouched between the cars. Maybe from the hillside behind the arena? No, too exposed. A long distance shot would require a telescopic sight which could reflect the light and draw attention. He or she was long gone, unless the rifle had been hidden while the perpetrator mingled with the crowds.

My police training warred with an overpowering urge to escape, to avoid any involvement. Private fear won hands down, coupled with the necessity to keep seventeen year-old Marli from experiencing the aftermath of violent death. A vivid memory of scolding a woman for fleeing the scene of a gruesome crime sprang to mind. 'If you ever get to walk in my shoes, officer, then you'll understand how I feel,' the woman had retorted. Now I, a Detective Senior Sergeant, recently Acting Inspector, was intent on emulating her. It was not an auspicious start to our stay in the country.

We arrived before lunch, to house-sit for my sister-in-law and her husband while they were in the UK on urgent family business. My other daughter, Marli's identical twin Brittany, had chosen to live in Sydney with their stepfather, Harry, and his new partner. In an effort to assuage my daughter's loneliness, I allowed Marli to buy a puppy from a breeder of border collies. We called at the local showground to collect it, but the woman was competing in the trials, so we found seats in the grandstand to watch the competition until she was ready to meet us.

Never having attended a sheepdog trial I was interested, but confused about what the competition involved. The farmer sitting beside us, leaning closer than strictly necessary, explained the procedure sotto voce, like a commentator at a billiards tournament. 'The man and dog are a partnership, see? They have to drive three sheep through the gates, over the bridge, then into that pen.' He pointed to the one near the exit to the arena and then continued. 'They have fifteen minutes to do it before the hooter sounds. The handler has to keep walking between the points without stopping or backtracking. He can signal or whistle the dog, but nothing else. We can't clap until he's closed the gate at the last pen, otherwise the sheep'll most likely take off and they could lose points.'

The canine half of the team cast a swathe around three recalcitrant sheep on the far side of the arena and turned them toward the next obstacle, whereupon they bolted in different directions. Undaunted, the dog streaked, a black wraith, around the arena and gathered them together again. Amid much stamping of feet and defiant glares, the sheep were herded into the last pen, whereupon the dramatic conclusion to the life of Jack Harlow had taken place.

The championship competition having been destroyed beyond repair, the farmer abandoned us with a regretful glance accompanied by a muttered apology, to join an agitated group in the stands below. Ashen-faced, Marli sat still, hands tightly clasped around the neck of the tote bag which carried everything she considered necessities of life.

'Come on, Marli, it's time we left.' Once we collected and paid for the pup, I intended to leave the area immediately and go to the farm where we were to house-sit, five minutes outside Emsberg.

Trying to hurry my daughter along, I grabbed the tote bag, stuffed Marli's iPod and hat inside and thrust it back into her hands. A police uniform moved into the centre of the crowd around the victim as we started down the steps to the exit gate. Almost immediately, an announcement came over the loud speaker ordering everyone to remain on the grounds until further notice. Some of the crowd moaned collectively but others, terrified, clutched their friends and neighbours. Protests flared, as people tried to control fractious children. Nearby, a newborn baby bawled and what appeared to be its toddler sibling set up a sympathetic wailing. A tired-looking young woman grabbed the child by the arm and jounced the pushchair down the steps making the baby screech even louder as they left the stands. A man rounded up the young soccer players on the other side of the showground, his body language indicating he was sending them back to their parents.

A man cupped his hands around his mouth and roared displeasure at having his family trapped at the grounds. A couple of small girls, giggling hysterically, jostled through the crowd, almost knocking Marli off her feet. I sensed tension rising; soon there could be a stampede for the exit. Unable to censure them without revealing myself as the "police," I ducked my head and pushed through the crowd, towing Marli behind, hoping any observers would think we were heading for the restrooms.

Within a couple of minutes we arrived at the back of the grandstand in the competitor's camping area, where I propped myself against a fence post and waited for Marli to locate the breeder. Happy, hairy faces beamed at me from behind mesh dog boxes; tails swished enthusiastically. Resisting the impulse to "sweet-talk" to the fur-faces, I hoped the promise of five hundred dollars would outweigh the woman's curiosity about what had occurred in the arena and she would wait for her young customer. James Kirkbridge, my brother-in-law, had already taken our dogs to a neighbouring property, before he and his wife, Eloise, had flown from Brisbane to the UK due back in a few months. The animals would be delivered to the farm later this afternoon.

The sun vanished behind the clouds again, as though to underscore the day's disaster. A chill wind rose, seemingly from nowhere. I was struggling into my coat when Marli arrived back at the car, clutching a curly-coated, squirming black and white bundle with beguiling blue eyes. Colour blossomed in her cheeks again as she smiled and nuzzled the pup, thoughts of the tragedy in the ring briefly forgotten in the excitement of the moment.

I paused, battling a modicum of guilt and indecision about leaving the grounds. 'Marli, I need to check out what's going on. Don't worry, I promise to be right back.'

'Mum, for God's sake, I'm seventeen, not seven! I'll be here, okay?'

I eyed my daughter's stormy expression and hastened to ward off a "teenage moment. 'I'm sorry, I didn't mean to treat you like a child.'

Marli shrugged, giving off an air of nonchalance,

though the expression in her eyes retained the shock of what she had witnessed. I left her struggling to hold the over-excited pup and walked to the corner of the grandstand to peer at the action.

The centre of the ring resembled a kicked ant heap, as agitated officials and competitors buzzed around bumping into each other. High-pitched screams, like the squeaks of a mouse, came from inside the melee. Any decision I might make to get involved after all, became irrelevant when an ambulance trundled through a side gate onto the grounds, closely followed by a red and white checked patrol car. A movement on the town side of the grounds revealed the arrival of a media van. Fear shot through me. The last thing I needed was anyone from the press to spot *me*. I slunk back to Marli.

'Come on, let's get out of here!' Doubling back, and then dodging behind trees and advertising hoardings as we passed gaps in the buildings ensured no one saw us, as did the circuitous route through the competitor's caravans and motor homes which enabled us to reach the car park without being prevented from leaving.

If I lost my hard-won control, my stress leave would be blown before it had even begun and the counselling I received after Detective Constable Danny Grey's death barely two months ago, would be all for nothing.

CHAPTER 2

A Whisper of Murder

Susan

Saturday: 12.30pm.

The mud-map which my sister-in-law had drawn was scanty to say the least. We called at the town Information Centre, after the episode at the showgrounds. Marli's puppy bounced at the car window, yapping his abandonment as we walked into the Centre, where the duty attendant was talking on the phone, her voice shrill with excitement. The town grapevine was already being enthusiastically harvested with news of the shooting. Reluctantly she said goodbye and tendered directions to the Kirkbridge farm, which was about ten minutes away. Before I could thank her, the phone rang again.

The small building housing a single toilet, situated at the far end of the crowded car park, was occupied. We waited patiently for several minutes when a thud came from inside, sounding like a sack of wet sand landing on cement. We glanced at each other apprehensively. I knelt on the concrete slab and peered under the door. The bejewelled feminine hand lolling on the concrete was attached a froth of material, encasing what was undoubtedly a body. *Not again.*

As my eyes adjusted to the dark inside the cubicle, an open-mouthed, ashen face emerged from the gloom, like a fish rising from the depths of the ocean. I scrambled awkwardly to my feet.

'Give me a hand here, Marli.' The door was bolted on the inside.

I kicked off my sandals, she cupped her hands and I placed my right foot into her palms and hooked my fingers over the top of the door. She heaved and I hauled myself up, muscles straining, to wriggle head-first through the gap under the architrave. The top of the door bit into my stomach; splinters caught at my clothing. I slid down the inside of the door like a python, bracing myself with a hand on the basin and toilet seat. An elderly woman dressed in polyester flowers lay in a crumpled heap. I folded myself into the gap between the toilet and the basin, placing my feet carefully on either side of her body. Her face had a bluish tinge; spittle flecked her lips. I reached across and opened the door outwards.

The small crowd clustered outside, attracted to the scene by the heady prospect of drama, gasped collectively with concern and excitement. Typically, no one seemed prepared to do anything, so I shouted for someone to ring an ambulance. Marli and I commenced CPR and a young woman rang Triple 0. Perspiration beaded on Marli's forehead; my arms ached with endless compressions. Finally, an ambulance arrived and the paramedics took over. We leaned against the brick wall of the toilet, drained and fearful of not having done enough. Oxygen was administered and the patient hooked up to an IV. With the economy of long practice, they loaded her into the vehicle and wailed their way to the local hospital.

As I turned away, the girl who called for the ambulance waylaid me. 'Poor Mrs Robinson, she's such a sweetie. I know she'd like to thank you, so can I pass your phone number to the hospital? The woman in the office is a friend of mine.'

I stared at her for a long moment. A split second of slyness in her eyes startled me, but vanished, leaving normal concern. *You're getting paranoid.* The woman was trying so darned hard to be helpful, I tendered the information and then bent to pick up my handbag which I had dumped against the brick wall of the toilet. My bag gaped open with my driver's licence jammed into a side pocket. I checked the purse, but my money was intact and the young woman had disappeared.

I shrugged, thankful there was no indication of my Detective Senior Sergeant rank, but why would someone want to check my ID? A nosy journalist? Or a bystander who thought there might be something worth stealing? I chalked the incident up to experience, because we had far more to worry about than the identity of a snooper. I was desperate to get out to the farm and settle in. We'd had one hell of a day.

Sunday: 9am

Memories of Jack Harlow's murder brought demons to torment me in a chase through the night. Marli, whom I expected to be traumatised, slept soundly, snuggled under the covers with her pup. The aftermath of the previous day is setting in. Decisions present mountainous obstacles which I have no inclination to scale–to stay in the police force or leave and do–something–is on hold. Marli clatters around the house, talking to the dogs, chatting on Facebook to one friend while she texts another on her mobile. The puppy, Titch, growls as he wrestles the legs of her jeans.

I want to stay right here on the side verandah, watching Eloise's Highland cows graze in the paddock below the house, listening to a light aircraft, a silver and red dragonfly buzzing over the nearby and hopefully, long-dead volcanic peaks. The country air, devoid of city sounds and smells, has a cleansing effect but is unable to quell the feelings which are threatening to destroy me.

I have always been moved to tears when observing the beauty of nature. An amazing sunset, baby animals and glorious paintings bring a lump to my throat, but now, gazing up at the great rocky crags of the mountains behind the small farm, I want to scream and fight the pain and anger inside me. Many cultures rend their clothes and shriek their agony of grief to the world. I take deep breaths and endeavour to force back the sobs which threaten to undermine my composure.

My memory parachutes back to the dreadful twenty-four hours two months previously and the terrible night when the youngest member of my team, Detective Constable Danny Grey, was shot dead by a vicious criminal. But, unable to cope, my thoughts curl away and alight on the disaster of my marriage and its ignominious ending. This is something on which I can vent my bitterness and rage.

The morning after the debacle of the warehouse siege, I'd awakened at nine, having only gotten to bed at five that morning. I remember staring at the ceiling for a few minutes, tracing the pattern of the old-fashioned embossed plaster. Through the fog of exhaustion, I knew there was something I should remember, and it crashed back to face me, a demonic wave of horror, with

Danny Grey's lifeblood a black river streaming down a concrete driveway. I never wanted to get out of bed again, to pull the covers over my head and remain hidden forever until blessed darkness claimed me. Reality had to be faced. I hauled myself into the bathroom to shower and dress.

Numb with shock and grief, I walked into the kitchen, not at first seeing the bulging bags standing by the back door. I had no premonition of anything out of the ordinary. My husband, Harry, ran his architectural business from home and frequently supervised building sites in far-off places. He was buttering his toast with short, angry sweeps of his knife and didn't look up when I entered. As I went to the electric kettle to make coffee, he made his announcement. 'Susan, I won't be here when you get home tonight.'

I was about to answer flippantly, then something about his tone of voice alerted me to other possibilities. I turned to face him, cup of coffee in hand.

'I'm leaving you for good.' He faced me defensively, handsome face rigid with tension, as though expecting me to draw a gun. I would have loved to accommodate him. 'The fact is, Susan. I've had it with you and your job. Your *career.* I've met someone who actually cares about me and who wants to stay at home fulltime.' He paused to stab me with an angry glare. 'I bought a house in Taringa and Sharon is coming up from Sydney to live with me.'

Up from Sydney? Who? He'd bought another house? What with? His money? Her money? Our money? My brain refused to compute. He noted my confusion with sly amusement. I took a sip of the hot liquid, trying for self-control, because throwing it over Harry would constitute assault, and wouldn't he just love that.

'I met her when she came to Georgie Hird's funeral,' he explained, referring to the passing of a close friend of Eloise, who had been murdered by one of my niece Ally's kidnappers, last year.

'They met when they were taking a course at the New South Wales Conservatory of Music, just before Ally left for London.' He smiled with cruel joy. 'We were introduced at the wake.' I seemed to remember her; a short, serious-looking girl with straight brown hair.

Harry waited hopefully for me to make a fool of myself by grovelling for him not to leave. I dumped the cup on the draining board and reached for my mobile to phone headquarters, but he stepped forward, took it out of my hand and set it on the table. He looked disappointed in my seeming lack of reaction to his exciting news.

'You may as well go to work, Susan, you're always there anyway. I'll come back tomorrow to collect the rest of my things. Of course, this house will need to be sold and the finances sorted. You can have all the furniture, except for the portrait of my parents and some photos of Brittany. I'll come back later and pick up my music collection and books, tools from the shed and things like that.' It was a fait accompli. No discussion or negotiation. Tiny beads of perspiration had broken out on his upper lip; I realised with savage pleasure, that he wasn't as calm as he pretended.

'I don't want to discuss anything with you. My solicitor will be in contact and we'll get a straightforward divorce–if you don't make trouble. I've relocated the office to Mt Gravatt. Mary's going on holiday, then moving with me when I get back,' he added, referring to his faithful secretary, who'd worked in his office at the back of our house for the last ten years and who loathed me. I hadn't realised his office was closed. Had I been that blind? Quick as a flash with the experience of thirteen years of marriage, he pre-empted my question. 'No, not even you could be that insular, Susan. I moved everything out yesterday while you were at work.'

An icy ball formed in my stomach, but I managed to focus on something concrete. 'The girls! What are we going to tell them?'

'Not we, Susan, you. When all's said and done, they're your daughters. I'll talk to them later.'

Rage and hurt flared through me. I wanted to strangle Harry. 'All of a sudden they're *my* daughters? You've been their father since they were four. Are you planning to leave them too?'

He looked at me coldly. 'No, of course not. I just meant–'

Out of the corner of my eye, I saw the edge of an envelope peeping out from under the daily paper. 'I suppose I would have found the traditional note, if I hadn't been here this morning? Or would your solicitor have sent me a letter?' His face said it all; I realised he was already long gone. 'At one o'clock this morning I was telling Helen Grey she's a widow at twenty-four. You couldn't have picked a worse time to spring this on me if you'd tried.' *Oh, Danny, I should have protected you.*

'I wasn't to know what would happen last night.' He flashed a nasty smile. 'As I said, my solicitor will get in touch with you. I'm going now.' He picked up his bags; the door slammed behind him.

The radio played softly from the other side of the room. I glanced at the clock. 9.10am. Of course, Danny's death would have been on the morning news.

My legs gave way. I groped for a chair and sank onto it, racked with grief and guilt, but before I gained any sort of equilibrium, the wall phone started to ring and as though choreographed by fate, or Harry, my mobile went off as well. I got to my feet, unable to decide which one to answer first, as the dogs started huffing at the back door begging to be let inside for their breakfast.

The clock ticked on the top of the refrigerator; down the street, someone shouted good-bye to his wife. Children ran past the front gate on their way to school, screaming with laughter as they bashed each other with their schoolbags. Life was going on and I stood in the middle of my kitchen not knowing whether to laugh or cry, while technology badgered me on all sides.

Sighing, I took my mobile out of my bag and flipped it open–DI Peterson, my immediate superior–shuffled to the wall phone–the press. I laid the receiver on the bench without answering and then spoke to the DI, ignoring the squeaks of protest coming from the house phone. 'Yes, Sir?'

He commiserated with me and wanted to know when my report on the "incident" would be on his desk. Through the fogged mire of my mind I must have made the right responses, because he asked me to be at headquarters in three hours. Asked? It was an order. I wondered briefly whether I should request the union rep be present, but then decided to see what panned out first.

The house telephone receiver squawked madly. The media were frothing because they couldn't dial out again. An insistent noise penetrated my mental fog. I opened the back door, let the dogs inside–I supposed Harry was divorcing them as well–fed them and then made another cup of coffee. The receiver started screaming.

Questions whizzed around my soggy brain, but I could only face the ones concerning my marriage, right then. 'Could I have been a better wife to my husband? At what point did a partner and wife renege on her responsibilities? At what point had I allowed my career to so totally take over my life that Harry's love for me turned to indifference? 'And your's to him?' my inner voice insisted. Annoyed by the persistent squawking, I dumped the receiver back on its cradle. Considering the number of times a case broke and I was late home, the occasions when Harry attended school concerts without me, I wondered why our marriage hadn't broken up long ago. Of course, Mary had been only too pleased to deputise. But what about Harry's betrayal at the start of our marriage? Not long after our marriage, he admitted–

The penetrating ring of the house telephone brings me back smartly to the here and now. I immediately fear bad news from either Brisbane or Sydney. After all, we have only just arrived and do not know anyone here who might call us.

'*Mum!* Nurse Someone-or-other from the local hospital wants to speak to you!'

'Who?'

'I don't know. I didn't catch her name. She wants to talk about the old lady you got out of the toilet yesterday.'

Dread curls like the swirl of a hurricane in my belly. 'Don't tell me she's passed away?'

'Dunno.'

I get slowly to my feet and pad barefoot along the hallway to the telephone. The voice is crisp, the tone professional. 'Mrs. Prescott? Nurse Rachel Armstrong from the Emsberg Hospital. I'm ringing on behalf of Mrs Edna Robinson. Apparently you attended her when she collapsed in the park toilet yesterday afternoon?'

'Oh yes, how is she?'

'Poorly, Mrs Prescott. She's asking for you to come and see her, if you would be so kind. She's very agitated, so could you please make it this morning?'

She's alive! *Thank you, thank you God.* Flushed with relief, I forget to answer.

'Mrs Prescott, can you still hear me?'

'Yes. Sorry, I was wool-gathering. I'll come in as soon as I can.'

I go back to the verandah to set the alarm on my watch for five minutes time, close my eyes and take several deep breaths. 'Better than drugs any day, my dear,' the counsellor had chirped in the infuriatingly practical tones adopted by the truly dedicated. Stifling the urge to arrest her for something, I tried meditation with some scepticism at first, but with increasing confidence as time went on. The final session, I took her a box of chocolates, which we agreed were the best therapy of all.

'Marli, I've got to go into Emsberg this morning. Want to come? You can mooch around the shops while I visit Mrs Robinson.'

She is not enthusiastic. Titch tumbles around, pulling at her clothes and licking wherever he can reach. I am anxious about leaving her here by herself, but what could possibly happen in the short time I will be away? She's seventeen and surrounded by dogs, for God's sake.

Emsburg boasts a 60-bed hospital situated in pretty, rose-bedded grounds on a hill overlooking the town. Warm smiles greet me on arrival at the reception desk and I am escorted to the Close Observation Ward–COW, they laughingly explain. Edna Robinson looks smaller than I remember and very frail. The well-padded frame which collapsed against the toilet door the day before appears to have diminished. Her hair is stuck to her skull in straw wisps. Luminous eyes, owl-like behind thick-lensed glasses, light up when I enter the small high dependency unit.

'I'm so glad you came,' she whispers breathlessly, gesturing for me to take the chair beside her bed. Instinctively leaning toward her, I whisper back–one tends to reciprocate on these occasions–and ask how she feels. Edna's 'I'm all right dear, thank you,' is an aside. There are more important matters on her mind. 'You must promise not to tell anyone this, dear. Please give me your word you'll not repeat what I'm about to tell you?'

'Well, I'm not sure. It depends on what your information is.' *Why tell me if you don't want anyone to know?*

Her face creases with the effort to impress me with the gravity of her message. 'You have to promise! I need to tell someone in case I die.' She clutches my arm so tightly that her fingernails leave half-moon indentations.

'Why, Mrs Robinson? If–' Her grip tightens; the wrinkles on her face crumple into a myriad of faintly blue petals.

'Shall I call a nurse?'

'No!' Edna almost shouts, and then lowers her voice to a hiss, pausing for breath between rushes of words. 'Listen to me, someone has to ... know. He had to be punished, so they beat him to... the dirty beggar ... the filthy ... beast.' Her lips turn down in disgust. 'He was always so careful to cover his tracks. Those things weren't talked about in those days ... and they had to do it. We made a vow not to ... say anything ... but now–'

She releases my arm and gropes with trembling hands for the glass of water by her bed. I pick it up and assist, as the old lady takes a huge gulp, gags and starts coughing gobs of phlegm. I jump to my feet, snatch a towel from behind her locker and thrust it into her hands. She plunges her mouth into the folds and scrunches her eyes shut. I reach for the bell to call for the nurse, but she wipes her mouth and gestures me not to. 'If anyone ever finds out I told ... they don't know about you. But now Jack's been killed ... that shouldn't have happened.'

My cop training springs to life, like a hunting dog chasing quarry. 'You know who killed Jack Harlow?'

'We agreed not to talk, but it was only a matter of ti–' Edna bursts into a paroxysm of coughing. A fleeting presence moves on the periphery of my vision, a shadow in the doorway. I glance across, but only the energy of someone's presence remains.

Edna Robinson doubles over and slumps forward, her skin translucent, exposing tiny veins running hither and thither under her skin, like ant trails. I ring for assistance, keeping my finger on the buzzer until a nurse rushes in, takes one look at Edna and hits Code Blue on the buzzer. The room swarms with medical staff. I slip out and head down the hall, carefully keeping my eyes averted from ambulatory patients, trying not to run to the exit. Beads of perspiration trickle down my back and prickle my skin; for my own peace of mind and recovery, I cannot allow myself to become involved.

CHAPTER 3

A Moment of His Time.

Sunday evening: at the hospital: 8pm.

The evening visitors had left. Here and there a bedside reading light glowed. A nurse re-made a patient's bed at the far end of the corridor. She flung the sheets across the mattress, and flicked the covers over the bed, tucking them into perfect hospital corners while the patient, sitting in a chair beside the bed, made low-voiced conversation. Her shadow flashing on the opposite wall cast an old-time lantern show.

Doctor Jason Hardgreaves gave a sigh of relief, as he hovered over Edna Robinson. 'She'll rest now. Take thirty minute obs, Cecily.' They noted the tiredness in each other's faces, the doctor from a long afternoon to evening shift, the nurse on her last night duty before her break and day shift. The staff had battled to keep Edna's heart stable.

Now, at nightfall, it looked as though she would live. The nurse left to monitor another patient. Hargreaves carried out a final check on Edna's vital signs, adjusted the oxygen and left the room, leaving the door slightly ajar. He was cautiously congratulating himself on a job well done, when a Code Blue alert sounded at the other end of the hospital. After a frozen moment, he rushed through the doors several metres away; the nurses charged in breathless pursuit, Edna Robinson momentarily forgotten.

None of them noticed the tall man who stood in the shadows of the hallway opposite, which angled away from the light and ended in a door leading to the outside of the building. He waited a few moments in case there was more than the three staff he knew to be on duty, but when nothing happened, he twitched the hood of his coat further over his face, stepped forward and emerged into the deserted corridor.

Nothing stirred; perfect conditions. A 'fair weather night,' but not for Edna.

The intruder knew his presence in the hospital, if discovered, would be sanctioned even at this late hour. He slipped quietly across the corridor to the Close Observation Ward, the hood of his jacket hiding his identity from the rifle-barrel gaze of the nearby security camera mounted high on the wall. He pulled the door half-closed behind him, leaving just enough of a gap to hear if anyone was approaching the unit. This would only take a moment.

The old woman slept peacefully, under the influence of a mild sedative, her face grey and haggard beneath the oxygen mask. He leaned over the back of the monitor, located the wall connection, moved the trolley forward with a gloved hand and flicked the switch off. He braced himself, listening for running footsteps.

Silence.

He turned to the bed. Edna's scrawny arms lay on the outside of the covers. Smiling, the visitor gently drew the sheet up to her chin and tucked the side edge under the mattress continuing along the bed on each side to "straightjacket" Edna. She stirred when the pressure registered. He lifted the mask off her face and picked up the spare pillow lying on the chair nearby. Her eyes opened, narrowing with short-sighted confusion, and then twinkling as she recognised her late-night visitor.

'Wha–? Oh, it's you, dear. I didn't tell–'

'You're not going to,' he hissed, as he dropped the pillow across her face and pushed down relentlessly. Edna's lips adhered to the fabric of the pillowcase; her mouth filled with soft, suffocating wadding. Faint noises came from her throat. She tried to kick free of the sheets which confined her like a straight-jacket. Her feet drummed weakly. He held the pillow down. Beads of perspiration popped out on his brow and spurted down his nose.

Hurry, hurry. Die, damn you! Die!

Terror and rage gave strength to his arms, but her struggles went on. When they finally ceased, he rested on her body for a moment, trying to slow his breathing before tossing the pillow back onto the chair. He pushed himself upright, whipped a miniscule mirror out of his pocket and held the cold surface against her lips. The glass remained pristine. He cocked his head.

Nothing.

He pulled the sheet out from under the mattress, put Edna's arms back on the outside of the bedclothes and re-settled the oxygen mask. At first glance, no one would realise she was no longer a problem to herself–*or to anyone else.*

Smiling, he slipped out the door, congratulating himself on a successful mission. He arrived for a visit that very morning as the old girl was about to spill the beans to the Prescott woman. His 'secretary,' Gloria's description of her was spot on, as was her impulse to ask the woman for her name and where she was staying. Was she mulling over what she'd been told? Or had she dismissed Edna's ranting as that of a demented old bat? He couldn't take a chance on allowing the secrets of the past to destroy the future. The Prescott woman was a liability.

He went to the door and peered into the empty corridor, before casting a pitiless glance at Edna's corpse. 'Everyone agreed we'd keep quiet, but after all the promises not to tell, you had to break ranks. But don't worry; we'll give you a good send-off.'

'He smiled grimly. 'Cheers, Aunty Edna.'

CHAPTER 4

A Good Place to Hide

The Doctor

Monday: 5.10am

Doctor Jason Hardgreaves lay in bed, watching dawn breaking over the trees outside his bedroom window. He shivered as he tried to force his mind away from the last nine hours. He'd only arrived home to bed at 4am. The Medical Superintendent told him to take the day off; the police would be in touch for a full statement.

He couldn't believe his ears when he was paged, raced back to the room prepared to do battle with another heart attack and found Edna dead. He had gently touched her grey, still-warm face and slid his fingers down to the carotid artery trying, without success, to find a pulse.

Sorrow for Edna, whose granddaughter he was engaged to marry, warred with terror. Had he missed a danger sign? There would be an enquiry, no doubt about that. 'Only half an hour ago, she was sleeping peacefully, her obs were fine ....we fought so hard to save old Edna, and then ... if only Code Blue hadn't pulled us away from monitoring Edna, she'd still be alive,' he heard himself wail.

Nurse Cecily Braum found the evidence which led

to the ultimate horror. As she moved the chair aside, a pillow on the seat tumbled to the floor. She picked it up, inadvertently placing her hand on a patch of sticky goo.

'Look! This pillowslip was fresh and now there's stuff all over ...'

'What do you mean?'

'I put a new one on just before we left Edna. Remember, Edna coughed water all over it? Well, Jason, this is *not* water.' Cecily's face turned ashen, as she realised the implications of her discovery.

He reached across, took the pillow out of her hands and held it to the light. What appeared to be a pool of saliva and phlegm, was partially soaked through the cotton slip. Had Edna pushed the pillow on the chair? No. She had been sedated, and she would not have been capable of putting the pillow over her head. Something terrifying began to form in a tight ball deep in his stomach.

Understanding of what the discovery might mean closed over him like a shroud. He wanted to throw up. The top of his head felt as though it had parted company with his skull. He leaned down and examined her face. Were those tiny blood vessels the result of petaechial haemorrhaging from being smothered? Or of age in geriatric skin?

'Hard to tell,' he thought, but because of the muck on the pillow combined with her blue lips–someone must waited for Edna to be left on her own after visiting hours.

He glanced wildly around, trying to identify a place of concealment. The bathroom? Nowhere to hide. Then a flash of the dark corridor opposite Edna's room, the one leading to the Diversional Therapy wing and boardroom, came to mind.

A good place to hide.

The flesh on his back crawled as he realised that he could have passed within centimetres of the killer, who might have been watching him run to the Code Blue emergency. But why on earth would someone want to murder gentle, inoffensive Edna?

'Put that back where you found it, Cecily. Don't handle it more than necessary and don't touch anything else. Close this room and don't let anybody in. I need to ring the police–and Mrs Eams.' Hardgreaves' voice came out high and squeaky. He made a determined effort to lower it. 'I'll have to phone her,' he said, referring to the Director of the hospital. He handed the pillow to the nurse who took a corner and carefully placed it on the chair, trying to position it exactly as she'd found it.

They scuttled from the room, death panting at their heels.

Hardgreaves refused to turn the lights on in the corridor, fearing the patients would be alerted. Explanations were not something he considered himself equipped to go into right then. He fled in the direction of the office, leaving Cecily Braum alone in the dimly-lit corridor. She trembled, her gaze drawn inexorably to the dark reaches of the hallway opposite, as she waited outside the door to Edna's room. *Perhaps he–or she–was still there ...*

If he sat down he'd never want to get up again, so Hardgreaves wedged himself into a corner between the desk and chair, leaned against the wall and unclipped the mobile phone from his belt. Deep breaths couldn't control the trembling which started in the very core of his being and distributed itself in cold, never-ending waves throughout his body. He dialled 000 and asked for the police. It took two attempts before he could keep his voice steady and advise a gravel-voiced officer of the situation, after which he dropped the mobile and slumped into a nearby chair.

'Shit. Why didn't it happen on someone else's shift?' Sighing, he initiated the second necessary contact. His call to the Superintendent went straight to voice mail, so he left a message, dreading the last one on his protocol list. Mrs Eams, a woman of somewhat masterful proportions, was not only the Director of the hospital, but also his fiancée's stepmother.

'What? Are you absolutely sure?' she screamed. 'You can't be serious! *Edna?'*

'Afraid so, Mrs Eams. I've notified the police and locked COW. They should be here soon.'

'I'm coming in!' she hissed.

'Yes, Mrs Eams.' He clipped his phone back on his belt and went to the tiny 'cafe' recess. He'd never craved a hot drink so badly. Drops of boiling water splashed over his trembling hands as he manoeuvred coffee mugs into position under the urn. Somehow he got the job done without inflicting more than minor scalds on his fingers and carried the steaming drinks to the corridor outside the Close Observation Ward.

The two of them stood in the corridor outside the door as they sipped. 'Libby and I only got engaged last weekend, so I've never met Edna's side of the family,' Hardgreaves explained.

'I meet some family members at events around town, but I've never got to make close friends with any of them. I dated Peter Robinson, one of the cousins, for a few months, but he was a bit of a waste of space,' said Cecily Braum. She took a slug of coffee. 'They're a pretty secretive bunch, actually. You never know what they're thinking. Sir Arthur got the 'sir' years ago before the Government got rid of knighthoods, but I can't remember what for. That idiot politician, "Slimeball" Murphy is Constance Robinson's son. He used to be a real estate developer.'

The doctor placed his coffee mug on a trolley nearby, then stepped into a small, empty side-ward and emerged with two chairs which he plonked against the wall. Gratefully, they dropped onto them.

'The women in the family are 'too posh to push,' if you get my drift? Especially Lady Ferna. Town's already in an uproar over the other day. You know, Jack Harlow.' The lighting in the corridor was just bright enough to reveal goosebumps rising under the pale hairs on her arms.

Hardgreaves feet and legs ached, but sitting comfortably in a chair felt disrespectful to Edna. More formality seemed to be called for. They'd forgotten their colleague working at the other end of the building.

Finally, the night buzzer squawked outside A & E. Jason rushed to open the door, unable to stop babbling as he led the police to Edna's body. The men whom he knew so well metamorphosed into grim-faced strangers. A faint, desperate hope that what he suspected was not so, made him lapse into terrified silence.

Then Mrs Eams arrived, and it went downhill from there...

He jerked upright, sweating, and brushed his hand over his stubbled chin. He'd nodded off without realising it. Slowly, he crawled out of bed and staggered to the bathroom.

It was going to be a long, *long,* day.

***

The Policeman

Monday: 5.10am

Senior Constable John Glenwood leaned against the wall in the hallway, watching the blue-overalled, masked figures of the SOCO–Scenes of Crime Officers–moving in and out of the ward where Edna Robinson's body lay. His mind scudded back to when City Despatch called him and his partner, Constable Loy Ng, off night patrol and directed them to attend an 'incident' at the local hospital. He grimaced, remembering how they'd joked about what could have occurred. 'Fighting cats had knocked over the pot plants at the front door, or maybe an ant crossed the path and set off the security alarm.'

Their first glimpse of the white-faced, agitated young doctor instantly wiped jokes out of their minds. As he and Loy gazed down at the bluish-grey face of Edna Robinson, he had been loath to consider foul play, but the reality was unthinkable. Perhaps if he went out the door and came in again, she would be alive?

The next step was to call the Criminal Investigation Branch.

The other night nurse, alerted by their voices, scurried along the corridor to join them. Cecily Braum put her in the picture, but before she could cause a scene, John bundled both women into the office, told Hardgreaves to keep everyone away from COW and called city station on his mobile.

Minutes later he had reported to the Duty Detective at CIB, then sent Loy to get a roll of checked tape out of the boot of the car. Having effectively secured the area by taping off the whole section of corridor around the crime scene, he reported to his station OIC, Senior Sergeant Harris. After he'd finished speaking, he posted the young constable back to complete the Saturday night street patrol. His final action was to commandeer a chair and a small side-table, place them beside the door and begin a crime scene log.

His mind swirled around the events of the last two days. They'd hardly begun the hunt for Jack Harlow's killer and now this? He didn't expect CIB would be best pleased. The two victims being related appeared significant, if indeed it proved that Edna had also been murdered, but that was for CIB to determine.

The youngest nurse approached, tip-toeing as though not to wake a reality she'd rather not confront. 'A cup of tea, John?'

'Yeah, that'd be good. Thanks Lynette. It's going to be a long night. CIB and Forensics'll be here in the morning.'

But before he could finish his drink, Beatrice Eams arrived, refused to accept the taped-off area as a crime scene and demanded to see Edna. A heated, though muted argument ensued and ended with the director charging the tape to get into COW, with John dragging her away and threatening to take her into custody. Jason Hardgreaves, emboldened by John Glenwood's presence, escorted the shell-shocked director to the office where he plied her with tea. A decision was made to wait until morning to advise the Robinson relatives of the tragedy.

At first light, Director Eams phoned her own daughter, who ran screaming to tell her husband. By the time she'd spoken to her best friend, who telephoned *her* mother, who advised the formidable president of the Women's Guild, the grapevine was buzzing. But no one thought to tell Edna's granddaughter, Libby, who visited on the way to work to leave flowers. Her stereophonic reaction to the news reverberated throughout the hospital. Mrs Eams grabbed Libby and hauled her into Accident and Emergency, where she was told to pull herself together.

The team of blue-clad figures carrying cases of equipment to the crime scene paused momentarily, glanced at each other then at John Glenwood and shrugged before continuing on their cumbersome way. Day staff tried to coax hysterical patients back into the wards, waving their arms like demented sheepdogs.

John briefed the two CIB officers, before posting a junior constable to prevent anyone from coming near that end of the corridor and signed over the crime scene log. All too soon, he would be back on duty in a town already rocked by the Dog Trial Murder. He shuddered, recalling Jack's widow, Penelope, kneeling by his body in the centre of the arena, ashen-faced, with a ring of faces gazing down like cows in a paddock. 'I didn't think she'd be so cut up about it,' he thought, 'I expect it was the shock.'

A memory flicked through his mind, something he should recall. He pulled into his garage, turned off the engine and sat for a few minutes. He knew it was very important, but if he didn't force it, eventually he would remember.

CHAPTER 5

One-Upwomanship

Daniella Winslow

Monday: early morning.

'Mum! *Mum?*' Carissa, Daniella Winslow's scruffy seventeen-year-old daughter sauntered into the kitchen, dropped on to a chair, crashed her elbows on the table and stared at her mother's back. 'Has Brendan rung yet?'

Daniella Winslow's position in society was under threat. The church ladies guild, the golf club, book club group and businesswoman's club, not to mention the hospital auxiliary would be on the one hand, wildly excited over the scandal and on the other, intolerant of a President whose relative managed to 'get himself murdered.

Daniella gazed over the escarpment, trying not to cry, barely aware of her daughter's presence. Introspection was not something in which she normally indulged, but the death of Jack Harlow brought back far too many memories than were comfortable. Even at thirty-eight years of age, she kept her secrets lest her friends despise the shameful person lurking inside of her. Jack had a lot to answer for.

'Mum!' The carping insistence of teenage angst finally penetrated her mental fog.

'I wouldn't know because I took the phone off the hook last night. Damned journalists,' Daniella snapped, a solitary mackerel surrounded by sharks. 'Do sit up straight, Carissa. What time did you get in last night?'

'Why? What's it got to do with you?' Her daughter yawned and stretched. 'Get off my back. And how do you expect me to get any calls? Brendan's supposed to phone.'

'What's wrong with *your* mobile, then?'

'I left it in Brendan's car,' snarled Carissa. A king-sized hangover was doing nothing for her temper. She sensed Brendan was using her as a stopgap until someone prettier or sexier came along. 'He hasn't even made a pass yet, for God's sake and we've been going out for two weeks!' She pouted, remembering the numerous times she'd stuck her boobs in his face, to no avail. Perhaps he batted for the "other side?" Or both sides. But surely she couldn't be mistaken about something like that.

But Daniella had other things on her mind. 'Since Jack got shot, I can't remember whether I'm coming or going.'

'Who?' Carissa asked, puzzled by the conversational direction.

'Jack Harlow. My cousin, your second cousin. Don't you read the newspapers or watch the news on TV? It's been all over the news. Are you so out of touch you didn't hear? They're calling it the "dog trial murder."' Her mother's voice cracked.

'What?'

'I said, Jack's dead. Someone shot him at the dog trials.'

Daniella checked the water in the electric jug, pressed

the switch and gathered two mugs from the cupboard. She spooned coffee into each and then took the milk out of the refrigerator, watching her daughter's face in the reflection in the gleaming stainless steel door.

'When? But we were camping, mum. Out of, like, radio range. What happened?'

'We don't know. Maybe someone bore a grudge against him. Or it might have been an accident. The police will probably want to interview us all. At the moment, I can't cope with any more people ringing. Ferna's phone has been engaged for hours,' she said, referring to the family matriarch. The kettle boiled and she began pouring boiling water into the cups. 'He was shot just as he was penning the sheep.' She reached for the milk.

'Faaaaaaaaar out.' Carissa's eyes widened.

Daniella agreed. She found it hard to believe that the ghost of the past might be vanquished. Perhaps a husband, father or boyfriend had finally taken action.

The fear and fascination with which she regarded Jack, hadn't abated since she was a fifteen-year old bridesmaid at a cousin's wedding. Daniella had returned from the women's restroom at the club to find Jack leaning against the wall, leering drunkenly at her. She'd tried to turn and run back to the reception, but he propelled her down the dark hallway and pushed her into a storeroom. Amid the choking smells of cleaning chemicals and solvents, he thrust his alcohol-coated tongue down her throat and stuffed his hand up her skirt. His fingers slid into her knickers and poked high up inside her, causing a sharp stab like a knife- thrust inside.

At first she'd been unable to react, but then she'd bitten his tongue and pushed him away, so hard he'd fallen into a pile of buckets and mop heads. She'd scrubbed her trembling hand across her mouth and rushed back to the reception.

Who could she tell? Her father? Uncle Arthur? But they would probably kill him. Her uncle John? No, not him. He was useless. Mum? Her mother was pontificating to a group of women from the bride's family. Not a good move; perhaps later, after the reception finished. Too frightened of spoiling the day for the bride and groom, she wandered among the guests, filled with indecision, forcing back tears, terrified of having to face Jack again.

She made her way to the ladies loo at the other end of the reception rooms and hid in a cubicle. She burst into tears when she discovered the blood and the broken elastic around the leg of her knickers. She cleaned herself up as much as possible and emerged, filled with shame.

Then she made eye contact with the one person she thought would understand, Mark Gordon, a cousin-by-marriage. Her teenage fantasies often featured Mark, though he treated her like a little sister. She sidled up and clutched his arm. 'Jack groped me!' she'd hissed into his ear as he bent down to listen.

'He did what?' He straightened and looked around the room. Unable to see the perpetrator, he leaned down again. 'What do you mean, he *groped* you? What exactly did he do?'

She opened her mouth to tell him, but was overcome with shyness, unable to find the words to describe how Jack rammed his fingers up inside her and wriggled them. Had, in effect, raped her. Remembering the scorn with which the older women in her family had flayed a girl from school who reported a rape–*she must have asked for it, respectable girls don't get raped*–Daniella was too frightened to reveal everything. 'He–um–stuck his hand in my pants.'

Mark's face flushed; his eyes narrowed. 'Right, I'll deal with this.' He rushed away, presumably in search of Jack. Daniella cowered in a chair, wondering what sort of explosion would follow. A vision came to mind of plates, glasses and wedding guests flying through the air while the newlyweds hid under the bridal table.

She bitterly regretted saying anything, but to her great surprise, nothing appeared to happen. The evening progressed smoothly; the bridal couple galloped out of the reception, hurled themselves into the best man's car and escaped. A regiment of aunts, other rellies and a motley collection of friends, hysterical with excitement and drunken exhaustion, waved from the front of the club.

Face battered, Jack left. When she'd finally sucked up enough courage to approach Mark, he'd said shortly, 'Don't worry about it anymore,' and, apart from asking if she was all right, refused to elaborate. Jack always pretended to have forgotten what he'd done–perhaps he was so drunk he really didn't remember, and Daniella was never game to front him about it. But sometimes he'd winked slyly at her and she wondered. Until the time he caught her in the horse box...

The news of Jack's murder was closure to her secret guilt. Mark was the only person who knew what happened, because she was never able to tell her mother or discuss the past with the now, Archdeacon Gordon–Jack's threats had put paid to that.

'So what happens next?' Carissa asked her mother, who was sipping coffee, staring at nothing in particular.

'Oh, I don't suppose it will affect us much. After all, we weren't at the showground. By the way, I want to call on the Kirkbridge's sister-in-law today. She's house-sitting for them and Eloise said she would leave eggs for me.'

'I saw her at the Information Centre Saturday afternoon. Getting directions.'

'What?' Daniella was all ears. 'I thought you only arrived home last night? I know,' she answered herself, 'you stayed with Brendan's family out in the bush.'

'Mum, you don't have to get your knickers in a twist. Brendan went to work, so he dropped me off on his way out,' Carissa muttered, burying her nose in her coffee mug. She raised her head briefly, to add, 'And I slept in the spare room, okay?'

Daniella closed the magazine and stared at her daughter. 'The news has been all over town. You must have heard about it.'

'Hey, Brendan's family don't have TV. And his parents weren't home anyway. Gross about Jack, but hey, shit happens!'

Daniella sighed, wishing she wasn't paying all that money out for private schooling only for Carissa to use vulgarities. 'The police will ask everyone in the immediate family for an alibi. What was the Kirkbridge's sister-in-law doing there? And how did you know it was her? And how come you didn't hear about Jack at the centre?'

'They walked into the Centre just as we were leaving. She was with her daughter, I think.' She gazed out the window for a moment, brow furrowed. 'We stopped to read the notices on the Centre verandah and I overheard this woman asking directions.'

'Are you sure it was the Kirkbridge's sister-in-law?' Daniella's eyes narrowed like a fox watching a succulent pullet.

Carissa shrugged irritably. 'Yes. Someone said.'

'You must know who said.'

'What does it matter?' her daughter whined.

Daniella folded her lips, but curiosity got the better of her. 'What's she like?'

'Who?'

'The woman, of course? Is she 'one of us'?'

Carissa squinted, trying to conjure up a face. 'Medium height, red hair. There was something about her ... can't put my finger on it.' She paused and took a gulp of coffee. 'Sort of serious. She's quite pretty for an old woman.'

Her mother persisted. 'How old *is* she?'

'About the same age as you. She looked sorta–sad.'

Resisting the urge to strangle Carissa, Daniella shrugged and returned to her magazine. 'Well, I'll go over later. You can come with me and meet the daughter.'

Monday: mid morning.

Two fat grinning Labradors raced down the driveway to greet them, a geriatric spaniel bringing up the rear. Daniella parked a little way from the bottom of the rather grandiose entrance. The colonial-style, straw bale building with ochre walls and deep-silled, huge, tinted windows glowed in the sun. Smoke wafted out of the chimney; a hint of spring spiced the crisp air. She had visited many times, and knew the home inside was elegant with a comfortable reception room, and lounge with a stone fireplace, the mantel of which was adorned with priceless object d'art.

A red-haired woman wearing jeans, a cashmere sweater, highly-polished boots and big, wrap-around sunglasses, waited on the verandah. The dogs panted up the steps and flung themselves at her feet.

Daniella felt upstaged. She stepped out of her car, marched up the first three steps, then stopped. Something about the woman made her uneasy.

'Hello! We thought we'd come and introduce ourselves,' she said, trying for cheery tones. 'I believe Eloise left some eggs for me.'

Her hostess stepped forward. The screen door behind her opened and a girl about the same age as Carissa, with olive skin and slanting blue eyes under dark brows, emerged. Her black hair was bound into a glistening French braid.

Daniella, feeling like a member of the hoi polloi, introduced herself and Carissa. The woman removed her sunglasses; Daniella cringed under the penetrating gaze. The silence stretched, seemingly forever, until the woman finally responded in a low, musical voice. 'De–Susan Prescott. This is my daughter, Marli. I'm Eloise and James's sister-in-law,'

Daniella, thinking there might be something caught in her front teeth, clamped her mouth shut and nodded. Scampering noises heralded the arrival of a tiny ball of black and white fluff.

'Oh, how gorgeous!' squealed Carissa, pushing past her mother to run up the steps and scoop the pup into her arms. Almost in the one motion, she breathlessly introduced herself to Marli Prescott, who smiled brightly and ushered her inside. Susan invited her visitor in for tea and told the dogs to stay out.

As she preceded her hostess through the great, wide hallway, Daniella realised, with some surprise, that for once she didn't have the upper hand.

CHAPTER 6

Scones, Jam and Cream.

Susan

Monday: mid morning.

My heart sinks when the dogs begin their 'Oh joy, oh Heaven, we've got visitors!' routine, as I finish speaking to my sister-in-law in England. The sound of an expensive motor approaching sends nervous flutters through me. 'For God's sake, visitors are all I need, right when I find time to ring the hospital about Edna Robinson's condition.' The information imparted by the old lady the morning before makes me sceptical. A tale of crime and retribution couldn't be discounted, but getting involved in townsfolk's problems smacks too much of my profession, about which I have somewhat ambivalent feelings.

As I lean against the side of the French door leading onto the side verandah, questions about my collapsed marriage keep returning to buzz around my head like flies. Depression, grief, guilt–the 'black dog' are not problems which I have encountered in any pressing way, being an exponent of the 'pull yourself together' school inherited from my grandma. Now my chickens are coming home to roost. *I've lost my lioness persona and taken on the mantle of mouse.*

How much did I contribute to Harry's abandonment of our marriage? Was it my insistence on keeping my career? At one time, in a futile bid to be the perfect wife and mother, I seriously considered resigning from the police force, but Harry, alarmed by the realisation that the extra money coming in was more than helping with the current slump in demand for architects, hastily talked me out of it.

Had I ignored my good-looking husband's affairs because I allowed chasing criminals to take precedence over Harry or the girls? But I did go to school plays and events ... often ... as much as I could. And I do–did –my share of the housework. *Yeah right, Susan, so that stacks up against what you didn't do?*

I reach for my sunglasses and walk onto the front verandah. A silver BMW is crunching its way to the house, accompanied by our dogs on escort duty. When the car stops, they stagger up the front steps and collapse around me.

A young girl of about Marli's age, the other a woman of my own, alight from the vehicle. The girl is dressed in tatty jeans, sweater, boots and a duffle coat. Her mother is truly majestic. Perfectly groomed tresses encase her regal head, long neck elegantly wrapped in a silk scarf, no doubt genuine Gucci, folded into a crisp, white shirt, which in turn snuggles into a pair of tight, black jeans. An expensive black duffle coat dangles from her shoulder; breathtakingly high-heeled black boots complete the ensemble.

Her eyes sweep me from head to foot as she climbs the first three steps. I'm sure she's guessed I wear washing-battered knickers. Old habits die hard. After she introduces herself and her daughter, I allow a lengthy silence to develop–a useful device for unsettling criminals and unexpected guests–until she starts to shift from one elegantly-clad foot to the other. Only then do I take my sunglasses off and introduce Marli and myself.

A moment of silence follows, during which my visitors don't quite know what to say, but then Marli's puppy wriggles onto the scene. With a happy cry, Carissa Winslow scoops him up, we all relax and the girls vanish to the back of the house. We mothers head for the kitchen.

Daniella sips her tea, grimaces and at my gesture, helps herself to more milk before diving headlong into the latest news in town, Jack Harlow's murder.

'So you see it was an awful shock when we were told about my cousin, Jack. I mean, I'm sure no one I know would do such a dreadful thing!' she finishes breathlessly.

Her cousin? Vaguely interested, I allow her to witter on, her voice providing a background to my thoughts which insist on returning to the morning Harry left–

'I don't know what the family will think, especially since Aunty Edna had another heart attack yesterday morning. Just as well she was in hospital already. If it hadn't been for some woman at the park, she might have dropped dead in the toilets...'

My mind snaps back to the present as Daniella's voice rams itself into my consciousness.

'Who?'

Daniella stops in mid-sentence, surprised, and then explains. 'Aunt Edna. She took a turn with her heart yesterday at the park -'

'You mean Mrs Robinson?'

'Why, yes. Do you know her?' Daniella's eyebrows hit full mast.

'I've met her. A very nice old lady. More tea?'

I wave the pot and thrust the scones, jam and cream toward her enticingly. She throws me a surprised glance, then holds her cup out and picks up another scone. 'How is she?' Perhaps it will save me a phone call.

'Oh, I rang last night and the nurse said she was stable. I haven't heard anything more, but no news is good news, as they say.' Daniella smiles complacently. 'You live in Brisbane don't you? Whereabouts? How long are you here for?'

Leaving me little time to answer between questions, Daniella's voice flows on, enquiring about my social standing and the depth of my relationship with Eloise and James. I parry her questions politely as my mind, in spite of my best efforts, shifts into cop mode. This woman knows "who's who at the zoo."

My guest waffles on about fashion, the local social hierarchy and all the volunteer groups to which she belongs. I can't resist the lure of the chase and cut into her babble. 'How well did you know Jack?' *Stay out of it, Susan.*

Daniella's eyes almost pop out of her head. For a moment, it appears as though she's not prepared to answer and I'm about to follow up with reassuring noises.

'Well, as I said, Jack was my cousin, but a good deal older than me. Our families lived next door to each other forever. Why do you want to know?'

I backpedal smoothly. 'I was interested, because I am an avid reader of crime. I don't mean to pry.' *Oh, you liar.*

After staring at me for a moment, she relaxes visibly and launches into a long and involved family history.

Jack Harlow was the oldest child of her Aunt Connie and trained sheepdogs all his life, as his father did. He left a widow, Penelope, but no children.

'Thank goodness Jack didn't breed,' she says with a sigh, 'but they have a lot of champion sheepdogs. Jack travels all over the country in the trial season, while Penelope looks–looked–after the farm. As a matter of fact, they live just over there!' She flings her arm out, indicating a point to the north.

'Jack was quite a bit older than you was he not? Did you know him when you were a child?'

'Yes, I remember first meeting him when I was about five.'

Something is urging me on. 'Did you like him? Get on well with him?' I nudge the scone plate toward her again. Softly, softly catchee monkey ...

She looks undecided for a moment then, obviously stalling for time, takes another, cuts it in half, slowly slathers on cream and jam and devours it.

'I believe his reputation with the women was not the best.' I almost miss the moment when something dark flashes into her eyes and a shadow passes across her face. Rage. Pure, distinct, hatred. *Enough to kill?*

'There was a scandal last year, but you don't want to know about that!' *Oh, don't I just?* I remember the farmer's voice–*'Half the town, I'd say.'*

'Can you think of any reason why someone would want to murder him? A rival competitor perhaps? '

She considers for a moment, opens her mouth to answer, then stares curiously at me. 'Why are you so interested? Did you know Jack? Do you ...' She snaps her mouth shut.

I hasten to re-assure her. 'No, I didn't know him. I'm

just interested because I was there when it happened.' *Shut up, Susan!*

Daniella jumps on my explanation like a crow on road kill. 'You saw what happened?'

I gave her a brief explanation of why we were attending the trials, and then was thankfully saved by the girls surging out of the family room at the back of the house to swoop like birds of prey on the remaining plate of scones, pieces of which they proceed to feed to the delighted pup. '*Mum!* Marli says the breeder had a few pups left in the litter! Can we get one?' pleads Carissa. Thank heaven for small mercies: a diversion.

Before Daniella can answer, the dogs shoot out from under the table, race along the wide hallway, toenails scrabbling for a grip on the parquet flooring and hurl themselves down the front steps. I get up, excuse myself and head after them to the front verandah where I watch transfixed, as a police car creeps inexorably along the rutted driveway toward the house.

My heart begins a courtly dance against my ribcage. Has something happened to my other daughter? A band of ice clamps itself around my body. I feel faint but Marli, recognising my plight, wraps her arm around my waist and holds on tight.

CHAPTER 7

Recriminations

Susan

Monday: late morning.

He is young, tall, broad-shouldered and, from what I can see of his face not covered by wrap-around sunglasses, devastatingly handsome. As he walks up the steps, Marli catches her breath. He takes his glasses off and to my surprise looks straight at the Winslows. 'Mum, Uncle Arthur said you were here. He tried to ring you, but your phone was turned off.'

Daniella steps smartly to the edge of the top step. *'What's happened?'*

The young constable glances at us and pauses. Daniella, remembering she is a guest, waves over her shoulder without taking her eyes off her son. 'This is Mrs Prescott and her daughter, Marli. My son, Adam.' He nods to me deferentially and then to Marli, his eyes narrowing ever so slightly, before he makes a determined effort to drag his gaze back to his mother. I'm relieved that he isn't the harbinger of Prescott bad news and he doesn't appear to recognise me. He steps onto the verandah to take Daniella's hand. His eyes are filled with dread. 'Er ... I'm sorry, Mum, I've got bad news.'

'Come, Marli.' I touch her shoulder. 'We'll give you privacy.' But as we turn to go inside the house Daniella grabs my arm, not taking her eyes off her son's face. 'No, it's all right.' She flashes me a 'please-stay-and-support-me' look. Reluctantly, I move back to stand beside her. Carissa squashes the pup to her chest and moves closer to her mother.

'Mum, Carissa–Great-Aunt Edna died last night.'

They gasp; Daniella's face turns ashen. Carissa's arms jerk convulsively and the puppy squeaks in protest. Marli gently removes him from her grasp. Sensing there is more, I look at Constable Adam Winslow.

'Ah, Mum, that's not all. We have reason to believe she was murdered. CIB and SOCO are at the hospital now.'

Daniella's scream seems to come from the soles of her high-heeled boots. Carissa starts crying; Adam wraps his arms around both of them. At my signal, Marli takes the frightened puppy inside.

'Shut him in the laundry,' I say quietly, struggling to suppress the onset of dread which would suck me back into the vortex of death and pain. How? Edna's words come crashing back into my mind. *'No one knew. He was always so careful to cover his tracks. It wasn't talked about in those days ... and they had to do it. It was a pact not to ... say anything ... but now–'* and I remember the shadow in the doorway. Had she been overheard?

Beads of perspiration break out on my torso, causing my clothes to stick to my skin. I knew what SOCO would be doing now, what the detectives were waiting for. So many times it had been me attending the scene. *I can't bear this. You have no choice.*

Marli nods and scoots inside. As I am about to

follow, a man dressed in a chambray shirt, black jeans and leather jacket climbs out of the passenger side of the patrol car and walks toward the front steps. The fine hairs on my arms prickle; my heart tries to abandon my chest. I pretend not to recognise him and focus on the visitors.

'Come along inside and I'll make more tea. We've some brandy too.'

Words tumble over themselves as I hasten to get away from Detective Inspector David Maguire. Acutely aware of his footsteps following us into the house, I usher the guests into the lounge-room and listen to myself gushing, as they settle into chairs. I point Adam Winslow in the direction of the liquor cabinet and glasses and then bolt for the kitchen. Maguire marches right after me.

My skin prickles when I sense him standing just inside the door, watching me making fresh tea. I try to prevent my hands from trembling as I take clean cups from the cupboard. *Oh my God, what am I going to do?*

'Susan?'

His voice is just as I remember it, hot chocolate but tough. Age has added marshmallows. I stop fluttering and turn to face him. The lines on his face are a little deeper, but his style-cut black hair still gleams. There are flecks of grey at his temples. Women deteriorate; men flourish. He takes off his Ray bans and I see that his brilliant blue eyes have lost none of their lustre. My gaze strays to his full, luscious mouth, which quirks up at the corners. Jangled feelings churn inside me. God, I'm having a hot flush! *Oh no, get a grip on yourself.* And please, God, don't let Marli come into the kitchen.

'How are you, David? I thought you were living in Cairns?' My voice is coming from somewhere outside my body.

'Fine thanks, but I've been with CIB in Ipswich for a couple of months. I got homesick for the southeast.' He parks his sublime bum against the kitchen bench as I refill the electric kettle and flick the switch with fingers which have developed the consistency of sponges. He picks up a buttered scone, slathers it with jam and bites with relish, chews appreciatively, before wiping his mouth with a paper serviette. 'You always made great scones, Susan. This your house?'

'No, my brother-in-law's. They're in England right now.' I don't want to elaborate. It is all I can do to keep a carefully assembled facade of calm in place.

'Melanie's living *here?'*

'No, it belongs to Harry's sister, Eloise and her husband, James Kirkbridge.' I meet his enquiring look with petty triumph. '*Sir* James Kirkbridge.'

He considers that for a moment and then decides to be satisfied with the answer. I can't go through the horrific kidnapping which brought Eloise, James and their daughter, Ally Carpenter, into our lives a year ago. The trial of the Esposito's and Robert Fox is still pending.

'Well, I certainly didn't expect to see *you* here, Susan. I wanted to talk to Daniella Winslow, so when I found out she was Adam's mother, I tagged along. I heard about Danny Grey and Harry leaving.'

I sit, unable to make eye contact for fear of what I shall see in his. David takes the chair opposite me and reaches across the table to pat my hand. His male aroma mingling with an intoxicating and erotic mixture of aftershave, combined with the leather of his jacket, send twitters of excitement into my mind. Something tugs deep in my belly. *Pull yourself together, stupid. Been there, done that. Got the scars.*

'I know it must have been hard for you, but I expect you handled it with your usual efficiency,' he says, coolly. Just then the electric kettle boils. Thankful for something to occupy my hands and the opportunity to turn my back on him, I get up, step to the kitchen bench and busy myself with making a fresh pot of tea. *Get a grip. Try for something light.*

'I managed to lose a colleague and another husband in just one day. It must be a record. And what are you doing here?'

'I'm leading the investigation into Jack Harlow's and Edna Robinson's deaths. We're staying here at the motel.'

'I see. How many are there of you?'

'Five, apart from SOCO. I'm sorry.' David looks at me with what I choose to interpret as pity, stands, turns his chair around and sits again, resting his arms over the back. His leather jacket creaks as he moves.

'Which one of the girls is *she?'* He nods in the general direction of the back verandah.

Rage whips through me like a gale force wind. 'Of course, you wouldn't know, would you? After all, you haven't seen your children since they were four years old!'

In a swift movement which sends me back against the sink, he casts the chair aside and jumps in front of me. 'And who wouldn't let me see them?' His eyes are cold. 'How many times did I phone? How many times did I write asking to see my children? You couldn't be bothered to even answer my letters! You just sent them back *unopened!* No photos, no contact. Almost all the birthday cards and presents I sent were returned unopened!'

'What are you talking about?' I hear myself squeak.

He is not listening. 'After we separated, I was

seconded to Toowoomba. I rang and said it would be awhile before I could get down to Brisbane. When I got back, I had them for the weekend. Do you remember that, Susan? But when I brought them back to your house, I was–barely politely–informed that you thought it would be better if I didn't see them until they were older. 'They were "confused and upset" after they'd been with me, was the excuse as I remember it.'

I struggle to control myself. 'Now just you wait a moment, David! You said it might be better if *you* didn't see them because you were going to be living too far away and didn't have anywhere suitable to take them. Not that you saw them much when you were down in Brisbane.

'I didn't say anything of the sort! I loved my daughters! I wanted to see them, but I was blocked every time. 'They've gone out, they've gone to the doctor, and they've gone to school ...' but I've kept paying maintenance for them all their lives and you *know* it!'

I stare at him in amazement. This is not how I recall the sequence of events. I waited in vain for him to arrange another outing, but time passed and there'd been no word. I'd rung his flat and then the station where he'd been working and was advised he'd been transferred. Where, the officer couldn't, or wouldn't, say.

'Let him sweat,' I'd been incandescent with rage.

Later, I'd heard he'd gone to the UK and joined the Police Force there. I could have tracked him down through my contacts, but what was the point? It became a matter of pride not to make any enquiry. If that was the way he wanted to play at being a parent, then too bad for him. Yet he'd not only paid maintenance for the twelve years he was required to, but still was, even though they had turned seventeen.

'Yes, I know you paid maintenance for them. Every penny is banked in a Trust account for them when they need it, but birthdays and Christmases have come and gone and you've never been there for them. Where *were* you all this time?'

'Keeping my distance, as you wanted it!'

'How dare you!' Waves of anger sweep through me; I want to drive my fist into his face–

'What's going on? We can hear you all through the house!'

Shocked into silence, we swing around. Marli is standing just inside the kitchen door. She closes it behind her and hones in on David 'And why are you bullying my mother?'

I move to stand beside him. 'We're having a discussion, darling, there's nothing wrong.'

I try to reassure her, but she is focused on David. 'Who *are* you?'

He takes a deep breath and flings an, 'I'll-tell-her-if-you-don't,' look at me. There is no help for it; we are going to hurt her. 'He's your father, David Maguire.'

Marli's face turns ashen, her eyes wide with disbelief. 'Him? But I *have* a father!'

'David is your biological father. You were only tiny when you last saw him.' I am unable to prevent myself from shooting a bitter glance at him. To my consternation, she rounds on me, face flushed with anger. 'So, an embarrassment of fathers! When were you going to tell us you were in touch with him? *On your deathbed?'*

'Marli, I didn't know he was going to be here. We haven't seen him since you were four.'

'Well, as they say, it's better late than never,' she snaps at David, who is gazing at her in wonderment and yes, pain.

Something wisps in my mind, as I watch my angry daughter front up to her father. He was a loving father when he was using his access rights, not working all the hours required of him by the Force and when he wasn't with another woman. *Don't go there, Susan.* I close my eyes and lean against the kitchen dresser. God only knows what's going on in the lounge room.

'Marli–Susan–' Grim-faced, David runs an agitated hand through his hair. 'Can we get together and talk? I'm caught up in these investigations, but I'll make time somehow.'

Our daughter looks at him thoughtfully. It's only right she's given the opportunity to hear what he has to say and from the glint in her eyes, I suspect David will need to talk fast. What am I saying? The sod can charm the proverbial birds out of the trees. The devastating smile which caught my eye all those years ago softens Marli in spite of herself. He whips his notebook out of his shirt pocket to take her phone number. 'Will you allow me to contact you? What's your mobile number?'

Marli blinks and smiles back. 'You're sure you'll ring?' she asks nervously.

David squeezes her arm, after he puts his notebook away. 'You can bet on it. So, where's Brittany?'

My daughter and I exchange a telling glance and then I answer for both of us. 'She's with Harry and they're still in Sydney.'

David doesn't comment, but his look says, 'What have you done now?'

Marli glances anxiously from one to the other of us before appearing to decide that she doesn't want to get involved. 'I'll go and see what's happening in the other room. Keep your voices down, you two,' she says. As she opens the door to the hallway, she flashes a glance at David. 'You might like to know that Mum saved old Mrs Robinson's life the other day.' She flounces out of the room. I begin to gather up the cups and plates, exhausted and unfit for anything more than lying on my bed with the covers over my head. David has other ideas

'You knew Edna Robinson, so would you like to tell me what you know?'

'First of all, when did she die?' He is not going to get a skerrick of information until I receive the details.

'She was murdered between eight and eight-thirty last night. The staff left her a couple of minutes after eight and immediately attended a Code Blue. When they got back to the Close Observation Ward, they found her dead. Someone got in and suffocated her. Autopsy will confirm.' *Scalpel flashes, splits from stem to stern, fat peeled back...the smell...*

Grief wars with rage. The woman who had such trust in me that she tried to tell me a secret which she had probably carried for years, would soon be lying on a steel table, with her body sliced open and her organs being weighed. My stomach turns over.

I fill him in on my acquaintanceship with Edna Robinson, the little I've gleaned about the family and the previous morning's activities. The fragile state of my mind and heart are under threat, yet again. I've been confronted with two dramas the first day of my stress leave, and now my past is sitting in front of me, scribbling furiously in his notebook. Not what my counsellor would advise. *Dear God, I just don't need this with everything else that's going on.*

When I finish talking, he absorbs the information in silence for a few minutes. 'A family secret and Jack

Harlow is related to her,' he muses, sucking the end of his pen. I can see the wheels turning rapidly and probably accurately.

'Yes, and I was there when *he* was shot as well.'

His eyes widen. 'What? If I didn't know you better, I'd wonder about you, Susan. You could help us because you know who's who at the zoo. Untangling these country family relationships is a bloody nightmare.'

'David, I don't know anything more than you do. We've only been here two days, after all.'

'But you're friends with Daniella Winslow.' The implication is that I will go undercover for the occasion. *No, no I can't do this.*

I take the opportunity to study him as he writes notes. The young, incredibly handsome youth I'd married is gone, leaving a beautiful, mature and, heaven help me, sexy man. His physique, I note, remains trim with broad shoulders and chest, and slim hips. He was always fit as a buck rat and age hasn't changed anything. He's as slick as a gravy sandwich. I look for a wedding ring, but there is none and unlike my own ring finger, no white mark to proclaim to the world, 'discarded spouse.'

'Like what you see?' He's obviously amused and gratified by my scrutiny. A blush starts at my waist, travelling up to suffuse my neck and cheeks.

'For the record, I'm not currently married, Susan. I married for a second time a few years ago, but it only lasted six months. Seems I'm not much chop as a husband because I didn't do any better than when we were together.' His eyes darken with something which looks remarkably like regret, but is then replaced by professional determination. 'We're going to get this bastard for both the murders. My gut feeling tells me he's responsible for both killings.'

He stands up, pushes the chair into the table and takes me by the shoulders. I feel the heat of his hands through the thin fabric of my shirt; warm twitters curl in my stomach. I feign nonchalance.

'Susan, I meant what I said. I want to spend time with the girls. When's Brittany coming back to Queensland?'

'I don't know. Brit always makes the most of her grudges.'

My eldest daughter has decided I am to blame for her stepfather's desertion. 'It's all your fault!' she'd screeched. 'If you weren't so obsessed by that bloody job, dad wouldn't have found someone else!' I know she's right. I've berated myself many times for my failings since Brittany and Harry left. That is, when I'm not breaking my heart and crawling with guilt over young Danny Grey's death. I've been absolved from responsibility for the fiasco. His widow and my colleagues don't blame me, but in my heart I should have been more vigilant and kept a tighter rein on my team. David releases me, pats my shoulder and then heads for the hall.

The Winslow women are wiping their eyes and preparing to leave. They thank me for my hospitality, Carissa exchanges mobile numbers with Marli, who stands beside me, as the BMW drives away. Adam Winslow, with a red-hot glance at Marli, intercepted suspiciously by her father, slips behind the wheel of the patrol car. With a wave, they're gone.

The silence is absolute. A chill wind has picked up, causing the heads of the dahlias to strain away from their stakes. The cows standing near the fence, watching the proceedings with great interest, start to wander off, their coats rippling as air currents ruffle their long, shaggy hair. In a couple of minutes, the patrol car is a speck in the distance. My daughter marches into the house, straight-backed and boot-faced. I follow slowly, bracing myself for what I am well aware is going to be a somewhat lively "mother-daughter" discussion.

I am furious with myself, a thirty-eight year old experienced detective senior sergeant, recently Acting Inspector, allowing myself to be completely thrown by the presence of my ex-husband, father of my twin daughters.

CHAPTER 8

The Face in the Crowd

The Policeman

Monday: late morning.

Part of Senior Constable John Glenwood wanted to be at the incident room, set up in the conference room of the town police station, but the rest of him yearned to stay in bed with the covers over his head until the detectives solved the whole ghastly case or Edna and Jack sprang back to life–whichever came first.

His wife had been dressed and ready to go out when he arrived home from the hospital. When he told her about Edna's demise, she hadn't wanted to know anything about it. 'I didn't like the woman when she was alive and I'm not going to change my mind now she's gone and got herself murdered. And that Harlow was a disgusting reptile.' She slapped his dinner plate down in front of him and snatched up her handbag. 'You've been up all night, so you'd best get to bed as soon as you've finished this.'

'Nola, you can't *get yourself* murdered,' he protested wearily.

'Well, mark my words; this'll be a family thing.'

'Yes, Miss Marple,' he replied, as she disappeared into the garage, jumped into her car and headed off to the shops.

The lamb roast, which had looked and smelled so appetising minutes before, turned his stomach. He covered the plate with foil, put it in the refrigerator and poured his cup of tea into the sink, after which he plodded into the bedroom where he wasted no time in showering, getting into his pyjamas and climbing into bed. He closed his eyes and willed himself to relax, but Edna's blue-white waxy face kept appearing inside his tightly closed eyelids. He tried to transfer his thoughts to the identity of the face in the crowd, but still couldn't remember who it was. Perspiration prickled his whole body, turning his fresh, crisply ironed pyjamas into sodden, rumpled cotton rag.

Determined to get the better of his wayward thoughts, he focused on the caravan trip Nola and he planned to take as soon as he retired. Coober Pedy, the opal mine capitol of the world would be their first stop, where many people lived underground in order to escape the intense heat on the surface. The township even boasted an underground motel and church.

He was looking forward to making the trip a late-in-life honeymoon. Dreaming, particularly of sex, made him feel like a sad wanker, hoping Nora might accommodate him sometime, but Edna's waxy, dead face kept looming into his mind, no matter how hard he tried to dispel it. The harder he tried to remember the face in the crowd, the more frustrated he became. He needed to focus on something else, but Nola's dry comment – 'this'll be a family thing'– kept recurring. Finally giving sleep away as a bad job, he threw the twisted, perspiration-soaked sheets aside, arose and made coffee which he took into the lounge room.

John let his mind drift to memories of growing up on

the small farm which adjoined the much larger Robinson property. He had mingled with the kids in the primary school playground, and joined them in "yabbying" in the creek which ran through both family properties. John smiled as his mind fast-forwarded to the early 1960s, when winter turned to spring and the all-important country dance season started. Hormonal tension vibrated in unison with bees' wings in the rising temperature.

A few days before the first event of the season, a committee of ladies descended on the bush hall, organised their men to chop wood, chase the mice out of the slow-combustion stove in the kitchen and top up the refrigerator with kerosene. John smiled wistfully as he remembered being co-opted to clean the outhouses–the dunnies–along with the Robinson cousins, Jack Harlow and George "Slimeball" Murphy, now a well known developer. The women on the committee, which included their mothers, would set them to clear the outside dunnies of possum excreta–and possums. The dance committees always hustled to bag the travelling piano tuner after he'd finished the church piano. The priest had the largest congregation and therefore first "dibs."

It was the happiest time of his life. From trawling for yabbies in the creek with the Robinson girls, John and his cronies progressed to chasing them, and any others they could get, during the dances, where an advanced form of 'doctors' was frequently played in the back seats of cars parked amongst the trees. Oh yes, he knew the Robinson tribe very well.

The murder of Jack Harlow frightened him. The man had always been inclined toward the ladies and had an unsavoury reputation, but John couldn't visualise any boyfriends or husbands actually *shooting* him for it. 'More likely they've have bashed him to a pulp behind the pub,' he mused.

The shooting was no accident. The shooter concealed himself–or herself, because they couldn't rule out a markswoman–somewhere in the vicinity of the grandstand and found Jack's heart with deadly accuracy. The weapon, according to preliminary reports, had been a rural favourite, the Enfield SMLE bolt-action rifle. The few registered in the district were accounted for, so would that indicate that the killer was an outsider? Possibly. Jack's appetites had been distributed without fear or favour.

John arrived at the arena as pandemonium began to erupt. His first job had been to ring for an ambulance, advise City Despatch of what had occurred and call for backup. His next action was to peel Jack's dog, Stephen, off his body and surrender it to shocked friends along with Penelope, Jack's long-suffering wife. The hardest task involved keeping the over-excited bystanders away and retaining as many spectators on the grounds as possible. He was aware some had left, but was gratified to know that by the time his colleagues arrived, he had rounded up plenty of eyewitnesses.

In all his years as a police officer, he'd not once had to control a murder scene, so it was a shock to his system to have not one, but two murders within forty-eight hours of each other. Why Edna? What could an old woman possibly do to deserve being murdered? Two members of the same family a coincidence? He could understand someone wanting to shoot Jack. A thought wisped through his consciousness, but he couldn't quite grasp it ... his gaze homed onto the bookcase containing the photograph albums which he and Nola had lovingly put together and maintained since their marriage. Something or someone he should remember.

He got up, took the oldest off the shelf and sat back to study the images, smiling as he ran his finger down the pages. There they were, John and Nola, glowingly bridal on the front page, on honeymoon looking silly and happy whale watching at Hervey Bay. He turned a page. Their first home, dog–and Nora vastly pregnant, standing under the Hills Hoist, rubbing her tummy and rolling her eyes. The baby, now twenty-five, a squashed insect at her christening then first day at school–*wait a moment*– the christening.

He peered intently at the gathering. One of the children's faces seemed familiar, not the same name, but one of them for all that. He thought the person he'd seen at the sheepdog trials was him, though he'd only seen a back view for a split second. The more his mind squirreled around the memory but he needed to check his facts before reporting to CIB. He'd only met DI Maguire briefly, but he realised that the man would not suffer fools gladly. However, there was one person whom he could ask about the long-forgotten figure in the photo.

He set the album back on the shelf and returned to bed, confident now he would be able to sleep. 'I'll catch him later this arvo,' he promised himself, as he sank gratefully into bed.

CHAPTER 9

Home Truths

Susan

Monday: late morning.

'So, you're telling me you could not only keep dad, but you and our real father could barely get it together either?' Marli bites the words like a wolf tearing hunks of flesh out of a carcase–mine. 'The great Detective Senior Sergeant–oh, I beg your pardon–Acting-Inspector Prescott–who never puts a foot wrong, stuffed up *two* marriages?'

'First of all, I'm no longer an Acting Inspector, I'm a Senior Sergeant. Harry and I lasted thirteen years and I was nineteen when I married David.'

Accusations fly thick and fast, as Marli spouts reasons why I am to blame for losing her 'real' father, everything from being 'like, wack' and not understanding him, to being obsessed with my job. 'You were never home, Mum.' Her harsh tone and set face shock me. I can't believe what's happening to my calm, unflappable daughter, the one who's always been my rock.

I start to draw a deep breath, but there is no oxygen available. I have no answer, for her accusations send me spiralling into guilt. Tears well into my eyes and spill down my cheeks. I dash them away, forcing back nausea. How could I have been so *stupid* and made such bad choices in my life?

Marli's vengeful demeanour cracks. She throws her arms around me and we sob for our losses, Marli for the loss of the only father she has known and for the years she hadn't known David, I for every mistake I've made. After a while, we calm down and just hold each other. The familiar warm, cinnamon scent she is wearing fills my nostrils; I can find her in the dark by smell alone, like a sheep at lambing time.

'Okay, Mum. We won't talk about dad for now, but I want to hear about the other stuff, David and you.'

'Yes, I will tell you about it, but I need to emphasise that there were a lot of pressures on us. We were both to blame for the breakup.' *Thank you God, I can focus on this. Even though I'm about to lay myself bare to her scorn.*

'Well, you owe me and Brit an explanation. If he hadn't come here today, how long would it have been before you told us about him?'

I move over to the window, trying to decide how much I can reveal. Little has changed outside. The wind is still getting up speed, the cattle have moved down to the creek and are standing up to their bellies in water. The hens, tail feathers fluttering in a stiff breeze, are propelled along like yachts. The air smells clean and fresh out here–a mock orange tree at the back door sends it heavy, almost licentious aroma through the window. A normal day outside, but inside the house–inside *me*–life has turned upside down.

Marli takes the initiative again. 'Mum, sit down. I'm seventeen and leaving school for good at the end of this year. Don't you think it's time you told me all about how you met–Da–David–and got married and everything? Just start from how you came to join the force and when you met him.'

My daughter swivels herself around in the armchair, leaning back against one armrest, her legs flopping over the other and waits. I wonder how to tackle this, then decide to recount it like the story of someone else's disastrous life.

'I'd always been a 'good' girl, the one your grandmother and my aunts said they could always depend on. This meant I got to mind my cousins while the adults played bridge or partied, and my friends and older cousins yahooed their way around the neighbourhood having fun. My bedroom was perfection. Even my dolls were well-behaved.' *My God, you were a sanctimonious little shit, Susan.*

'I bet Aunt Melanie wasn't perfect,' Marli cut in, grinning. My younger sister is a great favourite with my daughters.

'Definitely not. Her dolls were thieves and harlots.'

Marli smiled, sending relief coursing through me.

'But I made up for lost time when I became a teenager and I thought I knew what I was missing. Everyone else was having a fabulous time clubbing and chasing boys. Well, men. And I got sick of being goody-two shoes. How much to tell? Good Girl became Party Girl, became Bad Girl. Booze–boys, bands, all the hot stuff. Your grandfather, who was nursing at the time, usually worked night shift. He changed to 'days' so he could track *me* after dark.'

'You mean you were a wild girl, Mum?' Marli's eyes are as big as an owls.'

My face glows hot. 'Hm. Yes. I–er–got in with a rather fast crowd who lived on the edge. In spite of my best efforts, I came eyeball to eyeball with a number of juvenile police officers in the course of my short-lived career of mad abandon. One of them, who took a lot of trouble to find me a job, encouraged me to finish my schooling. I had an enormous crush on him for awhile. Fortunately, the dear man was honourable. I'd never actually been convicted of any crime, so when I was eighteen I joined the force.'

'And started on your climb to break through the 'glass ceiling'.' Marli is triumphant on my behalf.

'More like bounced off the tea urn; women still didn't get many chances to shine. Making tea, counter duties, typing, licences and lost property, which included children. They were the female officer's job. A lot of the men got a stunned-mullet look in their eyes and disappeared into the woodwork if a child was found wandering the street.'

Marli laughed. I sigh, remembering the times my contributions had been overlooked, and the slights, crude jokes and 'put downs' I suffered at the hands of my male colleagues.

'How did you get together with him? David?'

'I partnered David on street patrol. He was an absolute hunk, always had teenage girls vying for his lordly attention which of course he lapped up.'

'So, did he know you fancied him?' Marli asks, grinning.

'I doubt it. Too busy glittering. Of course, every time he came near me, I had a meltdown, but I had plenty of opportunity to make sure he knew I remained unfazed by his godlike presence.'

'I've always known you to be so cool and collected, Mum. I can't imagine you when you were young!'

'Thanks a lot.' In the latter stages of our marriage, I'd been a screaming, hysterical wreck, totally out of control. I'm grateful she is willing to listen. Perhaps she will understand after all.

'So how did you get together?'

'My aloofness intrigued him. He finally realised I wasn't grovelling at his God-like feet. He started hanging around–casually, of course–while I worked at the front counter in the station, and then began parking his car close to mine. He'd poke around under the bonnet of his car until I came out and allowed him to engage me in conversation.' *It's so easy to remember the good bits.*

'My girlfriends kept telling me he'd lose interest if I didn't sleep with him and find somebody else, but for once, I stood by my mother's advice. 'If he swans off just because you're not 'easy,' he's no use to you anyway, my girl. He's just as likely to go off after somebody else at the drop of a hat, and more fool them.'

Marli's eyes are like an owls. I've never spoken so candidly about my teenage years, but she's old enough now to know her mother is a human being. I wonder if David remembers the first time we went to bed together, something no one else needs to know about. *Don't go there, you sex-starved crone...*

'So where did you get married?'

'We married in the registry office on a sunny autumn day and had our reception in a local Chinese restaurant. Our honeymoon consisted of two days on Tangalooma Island.' I don't allow myself to remember that time.

'Mum? Earth to muuuuuuum!'

'Er–'

'Mum, you're actually smiling. You don't do that much now.'

Stunned, I realise she's right. Our wedding photos are in storage. I would have to take them out to show the girls. It was debatable whether Brit would want to see them.

'We were happy when you came,' I tell Marli. *Oh, you liar, Susan.* But how can I explain how we really felt about my pregnancy? My memories threaten to overwhelm me.

'So, when did you realise we were twins? ... *Mum?'* Marli thumps my arm to keep me on track.

'What? Oh, not for quite awhile. We lived in a one-bedroom furnished flat at the time. All we had were our clothes, linen, pots, pans, that sort of stuff, and a cat. So we needed to find a child-friendly landlord. The cat was more welcome in those days!'

'So? Come on, what happened next?'

She tucks her legs up under her and stares eagerly into my face. My heart sinks. David finally managed to settle down and accept that our plans to travel and have fun were side-tracked. He was coming around to the idea of fatherhood when the bombshell hit. Having to tell David we were expecting two babies took a lot of courage. *'How are we going to cope with this?'* he'd yowled, white-faced. The news and birth of the twins was the beginning of the end of my marriage.

'What do you want me to do? Have an abortion? Give one away? Cut one out of my stomach?' I'd shrieked.

'So, what happened after you told him we were twins?' asks Marli.

We didn't speak for twenty-four hours. We'd been so careful not to touch each other. It's not easy to hold a six-month pregnant 'twin' stomach in when you're trying to squeeze past each other in a doorway. Lying at the edge of the mattress was difficult. Every time I went to the loo

I had to roll out of bed. David always helped me, but he made no attempt that night. The standoff lasted until he left for work that day, after which I cried myself sick.

'Oh well, we managed.' In fact, an almighty row broke out over the cost of buying two of everything. David slammed out to storm up and down the nearby beach. I sat on the cover of the septic tank in the backyard clutching the cat and bawling my eyes out. Not so easy remembering the bad bits.

In the event, our family and friends rallied around. David's parents bought a double pram, my parents (grumbling) the cot and friends organised a huge baby shower which generated a cascade of nappies, bottles, clothes and goodies.

I admit something of our difficulty, because Marli is no fool. 'We were scared silly. All of a sudden 'playing house' was over. Even while we thought we were expecting one baby, it was like playing dolls. For me that is, but I don't think it was quite like that for your father.' *Too right it wasn't.*

He arrived home the following day and announced with quiet anger, that he'd found us a house where we were able to not only keep the cat, but they were "kid friendly." And he'd take on extra work to keep the roof over our heads and save for our own house which we realised we'd have to buy. We were overwhelmed by the double pregnancy and so worried about money, we'd forgotten to love each other.

I need to choose my words carefully and not infer that we destroyed our marriage because we were too immature to cope with two babies. 'Your father worked every shift he could cope with because we needed the money. I stayed at work as long as I could. My male colleagues jittered, as they watched my stomach expand, like a thousand kilo watermelon was waiting to explode.'

We laugh. 'I was hidden away in the bowels of the station checking on licences, criminal records and doing paperwork. They had to send to the uniform stores to find XXXL shirts which would cover my stomach.

'So what happened when we were born, Mum?' My daughter isn't about to let me close down now that she's got me talking. Strangely, this has never really come up before.

'As the doctor predicted, you came early. I was issuing a driver's licence renewal when my water broke. The men were horrified. Someone called the female cleaner to hold my hand and mop, not necessarily in that order. I was whisked off to hospital and your father arrived in time to see the pair of you in your humidicrib.'

'Was he pleased about us *then?*'

'Yes, he was thrilled.'

It wasn't long before he changed his mind: 'Susan, can't you keep them from screaming? I've got to get some sleep. I'm working tonight, can't you do something? How long is this going to go on for?' *Well, sort of forever, David.*

'How did you cope with us?' asks Marli, brow wrinkled with anxiety.

'Most of the time I took you out for long walks while your father slept.'

I wince, remembering my nipples cracking and bleeding, and the babies only sleeping for minutes at a time. Finally, the clinic sister discovered I didn't have enough milk and put them both on the bottle. At first we were ecstatic, but then they got colic. All I seemed to do was cry and screech at David who tried to be sympathetic.

When he was in 'help' mode, we would sit up half the night covered in regurgitated milk and poo, half-asleep, each rocking a baby. The house remained knee-deep in nappies and baby clothes. I couldn't keep up with the washing, which piled up behind the bathroom door. I stayed in my dressing gown for the day and had to rush like a maniac to get dressed before David got home.

We grew haggard and snapped at each other. We got no relief from the pressure of newborns who were afflicted with colic. David's mother and sisters always had something more important to do; my mother and father were overseas on a long-planned trip. My sister studied at an interstate university, and my girlfriends were working, only able to help out here and there on weekends.

Marli's voice snaps me back to the present. 'Mum? You can't stop now.'

'Okay. My friends came over as often as they could, washed all the dirty clothes, cleaned the house and even ironed your father's uniforms. I was so grateful.'

But finally the shit hit the fan well and truly. After yet another argument, David didn't come home one night. Unfortunately for him, a 'good' friend couldn't wait to ring and tell me that he'd been at a party with his mates and gone off with a skinny blond named Cherie. The fury with which I greeted him when he got home had to be seen to be believed.

I dragged a bag from the cupboard and started stuffing his clothes into it willy-nilly, not caring whether they were clean or dirty, and pelted him with his own shoes as he stormed around the room. I raced into the bathroom, swept up his toothbrush, toothpaste and shaving gear and hurled them at his head. He ducked and they bounced off the wall. To the accompaniment of a screaming wife, and of course babies, who joined in with their usual enthusiasm, he charged out of the house, threw a bag into the car and fishtailed up the driveway.

'So, how come you broke up?' She is not going to let it go.

'David decided he would sleep better at his mate's place, which didn't help me one little bit. On his days off, he did traffic duty for private contractors or security for industrial companies. Even I knew that he wouldn't be able to keep working such long hours with so little sleep and I couldn't seem to cope.' Remembering that terrible time brings the heartache surging back.

'Don't cry, it's all in the past now.' Marli hands me a tissue, as the tears pool in my eyes. *I'm so weak and needy. Stop this!*

'I need to make it plain that it was not the fault of you and your sister. The number of times I went to the doctor and was told to, 'Pull yourself together, mother. Lots of women have worse problems than yours!' I blame myself for not standing up to him and demanding proper help, but post-natal depression was regarded as a figment of a woman's imagination in those days.'

'But what happened with David? Did he come back?'

'Yes, a few days later, but not until after the grand finale. I had a particularly awful night with you both and "lost it" about two in the morning. I packed you both into the car, with bottles and nappies, and raced over to his mate's house.'

Marli leans forward in anticipation.

'I screeched up to the gate, jumped out of the car and tore up the path. I didn't even think. I picked up an aluminium dog's dish from the porch not realising it was full of water, and hurled it at the window. I was so mad it went up in the air, hit the porch light, which was on and the electricity sparked like fireworks. It was like a bomb going off! The house blacked out because the fuses were blown.'

'You didn't!' Marli is suitably impressed.

'I did. It shocked me senseless. There was a sort of scuttling inside the house and David and his mate burst out of the door in their under-daks with their guns drawn, shouting 'Police! Get down, get down!'

'What did you do, Mum?'

I had actually shouted, 'Piss off, you bastard!' but wasn't about to admit that to Marli.

'Well, everything was happening. All around the street lights were coming on. I refused to back down and threatened to turn the hose on them next, if David didn't come home.'

David marched me down the path, threw me in the car and shouted at me to stay put or he'd personally shoot me. He ran back into the house to get dressed and take me home. Right then, a woman, I never knew if it was Cherie, but David swore it was Mick's girl, drove a car out of the garage and took off.

'My mother, the gladiator!' Marli is laughing.

In retrospect it sounds funny, but I quickly remind her it was loss of self control and nothing to be proud of. 'I was stupid, love, and I ruined any chance of a reconciliation.'

'Did he come back home?'

'Yes, but not to move back in.' I remember how, a day or so later, he'd propped his gorgeous bum against the kitchen bench, arms folded defensively across his chest and watched me folding mountains of clean laundry.

'What are you going to do?' he'd asked briskly, not about to take responsibility for any of the chaos.

'How would I know? I'm stuck here with the kids and you're away doing God knows what with whom!' I'd snarled.

He stayed silent for awhile, before announcing that we would separate to, 'get our heads together.' Even after all these years, I can remember the utter despair of that moment.

I sigh, and look sadly at my daughter. 'If only I'd been rational and calm, I might have saved the situation, and if someone had been available to advise me. But I was so angry and too exhausted to cope. David wouldn't consider counselling because it was "your problem, Susan," I discovered later that David's station OIC had tried to talk to him. The Superintendant told him to take me to the doctor and insist I be given a check-up and medication to help, but David was so fed up he wouldn't listen. I, of course, was too afraid to ask for anything from the doctor, because he had already made me feel so guilty and stupid.'

'Mum, that's terrible. Even I know about post-natal depression. We learned about it in school. And then David left again?'

'Yes.'

She's silent for a moment before asking the inevitable question. 'Mum, would you marry David again if you had the chance?'

'No way. No chance. Never.' I jump to my feet and charge to the window facing the mountains in order to hide my flushed face from Marli. It is late afternoon. I lean on the broad sill, striving for calm as I look at the shoulder of the mountain with the sun glowing on the granite outcrop. A flash of light half-way up the steep slope flickers and then beams again. Shock sends ripples of fear through me.

Sensing something wrong, Marli jumps up and comes over to me. 'Mum? What is it?'

'Turn around slowly and wander to the kitchen. Don't look at the mountains. Go now.' I move casually away from the window. 'Pick up the binoculars on the table as you go and keep walking.'

She picks up the binoculars and tries not to run out of the room. I skirt around the settee, keeping close to the wall as I follow. Marli hands me the binoculars with a questioning look. I slide into the laundry and position myself where the sunlight can't bounce off the lens and reflect back to the mountain. I focus the glasses on the spot where I saw the light. My heart rate picks up and the skin on the back of my neck prickles.

Someone has a telescope trained on the house.

CHAPTER 10

Making A Good Impression

The Policeman

Monday: afternoon.

John Glenwood had slept fitfully for a couple of hours, before throwing off the covers, dressing and heading for the station to write the report on his attendance at the hospital crime scene. After he'd handed it in, he fended off the press who were camped outside the police station and set off down the street, ostensibly on patrol. In reality, he used the exercise to try to contact the person whom he thought had been at the dog trials. But each time he'd dialed, the message bank answered.

In all the places he visited, the supermarket, the greengrocers, the hardware, people were edgy and agog with the news of the murders. Some, he suspected, were trying not to appear too inquisitive in case he assumed their interest meant they knew more than they should. The women were afraid to ask questions for fear of risking a rebuff, but babbled incoherently about how dreadful it was: 'Thank goodness, Jack didn't breed,' was one camp's take on it. The other school favoured the, 'Poor Penelope, what a *pity* she has no children' approach. The men had a different perspective: 'Jack got caught on the wrong nest at last.'

John worked his way through town, listening and storing in his mind apparently insignificant pieces of information. Frustration built; would he *never* get a reply to his messages?

When his mobile phone rang in the mid- afternoon, he answered eagerly. After the usual greetings he asked the caller if the long-distance relative had actually been present at the sheepdog championship and if so his caller had seen what happened?

The reply came after a moment of silence. Yes, the relative had been there, but he himself had not witnessed anything untoward and he'd been as shocked as everyone else when Jack collapsed. Glenwood felt disappointed. He'd banked on receiving useful information. Then he remembered something vital. 'We believe Jack was shot from the eastern side of the stands near the announcer's box. You were standing there when I saw you.'

'No, I don't think so. I'm sure you're mistaken. I was near the announcer's box earlier, but I wasn't anywhere near it at the time. But now, I come to think of it, I do remember seeing ... look, give me a few hours to check something out and I'll ring you back. No, wait a minute. How about you pop into town tonight, join me for a drink and we'll do some catching up? Seven-thirty? I should have some news for you then.'

Glenwood scrubbed his hand over his eyes. Something didn't feel right, but exhaustion muddled his thoughts. He almost gave an excuse that he couldn't come because of being on duty, but Nola babysitting their grandchildren in their daughter's home put paid to that. The image of a silent house with television shows punctuated by canned laughter seemed unappealing. He wasn't actually on duty, so he could have a quick kip if he went home now ...

'Right, you're on! See you at seven-thirty, mate.' He snapped his phone shut and headed purposefully for the main street. Pleasure flooded through him at the prospect of an afternoon nap and an unexpected night out. He dismissed a moment's unease and doubled back to the station, taking a shortcut in front of the school playground where he looked forward to playing Santa in a couple of months time.

He glanced at his watch and realised he had time for a cup of tea, but hesitated, not wanting to run into the CIB team until he had some useful information to impart. When he spotted DI Maguire's car heading in the direction of the hospital, he quickened his pace. If he hurried, he'd get his tea and, if there were any left, a couple of biscuits.

He greeted the young constables at the front desk, who were flirting with a young woman making up her face for her driver's licence photo, and went through to the kitchen at the back of the station, passing the conference room, now the Incident Room. Relieved only by a photo of a much younger Queen on the wall, it was now decorated with several whiteboards, on which were diagrams, timelines, lists and photos of Jack and Edna. The extra chairs borrowed from the town cultural centre would be scattered around the room, the table littered with mugs ringed with coffee scum and three computers bulging with data. Folders and paperwork were piled at one end of the table.

Excitement flooded through him. For the first time in his career, he would be contributing what he hoped would be a vital clue to two high profile murder cases.

***

The killer needed to do something.

Fast.

He'd been on borrowed time as soon as John Glenwood mentioned spotting him near the announcer's tower. Any time now, Glenwood would put two and two together. The man might be a country copper heading for retirement, but he wasn't a complete fool.

He willed his mind to quell the rage bubbling within, to remain calm and think logically about how to save the situation. Perhaps he might jump in the car and head out to the Glenwood's house? No, Nola would probably be home. An idea rose, like pond-life in the scum of his mind and the solution fell into place.

The senior constable would have to travel along the country road to town. The sun still set early, so less chance of being seen. Of course, there was the problem of *lack* of light, but just how to accomplish it?

He gazed around the room, seeking something– anything. A small box directly in front of where he was sitting caught his eye. Ah. He pulled it down off the top of the cupboard, dumped it on the table and stood chewing his lip for a few minutes. Yes! Glenwood, the "punctuality freak," would leave home at exactly six forty-five and arrive right on seven-thirty.

He remembered the bend with a huge granite rock stuck up right next to the inside gutter, where the camber sloped to the outside edge, with a steep slope straight down to the creek bed. He knew it well. The locals had complained for years about that section. There'd been several accidents, particularly by teenagers driving too fast, and he had been as outraged as the rest of the community, but now he blessed the parsimonious inertia of the Main Roads Department.

Thanks to the copper's penchant for punctuality, he could calculate almost to the moment when the Land Rover would arrive at the rock. With a little regret, for he'd always liked the man, he took a small item out of the box and slipped it into his pocket. Plenty of time to get into position. He would park a couple of kilometres away–no, he would ride his mountain bike. With the road racer's regalia, helmet and goggles, no one would recognise him and the police would never find the lone cyclist who may have "seen something."

'Poor Nola–no caravan holiday for you, sweetheart,' he chuckled. John Glenwood's life was irrelevant in this high-stakes game, where a stupid man's ego and a pious old woman's words could have led to humiliation and disgrace. By morning another problem should be solved. After that, he'd follow up on the Prescott woman, who'd been visiting Edna the day she'd 'swallowed her pillow.'

His safety depended on *nothing* being left to chance

CHAPTER 11

Requiem for Edna

Sir Arthur and Lady Ferna Robinson

Monday: late afternoon.

'Arthur, go and put your teeth in!' snapped Lady Ferna Robinson, eyeing her elderly husband over the cornflakes. She needed answers from him, but couldn't understand what he was saying. She was prepared to wait for him to go to the bathroom and fiddle with his dentures, but not to wait while he meandered around the house looking at books on his way back to the dining room.

She was therefore rather surprised, when he fished a large white handkerchief out of his pocket in which nestled a pair of grinning dentures. He proceeded to fit them carefully into his mouth, to the accompaniment of a good deal of clacking.

As soon as he'd finished, Ferna persisted. 'Arthur, what are we going to do about Edna?'

'Why, nothing, dear. She's dead.'

'You know what I mean! Don't play games, Arthur. You may be eighty years old, but you've still got all your marbles.' Edna had let the side down badly by bringing wretched media clamouring at the front gate for "quotes."

Two of them had even climbed the fence and sneaked up to the house, and taken photos of Arthur in his dressing-gown with Genevieve wrapped around his neck like a fox fur, until Ferna had the gardener set the dog on them.

She barrelled on. 'Of course we'll have the funeral in St Matthews, a requiem mass, and then afternoon tea in the church hall. After all, it's too far for people to come out here and Edna belonged to the Country Women's Association.' Her sister-in-law had been a very popular member of the blue-rinse set. 'I might give Marigold Fensborough a ring. She thinks she's so wonderful being the President of CWA, so let her work for it. They may as well cater this, after all Edna's been a member for God knows how many years.'

Anger shot through her, when she remembered how she had been pipped in the voting for president. Then her mind swerved to the matter in hand. She would have to contribute to the wake, but what? Sandwiches would be easy and could be frozen beforehand. 'Mark will help me plan the service at St Matthews. Arthur can get the drink organised.' Edna, thought Ferna grimly, would get a better send-off than she deserved.

Arthur frowned. A requiem mass was too–Roman. Ferna was so High Anglican that she was practically knocking on the gates of Heaven. He decided to throw his weight around. 'The service will be the ordinary funeral one and the wake will not be in the church hall, Ferna. It's fitting that the wake for my sister be held in our family home.'

Once Arthur had made a decision, his wife had the very own hell's job of changing his mind. Ferna, who had been enjoying a pleasurable vision of herself playing the 'grande dame' to the sycophants who came to pay their respects–*'So good of you to come'*– snapped back to attention and sighed. 'I'll order flowers and talk to the undertakers.'

'Hadn't you better find out when the police are going to release her body?' asked Arthur, dryly. Ferna shuddered.

In the excitement of planning a central role for herself, she had almost forgotten why Edna was dead. 'Well, I'm sure no one we know could have been responsible. She must have upset someone ... perhaps from the Guild.'

Arthur looked at her over the top of his spectacles. 'The *Ladies* Guild? Don't be ridiculous, my dear. One of the family did it. There's no one else who would bother!'

Furious, Ferna heaved her not inconsiderable bulk out of her chair and towered over him. 'Who then? Constance and Grace are in their dotage, Kathleen's a weakling and always has been and John wouldn't do *anything* without your permission.' Her crisp tones uncharitably disposed of her elderly siblings-in-law. 'What I can't understand is why? What could Edna have possibly done to make someone murder her, apart from driving him or her stark staring mad.' Suddenly she paused and stared right into his very soul. 'You didn't have anything to do with it, did you Arthur?'

Arthur looked at his cranky wife without much pleasure. 'Certainly not. I don't know why someone would want to murder my sister, but the fact remains that someone did. You can speak to Mark if you want to, but nothing is going to happen until her body is released. And *I'll* decide what form the service will take and where it will be held.'

Ferna stood motionless for a long moment. When

Arthur spoke in that tone of voice, even she dared not cross him. Arthur was one of the executors, but she hadn't been able to discover the contents of Edna's will. Not that they'd be likely to get anything. There was the grand-daughter after all, being as Edna's second husband was long dead and Edna's son by him had very deep pockets. Of course, that second wife of his, Beatrice...it didn't bear thinking about. 'I'll be in the garden if you want me. And by the way, there's cat-sick on the hall carpet,' she snapped, glaring at her husband's feline companion who lay in the patch of sunlight under the window, staring at her with downright malevolence.

When the kitten had arrived as a stray and attached herself to Arthur, Ferna had become involved in a tug-of-war for her husband's attentions, from which the cat emerged triumphant. Ferna swore that Genevieve distinctly resembled Lily, Arthur's alcoholic bitch of a first wife. The moment she left the dining room, Genevieve would be up in Arthur's lap, eating from his plate. She winked insolently as Ferna swept past on her way out of the room, fully aware that both her husband and his cat were equally pleased to see the back of her.

As he got up from the table and went in search of a dust pan, brush and floor cloths to clean up after his cat, Arthur dallied with the possibility of hiring someone to murder Ferna. To his knowledge, she had not spent so much as a second to grieve his sister's death, a woman she'd known for more than fifty years.

Not for the first time, Arthur rued the day he'd made Ferna his second wife. He should have made do with a mistress, but then he remembered what she was like when he'd met her–elegant, commanding and the perfect hostess. And then there was the sex. Twenty-five years ago, Ferna could screw like a crazed weasel when she put her mind to it. He lowered himself onto arthritic knees and proceeded to clean the hall carpet of the clump of furball stuck in the fibres.

Genevieve wreathed herself around his hands, delighted to have caused trouble yet again. He made a mental note to groom her, but then decided to get her clipped. After lunch he'd put her in the cat box and take her, screaming, into town to the pet grooming parlour.

He didn't want to remain under the scrutiny of Detective Inspector Maguire and his minions. He had a fair idea why his nephew had been murdered–unless he'd finally diddled with the wrong man's wife or daughter. But if that were the case, Jack would have been shot or bashed up years ago. Jack and Edna had left immediately after the family meeting and were known to have talked since. Normally Edna wouldn't have associated with Jack, but they'd been adamant that ... but who could have actually killed the man? Arthur didn't really want to know.

Cleaning completed, he put the gear away and wandered down the tarmac pathway into the garden to sit on a seat in the shade. Genevieve jumped into his lap and puddled energetically for awhile before settling. Minutes later, Arthur and his cat were snoring in unison.

The Robinson family were the first to settle in the district. Arthur's great-great-grandfather had brought his bride out on the train in 1903 to the small rough-hewn hut where the dynasty began. From those first hard years sawmilling and dairying, the tiny farm had grown from a small crop pasture to a sprawling, cattle and grain-growing property. Arthur's land stretched across the undulating hills, most of it was leased due to its owner's age. A company had planted a tree plantation on one half, which brought in good money. A neighbour leased the rest. The noughts on the quarterly cheques were very comforting.

The small acreage around the house was more than sufficient for Arthur's garden and Ferna to flaunt her importance. Arthur roused slightly, remembering the 1940s when he'd returned from fighting in New Guinea, starved from being in a prisoner of war camp. But it wasn't long before he could manage to work his cattle and take care of the family. 'Yes, take care of the family in the best way possible ... please God the police will never find out what happened ... '

'Arthur! *Arthur!* Where are you?' Ferna's playful 'come out, dear, wherever you are' tones penetrated his sleep with all the gentleness of a buzz saw, a sure indication that visitors had arrived. Genevieve tore the fabric of his pants as she bolted for cover amongst the rhododendrons; Arthur wished he could follow her. He struggled to his feet, still half asleep as Ferna hove into view waving a trowel, smiling viciously under a huge floppy gardening hat. 'She looks like a constipated sheep,' he thought spitefully.

A tall figure loomed behind her. Detective Inspector Maguire stood just outside the kitchen door. Even though he was not currently guilty of anything, the elderly knight felt his insides curdle as he got slowly to his feet. *No one must ever know. Had Edna said anything about–*

'Sir Arthur?'

The detective came toward him, holding out his hand. The world swam around him, like heat haze coming off the bitumen. Arthur struggled to focus, but then his body started to dissolve. He just had time to register Ferna and Maguire's shocked expressions, before he sank into darkness.

***

At first he thought he was still sitting in the garden, but this idea was dispelled as Ferna's beady eyes glared down at him as he lay under a fluorescent light. He didn't dare look around in case he was at the undertakers. Cautiously, his fingers fluttered around. He was laying on something hard–not stainless steel–a padded board. Then a man's face replaced Ferna's.

'He's awake.' He felt his wrist being picked up, his pulse taken.

'Where am I?'

'You're in the hospital, Sir Arthur. You've had a little turn.' The face metamorphosed into ten-year old, Doctor Jason Hargreaves. 'But don't worry, we'll have you up and about in no time and home again.'

He turned away for a moment to repeat his re-assurances. 'Don't worry, Lady Robinson, you'll be able to take him home again soon.' *Oh please God, no ...not with Ferna.*

Arthur wished they'd all go away and leave him in blessed peace. Weariness slackened his muscles. Somewhere a machine beeped. His limbs felt so heavy, all he wanted to do was sleep.

As he drifted into unconsciousness again, he recalled Edna's death in the Close Observation Ward and hoped he wasn't occupying the very bed she'd died on.

But of course, he was.

CHAPTER 12

The Turning of a Worm

Marli

Tuesday: morning.

Marli always reckoned her sister, Brittany, stuffed her thumb in Marli's mouth instead of her own before they were born, because she'd been shutting her up since they started to talk. The night before was no exception. She'd rung to tell her about meeting their father, David. Brit became ominously quiet before lashing into her, citing everything she thought Marli had done wrong all her life and finished with an ultimatum.

'You're not to go near him, Marli, do you hear me? Otherwise, I'll never speak to you again.'

'Why not?' Marli felt hurt and utterly bewildered. She had thought Brit would at least be interested. 'Don't you want to find out what he's like? And why he didn't want to be with us?'

'No. Like, what's the point?'

'But–'

'*Harry*, is our dad,' Brit snapped, 'and our loyalty is to *him*. He's the one who brought us up. That creep didn't even want to know us. Like, if we weren't good enough for him when we were babies, why should we drop everything and let him see us now? And anyway, I'm not going to upset dad by seeing this–David–so you can forget a great hearts and flowers reunion. Okay?'

'But Brit, we need to give him a chance, he's really nice ... we don't really know what went on after Mum broke up with him.' She didn't dare tell her sister about her mother's confession. Brit would go ballistic and twist things around so that she, Marli, would be to blame for everything.

True to form, her sister honed in on her thoughts. 'If mother has told you anything about him, it's all lies. She'd say anything to get herself out of the firing line. Look what she did to Dad! I hate her, and as for *him*–they deserve each other. So don't you even *think* about going near him! I'm telling you, Marli, if you do, I'm never going to speak to you again!'

'You can't tell me what to do!'

'Yes, I can.' The phone went dead.

Marli didn't know what to do. Disappointment and anger intermingled with the realisation that her own opinions and feelings didn't matter to the one person she loved more than anyone else in the world, her identical twin. 'She hung up on me! Brit *actually* hung up on me.'

Tears welled up and oozed down her cheeks, but she lacked the energy to wipe them away. All the excitement of seeing David and being privy to their mother's story disappeared like water soaking into sand. 'Doesn't he at least deserve a *chance?'* If she told her mother what Brit had done, she knew all hell would break loose and it would make the situation worse.

She finally went to bed and cried herself to sleep. When she awoke in the morning, it was with a steely core of determination building inside. She'd boasted she was adult and been trusted with her mother's secrets, so now she'd need to act like it. She hurried to dress, make the bed, feed her pet rats and clean their cage before breakfast.

She was hungry, but indecision had her firmly in its grip. Somehow plain cereal and fruit didn't seem to cut it. Then she saw it. *Happy food.* She dragged the plate of jam tarts out and peeled off the plastic covering. There was still some whipped cream left from yesterday's scones, so she piled a spoonful on top of each tart, after which, she took half a loaf of bread for the cows, and carried her stash out onto the back verandah.

The wind had died down; the sun shone. The traffic hurtled along the distant main road, matchbox cars piloted by well-dressed ants scurrying about their business. Her mother, surrounded by dogs, walked across the back paddock. Titch bobbed up and down behind them, trying to keep up.

The cows looked up with great interest when Marli balanced the plate on top of a post, and took the bread out of her pocket. As the slices vanished into slobbering mouths and she stuffed herself full of tart, she vowed, 'This time I'll do what *I* want.'

When they were babies, Brittany got the attention because she was noisy. The times her grandmother made one of her rare "Royal Visits", her sister was always the first down the path to meet the car and wrap herself around the tall, autocratic woman's knees. For some reason, their grandma didn't seem to like mum, which confused Marli. Parents are supposed to love their children, no matter what.

One time when they were ten, Marli had been behind the sofa reading a book she'd sneaked off the shelf–one with bad words which her parents had placed off-limits– when her dad and grandma came into the lounge. She'd slid the book under the sofa and concocted a tale about why she was behind there, but something about the tone of their voices made her frightened.

'Harry, you've got to stop Susan from pursuing this ridiculous this ... career ... it's so low-class. A daughter of mine being a policewoman is unseemly. All that blood and those gutter types she mixes with. You have to make her stay home and be a proper mother to the girls. It's for her own good. And it's high time she had another baby. Too busy to take the time out from her precious career, no doubt.' Marli's eyes widened. Were they getting a little brother? She'd like that. Her father mumbled something, and grandmother continued.

'Well, how should I know? You must be able to figure something out. Make sure she's always late for work. Create an impression of unreliability ... perhaps I might have a word with Sally Harijan. She's the Commissioner's aunt, you know.'

They moved to the other end of the room and lowered their voices, so she couldn't hear any more. She wanted to jump up and tell them not to be so horrible to mum, but was too scared. Not only would she be caught eavesdropping, but they'd find out about the book as well. She'd stayed absolutely still until her muscles stiffened and she perspired with the effort of being quiet. She'd thought they loved Mum, but how could they, if they wanted to get her into trouble? Marli didn't know much about working life, but losing a job was a *major* disgrace.

She and Brit had always known Harry wasn't their natural father but it hadn't seemed important because he was devoted to them. Once, when she'd asked mum about their real father, she'd been vague. The only time she tried to talk to her dad about David, his face turned red and he'd gotten a scary look in his eyes.

Marli hadn't realised the cop who came to the house with Adam Winslow was David. She'd gone out to the back verandah to put Titch in his pen, but their voices had become so loud, she had to intervene. Carissa, her mum and brother were in the lounge room, for God's sake, talking about their dead auntie! She'd rushed in and been confronted by a man who looked so like Brit and her, it took her breath away. When she'd found out he was their father, she'd felt kind of funny about thinking him a hunk. Father's were not supposed to be good-looking, though their father–Harry–was handsome, but that didn't count because he wore cardigans.

When *would* David ring? Her mother's job entailed long arduous hours. When the investigation into her cousin Ally's kidnapping was on, it seemed like she hadn't been home for days. And now this David, also a detective, was in charge of the murder investigation.

Fear threaded through her. Someone had been spying on them. She knew her mother was concerned, because she'd warned–no, ordered her–not to stray away from the house, to keep away from the windows at night and not to walk in the paddocks with the dogs. Why should she hide because some looney sat on the hill acting like a dickhead? She'd pretty much managed to push the shooting of the Harlow man to the back of her mind, but it kept returning to make her sick to her stomach. And then the old lady's murder would come back to choke her. At night, she would start out in her bed, but inevitably scuttle in with her mother.

She left the cows, walked the short distance back to

the house, wiped her sticky fingers on a wet dishcloth as she passed the sink and stood in front of the mirror in the dining room, assessing her appearance, coldly and clinically in the dim light. Will he like me when he gets to know me? 'Maybe not,' a small voice inside reminded her. Their father hadn't seen them for years, so did that mean he didn't like them? Had never liked them? Perhaps going to see him might be more trouble than it was worth. Brit's heated, stubborn reaction hardened Marli's determination to hear his side of the story. A teacher at school told them, 'There's one truth, another truth and the real truth, which is somewhere in between.'

She would see David and listen to his version, but couldn't wait for him to ring. They'd know of his whereabouts at the police station and she'd chase him down from there. She looked out the side door and saw her mother digging vigorously in the vegetable patch nearby, an enthusiastic audience of dogs scattered on the lawn, waiting for something exciting to happen.

'Mum? I'm going to the library. Do you want anything brought back from town?' If she really went to the library, then it wasn't lying if she did something else as well. She didn't dare say what she was going to do. She would be safe with her father and if he wasn't available, she would come straight back to the farm.

As her mother straightened and turned, Marli gasped. The morning sunlight picked up Susan's rich, red hair, turning it into a fiery length of silk, highlighting her glittering, green eyes and turning her skin to pearl. For a moment, Marli felt she was looking at a stranger.

'Yes, could you take my book back, please? And you can get the local paper if you like and some sliced ham. Take the fifty in my purse. I don't think we need anything else. I bought milk and bread yesterday. Drive carefully.'

'I do have my P plate now, mum, so give it a rest will you?' Marli let her breath out with a great whoosh. *Sheesh.*

Susan turned back to the garden bed and became "just mum" again, looking like a dag, in tatty jeans and a green t-shirt with hair hanging down her back. Marli raced to her room, selected a white shirt, skin-tight jeans and black high-heeled boots. Her hands trembled with excitement as she slicked gloss over her lips and dragged a brush through her hair. Adam Winslow might be on duty at the front counter as well. She made kissing noises at her rats' excited faces peering out of their hammocks in search of treats. 'Sorry guys, you've had yoggie drops this morning! That'll have to do.'

She wasted several precious minutes looking for her mother's purse, which she found buried under the dog's blankets on the sofa, then swept up the library book, grabbed the car keys and flew to the garage before her mother could decide to come with her. Her heart pounded as she backed her mother's car out, turned toward the driveway and sped off down the road. Interrupting David while he was working didn't bother her. He'd have to suck it up.

'To hell with you, Brit! You might be my identical twin, but you don't own me!' she shouted defiantly, as she turned, too fast, onto the main road and sped toward town.

CHAPTER 13

Edna's Archives

Susan

Tuesday: morning.

After the usual courtesies, Daniella Winslow plunges into the reason for her phone call.

'Susan, I know it's probably an imposition to ask you, but would you please come with me to Aunt Edna's house this morning? The police have finished examining her things and no one else in the family wants to go to the place. Ferna refuses to go with me. She can be a bit difficult.'

I observed her Ladyship's iron grip on the local populace when I went grocery shopping late yesterday. The old bat had the supermarket staff grovelling.

'Well, I don't know whether I can be of any help, Daniella. Isn't there anyone else you can ask?'

'I can't find anyone else to go. Please Susan, you are so level-headed and I feel terrible.'

I've never met a family yet who couldn't wait to grab the goodies, so I am wondering why this lot isn't breaking their necks to get into her things. Then something occurs to me. 'Are you and they, afraid the murderer is hiding in Edna's home waiting to get you?'

'Of course not! But I–well, yes, a little. What if the person who did it is still around?'

'You can be sure whoever murdered her will be a long way away, Daniella. He–or she–certainly won't be hanging around Edna's house.' *I really don't know if I can do this.*

'But will you come?'

Years of training are telling me to go, to face down my demons and conquer the heartache which seems to fill my every waking moment. My psychiatrist advised me to take a break right away from crime, but she isn't on the fringes of a murder investigation. Edna's whispered hint of a long-ago murder flickers back into my mind, as does the memory of the shadow in the doorway just before she had her heart turn. Could I, as David suggested, do anything to help? Use my 'in' with the family to see what I can find out?

Daniella is speaking again. '...and I've got to go through her clothes and things. I just need for you to sit in a chair and talk to me. Keep me company.' *No, I can't.* There is something about her tone which alerts me to the fact that this proud woman is lonely. Against my better judgement, I feel sorry for her. 'All right, I'll come, but only for a couple of hours and you'll have to pick me up, because Marli took the car into town,' I hear my treacherous mouth spouting.

She is delighted. It's no trouble, she assures me, and she'll be here in half an hour.

'But Marli is in town and will come back to an empty house.'

'Carissa's home. Tell Marli to go to our place,' says Daniella.

I phone Marli to tell her where I am going, but only

get voice mail. 'Go to the Winslow's place as soon as you've finished in town,' I order.

I scoot into the shower and then change into a pair of chocolate cotton slacks, a cream shirt and boots. The face which stares back at me from the mirror looks like that of a doll abandoned in a cupboard. Dark shadows, bags under my eyes and scraggy red hair are the least of it. I plait my hair into a French braid and then slap some make-up on. My sunglasses, carefully chosen for their ability to keep the world at bay, do the rest.

Last night was hell. Marli ended up in my bed and kicked me for what remained of the night. The trauma of the last two months hasn't passed her by and a fight on the telephone with her sister hasn't helped matters. I eavesdropped on her side of the argument, but moved away quickly when she snapped her phone shut and headed for the kitchen, where I was cooking dinner.

'Brit says she'll never talk to me again, if I even, like, speak to David. But she can't stop me!' she announced defiantly.

'That's just talk. She'll come around eventually.'

I tried to be positive, but my eldest girl could be very stubborn – well, bitchy. But if I concede that description, I would then have to admit what a bad mother I've been. Long hours away from home are the job description of police officers and being a single woman with babies, then small children, had cut me no slack at the time. My struggle after David left had been horrendous, until my Aunt Beryl came to my rescue and moved into my spare room with her two cats. The trio had taken over the household.

'It's time you had a rest, Susan, and none of those useless women are being any help to you,' she'd announced, referring to my mother and David's toxic female relatives.

Open-mouthed, I'd stood with our cat and watched the little parade of aunt, pram and her cats make their way across the cul-de-sac in front of the house and wend their way through the trees. I remember being so stunned, it must have taken me at least an hour to fall asleep after diving into bed, after which I slept for ten hours, straight.

However, it wasn't long before everybody settled down, thanks to my darling aunt who purchased a house and moved us in, God rest her soul, and two months later I was back at work, keeping the roof over our heads and resuming my heady career of tea-making, looking after lost children and kowtowing to a paternalistic hierarchy.

I soon began searching for ways to inveigle my way into investigations. Fortunately, David transferred to another station after we separated and came to take the girls out once a fortnight. On those occasions I made sure I was working or out somewhere, so he only spoke to Aunt Beryl who adored him and tried to talk me into attempting a reconciliation. My stubborn heart made sure it didn't work... *for God's sake, Susan, stop harking back to the past.*

I check that all the windows are shut and back locked, then ring Marli one more time. She answers and snaps at me that of course she will go to Carissa's, how old do I think she is and to get off her case. Right. *That's put you in your place, Susan.*

The dogs in the back yard start a 'visitors' ruckus.

'Susan? I'm here!' Daniella's voice, coming from the top of the steps, is an elegant shriek above the cacophony.

'Coming!' I snatch up my purse and race out to the front verandah, but as I lock the front door, my eyes are drawn to the mountainside where I'd seen someone watching us with a telescope. *Oh God, what next?*

Daniella chatters happily as she drives, leaving me free to watch the rolling hills sweep by, the crops spreading over the valley, a symphony of brown, yellow and green patchwork quilt. The symmetry is broken here and there with a canopy of snowy white flowers.

Unsolicited information about Daniella's friends isn't my cup of tea, but years of practice at listening to several conversations at once ensures I can't help absorbing what she is saying even though I "tune her out." I am relieved when we arrive at the front gate to Edna's property. I am out in a trice, we are through and I latch it, watching out for Edna's herd of goats who, I'm assured, are lurking nearby awaiting the chance to make a quick getaway.

The small, gracious Queenslander stands on a river flat lined with willows. A row of gum trees cluster around the front garden and stand sentinel behind the building. Her garden glows with native shrubs and a gang of lorikeets scream in the grevillea blossoms. Momentarily, they stop to watch our approach with beady eyes, then sensing we are harmless, fall to fighting amongst themselves.

Daniella stops the car at the bottom of the steps to the verandah, on which stand a couple of easy chairs and a table. As we reach the front door, a majestic ginger cat dozing in one of the chairs, jumps down and runs over to twirl joyfully around our legs,

'That's Fat Albert,' Daniella announces, as she wrestles the key into the lock, gently pushing the cat aside with her foot. 'The neighbours have been feeding him, but I don't know what's going to happen to him. No one in the family will want to bother and I can't take an animal in.'

As the door swings open, we are hit with a blast of warm air, thick with the lavender and musky aroma peculiar to elderly ladies. The inside of the house is dark and secretive, resembling an underground cave. Albert slips indoors and runs ahead of us.

'I suppose he'll have to be 'put to sleep,' she confides, sotto voce, as though the cat might overhear, 'unless we can find a home for him.'

My heart sinks. There's been too much death, and now that of a helpless animal? My voice seems to have developed a life of its own. 'If you can't find a good home for him, then I suppose I could–'

She swings around. 'Oh, would you? That would be perfect. I'm sure Edna has–had –a cat carrier somewhere and I know there's a bed for him. We'll bundle him in it before we leave.'

Smiling with satisfaction and I realise, relief, she marches in and out of the rooms, pushing the windows up to let cool, fresh air in. I realise I have been cleverly manipulated. Daniella has discovered my Achilles Heel: cats. We reach the kitchen where she flings the back door wide, before filling the electric kettle, switching it on and taking cups out of the cupboard. 'Coffee?'

'Yes, thank you.'

Edna appears to have been a collector of pre-WWII Australian china. All available surfaces are covered with ornaments, knickknacks and vases of dying roses. On the refrigerator door, held in place by a plastic yabby magnet, is a shopping list. The contents, written in the loopy hand of the pre-1950s schooled, are poignant: milk, bread, peanut butter (crunchy), eggs and cat food. Idly, I wonder why she was in town the day Marli and I rescued her from the public toilet and who brought her car home. Or had she taken a taxi? If she was shopping, what had happened to her purchases?

Abandoning the coffee-making, Daniella goes out to the back verandah where a large pile of cartons is stacked. 'Adam arranged for boxes to be left here so I could make a start on packing up.'

She drags several out of the pile, obviously expecting me to do the same. Whatever happened to *'sit in a chair and keep me company'*? Reluctantly, I take three out of the pile and follow her into the depths of the house.

'How did Mrs Robinson get into town the day she collapsed at the park?'

Daniella stops and looks at me sideways, like a spooked horse. 'Ah ... let me think. She drove in and Adam or Euon, I'm not sure who, brought her car home on Monday. It's in the garage out the back. Why?'

'Just curious,' I reply, casually. Daniella shrugs and leads the way back to the lounge room. The back of the large settee is covered with tapestries which apparently Edna embroidered herself. The whole job of packing everything away looks like a week's work for ten people. I could be so easily sucked into the investigation. The cop side of me itches to prowl through the house; perhaps it won't hurt just to see what sort of impressions I can pick up.

Daniella leads the way into a small study. Books have been pulled out of the shelves, drawers left open, the contents disturbed. David's troops have been thorough. I meander over to the desk and idly glance at her papers. Accounts, letters, ink splatters over several documents. Looks like someone dropped a fountain pen. Do people still use them nowadays?

Daniella bounces over and begins to sweep everything

into a plastic bag. 'These have to go to the solicitors,' she announces, 'for probate.'

'Are you the executor of her estate?' Daniella shouldn't be touching the contents of Edna's desk if she is not. What *were* the contents of Edna's Will?

She looks at me as though I was mad, and she could be right. 'Yes, I am actually. Myself and Arthur Robinson, but he's too old and tired to be involved in this. I'm not letting that old cow, Ferna, near the place.' She fossicks in a pocket and comes up with a couple of sheets of paper stapled together. 'I have a list of what everyone is supposed to get, apart from what's in the Will. Everything else is to be sold.' She puts them down on the desk and places a glass paperweight on top. I edge closer, hoping to get a glimpse, but she steps in front of me to pounce on a pile of letters, which she throws into the bag. 'I'll go through them when I get home. There's no time for that now.'

The opportunity to snoop at the list is gone. I glance around, uncertain as to what Daniella expects of me.

'You can start gathering up those photos if you would be so kind, Susan?'

An imposing bookshelf has been given over to dozens of framed photographs. I pick up the nearest, a sepia of a group of men standing beside their draught horses with a load of logs on a wagon They're all wearing suits with vests, sombre faces almost obscured by their hats and, so common in days gone by, the photo has been taken with the subjects squinting into the sun.

I am about to place it in the box, when I remember Edna's last words to me. *'It was a long time ago, but someone needs to know. He was murdered on the farm ... if anyone ever finds out I told ... but they don't know about you ... and now the sheepdog trials. That shouldn't have happened!'*

Edna and Jack Harlow; cousins. Had Harlow been privy to the secret which Edna had tried to tell me? Too much pain, too much death. My stomach swirls, beads of perspiration form on my brow and trickle down my cheeks. The light in the room darkens, to the accompaniment of rushing in my ears. I grope around and almost fall into a chair near the desk. I must have made some sort of sound, because Daniella is alerted.

'Susan, what's wrong? Are you ill?' She drops the box she's carrying, hurries over and crouches down beside the chair. 'Can I get you a glass of water? You said you haven't been well. I'm so sorry. It was thoughtless of me to ask you to come here. Perhaps I'd better run you home now.'

I pull myself together quickly. Something is telling me to stay here in this house. 'No, I just felt a bit faint. No breakfast,' I lie. 'Perhaps the kettle might be boiled by now?'

She is immediately contrite. 'I forgot all about it! Let's go out to the kitchen and have coffee, then if you still don't feel well, I'll take you home.' She glances around and her eyes focus on the photo which I've just examined. 'Mad weren't they? Fancy dressing in suits and woollen vests to go logging in this heat, and the women weren't any better with their long dresses and stays!'

She picks up the photo and holds it to the light. 'That's great-grandfather Robinson and his sons hauling the timber to build the original house on the family property. Of course, the main parts, the kitchen and bathroom have been modernised. Ferna insisted on that and I don't blame her, but it's still around fifty percent original.'

'What year was that?'

She turns it over and examines the back. 'This was before the First World War–1898 actually– but the photos for that time are all mixed in together. The more recent ones are there.' She points to the far wall, where modern photos are side by side with the ghosts of yesteryear.

'Do you know who all these people were?' I ask, craning my neck to see if there's any means of telling what vintage they are.

'No, but Edna was meticulous about writing all the names and dates and a paragraph or two about what was going on when the photo was taken.'

Was she indeed? The detective in me rises to the surface. 'Are any of them still alive?'

Daniella shrugs. 'Oh yes, some. Arthur, his brother John, sisters Connie, Grace and of course my mother, Kathleen. Only Edna has ... gone.' Her voice breaks. Daniella isn't as unmoved as she appears, but my experience is that families tend to crack hardy until the funeral and then break down. There is something about the open grave, the slow moving bier or the curtains creaking shut behind it in a crematorium, which can break down the most stoic, especially a guard of honour. *Don't go there...*

We sit in the kitchen and Daniella organises coffee. The hot liquid makes me feel better, but apart from slightly reddened eyes, my hostess shows no sign of distress. 'How old was Edna?'

'Seventy-six,' replies Daniella, blowing on her coffee to cool it.

'And did she keep photos of everyone in the family?'

'Oh yes, I think every single person who has ever been connected to this family is somewhere in Edna's archives, even the bastard vicar, great-uncle Roland, who bashed his wife senseless on her wedding night. The Bishop ordered him to get married because he batted for the other side, and that was a potential scandal for the church. He had a predilection for pickups in city parks. So they picked an elderly virgin out of the parish ladies guild, then forced him to court and marry her. Of course it was all hushed up, but a few people knew about it. The poor woman had no idea what a homosexual was–mid-1950s–and committed suicide six months after they got her away from him. It was all hushed up, of course, but these days she'd have had him up for assault and "outed" him on Facebook.'

'Good grief! And nothing was ever done about – this, Roland?'

'Oh no, he apparently lived to be an old man. "The devil looks after his own." The Robinsons have had their share of crazies, believe me.' She sips her coffee, eyes shadowed. Is *this* what Edna was referring to?

Suddenly, a way into the family archives springs to mind. A big fat lie blurts out of my motor-mouth. 'I did part of a librarianship course before I joined the–er–public service. It involved some cataloguing of photography, so I could sort all the photos for you. You really won't have time with everything you have to do and it would be most unfortunate if any get lost. Edna has gone to so much trouble to keep them. Adam and Carissa and the other children in the family might want to do the family genealogy one day.'

I've only done the training at the academy and read a comprehensive course which a friend was doing, but I have catalogued murder exhibits. When Daniella asked what I did for a living, I said I worked for the Justice Department which seemed to satisfy her at the time, but would she go for this whopper? I feel the idea appeals to her, but good manners prevent her leaping at the suggestion.

'Susan! That's an enormous job. No, it's too much to ask anyone to do.'

I take ruthless advantage of her social graces. 'I'm here for at least a couple more months and it would be good to have a project to keep me occupied. Really Daniella, I would be delighted to do it. You can come and help when you have time– and we'll crack a bottle of James's best wine!' I add slyly.

She looks undecided for just a few seconds, genuinely not wanting to impose. 'Well, if you're sure ... I really don't have time. All right! Thank you, Susan. Shall we just box up all the photos today and take them back to your place?' She's forgotten I am only house-sitting. We pack up the photographs. There are endless albums and boxes in the cupboards all bulging with photos. Fortunately, Daniella knows how many boxes there are.

We are covered in dust and exhausted, after loading the last of the boxes into the back of Daniella's station wagon and putting all of Fat Albert's personal effects into a garbage bag. Albert squirms, kicks and yowls as we stuff him into his carry case, all fat furry arms and pleading paws waving through the bars, claws extended. It takes the two of us to lift his case and poke it in beside the boxes. 'I'll shut him in the guest bathroom when we get back,' I puff. 'Do you think he'll cope with the dogs?'

'I know he will!' Daniella wipes her hands on a towel which she throws over the cat box, effectively blotting out the pitiful sight of Fat Albert's big, round, orange eyes. 'Edna had two dogs until last year when they died.'

It is just after lunch-time by the time we get back

to the house, run the gauntlet of the dogs and carry a furious Albert to the bathroom where he immediately kicks most of the litter out of his sand-tray and knocks over his water bowl, before settling down for a good sulk. Afterwards, we unload all the boxes into a side room.

Daniella declines lunch, saying she has a hairdressing appointment. As I watch her drive off, waving, I realise with some surprise that I actually like her. But I wonder whether we will still be friends when she finds out I am a police officer, and if I discover that at least one of the faces in the old family photographs was a murderer?

CHAPTER 14

The Empty Bed

The Policeman's Wife

Tuesday: mid morning.

Nola Glenwood felt something was wrong. John had an afternoon to late evening shift and should be home during the morning, but she couldn't hear the radio playing, hammering from the shed or whistling in the bathroom.

Nervously she closed the garage door, set her overnight bag on the concrete, picked up the bags of groceries, walked into the kitchen and dumped them on the bench. Automatically, she looked at the table. In thirty-five years, if he had been called out, John had *never* failed to leave a note for her under the garish rooster and hen salt and pepper shakers which they'd been given as a wedding present.

She slid her handbag off her shoulder onto the counter, took off her coat, checked the water level in the electric jug and switched it on. She walked along the hallway, glancing into the lounge room, slowing as she reached the bathroom. 'John? John, are you in there?' She cocked her ear to the door, listening for masculine sounds.

Nothing.

She moved on toward the bedroom, glancing into the rooms lining the hallway as she went, pretty much prepared for anything but the sight of the bed, neat as she'd left it late yesterday. Her heart rate picked up; he hadn't slept at home. Had he gone in for another night shift? But he would phone her if that were the case. She went into the en suite, felt his towel and looked at his toothbrush; they were both dry.

He'd phoned her at their daughter's where she baby-sat the previous evening to tell her he intended to go to the city, but refused to say why. 'Luv, I can't tell you what it's about right now, but I'm hoping to get some information.'

'Silly old fool thinks he's going to earn kudos from the CIB. They'll take whatever he gets and make out they thought of it themselves. John thinks the world of his job and the sun shines out of George Harris's bum,' she'd muttered bitterly to herself. She hadn't been able to argue the point, because she'd had to slip out before the supermarket closed to buy some chocolate treats for their grandchildren.

Had he received a message on his mobile while in town and gone straight to the station? Surely after sitting outside Edna's room all night, he'd taken time off. He must have been called out again. Nola had no faith in the police hierarchy to consider a person's feelings after guarding a dead body. She'd experienced too many years of caring for screaming babies, and later the children on her own while John was on duty. Nola could count on her fingers, the number of public holidays they'd enjoyed as a family when he worked in the city.

'He didn't leave a note ... he's never forgotten before ... but we've never had two murders in town before either,' she chided herself. 'That must be it. John's been called in early and what with one thing and another, he's forgotten.'

The electric jug was boiling. She took a last glance at the pristine bed before hurrying back to the kitchen. She thought she might give the station a ring to see if he'd gone in. 'I'll wait until I've finished putting the groceries away. Don't want to look like a fool if he's there,' she muttered, having forgotten her overnight bag left on the floor of the garage.

***

Tuesday: late morning.

Adam Winslow was not unduly disturbed when Nola Glenwood rang the station. 'No, Mrs G, he's not due in until this afternoon. Is there a problem?' He grew increasingly perplexed, as he listened to her agitated voice.

'No, he called in sick late yesterday afternoon. Loy covered for him.' He turned to his colleague. 'Did you hear from John last night?'

'No. Why?'

'His wife's on the phone. Says he's not at home and the bed's not been slept in. Apparently she stayed with the grandchildren in town last night and only got back this morning. She's worried he might have had an accident.'

'What's he up to?' They smirked at each other. Being young bucks on the prowl to get laid, their minds immediately sprang to the one conclusion which made sense to them. But Senior Constable Glenwood was the last man they'd expect to be playing away. Too old, for one thing and not enough imagination for another.

Adam knew he would need to cover all avenues of enquiry. 'I'll ring Loy and see if he knows anything. He was on last night until midnight.' Loy Ng, the senior's usual patrol partner and rostered with Glenwood on Sunday night.

'Hold on a minute, Mrs G, I'll make a call and ask if he came in this morning.'

He laid the receiver on the desk and went to use another phone, only to be advised that Constable Ng didn't know the whereabouts of John Glenwood.

Reluctant to return to Mrs Glenwood with no news, Adam inquired of the civilian clerks in the back office the whereabouts of the Station OIC and discovered that Senior Sergeant Harris had been called out. Only Ron and he were available. He heard a steady murmur from the station conference room, now a major incident room. Should he ...? Maguire was the senior officer currently in the station.

Adam hurried down the passageway and peered around the door at the far end. Detective Inspector Maguire, talking on the telephone but noting the constable's anxious expression, signalled he'd be a moment.

As he waited, Adam speculated on Maguire and his relationship to Mrs Prescott and her gorgeous daughter, Marli, with her father's penetrating gaze, his square jaw line, high cheekbones, olive skin and lustrous dark hair. The DI hadn't said anything as they drove away from the house the day before about catching him eyeing up his daughter, but Adam realised he'd better watch his step.

Seemingly endless minutes passed before Maguire finished his call and turned to Adam, only too eager to unload the puzzle onto senior shoulders. When he finished talking, the DI was silent for awhile before asking, with a wry smile, 'Senior Constable Glenwood isn't one of your tribal connections, is he?'

Adam almost choked. 'No, he's not. Do you think–?'

'Relax, Adam. It's most unlikely, but with two killings involving Robinson rellies ... on the other hand, didn't I hear that he likes to walk around town talking to people?'

Adam's expression lightened. 'Yes, sir. John knows which cupboards hold the skeletons in this town. But Mrs Glenwood said John always left a note to say where he was going if he left before she got home.'

Frowning, Maguire got to his feet and headed for the outer office, followed by Adam. 'Is she still on the phone?'

On being told she was, he went to perform damage control, but before he picked up the receiver, a weary-looking OIC walked in from the car park.

The tension in the room sent Harris into full alert. 'What's happened?'

Adam Winslow filled his boss in on the problem; Harris reached for the phone.

'Sorry you've had to wait, Nola. No one seems to know where John is right now, but he's due in this afternoon. He rang in sick late yesterday. You say it appears he didn't sleep at home last night?'

As the squawks from the receiver reached epic proportions, the Sergeant made soothing noises. After he'd finished calming Nola and hung up, he stared thoughtfully at the carpet and then looked anxiously at his colleagues, perhaps hoping for enlightenment.

'Is the man *likely* to be playing away?' asked Maguire.

'John? I'd never have thought it.' Startled,

Harris looked a question at the two young constables, who shook their heads, guiltily remembering their snide joke at the older man's expense.

Harris glanced at his watch. 'I can't remember the last time John took sick leave. Well, we'll have to wait and see if he turns up at four. He's always in early. In the meantime, I'll put out a call to see if anyone's seen him, just in case something's happened.'

Maguire nodded and went back to work. Shrugging, the two young officers turned to the front counter where one libido perked up considerably. A young, attractive dark-haired girl had arrived and asked to speak to DI Maguire. The other, belonging to Adam Winslow, couldn't even raise a twitch–her father was only metres away.

Inspector Harris reached for his mobile, but before he could flip it open it rang with an urgent message, the content of which rendered them speechless.

***

Nola could hardly breathe for the fear which flooded through her. No one knew where John had gone. She felt much as she had when her daughter, aged two, had gone missing in a department store. They'd finally found her an hour later, playing in the toy section a floor below.

Where *was* John? He never "chucked a sickie." But not coming home ... could he have had a heart attack? Was he lying in the hospital right now? But his fellow officers would have known if that were the case. What if he was lying injured somewhere? If only she'd known who he was going to meet last night. Why of *all* times did he have to turn off his mobile?

She cursed the Robinsons and their shenanigans. She didn't care about Edna or Jack Harlow. So what if they'd gotten themselves murdered? His wife, Penelope had probably ignored Jack's infidelity because she understood on which side her bread was buttered. Everyone in town knew that Jack was a disgusting creature who'd played around with other women all his married life. Jack had not been too fussy and if a jealous husband finally snapped and shot him, in Nola's less than humble opinion it was no more than he deserved. She hoped someone had told CIB about his carryings-on.

She brightened as an obvious explanation for his absence occurred to her. 'John's come home from town, fallen asleep in the lounge watching TV. I'll bet he's woken up and gone off down the street, talking to people. He knows everything that goes on around here.' The fact that under the circumstances this might be dangerous didn't occur to her.

'For God's sake, woman, pull yourself together,' she said loudly, embarrassed because she'd rung the station in a tizz. 'What they must think of me!' she giggled. 'Young Adam must be thinking I suspect John of having an affair. The very idea!' This was no way for a police officer's wife to behave, especially after all these years.

She marched into the kitchen, turned the stove oven on 'high,' smiling at her foolishness as she put flour, butter, soda water and eggs on the kitchen table. 'A batch of scones will go down a treat,' she said to the cat, who had arrived in the kitchen as soon as the refrigerator door opened. She sifted the butter through the flour, mixed in the soda water, egg and milk, then lightly kneaded and rolled the mixture. When it reached the desired consistency, she put it back into a deep bowl, popped a clean damp tea towel over the top and then put it into the refrigerator to cool while the oven heated.

Relief flooded through her as a car pulled into the driveway as she finished washing her hands. She quickly wiped them dry, smoothed down her apron and headed for the door.

'You silly old fool! Where have you been?' She flung the door open and came face to face with a grim Senior Sergeant George Harris.

CHAPTER 15

Breakthrough

Detective Inspector David Maguire

Tuesday: mid morning.

Detective Inspector David Maguire's patience had quickly worn thin when he interviewed Lady Ferna the previous afternoon. *Bloody hell, why didn't I bring the old battle-axe into the station before she got a chance to ring her mates?*

Lady Ferna had been in contact with the Police Commissioner and the local Federal and State members, not to mention the Premier, the Mayor and, 'God only knows who else.'

He tried for the umpteenth time to get Ferna to talk about her deceased relative.

'I really don't know, Inspector. Jack Harlow was not a close relation. Is there anything else?'

He wanted to strangle the old bag with one of the thick plaits wound around her head. She had done everything she could to obstruct him, even ordering him to the back door when he arrived at the house. He'd ignored her, of course. Having taken a chance and driven out to the homestead to catch the elderly couple in their lair, he hadn't been about to give up when Lady Ferna had begun her shenanigans.

'Madam–'

Her arched eyebrows did their dangerous best. 'Lady Robinson, if you don't mind.'

'Lady Robinson, you are not legally obliged to answer my questions, however, failure to do so will cause me to suspect you are withholding evidence. Now, let's start with Jack Harlow. I am informed he is your husband's second cousin and he lived in your household for about a year prior to his marriage eleven years ago and you have been in regular contact with him? So how well *did* you actually know him? I expect you to answer the question, thank you.'

'If I must. He was a perfectly ghastly man. Sir Arthur insisted he stay with us all those years ago. It was not long after his mother passed away.' Her mouth folded into hen's bum mode. 'He had a room out the back of the house.' Where he couldn't contaminate us,' was the inference.

Maguire clenched his teeth so tightly that his gums hurt. 'Did Jack have many friends?'

It transpired that Jack's friends were numerous and of the hoi polloi–farmers, truck drivers and *sheep* people. 'He was a disgusting reptile. Far too many dogs and an eye for the ladies,' spat Lady Ferna. Could a disgruntled husband have gone over the top? Maguire wished a wife had gone over the top and "done" Ferna, but having seen a photo of Sir Arthur, conceded it was an unlikely scenario.

Relations between Maguire and the old woman had deteriorated somewhat by the time Ferna led Maguire into the garden in time to see Sir Arthur collapse. The DI administered CPR while her Ladyship phoned, reluctantly he suspected, for help.

The paramedics bundled the old boy into the

ambulance and Lady Ferna, who seemed to feel her husband had let the side down badly, aimed a surreptitious kick at a fat, white Persian cat lurking nearby, then climbed into an ancient Bentley and followed the ambulance.

His team had brought in reams of statements from townsfolk and the general consensus from the locals was that, 'Jack was a good bloke. No one would want to shoot him, unless it was over a woman.' Further inquiries amongst the relatives and friends yielded similar information. Uniform branch only recounted rumours. John Glenwood, who apparently knew in which cupboards all the local skeletons were hiding, seconded general opinion.

'Was the old bat trying keep me from asking too many questions, or is she a just crazy old cow who like to treat the police like dog shit?' Maguire suspected a bit of both. After two days there'd been no progress on the Harlow case and during that time, someone had 'nailed' Edna Robinson.

The CIB team seethed with frustration. The perpetrator wasn't about to leap into the arms of the law of his own accord. Short-staffed, Maguire ploughed bad-temperedly through the interview reports. The security camera recorded the perpetrator of Edna's murder as around 190cm and of male build. A bulky, hooded coat precluded any identifiable feature, including the proportions of the killer's form.

Two members of his team interviewed the patients who were in hospital at the time. Most were elderly and those who still had all their marbles maintained they hadn't heard anything. His partner, Detective Senior Sergeant Pete Hansen, commented wryly that as the majority were wearing hearing aids, it wasn't surprising.

Before the first killing, the press consisted of one local reporter, who could be intimidated and was grateful for any scraps of information the local station tossed him. Now, when the city press weren't propping up the bars in the hotels, they were camped on the steps and in the forecourt of the station.

Forensics advised Harlow was shot in the heart with an Enfield SMLE bolt-action rifle and as Susan had surmised, the sniper was probably positioned amongst the cars parked below the ring announcer's box, around fifty metres from the victim. The point that the perpetrator was a marksman of some talent hadn't gone un-noticed, but so far none of the Robinson clan fit the bill. Enquiries of the local rifle club had yielded nothing useful, although there were several members who had the skill to have picked Jack off at a considerable distance, CIB had uncovered no motive for the crime. The commentators in the announcer's box at the sheep-dog trials swore they weren't aware of what happened until everyone started gathering around Jack. Maguire was incensed. 'Bastards had a radio up there and were listening to the cricket, more like.'

He peered crankily into his almost empty coffee mug. It was too much trouble to get up, re-heat the electric jug and make a fresh cup. His mind went back to Edna. How long, he wondered, had the killer stood there, watching and waiting for an opportunity to get the poor old thing? When his chance came, it wouldn't have taken long. Say, two minutes at most to suffocate her, a minute to check he'd left no trace and get out of there. The monitor must have been turned off before the killing. To do all that without being seen? An idea fluttered at the edge of his consciousness ...

He shook his head, unable to retain the thread. Frustrated, he got up to make yet another mug of coffee and root through the caddy, disappointed to find all the chocolate biscuits gone. Thinking dark thoughts of his colleagues, he selected a shortbread and carried his coffee to the end of the corridor. A police cruiser and four nondescript sedans were the sum total of vehicles in sight. The station OIC's goats grazed in the paddock behind the car park, stopping occasionally to rear up and grab leaves off the lower branches of the wild apple trees. An idyllic scene which had nothing to do with hatred, greed, jealousy or secrets.

He finished his drink and went inside to stare at Edna's gentle, sheep-like face on the whiteboard, side by side with the long, horsey face of sly Jack Harlow, who had left a large superannuation and generous life insurance policy, which was inherited by a noisy wife, ten dogs and some sheep. The insurance company would no doubt be praying that Penelope would prove to be the murderer so they didn't need to pay out. Beside that stood the diagram of the trajectory of the bullet and photos of the outlines of Jack and Edna's bodies–though the old woman's was safely tucked into a bed at the time of her death. The diagram of her room showed there was no way her killer could have hidden until the doctor and nurse left on their Code Blue emergency.

Heavy footsteps heralded the arrival of three detective constables, who gave verbal reports then clustered around the coffee maker, mourning the paucity of biscuits. After they left to follow up more interviews, Maguire re-read a copy of Edna's will.

She left a more than comfortable bank account, a cottage on forty acres, antique furniture and some valuable rings. *Worth doing her over for?* 'People have been done over for less,' he reminded himself. She had left her property to Libby and divided her cash and investments between the RSPCA and her son. 'Can't see one of them knocking Edna off,' Maguire muttered, 'but we'll check the grand-daughter.' Daughter-in-law, Beatrice Eams. Hm.

He'd heard that Libby had screamed the hospital down when she'd heard about her grandmother's murder. Fake? Unlikely, but possibly in partnership with someone? She was engaged to Dr Jason Hardgreaves but fortunately for him, the doctor's alibi had been provided by two nurses and a patient. They'd also established that the two victims, although related, hated each other's guts. Their only point in common seemed to be their membership of the same family, and Edna had strongly disapproved of Jack's extra-marital activities.

'There has to be a good reason why the old girl was killed, but what in God's name could she have done?' he muttered. The only person, other than hospital staff, to have spoken to Edna on the day she died was Susan. A giant hand had squeezed his heart when he saw her standing at the top of the steps to the farm house. The past thirteen years had been kind. Her glossy hair smelt of flowers. Her skin, always fine and clear, looked as smooth as silk. He had wanted to reach out and run his hand across her cheek.

'Jesus, don't go there ...' He shifted uncomfortably as he felt the beginning of a boner. Having just broken off a recent relationship, he had fled to the southeast to escape recriminations. The last thing he needed was more complication in his private life.

The phone beside him rang, startling him out of his reverie. He was soon brought down to earth by a lengthy discussion with CIB headquarters, during which Adam Winslow came into the room.

Maguire observed the young constable from the corner of his eye as he finished his conversation. Young and ambitious, it could have been himself standing there, jittering while a senior officer set him straight. Unbidden, a former Superintendent's voice flashed its unwelcome way into his mind. 'Maguire, you're too quick to judge. You don't listen to what people, Susan included, are trying to tell you. And one day that'll be your downfall.'

Not long after he'd left his marriage and four years later, lost his children. 'Damn. Why is it all of a sudden I can't function without thoughts of Susan?' The realisation that maybe he had never stopped loving her, was unpalatable.

After Adam had explained that the senior constable appeared to be AWOL, Maguire followed the constable to the front office to make soothing noises to Glenwood's wife, but was saved by the Sergeant George Harris's arrival. After expressing his concern, Maguire left them to it and trudged back to the computer, only to be recalled because his daughter had arrived at the front desk.

'I know you said you'd call, but I couldn't wait to talk to you. Am I interrupting your work?'

Maguire pulled a chair forward and gestured for her to sit. 'Nothing that can't wait. Coffee?'

'I'd love some, white, no sugar,' she replied shyly. He made two cups, set them on the desk and sat down. He felt nervous, unable to think what to say to this child he had not known since she was a toddler. They stared at each other, and then Marli took the initiative. 'Will you be here in town long?'

'I don't know. It depends on the cases we're working.

Of course, that makes no difference to you and me. Now I know how to contact you, we can get together. And I'm living in Ipswich now.'

She smiled and relaxed. He listened to her chattering, between sips of her coffee about her life, sister, pets and friends. His heart twisted with regret because he'd not been around to share all those things. *Damn you Susan, and damn me for not forcing the issue years ago.*

Harris bustled into the room. 'I'm sorry to interrupt, Dave, but can I have a word?' His look said, 'Outside.'

Maguire stood up. Harris nodded to Marli and backed out into the passageway. Her father placed a re-assuring hand on her shoulder. 'I won't be a moment. Wait here, okay?'

'We've had a message that John Glenwood's car was found down the side of an embankment on the road to town. The ambulance is on its way and I'm going have to go and tell his wife.'

'How badly hurt is he?'

'Not good. It appears he was there all night. Significant head injuries.' They shared a few words, and Harris accompanied by an officer, face tight with worry, hurried out to the car park. Moments later, the cruiser left.

'What's happened?' Marli asked, when they were alone again.

Maguire, knowing the word would be out in no time, filled her in on the details 'We'll have to wait and see how he is. Did you know him?'

'No. We've only been here since Saturday afternoon, remember.' Maguire could see her hands trembling.

'A lot's happened since then, Marli. I'll need to talk to your Mum again. Is she home today?'

'She was, but she phoned me and said Mrs

Winslow asked her to come with her to old Mrs Robinson's cottage. I'm going shopping with Carissa after this.'

'Constable Winslow's mother?'

'Yes,' Marli replied, puzzled.

'Why would Mrs Winslow take your mother over there?' he mused, chewing his lip. Susan getting together with the Winslows could be very useful, if only she would co-operate.

'Apparently she wanted mum to keep her company while she packed up Mrs Robinson's stuff. None of the family wanted to go over and mum thinks Mrs Winslow was scared to go by herself.' She rolled her eyes.

Would Daniella Winslow want Susan to attend Edna Robinson's funeral? The wake would be at Sir Arthur and Lady Ferna's property. Sir Arthur was still in hospital, but Maguire would bet his pay cheque on the old knight hosting the party. From what he remembered of his ex-wife, she'd had a strong sense of what was right and felt confident she would regard it as her duty to attend the funeral. He realised his mind was wandering, when Marli tugged his sleeve. 'So you will phone me won't you?'

He looked down at her, surprised by a great rush of tenderness for his child. 'Of course I will. In fact, if I can manage it, I'll take you out to dinner tomorrow night. Where would you like to go?'

Her face suffused with pink and her eyes sparkled. 'That'll be fabulous! Have you heard of the Dale Restaurant?' she asked, naming a trendy place up the road which he'd heard was the latest excitement in town.

'Okay, Dale it is. I'll have to confirm it with you, though. Anything could crop up.'

She looked resigned. 'Yeah, like, same old same old. I'm used to it with mum. It was nearly always da–Harry or sometimes his secretary, grumpy old Mary who filled in when she had to stay at work and there was something on at school.'

His heart ached with guilt. He knew he could have changed the situation at any time over the years if he'd really tried. He put his arm around Marli's shoulders, hoping she wouldn't shake him off and walked her back to the main office where they paused, riveted by a tirade from Adam Winslow. His colleague was listening, open-mouthed.

' ... old bastard Jack. I just know he said or did something to Carissa at Caroline's wedding a couple of years ago. She won't say what or I'd have done him over by now. I hated the bastard.' He pulled up short, flushing when he saw his audience. Maguire dropped his arm away from Marli and walked over to lean close to him. 'I'd be very careful of what you say, son. I'll see Marli to her car and then we'll have a talk.'

He ushered his anxious daughter out to her mother's car, saw that she was strapped into her seat belt and promised to confirm dinner. From her expression as she drove away, he knew she was hopeful, but bracing herself for a disappointment.

The angry expression hadn't left Winslow's face when he walked back into the office. Jerking his head in the direction of the Incident Room, Maguire stalked off followed by Winslow.

'Now, what else do you know about Jack Harlow, Adam? And for fuck's sake, this time tell me everything!' snarled Maguire.

'There's nothing I can put my finger on, but ...'

Adam went on to describe a possible incident involving Harlow at a family wedding previously, emphasising that he hadn't been able to get his sister to confirm Jack had actually made a pass at her.

'And she didn't tell anyone else that you know of?'

'No, I didn't see her talking to anyone after that. It was more of an impression I got because she was shying away from Jack. He was drunk, but not out of control I would have thought. It was more that Carissa was in tears at one stage and she didn't go near Jack again that night.' He paused, a faraway look in his eyes as he searched his recollection of events, past and present. 'In fact I don't think she ever went near him again. We didn't see much of him, except at family events.'

'How often do the Robinson's have gatherings of the clan?' Maguire asked quietly. Weddings could have been a fertile hunting ground for Jack; lots of tipsy women.

'We had one recently for Lady Ferna and Arthur's anniversary.'

'And did anything out of the ordinary happen at the anniversary party?'

Adam frowned. 'No, I don't think so.' Then his face lit up. 'Hang on! There was something different. There was a private meeting between the oldies which might have ended in a row. Now I come to think of it, Aunt Edna and Jack left early.'

Maguire was all ears. 'What? Jack and Edna? Together?' The first possible connection between them. 'Did anyone else see them?'

'No. I don't think so. It was all over and they were gone before most realised the meeting had even taken place. Aunty Edna didn't actually leave *with* Jack, because they don't like–didn't like each other. I was nearby when they came out of Arthur's office. There was Ferna, Arthur, Edna, Connie and Kathleen and of course, John. I think the meeting might have had something to do with Arthur's autobiography and the Order of Australia.'

David could cheerfully have wrung Adam Winslow's neck. The whole bloody coven was there, and this young idiot hadn't thought to mention it? 'Why didn't you tell us this before? You knew we needed to know everything about Jack and Edna. Did your mother and sister know about this meeting?'

Winslow straightened, flushing. 'I'm sorry, sir, I really did forget to mention it. They knew, but they weren't included, only the older family members. And they didn't say anything about hearing the row.'

'Right. Go and write a report for me and for Christ's sake, put *everything* in it. Who said what to whom, who was doing who under the rhododendrons. Got it?'

'Yes, Sir!' He scuttled back to the front office.

'Now we'll have to start questioning the Robinson tribe all over again.'

Maguire cursed, contemplating the bearding of Lady Ferna in her den for a second time. 'Perhaps I can get her in to the station and scare the bejesus out of her,' he muttered, with grim relish.

He'd been working on paperwork for over an hour, when his mobile rang.

'Maguire.'

'Dave, it's George Harris. Listen, John Glenwood was attacked with what they think was an iron bar, possibly a tyre lever.'

'What? I thought he had a car accident!' His gut

metamorphosed into a cold, hard ball.

'Yes, he did, but the doctors think he was attacked after the crash. That someone tried to kill him.'

'Tried?'

'Yes. He's in a coma, and not expected to live.'

CHAPTER 16

The Best Laid Plans of...

The Killer

Tuesday: midday.

The murderer enjoyed porridge with honey and cream, two soft-boiled eggs and hot toast with English marmalade for a late breakfast. He'd slept well; with the exception of sex, nothing ever disturbed his repose. Jack Harlow deserved to die. His hatred of the man almost overcame him, but he managed to force it down. On the other hand, he hadn't given Edna a thought from the moment she'd ceased kicking.

John Glenwood's death had been so easy to carry out. He had stowed his mountain bike in the bush a good kilometre from the fatal bend, hiked in and set himself into position behind the boulder with the equipment. All he needed to do when the Landrover hove into view, was point and press the switch. He had blinded John Glenwood with the device as he drove into the bend and watched avidly as the senior constable's vehicle swerved and then rolled down the hill. He'd scrambled down the embankment and shone a torch straight into Glenwood's eyes, before whacking the man over the head with the tyre-lever.

Twice.

Bone had crunched under the impact.

He leaned back in his chair, sipping a large mug of cappuccino, as he listened to the news on the radio. The announcer's voice washed over him. A disgraced politician was going to retire in order to spend more time with his family, the director of a well known bank had been booted out, taking millions of customers money in "bonuses" and a country policeman had been seriously injured when his 4WD ran off the road on the way to Ipswich.

Injured?

Pin-points of ice swarmed over his skin, penetrating folds and orifices like an army of ants. His handle trembled, as he leaned over to turn up the volume of the radio. The voice went on and on, the words ricocheting around him like bullets. 'Senior Constable John Glenwood is in a coma ... deliberate attack with a blunt instrument ... '

Glenwood was alive.

Fear rippled through him. What if the man awakened and remembered what he had seen? No, the torch had taken care of that. But what if he remembered who he was going to meet? But Glenwood hadn't suspected him. Even if John did remember, there was nothing to connect *him* with the shooting. All he needed to do was to be as shocked as everyone else by the attack.

The murderer stood up, carried his plates and coffee cup to the sink and placed them carefully in the bottom, turned on the cold tap to rinse, then methodically wiped his fingers on a handtowel.

'Keep calm,' he told himself, 'John Glenwood will die, no doubt about it. But first things first.'

Comforted, he moved to the window and stood for a long time, gazing out over the garden, an aura of calm wrapping around him like the arms of a lover.

'Now for the Prescott woman. My alibi's ready and everything's set for tomorrow night.'

CHAPTER 17

A Moment of Inattention

Susan

Wednesday: evening.

Fat Albert watches me cynically from his look-out post on the top of a bookcase. I was concerned he would fret for Edna and that strange dogs might frighten him, but Albert is made of sterner stuff. Having established his superiority in the household with one swipe of his paw across the nose of the leader of the pack, he slept on my head last night. We came to an amicable arrangement the first night he arrived; ninety-five percent of the bed belongs to Albert.

Marli spent the day trying on all the combinations of clothes she possesses and sending images of herself to her girlfriends on her mobile so they can give her the thumbs up and or down on her appearance for dinner with her father. Facebook chatter, emailing, washing her hair, doing her nails, playing with her rats and pup has been interspersed with worry that David might not be able to make their date. Finally, he rang late this afternoon to confirm their outing, so she was beside herself with excitement.

I was exhausted, though I had been sitting down most

of the day with Edna's photos. I tried to phone Brittany but her mobile was switched off. She probably wouldn't have spoken to me anyway, but I had to try. I lean back in my chair and rub my eyes as Marli appears, looking gorgeous.

'Love the black skirt and funky top, darling. Where did you get that outfit?'

'The shop at the far end of High Street,' she replies.

'Those boots look a little unstable to me.'

But she insists they are super-cool. Her hair falls to her waist in glossy black waves, her eyes sparkle with excitement and she has filched a pair of my garnet earrings. 'I won't see *those* again unless I hunt them down in her rat's nest of a bedroom,' I mutter to myself.

'You look lovely, sweetheart.'

'Thanks Mum. Do you really think Dad will make it?'

Dad? The dogs start barking and tear, en masse, down the hallway, their claws scrabbling for a hold on the tiles. David has arrived. A jolt of electricity shoots through me. I want to beat the dogs to the door, but I follow Marli sedately to the front verandah. Before her father can switch off the engine, she totters down the steps and throws herself into the car. With barely a wave, they are gone.

Feeling decidedly sulky and hard-done-by, I slosh whisky into one of Eloise's most expensive crystal glasses, wrench the refrigerator door open and savagely hurl ice-cubes into my drink. Am I jealous of my own daughter? 'Oh yes. You've joined the ranks of the truly desperate, girl. Get over it.'

Half of me wants to know David again, the other half wants to smack him out. He neglects his daughters all these years, then swans back into their lives and effortlessly bewitches Marli. Typical. But there is a conflict in our recollection of past events and I can't rest easy until I get to the bottom of it. Something doesn't add up.

I head back to the lounge room and sit down at the table in front of the piles of Robinson photos. Poring over Edna's vast collection, sorting them into years, I asked myself why I am putting myself through this. Is it because my police training won't let it go? Or do I want to redeem myself, at least in my own eyes, for Danny Grey's death? Instinct says the answer to Jack and Edna's deaths lies within the family. Sir Arthur and his siblings were born, grew up and raised their own children here and in the process became inter-related to other families nearby. Just that fact might have set up inter-family angst. 'Just what sort of motive would you have for murdering two seemingly innocuous people?' I ask myself, 'unless old Edna turns out to be practicing witchcraft. Or blackmail.' *Hm.*

Jack was less than the gentleman he pretended to be. It's more what Daniella *didn't* say about him which caused me to suspect he'd sexually harassed her at some time, if not more. And if indeed he did it to one, then it was unlikely he would have stopped there. What about Daniella's daughter? Did he have his eye and heaven only knows what else, trained on Carissa? Did Daniella own a rifle? Or access to one? And the skill to use it? And what about Libby? If he'd interfered with her, her fiancé, the young doctor might have taken matters into his own hands, no, I remember that his whereabouts are vouched for by colleagues during both murders.

Whose brain can I peck into? Adam Winslow. He might be a tougher nut to crack being a cop, but he is young and if I really wanted to pull rank, a constable. But do I want to break my cover of an ordinary mum on holiday with her teenage daughter? 'No, definitely not. I hope Marli hasn't blurted out it out already,' I say to Fat Albert, who is washing his furry bum, with fine disregard for modesty.

I promised myself I wouldn't allow David's presence to affect me. Fat chance. I try to think about Harry and what *he's* doing, but if I'm honest, I don't really care, except that Brittany has chosen to stay with him. But Harry was dad to my girls, and when all's said and done, David is an absentee biological father.

Finally, I throw open my quivering memories and allow my thoughts to free-range over the shambles which my life has become. The last two months have been appalling. I'm trying to follow the advice of my psychiatrist and not allow my mind to dwell on what I can't change, to allow the memories to come as and when they may, examine them, then put them aside.

I focus on my girls, but of course this brings me back to wondering why David didn't bother with them after they were four years old. I remember him standing on the pathway at the bottom of the steps of the house I shared with Harry, a toddler on each hip, covered in sticky lolly and tomato sauce, surrounded by the paraphernalia necessary for the comfort of tiny children. Reluctantly, it seems now, he returns the babies to Harry, who almost snatches them away. David passes the bags containing nappies and soiled clothes to me and hesitates. 'When can I see them again?'

'In a fortnight, as we agreed.' After all these years I can still hear the bite in my voice. Without a word, he turns away and stalks back to his car. Before I closed the door, he pulled away from the curb, wheels spinning as he vented his anger. We never saw him again and I didn't pursue it.

Neither of us wanted to go to court. I think as police officers we had our pride. David faithfully paid his child support payments, but I only remember cards and parcels arriving for a short time–and I thought he really loved them. Something flickers at the back of my mind and wisps away before I can catch it. A vaguely remembered look ... or word said long ago. I take a few deep breaths and damp the flame down to a simmer. I will get to the bottom of it one day, but not now.

I take a sip of my drink, carefully place it on a coaster and look at the photos on the desk. Countless relatives stare back at me with the stern, "take no prisoners" look which appears traditional with pre-1900s photos. Someone once told me that the reason they didn't smile was because their teeth were so bad. Babies, no matter their gender, were garbed in dainty dresses with turn of the century curls. Why didn't they put names on the back of photos in those days, for God's sake? Edna's cataloguing only started after about 1927.

How far back do I go looking for evidence of murder? Edna was seventy-six when she died, so post 1934. How old would Edna be when, presumably, she was mature enough to know about a *'dirty bugger'*?

My mind finally clicks into gear. Teenage to young woman would be a start. I sweep the current box of photos aside and start fossicking through the others until I come across a carton labelled 1948. Edna would have been around fourteen then. It was as good a year as any to make a purposeful start.

'God, look at the time!' I push my stiff body out

of the chair and walk around the house, stretching my aching limbs. Tired of their enthusiasm, I had shut the dogs in the back sun-room because of their tendency to lick my knees under the table. Titch is asleep in Marli's bed.

I peruse through the titles of my brother-in-law's classical music collection until I see one which looks familiar, Schubert's Impromptus. I remember his concert pianist daughter, Ally, playing it for us one night at her home. It is the work of a moment to turn on the stereo. I wander out onto the small side verandah to sit in the squatter's chair and gaze out onto the dimly moonlit countryside, allowing the glorious music to soothe my tortured mind.

There's been no discernable progress in my investigation of the photos. All the men look shifty and there doesn't seem to be anyone who disappears suddenly from the chronicles. 'Some detective you are,' I tell myself. This leads me again to thoughts of the past. Unable to stop myself, I relive that terrible night when tragedy struck.

Danny Grey's young, eager voice storms into my head. 'What do 'ya reckon, ma'am? Shall I take a look?' He wants to follow a lead to a Brisbane south side warehouse.

'No,' I hear my voice saying sternly, 'it's north side. That's where Delaney said. We're still waiting for Crimmons to show up. You're supposed to be checking phone records, Danny. So get on with it.'

'Yes, ma'am.'

It was the last time we spoke.

While the rest of my team and I fruitlessly chased a tip-off kilometres away, Danny disobeyed my order and went to a warehouse on the south side of the city on his own. By the time we realised we had been out manoeuvred, our youngest team member had walked into an ambush.

Danny radioed that he'd been shot and called for backup. We stormed south side, the SWAT team and Dog Squad joined us at the warehouse. The killer was somewhere inside and cut the electricity supply to the building. Rage and fear almost swamped me as we got into position. The scene runs through my mind like a movie reel, over and over without let up:

We position ourselves around the building, frantic to get to Danny. Efforts to negotiate with the criminal are fruitless. After a final warning, I nod to the dog handler and the hairy cop becomes a silent missile in the blackness, followed in by his master. Minutes later, the night is rent with a shotgun blast, followed by falling timber. During the commotion the dog makes his capture. The SWAT team thunders past me to secure the area and take the criminal into custody.

But it's too late for Danny, sprawled inside the warehouse on the concrete floor in the dark, bleeding to death.

Tears pour down my cheeks. I dash them away with the heel of my hand. My heart feels as though it is breaking in two. Why, why, why didn't he wait for assistance before following a dangerous criminal on his own? Damn the impetuous, ambitious young idiot. I'm angry with Danny for dying, I'm furious with him for making me angry and I want to kill him myself because his death has turned me into a card-carrying, snivelling, frightened mouse and right now, I can't see any way to climb out of the hole he has–no, *I* have–dug for myself.

Telling Danny's wife, Helen, that her husband wouldn't be coming home was the worst thing I've ever had to do. Her screams still ring in my memory. She hadn't wanted my colleague, Evan, or I to stay with her; I expect she couldn't bear to look at us. All we could do was wait until her family arrived, then leave.

The ensuing investigation and funeral were appalling. Amidst our personal and collective grief, my team continued to operate efficiently, though our minds and hearts were shattered. The media gathered around the tragedy like wolves circling a carcase, mine being the most visible, but I didn't care about that. Castigation has become my second name. 'Oh dear God, why didn't I listen properly, when Danny insisted we go to the *south side warehouse?* Why didn't I twig the other was a decoy?' If we, the team, had listened to Danny, the Dog Squad and Tactical Response would have been there to go in first. Being exonerated from blame makes it even harder to bear. Will I ever be able to get on with my life and function as a whole person–a police officer again? I have to forgive myself and that is the hardest of all.

I look at my watch; nine-thirty. Marli and David have got a lot to talk about and I should be in bed before he brings her home. I can't let them think I've been waiting up like a needy crone, longing for company.

I wipe my eyes, blow my nose and pick up my empty wine glass, but as I turn to walk back inside the house, over the music I hear the dogs growling in the laundry.

My skin crawls.

The air moves behind me.

Before I can turn, a hard body slams into the back of me.

Hands lock around my throat and squeeze.

The glass flies out of my hand.

My head is smacked onto the floor.

I am fighting for my life.

CHAPTER 18

Dinner with Daddy

Marli

Wednesday: evening.

Marli could hardly keep from pinching herself. 'I can't believe it. I'm actually in the car with my real dad!' She longed to reach out and touch him, just for him to look at her and maybe smile. Vague feelings of guilt for disobeying her sister twittered here and there, but quelled before they had a chance to take hold. Over the past couple of months, their stepdad, Harry, had slowly ostracised her only speaking directly to Marli when mum was within earshot. Hurt and bewildered, she had clung to her mother, withdrawing even from her sister.

'But now I've got our real father to myself. So suck it up, Brit!' No sister to scream at her, no mum to divert his attention, though she felt awful when she remembered her mother standing alone on the verandah watching them drive away. 'It'll be mum's turn next time. Tonight's my time.' She wriggled excitedly, stealing shy glances at his profile as they drove to the restaurant. It cost so much to eat at the Dale, but her father hadn't so much as blinked an eye when she suggested it. Perhaps he didn't know how much it would cost?

'Er, it's a very expensive place. If you wanted, we could go somewhere else?' she offered. *Please say we'll still go.*

He raised an eyebrow and glanced at her. 'You mean you want to go into town and eat at McDonalds?'

'If you think so.' A wave of disappointment swept through her.

David grinned. 'And deprive me of a decent meal? No way. You'll just have to force yourself to eat whatever rubbish they're serving here!'

He was rewarded by her brilliant smile, as he swung the car into the forecourt.

She cast him a coquette's glance. 'You're going to deprive me of a Big Mac? My heart is broken!' She burst out laughing and when he joined in, she realised with some surprise, that it was the first time she'd shared a joke with her *father.*

David glanced around, surprised by the modern ambience of the restaurant, softened with original paintings on the walls. It was not the sort of establishment he expected to find in a country town. Their plates of grilled seafood glistened in the sparkling lights. Marli was beside herself with excitement. She ate a few mouthfuls and washed them down with a Squashed Frog. 'Are you going to be in town for long?'

David finished his mouthful. 'Depends on what happens with this case. It's early days yet. We've interviewed the main cast, but there's lots more to go and so many times, Marli, enquiries come to nothing and you need to start over again. With any enquiry, you sift through a lot of facts, until one leaps out at you and this is either the one you want or it leads you to the one which will solve your case. We've talked to all the people who were at the dog trials, the judges, the announcers and the sheep handlers. A lot of people left before an announcement could be made telling them they had to remain.'

Marli ducked her head, letting her hair fall forward to hide her flushed face. "Lots of people" included her mother and herself. She exhaled slowly, trying not to let her breath out with a whoosh. She would be mortified if David knew they'd sneaked away from the trials. How would she explain that mum had rushed her away? She'd get Susan into trouble for sure.

'Did your mother have a good time with Mrs Winslow yesterday?'

Marli looked up and smiled. 'Oh yes, and she came back with Fat Albert, Mrs Robinson's cat. She said he needed a home and he slept with her last night. I went in and he was lying on mum.' She giggled. Her father laughed, and muttered something under his breath which sounded like, *'Lucky Albert,'* but she must have been mistaken. That didn't make sense.

Her father went on to ask her about what she was going to do now that she'd finished school.

'I want to be a vet. I'm hoping to get an OP1 so I can apply for a place at Queensland Uni, Gatton Campus. Brit wants to do medicine, but she has to get another degree first, so I think she's going to do Biology.' She chattered on, painting a word-picture of herself and her sister. David leaned back in his chair, bitterly hurt by what he'd missed.

'Is Brittany like you?' he asked, when she paused for breath.

'No, I'm a wimp. Brit's a Rottweiler. She told me not to ...' she stopped, clapping a hand over her mouth. A lifetime of loyalty held her tongue.

David's eyes twinkled. 'Not to speak to me? Don't worry, Marli. I'll deal with it when the time comes.'

'So why *didn't* you want to see us when we were growing up?' Marli couldn't restrain herself a minute longer. 'Mum told me what happened between you, but now I want your side of it. The truth and nothing but the truth!' she parroted, trying to make light of the tension she could feel rising between them.

Relieved she'd brought the issue into the open, he looked back at her, staring defiantly at him, biting her lip to keep control. Anger against Susan roiled in his stomach. She'd not dodge the issue again; he'd make time to corner her and demand some answers. He wiped his mouth with his napkin, wondering what Susan had said about him. He suspected he hadn't come out of it too well, but she'd been less than helpful all those years ago. Playing for time, he invited Marli to choose dessert, which he ordered along with coffee.

Then his phone rang. Signalling he'd only be a moment, he turned aside. Marli's heart sank. She just knew her perfect evening and her chance to really talk to her father was going to be disrupted. It had happened too many times with her mum when she was growing up. In fact, she realised with wonder, the last two weeks were the only time she'd enjoyed her mother's sole attention. 'Thank you, God, Brit's in Sydney and can't mess this up for me as well.'

David snapped his mobile shut and turned back to his daughter.

'W–what's happened? Do you have to go?' she asked through stiff lips. *Don't cry, just don't cry.*

'No, I don't, Marli.' He was silent for a moment and then made up his mind. She'd hear it all anyway with him living at the house. 'I asked for an update on Senior Constable John Glenwood and I've just been advised he's still in a coma. The doctors don't expect him to come out of it any time soon. In fact, he may not make it.'

His thoughts shot back to the rest of the information which Senior Sergeant Harris had imparted. John Glenwood's wife, Nola, remembered that her husband was going to town to follow up a lead into the Harlow shooting, but hadn't told her who or what it was about. Ultimately, they might be dealing with a cop killer.

'Poor Mrs Glenwood. Do they have children?'

The arrival of their dessert interrupted, but it didn't look as enticing as she had expected. David picked up his spoon and gestured to her plate. 'His kids are all adults, thank goodness. You not eating your tiramisu won't help Senior Constable Glenwood. Come on, chin up!'

He thrust thoughts of the investigation aside. That would come tomorrow; his daughter had priority.

Marli smiled reluctantly picked up her spoon and dug into the cake. At least there weren't little children waiting at home for their dad, like she was sure they must have missed him when they were little. He mustn't be allowed to get away with not answering her question.

'Please, can we return to you not coming to see us? I really need to know why!'

Tears shimmered in her eyes, turning his insides to mush. He would give anything not to have caused his child the pain of bad-mouthing her mother. Twisting the truth would do to save her reputation. 'Harry, your mother and I thought you'd become confused by having me popping in and out of your lives, and I needed to go away and work. I was in the UK police force and only came back a couple of years ago to Cairns.

I've been down here for two weeks. Marli, you and Brittany were always in my heart. I never missed sending you both birthday and Christmas presents.'

He didn't mention the child support payments which he'd never reneged on and which Susan said she'd banked for the girls.

She wiped her eyes with her napkin and glared at him. 'That's not what Mum said. She couldn't understand why you didn't come, and we didn't get birthday or Christmas presents from you after we turned six.'

David gaped at her. 'What? I don't understand.' He cast through his mind, trying to remember where he'd been when his daughters were six. He couldn't remember, so latched onto a present he'd sent for a recent birthday. 'I sent two hand-painted mugs to you for your last birthday. Do you remember?'

'No. We never got any mugs. What was painted on them?'

'Er, rats actually.' It seemed such a childish present now he was looking at a young woman, not the little girl he'd pictured her as.

'I've had pet rats since I was eight! I have two of them now, back at the farm!' Her dad liked rats? She gazed at him, momentarily diverted from her purpose.

David frowned. 'Perhaps they got broken in the mail and your mother didn't tell you?' He was trying hard to find a reason for the non-appearance of that particular parcel, and deep down, relieved that she didn't appear to think the present was childish.

'No. I overheard dad–Harry–saying to mum that the bas–you'd forgotten us again.' She caught her breath, hoping he'd not realised what she'd almost repeated.

'Marli, I sent those mugs by registered mail. I'd have

been notified if they hadn't arrived and the parcels would have been sent back to me.' His expression hardened; his eyes were like ice. 'Tell me something,' he paused for a moment, 'how well did you get on with Harry, your stepfather?'

'He did everything for us. He taught us to swim and went to school things. He even went clothes shopping with us sometimes and sat outside the dressing room while we tried on oodles of gear.' Marli smiled, remembering the good times. She didn't want to think about the last few months.

'Do you know why your Mum and Harry never had any children of their own?'

'Oh yes, we put in an order for a baby brother when we were about five, but then they told us Harry wasn't able to have children. He always said he didn't need any more because we were the lights of his life and he was happy with his girls.'

David forgot to breathe. The windows of his mind had been thrown open: Harry Prescott had deliberately stolen his children. *And he, a perfect idiot, had let him.* But Harry would have had help. Did Susan–? A snapshot of Susan's incredulous expression when he'd faced her in the kitchen on Monday morning popped into his mind's eye. No, not Susan, but someone had aided and abetted; someone who hated his guts. The perfect candidate came to mind.

'Was your grandmother there very often?' Susan would be working her backside off and they'd be conniving behind her back. .

'Yes, but she usually came during the day when mum was working and if dad wasn't home, she'd spend a lot of time with Mary. Sometimes she came over on the weekend and for our birthdays and Christmas. She usually only rang mum to tell her off.'

Marli's face clouded as she remembered past slights: 'Getting a little pud, aren't you Marli? Perhaps you'd better give dessert a miss tonight ...'

'Who's Mary?' Her father's voice pulled her back to the present.

'Mary Jellow, dad's secretary.'

David's eyes narrowed. 'Tell me about her,' he invited, signalling for more coffee and a coke for Marli.

'She's been dad's secretary for years, ever since we were little. He built an office out the back of the house with its own entrance and she worked out there. She's madly in love with dad. Mary used to stand in for him or for mum when neither of them was able to do things with us, like shopping and stuff. She's a bit dippy, and she gave us things, like books and ornaments she'd picked up at op shops. She'd walk the dogs and answer the phone, take in our private mail, take messages. All those sorts of things–'

It clicked.

Marli's face whitened; her eyes grew wide with shock.

David nodded slowly. 'So damned easy. Every time I tried to contact you, Brittany or your mum, either Harry or some woman would answer the phone, with messages purporting to be from Susan. I tried writing too, but never received an answer. I even went to a solicitor once to see what could be done about getting access, but while I was living away from you there wasn't any point in pushing for it. I admit that in recent years I didn't phone or write at all because ... but I'll go into that with you some other time, I promise.'

'It's all right.' Marli's heart felt as though it was

curling up in a ball of pain. The father she'd known since she was a little girl and whom she thought loved them had betrayed their trust. Because he'd done it to Brit as well, though of course her twin wouldn't care about it. Not like she, Marli, would.

David picked up her small, slender hand and continued. 'I thought your mother blocked me from seeing you and Brit, that she didn't want me anywhere near you. It had to be Harry and this Mary character, because there's no other explanation.' He thought for a moment. 'Were Mary and your mum friends?'

Marli bit off a giggle. 'Not like you'd notice. She hated mum. She's supposed to be joining dad in his new office. What a doormat! Anyway, he's got someone else now. Sharon in Sydney.' Her mouth turned down at the corners with the scorn of the teenage and untried in life.

David almost laughed, as he thought about the prospects of future boyfriends who thought they might treat her carelessly. This brought him to good-looking Constable Winslow. Better tread carefully, not make an issue of it.

'How well do you know Adam Winslow?'

'I only met him when he came over Monday morning. Why?'

'No reason. Just be careful. Are you ready to go?' he asked, as he reached for his wallet. *And I'll cut his balls off if he hurts her.*

'Did you ever think about us?' Marli's voice came out high and squeaky.

David looked at her anxious face. 'Yes I thought about you often, Marli, and Brit, especially when I had to deal with girls your age in the course of my job. Those were the times that no matter what I wanted, I was glad you were safe with your mother and stepfather. In spite of everything we can now guess about Harry and Mary's part in our separation, I am still grateful for that.' They smiled at each.

She couldn't string the evening out any longer. There was only one other couple in the restaurant and the staff were getting restless. Marli got up from the table, gathered up her purse and listened to her father joke with the manager as he paid the bill.

They didn't speak much on the way back to the farm. David seethed with anger over the conspiracy which he was sure he'd uncovered. Marli, revelling in the comfortable rapport between herself and her dad, quivered with suppressed excitement. Mum needed to know what they'd discovered and she longed to squeeze Susan as hard as she could, to show how much she loved her. She'd always known granny preferred dad–Harry– to mum. Fancy a mother loving your daughter's husband more than your own child. Surely ... no, granny was too old to be *'in love'!*

Her mind twisted away from the thought. Sarah McQuorqudale was sixty-five, but she'd always been ancient as far as Brit and Marli were concerned. All she knew was, granny didn't like mum's job and didn't approve of anything that Marli did. But she loved Brit to pieces. Pain arced through her. She didn't love her grandmother, but the knowledge that the old woman preferred Brit, still hurt.

As the car started up the long driveway, the sound of high-pitched hysterical barking racketed in the night air. Something was very wrong. David jammed his foot hard on the accelerator. The car roared toward the house, sending gravel flying, bottoming out as they rocketed over a culvert.

He slammed the vehicle to a halt at the bottom of the steps. Breaking glass and a heavy thud were followed by a muffled scream. David took the distance from the ground to the verandah in one leap and tore around the side of the house. Heedless of danger, Marli ran up the steps and followed, to pull up short at the side recess in the verandah.

The still form of her mother was just visible in the shadows, sprawled face-down on the floorboards.

Marli hurled herself to her knees, fumbling for a pulse.

CHAPTER 19

A Suitable Arrangement

Marli

Wednesday: late evening.

The dogs kept up their desperate barking.

'Shut up!' Marli screamed. Her fingers caught in her mother's hair as she fumbled for a pulse in Susan's throat. Gritty pieces of glass pierced the fabric of her jeans.

'Shut up! I can't do this, mum ... mummy, please ...no!' she heard herself sobbing. From the back of the house, the dogs continued to bark hysterically. Then her father bounded up the side steps and crunched across the glass to turn Susan over. He also felt for a pulse in her neck. 'Get a light on out here!' he shouted, 'and let the dogs out, for Christ's sake!' The music in the background rose.

A croaked, 'No' vibrated against his probing fingers, stopping him in his tracks. He peered down. Susan's eyes opened and she brought her hands up to her throat.

'Wha ... where ... no ... ambulance. 'Her hair smelled of flowers.

'Don't try to speak! We've got to get you inside. Get her some water while you're out there!' He dragged his mobile phone out of its pouch.

'No...ambulance ...' her mother croaked. David frowned, and put it away.

Marli hovered, undecided. 'And tea?'

'Whatever. Now get going! And turn that music off!' her father snapped, as he slid his arms under Susan's back and knees, preparing to carry her inside.

Marli flicked the switch; pieces of wine glass glittered in the light. She raced to turn the stereo off then ran to the laundry, where she waded through the frantic bodies to the back door. The dogs beat her to it, leaping up against the timber, pushing against the door as she tried to open it. She couldn't hear herself think over the pounding of her heart and the yelping.

'Shut up! Just shut up!' she shrieked, tears pouring down her cheeks. She wrestled the door open and was knocked sideways as they tore into the garden. Sobbing with relief, she slammed it shut and shot the chain across and leaned against it for a moment, breathing heavily. Then she grabbed a tea bag, dropped it into a cup and held it under the instant hot water machine. Her hands trembled as she poured a glass of water, retrieved milk from the fridge, got the sugar out and made her mother sweetened tea.

Back in the lounge room, tears poured anew as she looked at her mother lying on the sofa. Shards of glass twinkled in her hair; ugly red marks circled her throat. The top buttons of her blouse had been torn off in the struggle; her hair flopped around her white face. David helped her to sit up and propped cushions behind her back.

'I'll call an ambulance,' he announced, reaching for his mobile again. 'You might have internal injuries to your throat. And don't try to talk.'

'No!' Susan's eyes widened, her face working in

protest. Marli placed the glass of water and mug of tea on the coffee table and then plopped onto the sofa beside her mother's legs.

'Mum, he could have killed you. Dad's right. We have to get you checked out.'

Eyes wide with shock and anger, Susan's hand shot out and grabbed hers. 'Marli,' she rasped, 'we have to keep ... him guessing ... no, Dav ... David ... let's ...talk first.' She held her throat and coughed carefully.

David's face was granite. He grasped Susan's chin. 'Let me see?' The red marks stood out, where large finger-bruises were forming already. He pushed her hair back with gentle fingers and ran his hand over her head. 'You've got a lump forming, but the skin's not broken. You might have concussion.'

She turned her face away from his hand. 'I'm sure it's ... not ... too bad ... it's throbbing a bit but I'll be okay. It's easing... off already. I'll tell...you...if I feel...sick or... drowsy.' She swallowed painfully, and reached for the glass, but her hands shook so much she couldn't grasp it. Before Marli could lean forward to help, David picked it up and tilted it for her mother to sip.

'What about a brandy?' His eyes flashed a question at Marli.

She nodded and rose, but Susan grimaced, gingerly shaking her head. Marli wanted to cry; she'd never seen her mum look so vulnerable, not even in the terrible days after Danny Grey had been shot and Harry left them.

'No. Thank you.'

'I thought–' Marli stopped.

'So did I,' her father agreed. 'How are you now, Susan?'

Susan nodded. 'Just a little ... but... it's getting better.'

Her voice sounded as though she'd been at a party with a hundred chain smokers. 'How ... could I ... allow ... myself ... ?'

Marli felt perspiration break over her body, as it slowly dawned on her that a few minutes ago, the person whom she loved most in the world could have been brutally murdered.

'It didn't happen, so get over it!' she told herself sternly, reaching for the travel rug lying on the chair next to the lounge.

'Susan, it's not your fault. You couldn't know someone was out there ready to attack you,' said David.

'I should ... have realised there might be... a possibility.' She ran careful fingers over her throat. David looked the obvious question.

'We saw someone watching the house through a telescope from the mountain on Monday afternoon. Mum and I saw the sun flash on his telescope and mum got the binoculars,' Marli explained, trying to be helpful, as she tucked the rug around her mother.

'Why didn't you tell me?' Maguire snapped, sharing his anger between them. 'You should know better than to keep something like that to yourself, Susan. You *are* still a police officer.'

Susan waved her hands in dismissal. 'It ... could have ... been a farmer looking for cattle.' She coughed and took another sip of tea. 'We only saw a figure. Not even... whether it was male or –'

Marli broke in again. 'Did you see him properly ... Da–David?'

The corners of his mouth twitched as he made eye contact with Susan. 'Dad' will do nicely, if you like.' He placed the glass back on the coffee table and offered the mug of tea to Susan who shook her head.

A blush crept up from Marli's neck, flooding her face. 'It just feels right somehow,' she said, shyly. But her sister would go apeshit. *Stuff you Brit. Like, piss off!*

'It is right, darling.' Susan's voice sounded stronger. She hitched herself higher on the cushions, attempting to swing her legs off the sofa. David reached out, laid his hand on her thigh and held her back. Their eyes met. Something–an awareness–arced between them, then her mother put a hand to her throat. The marks were almost indistinguishable from the rosy flush which suffused her face.

Marli caught the glance and looked away. Deep inside, excitement twirled with embarrassment at catching her parents, at their age, fancying each other. On the other hand, perhaps they might ... no, don't even think about it. The notion of them actually doing anything ... like, yuk.

The moment over, David offered her mother the glass of water, which she accepted, concentrating on holding the vessel with both hands. His eyes roamed around the room, coming to rest on the piles of boxes scattered on the table and the piano. He frowned, stood up and walked over to them, gazing intently at the photos fanned out and piled in years taken.

'Whose are these?'

'Edna Robinsons.'

Marli took over the explanation. 'Mum told Mrs Winslow she'd catalogue them.'

Susan sucked in a painful breath, set her cup aside, lay back into the cushions and pulled the rug higher. David moved a few photos around and then turned to her, eyes gleaming. 'You mean you have the *entire* collection of the Robinson family here?'

Susan nodded. 'I think so. They go back ... for years.'

He almost leapt back into the chair beside the sofa. Marli leaned forward, listening with wide-eyed intent.

'Keep this to yourself, Marli, okay? We believe both Jack Harlow and Edna's murders are linked to a conspiracy someone wants to keep hidden.' He went on to expand on the CIB theory, including Adam Winslow's recollection of the family meeting at Sir Arthur's birthday party and the apparent dissension between some of the members. Then he filled them in on the details of John Glenwood's attack and Nola Glenwood's statement about John's reason for going to town.

'We believe it had to be in connection to Jack's murder. The answer could be somewhere in those.' He said waved his hand at the table. 'What are you planning to do with these? Have you seen anything interesting?'

'I'm still getting them in order.'

Outside, the dogs slumped into hairy heaps, looking like sacks of grain dumped willy-nilly on the lawn, exhausted from their fruitless chase through the garden.

'All right, I agree.' Susan drew in a deep breath, exhaled slowly. 'I think there's something in what ... you say. But I haven't ... found anything yet.' Her voice sounded like that of a frail, old woman.

'But if you do, you'll tell me. Right?' He reached across to squeeze her arm. 'And now, do you think you can tell me what happened? Out there?'

'Not sure ... yes. Yes, I can.' David whipped out his notebook and glanced at Marli. 'Could you get some more tea for your mother, please? And coffee for us,

Marli? If you want some, that is.'

'Not for me thank you, Marli,' her mother intervened, 'I've haven't finished my tea.'

Reluctantly, Marli got to her feet. She didn't want to miss out on anything interesting but, totally under her father's spell, headed obediently to the kitchen. She left the door open to the hall and listened to her mother's slow and husky voice.

'I was working on the photos for an hour or so, after you left. It was just before ten when I went outside and sat on the verandah.' She pointed to the sliding doors leading outside. 'I sat there for, oh, about fifteen minutes, having a glass of wine.' She paused, frowning.

'What made you come back inside? Did you hear something?'

'No. I didn't feel anything untoward, but he...must have used the music to sneak up to the house. I stood up to come inside, the dogs growled–no, snarled–just as I turned to come inside. He slammed into me and tried to strangle me. I fought, but he got the drop on me.' Her voice broke.

'It's okay now.'

Marli arrived in the doorway, carrying a tray with two coffee mugs, eyes wide as she looked at her mother leaning against her father, his arm encircling her shoulders. David grabbed a handful of tissues from a box on the table, which he thrust into Susan's hands. The diversion of making room for the tray and Susan trumpeting into the tissues allowed them all time to regain their composure. When she was settled again, he continued. 'How much can you remember about him?'

Susan sipped her tea and stared into the distance, eyes narrowing as she went back to the terrifying moment when she thought she would die. 'He was tall, probably a good 198cm. He breathed from above me, if you know what I mean?'

David nodded. 'I'd go with that. I didn't get a good look at him though. He legged it up the slope like a mountain goat. No hope of catching the bastard.'

'He *was* very fit. He slammed–' she coughed and cleared her throat before continuing. '–his body into my back and it was all muscle. His hands were like a vice.' Her voice wavered, momentarily. 'He wore gloves, those thin surgical ones. We struggled for a few moments but it felt like forever. That was when you came.' She glanced at David and then closed her eyes. 'He had no smell. I remember that. There was nothing, no aftershave, no personal smell. He'd washed himself and wore clean clothes?'

David scribbled in the notebook. 'So it wasn't a random attack. Anything else?'

She was silent for a moment. 'Yes. I think so. Nothing about his clothes... oh, he was wearing a tracksuit. Thick material. I grabbed his trousers and tried to roll him off me.' She sat up, almost spilling her tea.

David reached over and took the cup from her.

'Anything else? What about his hair?'

'No. I didn't get a chance to touch it, but I'm sure he was wearing either a mask or a balaclava. I caught a glimpse of either eyes or eye sockets.'

'And of course you couldn't tell whether he was clean-shaven or bearded?'

'No, he was behind me, but he has to be the one who almost came into the ward the day I went to the hospital. Thought Edna told me more than she actually did, or perhaps someone else did. Then told him what she was saying to me. Why else would *I* get ... attacked?

'She coughed. 'But I only had an impression of someone standing in the doorway and then vanishing. '

Marli thought if she had been in her mum's position, she'd not be able to remember a thing. Nausea swirled in her stomach. How could her father calmly sit there and write it all down like mum was nobody special? She had to be sort of special to him though, didn't she? After all, they'd had her and Brit, no matter what happened when they were married.

Then Susan spoke, her voice rough with pain. 'I'm angry with myself. Over the years I've been–exasperated –with women who've been attacked and who can't seem to give an account of their attacker, or didn't appear to want to and here I am, the senior sergeant, trained in self defence who couldn't even save herself.' Tears glittered in Susan's eyes. 'Some cop I turned out to be. First Danny and now–'

'Sh, sh. I understand,' David comforted. They sat in silence for a few minutes, each deep in their own thoughts. The only sound was the ticking clock over the fireplace. The thick strawbale walls gave an illusion of safety.

Marli jumped when he spoke again. 'Are you going to Edna Robinson's funeral, Susan?'

She started. 'Er, yes. Daniella Winslow asked, well almost begged me to, because of my so-called association with Edna. Why?'

'You know why. I need you to suss out the clan. Would you do that for me?'

'Aren't you going?'

'I'll attend the service. But they'll talk to you because they don't know you're a police officer and you'll go to the wake.'

'Well, they don't know yet,' Susan commented dryly as she sat up, swung her feet to the floor and stood for a moment, testing her balance. Marli prepared to grab her mother if she was unsteady. David closed his notebook and went to her side.

'Are you okay? Do you want help?'

'No thanks, David. I need to go to the loo. And no, I'm not frightened to go alone, thank you both. He won't dare come back here tonight.'

She staggered a moment, but waved them off as they attempted to range either side of her. They watched anxiously as she tottered out of the lounge room. Maguire put his notebook in his briefcase, satisfied he'd brokered a suitable arrangement between them.

Marli collected the empty glass, mugs and tea cup. 'Do you think she'll be all right?' she asked her father.

'Your mother's a tough old bird, love,' he replied with a smile.

'Old bird?' Marli feigned indignation. 'You've got to be joking! Half the force was in love with her when she was in Brisbane, even the young ones!' That'll show him.

She trekked to the kitchen, placed the tray on the sideboard, turned on the hot tap and rinsed out the crockery.

David followed, knowing his daughter had a romantic fantasy about getting her parents back together. *That just isn't going to happen.* His thoughts flicked to Donna, his ex-lover, with whom he'd broken up a fortnight prior to arriving back in the southeast corner of the state, but these were interrupted by a gnawing sound.

'Where's that coming from?'

'Somewhere under the sink. We've searched and

searched for it,' Marli replied, opening the cupboard door to reveal a humane mouse trap nestling beside the garbage bin.

'What's your mother going to do with a mouse if she catches it?'

Marli giggled. 'Probably put it outside!'

'It'll just come back again to join its family and friends,' he objected lightly.

'Oh no, there's only one mouse in here.'

'Marli, I've got news for you both, there's no such thing as a celibate mouse!'

'Oh yes, there is!' She gave a shaky laugh and bent over to stroke Fat Albert, who had emerged from under the grand piano where he fled when her mother was attacked. Marli quickly closed the cupboard door and reached for a packet of dry food, which she proceeded to shake into his bowl. 'What about Granny and Harry and Mary? You know ...?' How could she refer to Harry as "dad" when her biological father was standing beside her?

'It might be better to keep that between us for a day or so, while I think about it and to give your mum time to recover from tonight. I'll put a report in about this attack and we can get forensics out here discreetly to search for evidence, but there won't be any. This bloke's thought of everything, but he won't know what we're going to do about it. Sooner or later he'll slip up and we'll get him. So, no mentioning it to anyone, understand? Stay away from that part of the verandah and keep the dogs off it. No wandering about the place on your own, either!'

Glowing with joy at sharing a conspiracy with David, Marli would have promised anything. Susan came into the kitchen, her face tight and pale. Shadows lurked under her eyes; she'd changed her clothes and buttoned her shirt right up the top. Marli went over, put her arms around her mother's waist and buried her head in the soft breast. 'Mummy, can I sleep with you tonight?' she begged childishly, tightening her hold as she felt tremors course through her mother's body.

'Yes, of course you can. I'll be glad of the company.'

David watched them, memories of the past crowding into his mind, recalling the Susan of almost seventeen years ago, clutching two black-haired bundles at her beautiful, engorged breasts. A memory of the warm, sweet smell of milk, mingled with freshly bathed and powdered baby filled his nostrils as strongly as if it were yesterday. *That fucking bastard Harry and her old cow of a mother.*

An unwelcome reminder that he had generously contributed to the breakup, crept into his mind, and anger, compounded by his own guilt coursed through him as he thought of the wasted years. Without a shadow of a doubt, if he caught the bastard who tried to hurt Susan, he'd shoot to kill. Having missed getting her tonight, there was nothing surer in Maguire's mind than that the murderer of Harlow and Edna Robinson would be back, for who else could it be? He straightened purposefully and walked to the kitchen door where he stopped, turned and glared at the women.

'Well, you're going to have more company. I'm moving in.'

CHAPTER 20

Before Dawn

Detective Inspector David Maguire

Thursday: 4.30am.

'Maguire. Yes? *What?* Wasn't he being guarded?'

Stereophonic squawks announced that the hospital was on fire; Senior Constable Glenwood had been attacked in ICU and the constable on guard missing.

'Okay, fill me in when I get there.' Maguire cut the call short and pocketed his phone. Then he grabbed a piece of toast, threw on his jacket and sprinted for his car, shouting for Susan and Marli to lock the doors. Seething, he put his foot down hard on the accelerator, confident that he wouldn't be pulled up by traffic colleagues at this time of the morning. If it wasn't bad enough Susan being attacked, he was now faced with a second murder attempt on a fellow police officer. He was afraid to speculate on what might have happened to the young constable guarding him.

'Fucking hell,' he growled, as he tyre-squealed a tight bend in the road and was brought to an abrupt halt as a fire truck stormed toward him then cut across in front of his car and turned into the hospital driveway.

Numerous black and fluorescent-yellow figures scurried between two other fire engines and the back of the hospital, manipulating gleaming water hoses. Maguire pulled into the far corner of the car park, and pressed the speed-dial on his mobile. His partner, Detective Senior Sergeant Peter Hansen answered.

'Dave?'

'What's going on up there, Pete?' He climbed out of his car and squinted into the glare of the emergency lighting.

'The bastard set fire to one of the offices and then threw a smoke bomb. That's how he got to Smenton and Glenwood.'

'Christ! No sign of Smenton?'

'No, not yet. I'll meet you around at the morgue, Dave, we can talk there.'

Maguire snapped off the phone and edged his way between the vehicles, aiming for the narrow alleyway between the main building and the separate unit which served as the morgue. The stink of wet ashes invaded his nostrils. As he drew closer, he saw his colleague picking his way by torchlight.

As Hansen came up to him, Maguire took a deep breath. 'Tell me, from the start, Pete.'

'It's up the shit, mate. The nurse on duty at this end of the hospital was running past the ICU after the sirens went off, heard the alarms on his monitors, but couldn't see Smenton. Then she found Glenwood in a coma. All hell broke loose. The fire was lit at the other end of the building, obviously to draw attention away from this end. The brigade took the call at 4.20.'

He nodded toward the engines. 'It was a pile of newspapers and cardboard boxes, nothing serious, and they evacuated the patients into the gardens. The team's inside hunting for Smenton ...' Maguire realised the situation was getting out of control. Not only did they not have a motive for the killings, the murderer was doing whatever he wanted–no, not strictly true. The bastard had been foiled last night, and John Glenwood was apparently still alive, for the moment.

'We've got to find Ken Smenton ...' His voice trailed away as Constable Loy Ng raced out of the building and came up to them.

'We found Ken, sir, knocked out in one of the visitor's toilets.'

'How badly is he hurt?' asked Maguire.

'Head wound. They've got him in A & E.'

'Where's Senior Sergeant Harris?'

'Inside waiting to see how Ken is.' The young constable was breathing hard.

'Okay, can we get in there now?'

'I'll ask the chief,' Hansen offered and headed in the direction of the fire crew.

'You all right?' Maguire asked Ng.

'Yes, thank you, fine sir. I got some information about what happened to John while we were searching for Ken. Somehow he got an overdose of insulin. The nurse who found him has a sister who's a diabetic. She recognised the symptoms, took a chance and injected him with glucose. '

'Thanks, Constable. We've got a right one here, that's for sure,' Maguire answered grimly, as he watched the fire chief supervising the rolling of hoses and stacking away of equipment.

'We can go in, Dave,' called Hansen. They all headed into the hospital where an ashen-faced Director Eams, lips folded in a thin line, met them outside the ICU. 'Mr Glenwood was given insulin, Inspector. When the nurse answered the monitor alarm, she found his bedclothes were disturbed. Blood was seeping out from under the nail of his left big toe. It would be the work of a moment to whip the sheet up and inject him. I have no idea how this happened, but in view of Edna's murder, I assume whoever did it has a key to an outside door, or some other way of getting in.'

Mrs Eams leaned back against the wall, her face white and strained, hands pressed to the front of her smoke-blackened clothes. She looked as though she was about to collapse.

'The bastard thinks of everything, but we now know he has access to insulin,' replied Maguire.

'Are all your patients safe, Mrs Eams?' asked Hansen.

'Yes, thank you, we got them out safely. And the bedridden ones haven't appeared to suffer any smoke inhalation, no thanks to your murderer!' She straightened her back, nodded abruptly and then returned to the ICU. Maguire poked his head around the door, but couldn't see Glenwood for the staff hovering over him.

'How's Smenton?'

'He's still in Emergency, sir.' replied Loy Ng. 'Senior Sergeant Harris was there, but–here he is now, sir.'

Harris barrelled toward them, his face tight with anger. 'This fucker's got to be found, Dave. Ken got a massive blow over the right side of his head. I've got to let his parents know, so I'll see you back at the station. I sent someone to get the CCTV footage. Don't suppose we'll find anything useful. This bastard's too clever by half.'

They watched in gloomy silence as Harris, followed by Constable Ng, charged through the doors at the end of the hall. Maguire looked around, surprised to see dawn breaking outside the windows. He glanced at his watch; 5am. Time to explore the scene of the crime.

Each took a side of the long, L-shaped building. There didn't appear to be a door through which someone could have come without being seen, except for that which led to the outside from the boardroom, where they'd determined the killer had gone after he killed Edna. It was supposed to be locked unless the hospital board met. So how had the perpetrator gotten a key? Could one of the board members be a murderer? Or the hospital staff –cleaners, visiting doctors, casual staff, kitchen–even the hospital auxiliary. Maguire considered the logistics of interviewing them all again and shuddered.

'Pete, looks like we're going to have to check the board members again and get alibis from everyone,' he said tiredly. 'Uniform's collecting the tapes from the security cameras, for all the good it will do us. Advise Mrs Eams to get all the locks changed. I suppose she'll have to go through the Health Department to do that.' They shared a look of commiseration. The chances of finding anything incriminating were minimal, but there was a possibility of confirming whether the same person who killed Edna had attacked Glenwood and Smenton.

Hansen left to talk to the director and Maguire headed for his car for the short drive to the motel. He could guarantee the killer would be back for another try. Had Glenwood confided in *anyone?* He certainly hadn't told his wife who he was going to see that night. 'Stupid old fart. If he'd shared his suspicions, instead of heading off to see the bastard, he wouldn't be half dead in ICU!' muttered Maguire, as he opened the door to his unit. How totally naïve to go and talk to someone you think might be a killer. But perhaps he'd only been on an inquiry and inadvertently picked on the actual murderer.

As he stood under the shower, for what seemed to be the thousandth time, Maguire sifted the sequence of events through his mind. Why didn't Glenwood tell one of his fellow officers what he was going to do? Why hadn't the man come and told him? But as he reached for a towel, he was seized by the unwelcome suspicion that his own reputation for not suffering fools, might well have led to Glenwood wanting to verify his facts before he spoke up. *Bloody hell.*

Maguire finished drying himself, wrapped the towel around his waist and started shaving. His tired face stared back at him from the mirror. A fresh wave of anger at Glenwood's supposed stupidity began to roll in, but was replaced by the knowledge that indeed it was his, Maguire's, fault. He was well aware of his formidable reputation for perfection. No one was allowed to make a mistake on *his* team.

He finished shaving and swiped cologne around his cheeks, thoughts straying into uncomfortable territory. How many times had he bulldozed his way through investigations and his life? Unaccountably, a picture of a young Susan, clutching their babies to her breasts, all of them crying, flashed in his mind, followed by one of his immediate superior's calm measured tones, trying to explain post-natal depression and his own voice snapping in pig-headed denial.

So just how much of the debacle of his first marriage had been his own fault? He'd always dismissed the notion of himself fleeing the situation, leaving Susan to cope on her own. She'd had her sister and mother, hadn't she? But Melanie had been in New South Wales at the time and Susan's parents overseas. He also recalled telling his own mother and sisters–who didn't like Susan and were intimidated by her–that his wife didn't need their help. He'd hoped Susan would have learned her lesson and come crawling to him for help, so he could return without losing face. So, what lesson? She had been a struggling mum with twins and he'd thrown it all up and opted out. She'd had to rely on her elderly Aunt Beryl, who'd tried so hard to get them back together.

He cringed, remembering his own arrogance at the time. A fat lot of help he'd been–and Susan hadn't come begging. So he'd hidden his own heartbreak, retained his so-called dignity and lost his marriage and children. He didn't want to think about his second attempt at matrimony which had ended as ignominiously as the first. Now, he needed to acknowledge that he could have been a lot more accessible, particularly in this instance. Senior Constable Glenwood was not part of his team; he was George Harris's, but he, Maguire, was responsible for the man's situation and Smenton's cracked skull.

He clicked on Susan's number, feeling thoroughly chastened. On being assured that she and Marli were safe, he dressed, gathered up his belongings, stuffed them into his bags and met Hansen around the back of the unmarked police car.

'You going back to town, Dave?' Pete asked.

'No. I haven't had time to tell you, but my ex-wife and one of my daughters are staying on a farm near here. Come and have some breakfast; I need to discuss something with you.' Ten minutes later, having checked out of the motel, he met Hansen over breakfast at the roadhouse cafe outside of town, where he brought him up to date with the happenings of the previous night. 'So you see, we decided not to let news of the attack get out to keep the bastard guessing,' he ended.

Hansen looked at him in surprise. 'I didn't know you'd been married to DSS Prescott, Dave. You said you had daughters, but I wasn't aware your ex-wife is a police officer. Moreover, just *who* she is. I've seen her photos in the paper. Sad business, that.'

'She's on stress leave. Blames herself for the debacle over that young fool, Danny Grey.'

Hansen nodded. 'It's not surprising. She has a good reputation as a top class investigator. There's plenty who'd be happy to work with her. I know I would.'

'Well, her second marriage broke down and she's suffering from that too, but she's going to try and help us out.' Maguire went on to detail Susan's role in Edna Robinson's last days, explain her 'in' with the family, including cataloguing the photographs. 'So you see, Pete, she's in a good position to find out what we can't. I wonder if this arsehole knows she's with the force? He obviously thinks she saw him when she was with Edna Robinson. I'm going out to stay at the farm, so if this bastard tries again, I'll be right there.' Maguire's eyes glinted. 'The funerals are on Saturday afternoon, Edna's at 2 and Harlow's at 3. Apparently they're having a joint wake at Sir Arthur Robinson's home. I'm hoping Susan will attend Edna's funeral and wake.'

Back at the police station, they met the rest of the team in the Incident Room, where they stood in front of the white board looking at the time lines and faces of the major players. On the left, the women, aged sixteen up, on the right the fit men of the family, including fiancés, and Constable Adam Winslow. Hansen raised his eyebrows, saying nothing, but Maguire picked up his thoughts.

'I have to include Winslow because he's a close relative of the Robinsons. Almost all of the buggers came up with alibis, including Winslow who was actually on duty. But he could have sneaked away. There's time unaccounted for, because he wasn't answering his mobile for at least half an hour,' growled Maguire.

'You a bit sorry Winslow's not a serious suspect? Since he's after your daughter?' He'd overheard Adam and his sidekick at the front desk enthusing over Marli Maguire.

Maguire looked sheepish for a moment. 'Yeah, but I can't nail every bloke who looks at my daughter. The gaols would overflow.'

They chuckled. 'Some of these bozos only have their wives, girlfriends, husbands or whatever, to vouch for them. We can't prove they weren't home watching Top Gear or the footy when Edna got done,' Hansen reminded Maguire.

'Going on what Edna told Susan, which is all we have so far, I'm tipping it's a family thing. Of course, I haven't discounted Jack's penchant for women, young ones, middle-aged. From what I can gather, even a sprightly granny probably wouldn't have fazed him.'

He went on to bring Hansen up to scratch with Adam Winslow's account of the family birthday party and meeting. 'Winslow thinks someone else left just after, too.' He screwed his face up for a moment as a fragment flashed into his mind again and fled. Something he'd heard or someone had said recently ... damn, lost it again.

After Hansen left to check alibis for the latest attack, Maguire made himself a cup of coffee and then sat down at the computer to send the Significant Event Message–Sig Event–to the Ipswich CIB. A stack of reports lurked on the table beside him. The answer had to be in there.

Somewhere.

CHAPTER 21

The Luncheon

Susan

Thursday: late morning.

Mother's phone call is the eleventh this morning. My neighbour in Brisbane rings to tell me all is well at the house, but old Mrs Phillips' geriatric dog has been digging the hydrangea bushes up again. Two close friends and four colleagues, including my work partner Evan, phone to ask how I am. Eloise calls from the UK to let me know they need to stay for at least another three months, and David checks that we are still alive and fills us in on the attack on Senior Constable Glenwood. The constable guarding him is lucky to have survived. We are sworn to secrecy once more, a stricture which is aimed at Marli.

Mother has never missed an opportunity to take jabs at my work or to mention Harry, whom she adores. I resist the impulse to retort that he couldn't care less about any of us, including her. 'Susan, you know what I've always thought about your job and now these murders in Emsberg. I think you should go home, because it's not good for Marli and Harry won't like you putting her in danger!' Like Harry would care? *He can get stuffed.*

Off-hand I can't remember the sentence for matricide, but if the jurors had ever met my mother, I'd get off, scot free.

'Mum, Marli's okay and I'm fine. The house is empty and up for sale, so we've nowhere to go.'

'Everything's not fine, Susan. And you're coming down with a cold. I can hear it in your voice. It's not surprising since you never wear good woollen underwear.' A flash of memory reveals myself, at four years of age, being spectacularly sick into a pair of huge, pink 'passion-killers' which belong to my grandmother

'Mum, I'm resting, not ill and the trouble here has nothing to do with me. I'm an ordinary citizen as far as that's concerned.' *Oh yeah, right.*

God help me if she discovers my ex-husband is leading the investigation. The only time I heard my mother swear was during one of her and David's vicious clashes following the twin's birth. The score was 100% in his favour and she's never forgiven him for it.

'I've a good mind to come and take over. Has Brittany rung you?'

'No, mum. You know she's not speaking to me.'

'Hurrrrrrph' No one can snort as triumphantly as mother. 'Well, it's not surprising, is it? After the way you treated Harry.' *Give me strength.*

'Yes, Mum. I *know*. It's my *own* fault he left.' Pain arcs through me. My two failures as a wife have bitten deeply into my self confidence.

'What does Melanie say about it? I don't know what's wrong with that girl. She never returns my calls.'

Mother rambles on, running down my sister, the Reverend Melanie Burgess, whose religious calling she couldn't understand but boasted about at every opportunity. My throat is too sore to argue and I am exhausted from lack of sleep.

When we went to bed last night, Marli moved in with me, as of course did Fat Albert, who stretched himself until he had both of us at the edge of the mattress. Her gentle breathing and occasional snores were comforting and even Albert's purring was a blessing. Titch slept in Marli's left armpit. It was a cosy, but crowded arrangement. I dozed intermittently throughout the night, waking at every call from a night bird. David settled on the lounge, taking his self-imposed guardianship to the point where he patrolled the house at the slightest sound, causing my heart to thud and perspiration to break out every time the floorboards creaked. His opening the door each time he prowled and asking, 'Are you all right?' didn't help either.

At 4.15am, Albert tipped Marli out of bed to land with a thud which shook the floor. Her pup let out a high-pitched squeal. David bounded into the room and tripped over the old spaniel sleeping on the mat on my side of the bed. He put a hand out to save himself and squashed Albert who, justifiably annoyed, swiped his claws across the back of David's knuckles. The younger dogs, alerted to the excitement, yelped in their enclosure outside.

My ex-husband's reaction was predictably male and involved curses. By the time Marli picked herself up and we recovered from our fright, the house was in an uproar. We trooped out to the kitchen, calmed the dogs, put the kettle on and plastered David's bleeding hand. Another spirited debate ensued over whether I should be examined by a doctor. I protested vigorously. 'No one will talk to me if they know what I do.'

'You weren't going to involve yourself,' my saner side reminded. *'Oh shut up,'* my professional self snapped.

After much protestation and checking my throat, David backed down. He and Marli were making toast and drinking hot chocolate when his mobile phone rang with news of more trouble at the hospital–

'Susan? *Are you listening to me?'* Mother's shriek snapped my attention back to our conversation.

'What? Sorry mum, I was distracted for a moment. Look, I've got to go; someone's coming up the driveway.'

'All right, then. But make sure you ring me back and let me know what's happening. Perhaps Brittany should come and stay with us, you know she's impressionable and since Marli's with you and you're not there to protect Brittany–'

Brit could take on a rabid Rottweiler and win with one hand tied behind her back. 'Mum, I'll ring you tomorrow. Sorry, bye.'

'Marli, stall whoever it is. Tell them I'm getting dressed and won't be long.' It's eleven o'clock, for God's sake. Whoever it is will think I'm a lazy cow. I bolt for the bedroom, drag on clean jeans and a reasonably respectable shirt, and then examine myself in the mirror. If I pull the collar up, fold a scarf inside the neck of my shirt and keep my hair down, with any luck no one will notice the bruises. Panic shoots through my veins like a hoon through a backstreet after midnight. If David and Marli hadn't come home when they did ... I force myself to calm down. *Will I ever get my mojo back?*

'Mum! Mrs Winslow and Carissa are here!' shouts Marli. Oh, my God, what's happened now? I smooth my hair down around my neck and twitch the scarf higher inside my collar, just in time to greet Daniella and Carissa at the front door.

Daniella is apologetic over not ringing before she came, but she would like me to do her a favour and: 'How am I? You're so pale, Susan! Marli, you look tired too. Late night?'

We usher them into the kitchen where it transpires that Daniella is taking me to lunch at Sir Arthur Robinson's lair and Carissa wants Marli to help "re-do" her website. Carissa has a website? What am I thinking, of course she does and a Facebook page and she's on Twitter, as are my daughters. *And I'll bet Brit's unfriended me by now.*

Daniella's voice penetrates the fog in which I am swirling. 'Some of the family are dropping in, and I'm sure the girls will be fine here.' She doesn't realise how dangerous it is to leave them on their own.

'How about if you two go to Ann's place and work on your stuff there? I hear she's an expert on websites,' I add, slyly. Carissa's friend, Ann, lives in town.

Carissa looks rebellious. Marli "twigs" what my problem is, but doesn't want to co-operate. 'Look, mum, we'll be okay here. Its broad daylight and we've both got mobiles, okay? I'll even lock the doors when you go.'

I try to find a good reason not to agree, but for once can't think of anything without blowing my cover. Daniella is jiggling her car keys impatiently, so I let the dogs into the house and race around locking the outside doors, because I don't trust my daughter to remember. 'I'll be ringing you,' I announce, with a telling glance at Marli, who rolls her eyes with wounded patience.

'We'll see you later, mum.' They head off to her bedroom, where she is about to discover that her pup has torn her best shoes to pieces, because she's too lazy to put them where he can't get them. Tough.

'Thank you, Daniella. Can I contribute anything? A bottle of wine, perhaps?' James has told me to make free with his collection.

Daniella lifts her nose like a hunting dog. 'Have you a nice 'red'?' she enquires enthusiastically.

Before I can gather my wits, two bottles of Riversands Doctor Seidel Soft Red and I, are managed into the BMW and on our way. I've seen Lady Ferna in action, when she'd sailed into the local bakery like a modern-day Boadicea, sans chariot, so I am not looking forward to meeting her formally, much less being her guest.

Small villages nestle in the curves of a winding river; numerous dams reflect the sky, littering the landscape like blue puddles. The Robinson mansion, a huge two-storied Queenslander, perches on the side of an escarpment overlooking a wide, shallow valley. Daniella parks in a space beside several luxurious cars in the circular driveway.

Can I cope with this? Too late. I'm being herded up the stone steps to meet Lady Ferna, who is standing sentinel on the verandah. A group of people behind her fall silent as we arrive at the top. Daniella, having relieved me of the wine, kisses Lady Ferna's cheek, introduces me and swans toward the assembled company, waving the bottles in the air. She puts them on a broad windowsill which is doing duty as the bar. Caterers are setting a long, white-clothed trestle at the far end of the verandah.

'So good of you to come,' announces my hostess, sweeping me with a penetrating glance, as she holds out a svelte paw for my garden-stained clasp. She has a grip like a boa constrictor. Within moments, I am seated in a comfortable chair beside Sir Arthur, wriggling my hand to make my circulation return. A huge cat, who looks at me as though I am a morsel it's dragged into the house and then rejected, is sitting in his lap.

Sir Arthur focuses his owl-like gaze on me. 'You're a relative of the Kirkbridge's?' and, 'You work for the government, I believe?' are swiftly dealt with. I wonder why I am here, because Daniella doesn't appear to need any support, but it transpires that they wish to thank me for reviving Edna during her ill-fated visit to the loo on Saturday.

'I am so glad you were there when Edna fell ill, Mrs Prescott,' gushes Lady Ferna.

'I was glad to do what I could,'

There is no merit in doing what one must, but they will not let it alone. Intrusive questions fly thick and fast, but I parry them with practised ease, itching to ring Marli. When they finally back off, I tune into the snatches of conversation flowing around me. One or two cause my eyebrows to hit my hairline.

'Of course, Ferna has that dreadful Quincy to do the garden ... yes, I know Ferna does do a lot and Arthur takes the credit ...'

' ... I gave it to the cat, but he said he didn't like it ...' *Huh?*

'... those cuttings you took ...'

'Of course, it's going to be a good show, Ferna's arrangements always go to plan ...' Edna's funeral?

'Libby's behaviour is disgraceful, considering ... and she gets half of all Edna's money ...' *What money?* My ears are quivering like a Fennec Fox. More luncheon guests arrive and the assembled company greets them enthusiastically. Each one emerges from Ferna's voluminous bosom and races to the windowsill to fill a glass. I sneak into the loo and phone Marli, who snaps that she's, *'Still alive thank you, mother,'* and hangs up.

Surreptitiously I examine the clan, which ranges in age from twenties, early forties or thereabouts, to the eighties. The older members, apart from the hosts, are a couple of geriatric identical twins with a distinct resemblance to Arthur, sitting apart from the crowd, whose names are Connie and Grace. They are holding hands and whispering to each other, seemingly oblivious to the conversation. I am about to turn my attention to the younger members of the gathering when I realise their body language shrieks tension. *Interesting.*

I focus on the men, saving Libby, Edna's granddaughter and co-inheritor of her estate, for future reference.

Euon Jellicott, Lady Ferna pronounces his name, "yew -on" is fifty-ish and a solicitor. He is not wearing a wedding ring, so I assume is maritally unencumbered. An expensive-looking briefcase is on the floor by his seat. It's open and bulging with official-looking papers. My fingers itch to fossick through them. He arises and trots down the steps to stand on the driveway, smoking something revolting. He is about 190cm, narrow-shouldered, but wiry with muscular legs. One could easily imagine him legging it up the mountain behind the farm.

The thirtyish, good-looking man sitting opposite is Jason Hardgreaves, the doctor who attended Edna the night she was murdered. His ear is wet from Libby's whisperings. She sees me looking at him and slips her hand into his, making sure I see a flash from her diamond ring. I'm amused at being warned off; if I'd started breeding at thirteen, I'd be old enough to be his mum.

Lady Ferna is leaning over, clutching the arm of another family member, hissing into his face. A muscular, sporty little rooster in his late forties, he is not tall enough to be my assailant. He meets my gaze with a lustful gleam in his eye. Why? I am not sex-on-legs. Encouraged by my regard, he makes a beeline for me and introduces himself as Peter Robinson, the son of Arthur's younger brother, John and his wife who are absent from the party. 'Uncle Arthur and Ferna's landscaping is famous. I'd be happy to show you around before lunch,' he offers, sliding his arm around my back.

Before I can step away, Euon Jellicott jumps up and joins us. 'You're taking Susan around the garden?'

Is this a set-up? Before I can reply, I find myself being escorted down the steps to the lawn, a stalwart on either side.

'Show her the rose garden!' bellows Lady Ferna. Obediently, they wheel me to the left.

'So, Susan, how long are you visiting our part of the world?' Peter's manner is sly and flirtatious; I'm not fooled for a moment. This is an exploratory expedition to find out who I am and why I am staying in this rural community. "A holiday" is not on their agenda.

'I'm sure I've seen you somewhere before, Susan. Are you famous?' asks Euon. Oh God, have they seen my picture in all the papers? It's been awhile now; surely I will have been forgotten. They enquire my profession.

'I do something boring for the government.' I, too, can play this game. For God's sake, don't let them find out about me.

'Don't tell us you're a cop or in ASIO, Susan,' they joke. 'You're too pretty for that! So what are you doing in Emsberg? Have you got a boyfriend down here?' A boyfriend? Do I look like a cougar? I am forced to use all my skill to evade their probing. At the centre of their interest are Edna's photos.

'If you're cataloguing old Edna's snapshots you must be bored sick,' says Peter. 'How about we go out one day and I'll show you the sights?'

'I'm doing it for Daniella,' I explain. 'As the Executor of Mrs Robinson's Estate, she's pushed for time.' I don't miss the look which flashes between them. Euon moves closer, urging me toward the distant roses; Peter lays a heavy hand on my arm and squeezes. We are headed for a secluded part of the garden. I sidle away, removing myself from his grasp. He can't snatch me back without making it look like an attack.

Have I lost my nerve?

Yep.

I pretend to admire a flowering shrub almost at the side of the house and hit redial on my phone. Marli's numbers rings twice and her voice answers curtly, 'Yes, mum, we're all right. We're almost at Ann's house, okay?' She hangs up and I turn reluctantly to my escorts.

'We are supposed to show you the rose garden, Susan,' says Euon, purposefully taking my arm again.

I jerk my arm back. 'I'm allergic to roses!'

Everyone at the house knows where I am. You fool, Susan. They couldn't do anything to you. Not here. Has last night spooked you? Too right it has. My heart is pounding so hard, I'm sure they can hear it. Perspiration breaks out all over my body, beading on my face.

'In that case, Lady Ferna's iris beds are spectacular,' persists Peter, endeavouring to turn me in another direction. I need to take control of this situation. Get a grip, you fool.

'Perhaps later. It's almost lunch time. I want to talk to Sir Arthur and ring my daughter.' They're taken by surprise as I break away and march back toward the front of the house. *I am woman, hear me roar! More like squeak, squeak.*

Courtesy demands they follow and we arrive at the verandah before they can complete their interrogation. 'That didn't take long!' booms Lady Ferna. I excuse myself and move away from the crowd. Marli's mobile almost rings out before I hear her voice.

'Are you alright, darling?'

'Mum, give it a rest, okay? Ann phoned and we're at her house *right now*. Titch is with–'

The line drops out, but she's safe. I sit beside Daniella, who is talking to a tall, languidly graceful new arrival, Father Mark Gordon, Archdeacon of St Matthews in the city and Lady Ferna's son, mid to late fifties, but very well preserved. He is obviously not the progeny of Sir Arthur. As I respond to his polite conversation, his eyes focus on my scarf, which I casually smooth across the front of my throat. *Has he noticed the bruises?*

My erstwhile escorts take their places opposite and to my right at the table. The elderly knight and his Persian Familiar sit beside me, on my left. The relief of being safe is such that I'm even prepared to put up with cat hairs in my food. Mark Gordon takes the chair directly opposite, next to one of two stalwarts to whom I have not been introduced. Lady Ferna, who is commanding the troops in the kitchen, directs Daniella to sit beside a rather determined-looking young woman, who is apparently Sir Arthur's biographer.

Dianella rises obediently, gives me a wry smile and a

shrug of her shoulders, an apology for not keeping me company. Now I am surrounded by Robinson men and I don't believe for a moment it's because of my 'beau yeux.' A moment of panic almost overwhelms me as my radar picks a singular vibe:

There is a malevolent presence at this table.

CHAPTER 22

Sprung

Susan

Thursday: late afternoon.

Daniella spends endless minutes with each person sitting around the table. We've been at the Robinson stronghold since eleven o'clock this morning, but she continues to evade eye contact. I've rung Marli several times to check on her. Although I've been advised that this is a bad mobile phone area, each time I've at least been assured she is safe.

After some forced 'girls-together' monosyllabic conversation, I've arranged to 'do' coffee with Sir Arthur's biographer and exchanged phone numbers. I wonder if Briony Feldman will be any more forthcoming on paper than she's shown herself to be verbally. She doesn't strike me as a shrinking violet type and wonder why she is pretending to be submissive.

If I don't make a move to leave, Daniella will stay for dinner as well. I stand up, sweep my handbag off the chair and announce that I need to get home to my daughter. 'Oh my goodness, Susan, I didn't realise it was so late,' Daniella trills, feigning surprise. 'You should have told me!' Itching to slap her, I say my goodbyes with determination. In a matter of minutes, we've trundled down the steps to the car and driven off, amidst a spray of gravel and waving hands from the house.

Daniella apologises for keeping me and then chatters about the family all the way back to the farm. This time I'm paying attention: Euon, a champion marksman in archery, Olympic standard, is the grandson of Grace Jellicott, one of the twins who were doing tapestry before lunch. Does his skill with a bow extend to a rifle?

Peter Robinson, nephew of Arthur, is an architect. George "Slimeball" Murphy, who arrived last, is apparently the much-admired son of the other twin, Constance, and her deceased spouse, Keith. 'He's doing so well, you know,' boasted his mother.

Two forty-something men whose names I didn't catch, revealed themselves to be Ferna's younger brothers. It transpires that they're unmarried, and consider themselves extremely eligible. Keen cricketers, they regarded me with licentious intent until I revealed that watching an ant cross the path is more exciting than a game of cricket. Their farm-roughened hands expertly twisted the tops off beer bottles, reminding me of the ones which had been wrapped around my neck. Perhaps I can find out about them at the joint wake for Jack and Edna, to which Arthur has invited me with great enthusiasm. Genevieve, his cat, signified her approval by permitting me to pat her.

Last, but certainly not least, there are young Doctor Jason Hardgreaves and Mark Gordon, the Archdeacon. I was unsuccessful in coaxing the doctor to discuss Edna. This was partly due to Libby, who wrapped herself around him like a python and sucked his earlobe.

I dread to think what she did to him under the table; he squirmed rather a lot.

The Reverend Gordon is another proposition altogether. He oozes charm, no doubt a successful tactic to keep the Mothers Guild at the church enslaved, and asked me to dine with him at my earliest convenience, making it very clear this is a date, man/woman stuff. Grrrrrrrr! I manage to make a fool of myself, stammering and spluttering. Being out of circulation for thirteen years puts one out of practice, but of course my busy mouth helped me out: 'Oh that would be nice. Thank you, yes, I'd like that.' *Shut up, Susan.*

He beamed with satisfaction and whipped out his diary. Before I gather my wits, I agreed to be ready at half-past six the following evening. He would collect me from the farm. How did he know where I lived? 'Everyone knows where you're staying, Susan,' he assured me. That kind of local knowledge I can do without. What the hell am I going to wear? And who would stay with Marli? Although she is seventeen, circumstances being what they are–I stifled a chuckle. *David!* Yes, why not? After all, he is moving in to protect us and wants to take up his mantle of fatherhood. Having him watch me date an attractive man will be a boost to my ego. *You're so petty, Susan.*

As we turn in at the main gate to the farm, a car horn starts tooting behind us. It's Marli and Carissa in my car, smiling and waving. 'Thank goodness they're safe,' I exclaim.

Blissfully unaware of last night's attack, Daniella smiles and shakes her head at me, 'You're such a worrier, Susan. What possible harm could they come to in Emsberg?'

Fearing I'm about to let my tongue run away with me again, I smile weakly and for the umpteenth time, make sure my scarf hides my bruises. We park at the bottom of the steps, as Marli drives my car into the garage at the side of the house. The dogs break into glad cries. Daniella elects to wait in her vehicle for Carissa, so I stand by the driver's door talking idly until the girls appear. With a, 'That was, like, awesome,' from Carissa to Marli, and, 'I'll ring you soon and we'll "do" coffee,' from Daniella to me, they pull away.

Apparently, Ann, Carissa's friend has a rather attractive brother who is nineteen. As we walk up the steps, my daughter enthusiastically compares the charms of this undoubtedly licentious youth to those of Adam Winslow. Adam is on shaky ground, when we realise the door is ajar. I put my hand out and hold her back.

'I told you to lock all the doors, Marli!' My voice is husky with fright.

'I definitely shut and locked it, Mum.' She dangles the key on a loop in front of my nose. I jerk my head back, signalling silently for her to get behind me.

The hallway is full of a hollow silence. As I move further into the house, the pendulum ticking in the grandfather clock is the only sound. I pick up a jade statue from a nearby stand and start quietly toward the lounge room. At first glance, nothing is amiss, but then all is revealed. My carefully arranged piles of photographs are missing. Empty frames lie scattered on the floor; glass pieces litter the carpet. Cushions have been flung on the floor; books are half out of the shelves. My heart pounds; fear slithers down my arms like pins and needles. *He's been back.*

'Mum, what's happened?' I set the statue down and

we approach the table. A few photos remain, but liquid paper has been splattered over the subject's faces. Unless I can gently scratch it off, they're ruined. 'Marli, put him away,' I nod at the puppy she carries, 'and get back here fast.' She scuttles to her room, pops him inside and runs back to me.

'When exactly did you and Carissa go out?' I am aware of a whiff of a familiar smell.

'Not long after you, mum. Ann rang and we left here at a quarter past eleven. I know because we were to pick up a video and I wanted to be sure Video Ezy was open.' Her eyes widen as she realises the implications of what could have happened. 'I'll let the dogs out.' Her words come out high and jerky.

A smell of burning–that's it–gets stronger as I succumb to a desire for coffee. To my consternation, a heap of cold ash is in the kitchen sink. A few tiny photo fragments on the floor. What the hell am I going to tell Daniella? I am supposed to be looking after these family mementos, not losing them. But, did she get me out of the way for the day so someone else could destroy the photos? But she brought Carissa over to stay with Marli. *Stupid, stupid. Wake up to yourself, Susan.*

Tears well up. I force myself to get control, because I don't want to frighten Marli any more than she is already. I fling the windows and back door open to get rid of the smell. Can I still live here, now that our security is breached again? Maybe Marli really didn't lock the front door properly.

I jump as a sound of nibbling comes from underneath the sink. 'You little shit, this time I'm going to get you! You're *sprung!*' I snarl and fling the door open. A furry blur streaks into the cleaning utensils. Angered beyond reason, I drag bottles of cleaner out, cursing. Then I see it. A perfect mouse nest, lined with rags and–forming an outer shield–photos. In the middle are a squirming pile of pink nodules. Our mouse is definitely not celibate.

I lean down, carefully pry the celluloid walls away from the nest and examine them in the light coming through the window. An innocuous scene of the mountains is torn, but the other is of a group of people looking embarrassed, possibly not used to being photographed. I recognise teenagers Grace and Constance, but the rest are strangers. I turn it over and try to read the faded inscription: "Grace and–" I can just make out the year, 1946. Perhaps they wafted over the side of the sink and floated under the table? A small piece of food is smeared on the back of the mountains, which may be what attracted the mouse.

Something is off-kilter about one of the slightly blurred faces in the second black and white photo. There's a magnifying glass in one of the kitchen drawers, amongst the loose rubber bands, paper clips, half-empty reels of cotton and biros which only work when they feel like it. Even with its help, I need a couple of minutes to work out that someone has very carefully and from what I can see, deliberately put a pin hole straight through each eye of one of the men. The perforations are minute, but I'm shocked by the hatred implied by the mutilation. Perhaps another photo has been tacked over the top? No, it's a deliberate stabbing.

Just then, Marli rushes into the room. I'm about to blurt out what I've found, but her words forestall me. 'Mum, dad's coming!' she squeaks. *Harry?* No. Of course not, it's David. My pulses rev up their tempo. *God, what are you thinking, you silly old fool.* I hastily shove the photo into my pocket and squat down in front of the cupboard. 'I found the nest! Now all I need to do is catch the mouse,' I announce lightly, but there is no answer. A hullabaloo from the verandah greets the conquering hero. I quickly re-arrange the bottles and tins to hide the nest, shut the cupboard door and stand up. If my instinct is correct, I need to focus my search on the 1940s. My search? 'When did it become your mission, Susan? You weren't going to get involved. Remember?'

I'm tired of being a wimp, tired of guilt. How could I allow two silly corporate rogues to "get to" me today? I should have made mincemeat of them. I've been handing my life to other people on a platter because I've allowed myself to wallow in self pity. I will not be driven from this house in which I feel comfortable, if not exactly safe at the moment–and I'm going to find this murdering bastard if it kills me, and him.

Detective Senior Sergeant Prescott is back in business.

CHAPTER 23

Body Blows

Marli

Thursday: late afternoon.

Marli nearly cried with relief as her father's car stopped in front of the house. The attack on her mother the previous evening and arriving home that day to see the destruction wrought by the intruder, brought home to her how vulnerable she and her mother were. Much as she loved her aunt and uncle's house, it felt scary to be there.

Maguire collected a bag from the back seat and set it on the ground, took out a laptop which he tucked under his arm and closed and pressed the remote locking device. *'Hurry, hurry!'* her mind shrieked, as he stopped to pick up the bag and then paused for a moment to kick the right front tyre. He was smiling at her as he came up the steps, but when he reached the top, Marli burst into tears and hurled herself at him. He eased his laptop to the floor, dropped his bag and wrapped his arms around her. 'What's happened? Are you hurt? Is your mother–'

'No, no, but the man's been back!' she shrieked. 'He's wrecked mum's work with the photos. I don't know how he got in. I locked the house!'

'Were you here?'

'No, no. We–Carissa and me–went into town.'

'Thank God for that. Let's get inside ...'

Marli backed off and picked up the laptop, Maguire, the bag. As they entered the house, she filled him in on the day's events.

'Does Mrs Winslow know about the photos?'

'No, she waited in the car for Carissa and then they went home.'

Maguire advanced on the desecration in the lounge, carefully edging around the broken glass and twisted photo frames to stand staring at the debris. 'Are all the photos missing?'

'Yes, he burnt them,' Marli sobbed.

Susan walked into the room and explained what she had found in the kitchen. As her parents examined the remaining two photos, Marli noticed something different about her mum. The anxious woman who'd arrived home not fifteen minutes ago had vanished, dispelling memories of the distraught woman of two months ago.

Unable to find her sister, Brittany, she had caught the bus home alone that terrible day and been shocked to see news vans parked along the street. Journalists and photographers were crowded around the front gate, waiting for a statement about the shooting of Danny Grey. Marli pulled her school hat down to cover her face and ran to their neighbour, old Mrs Phillips, who let her go out the back of her house to sneak through the side fence and crawl across the lawn under the shrubbery to reach her home. Their two dogs rushed at her when she opened the kitchen door. She swatted them down and pushed them into the backyard.

Her mother sat in the dark with the curtains

drawn, while the doorbell rang and rang. 'Mum! What's happened? Has something happened to Brit or Dad?' she'd cried, dumping her school backpack and sports bag on the floor. She turned the lights on and went to wrap her hands around her mother's frozen ones, afraid her mother had had a stroke or something. The doorbell kept ringing. 'Piss off!' Marli had screamed and for a moment the incessant ringing ceased, replaced by shouts to open the door. She forced herself to ignore them.

'Squeeze my hands and smile, mum!' A first-aid course had been part of their school curriculum. Her mother's hands were lumps of ice. Receiving no response, Marli waved her hand in front of her mother's face, finally bringing a blink and recognition. Relief flooded like warm water through her body. Not a stroke.

'Oh, darling you're home,' Susan muttered.

Marli ordered her to stay where she was, though her mother showed signs of being welded to the couch. She'd fled to the main bedroom to grab her dressing gown. There was something different about the room, but she was in such a hurry it didn't register until she'd forced her mother's arms into the sleeves and tied the belt around her waist. 'Dad's things are gone!' Fear shafted through her; the wardrobe had been wide open and half empty.

Eliciting no information from Susan, Marli ran back upstairs to the en suite. His shaving gear and toilet articles were gone. He wouldn't have taken it on a job because he had a separate lot for work trips. She could ask Mary–no, Mary was on holidays. She charged into her sister's room. One look revealed that clothes, make-up and shoes were missing. Terrified, she pulled out her mobile to text her sister as she flew down to the kitchen, only to see photographers hanging over the back fence. The dogs were going berserk in the back garden, keeping them at bay. She pulled the blinds down, put the electric kettle on and got bread, butter and some packets of soup out of the cupboard. Eventually, she managed to get Susan to the kitchen table to drink some soup and tell her what had happened.

Not only had her father left them, but one of mum's officers, Danny, whom Marli fancied something rotten for all that he was married, had been shot dead the night before. And it happened when mum was there–well, almost there. Now she was on stress leave and there would be an investigation.

'It'll be bad here for awhile, darling. The media will be everywhere. Perhaps you'd better go to Granny's until it's sorted out.'

'No way. I'm staying here with you. And where's Dad gone? Brit wasn't at school. Does she know about it?' Her mother turned her white face to Marli, but didn't speak. She was about to repeat the question, when Susan responded in a drained whisper.

'Yes. He phoned Brit at school and she took off with him to Sydney. He's found someone else. Apparently they're all going to live together and be happy ever after. He picked her up from school and they came back to collect some of her things. She left a note.'

Marli couldn't believe it. Dad had gone off with another woman and her identical twin went with him? Brit's classes were different, so she hadn't realised her twin had abandoned her without a word. She burst into tears.

It was on for young and old then. They bawled in each other's arms until they were brought around by the dogs insistent scratching at the back door, frantic for their dinner. Since her mother didn't seem to be able to function, Marli opened the back door a crack to let the animals inside for their dinner, threw out the tepid soup, heated a tin of spaghetti and made toast and then rang Brittany again.

An unholy row erupted, not the first by any means, but this time the ferocious nature of it shocked Marli to the core. Brit wouldn't be returning. 'You're like, so beyond sad, Marli. If you stay with her, you're just as much a loser as she is! It's her fault Dad found someone else. If you come to your senses, let me know. And I'm unfriending you from Facebook and telling everyone we know to do it too.' She hung up in Marli's ear.

Having to take stress leave was the final straw for Susan, who sobbed in her bed every night. Friends, colleagues and their wives phoned, offering to come and help out. Susan refused their help, especially granny, and even her sister, Melanie and sister-in-law, Eloise. The only people she would speak to were her partner, Detective Sergeant Evan Taylor, members of her team and the union rep.

The press, who were camped in the park opposite the house, constantly formed a howling mob when anyone came or went from the house. The phone had to be left off the hook. Neighbours were quizzed; TV crews arrived and over-excited female journalists with sincere expressions, issued reports on the front footpath. Marli kept the curtains and blinds drawn and the lights turned on. Even the dogs got photographed as they ran around the back yard, barking hysterically.

The family cat slithered under Marli's bed and refused to come out, so she put the sand-tray in her room and fed the terrified animal in there. About the third day they were under siege, the geriatric cat died and Marli lost her composure. Sergeant Taylor sent two young constables over to bury the cat, again a much-photographed event. Meanwhile, Susan flatly declined any help in the house.

Over the next few days, Marli discovered that the "get-up-now-you'll-miss-the-bus" fairy was hunkered down with the bedclothes over her head, crying along with the "doing-the-washing-and-make-the-beds-fairy." The "iron-the-school-clothes" and "cooking-meals-making-lunches-fairy" was definitely on strike, and worst of all, the "load-and-unload-the-dishwasher" and "feeding-the-dogs-fairy" had run away from home with the "chauffeur" fairy.

Marli became exhausted from trying to do everything. She wanted to scream at her mother to "get with it" but controlled herself with a supreme effort. She'd rung school and spoken to the principal who also wanted to help and gave her time off. She felt bad turning family friends away, but her mother remained adamant.

Following the heartbreaking funeral, media attention turned to the next scandal and Marli continued to cope with Susan, who awaited the investigation.

She returned to school for her final exams, but it was scary to come home and find her normally immaculate mother still in her pyjamas, lying on the lounge staring at the ceiling, dishes unwashed in the sink, soiled clothes piled up in the bathroom and the dogs barking madly in the back yard.

Sergeant Taylor had turned up again late one afternoon, taken one look at the house and suggested for the umpteenth time that his wife, Genevieve would come and stay with them for awhile, but mum maintained that she couldn't bear to face anyone.

'You made it to the funeral, so you need to pull

yourself together. The investigation starts tomorrow,' Sergeant Taylor had reminded her mother, a little sharply.

'I've already made a statement, been interviewed and done the reports. What more do they want?' she bleated.

'They'll want their pound of flesh, Susan. You know that, as well as I do. Everyone knows Danny was a young hothead and you're not to blame. I was on that case, too, and I've made my report. Harry buggering off and taking your daughter with him is an added blow on top of everything else. Having to cope with that as well must be terrible, but Marli needs her mum back, she can't cope with all this–' he indicated the house– 'on her own and finish school. This is an important time for her.'

Mum insisted she didn't need her family's interference, but the sergeant told Marli to ring her mother's sister, Melanie and beg her to come. 'Tell her it's urgent, love. She'll pull your mother out of it.'

So, after another fruitless day of trying to get her mother to eat and wash herself, Marli rang Melanie and begged her to come.

Susan was standing staring out of the window, when her sister's car pulled up in the driveway. 'Marli, I told you I didn't want anyone coming here, even Melanie!' her mother snapped, correctly deducing from her daughter's guilty face that she was to blame for this latest development.

'Mum, I can't cope with you, so kill me if you want, but I *had* to call Aunty Melanie,' she replied defiantly, opening the door to her mother's tall, attractive sister. She dumped her bag on the floor, kissed Marli, walked straight over to her angry sibling and wrapped her arms around her.

Marli waited until her mother burst out crying again, then sloped off to the kitchen to make yet more coffee. She rabbited around and discovered some cake which one of the police wives had sent over, laid a few slices on a plate and served it, with coffee, to her soggy mother and stoic aunt. Aunt Melanie marched to the liquor cabinet, grabbed a bottle of brandy and poured a hefty dollop into the coffee.

Marli took the opportunity to slip upstairs to shower and dress, then raced into her mother's bedroom and changed the bed linen. On her way back to the lounge, she met the two women on the stairs, her aunt pushing her red-eyed mother ahead.

'Susan, Harry's a prick. Now shut the fuck up and get in the shower. You stink!' she heard the Reverend Burgess, chaplain of the women's prison, say forcefully, just before she shut the door of the main bedroom behind her. Minutes later, hearing yells coming from her mother's en suite, Marli suspected her aunt had pushed her mother into the shower, clothes and all.

They'd come downstairs soon afterward, her mum in a tracksuit with her hair wrapped in a towel. Aunt Melanie forced her to eat an omelette and toast and more strong coffee laced with brandy. When Susan finished, Melanie propelled her back upstairs and tucked her into bed. 'You need your strength for the investigation. So don't come out of here until you're human again. And give Marli a rest.'

Her aunt stayed with them for ten days, during which time she'd dragged her sister to a good solicitor. 'This one's a gladiator, Susan. She'll stake Harry out and stick his dick in a jar full of fire ants. And you should take advantage of the police force counselling service. You might be able to run a murder investigation with both hands tied behind your back, but even you can't do this on your own. You've suffered shocking body-blows. You're not a bloody psychiatrist!'

After Aunt Melanie returned to work, Aunt Eloise, her dad's sister, arrived to look after them, much to Marli's relief, thankful granny hadn't come. Her carping disapproval would cause mum to commit matricide.

Her mother finally pulled out of her fog, went to counselling and sorted out her legal position with regard to her marriage. Marli didn't know what arrangements they'd come to, but mum assured her they were financially okay, but that dad was forcing the sale of their home. 'We can't plan an overseas trip just yet, love,' she'd said with a watery smile.

Her father, Harry, did not communicate, but Brit kept up a steady stream of text messages and phone calls, issuing instructions and wanting to know what mum was up to. 'Why don't you speak to mum yourself?' Marli braced herself for the wrath which she knew would break over her at the very suggestion.

'What do you mean? It's mum's fault Dad left!' Brit shrieked. 'You always sided with her. Get real!' Their relationship had gone downhill from there. Now, as she listened to her mother's account of finding the burned photos and events at the luncheon, she realised mum was back, strong as ever and Marli had their real dad too. Brit was missing out big time.

She sat on the lounge, tucked her legs up under her and leaned back, glowing with secret joy. If she kept very quiet, they'd forget she was there. She glanced at the bag he'd dropped on the floor beside his chair. He was going to stay with them! Her heart felt as though it was being squeezed beyond happiness.

But just then, her father's mobile rang. Her heart sank as she watched the expression on his face change.

CHAPTER 24

Making Tracks

The Killer

Friday: 5pm to dawn.

He couldn't keep still. The fear and rage bubbling inside him found its outlet in smashing things; cutlery glass–anything which came to hand. Fear oozed out of his body, permeating his nostrils. His stomach roiled.

Shards of glass flew around the room with cyclonic force. Kitchen implements bounced off the walls, the doors, and clashed in mid-air as they crossed flight paths.

It still wasn't enough, even as he leaned, exhausted, against the kitchen dresser.

Something had to give.

The family secret could not be allowed to choke his future. Surely Arthur wouldn't be so stupid as to even *hint* ... no, they agreed at the family meeting, that nothing would be said. Arthur had been the most vigorous supporter of silence. Well, he would be. His biography could blow the past apart and there was no way to stop the bloody thing from being written. The book had been commissioned and paid for by the Historical Society. If he intervened, people would want to know the reason why.

He looked at the clock. His girlfriend, disguised as his current secretary, Gloria, would arrive shortly. How to explain the devastation in the room? What to do? A solution came to mind.

He crunched across the glass fragments to the sink, took a full bottle of detergent from the shelf underneath and squirted a huge swathe of the liquid onto the floor, trailing it across the draining board. Then he reached behind, squirted some over his right buttock and smeared it down the back of his trousers. Then he drizzled it over his shoes and swiped his hand along the underside of his sleeve and over his shoulder. He followed up with a stream of detergent on the right side of his face, hair and ear. He dumped the bottle and edged carefully around the mess to the laundry.

His cleaner tended to put things in the wrong place, but this time the mop was where it belonged. He half-filled the bucket with hot water and carried it back into the kitchen, dunked the mop into the bucket, squeezed it and swiped at the detergent, skilfully cutting wild paths from the sink to the table. The resultant tracks looked for all the world as though he had slipped and fallen on his right-hand side.

He finished just in time. As he reached the end of his track-making, Gloria's high heels tapped along the path at the side of the house. He dropped the mop into the bucket, grabbed the dustpan and brush, and was diligently sweeping up crockery and glass from the other side of the room when she walked in the back door.

'Oh my goodness, what's happened here?'

'I spilt the dishwashing liquid and slipped in it while I was filling the dishwasher,' he explained, with rueful charm.

She gave a "poor man let me do this and I'll show you what a good wife I'll make" smile and took the implements from his helpless hands.

Three quarters of an hour later, he'd had a shower and Gloria had cleaned up the chaos. He took two glasses from his crystal collection, normally kept for special occasions, poured them a glass of wine each and chatted to her as she loaded the dishwasher with what was left of the china.

Then he took her out to dinner, fed her, brought her home, "did" her and was forced to listen to her breathing beside him for the rest of the night. But it was a small price to pay for her naiveté in accepting his fairytale, and too stupid to question why he was filling the dishwasher. His housekeeper *always* did that.

He hadn't given up the idea of returning for Susan Prescott, but the police hadn't done anything more than question him along with everyone else in the family. He wasn't worried; she hadn't seen him at the hospital after all. For some reason his attempt to strangle her hadn't been reported, which made him a little anxious, but there was no way she could identify him. And now he'd managed to destroy the photos as well. He'd made sure no clues remained.

He stirred uneasily, reliving the moment on the six o'clock news while the announcer reported the fire at the hospital. Images of the fire engines and crews mopping up the mess played themselves out on the screen, while he seethed with fear and anticipation. Glenwood must have died. The dose of insulin had been enough to kill three men. Perhaps the police were not going to make the attack public? The young constable had his back turned when he was hit, so no danger there. And The CCTV footage would only show a tall, hooded man.

He clenched his teeth as he waited for some mention of a death–two deaths–for he'd belted the constable so hard, his skull had cracked.

Gloria stirred, rolled over and draped her leg over his. He wanted to smash her face in, but she was so damn useful and just how he liked women–stupid, pretty and skeletal. Having a woman around was the only way he could conceal which side he really batted for. He always took his lovers to out-of-the-way places, where no one knew either of them, but he'd begun to lay the groundwork of Gloria's instability in case she went public with their relationship. Discreetly, he had told his colleagues she was crazy and coming on far too strong. If necessary, he would ask one of them to quietly advise her to back off; perhaps even to counsel her.

He rolled her over, heaved himself on top, rammed into her and began to ride her as though he was winning the Melbourne Cup.

Her eyes flew open, startled. She wrapped her arms around his neck and locked her legs around his waist. The faster he got to the finish, the sooner morning would come and he could find out if John Glenwood was still alive.

Then he would reconsider his position.

CHAPTER 25

Condemnation

Susan

Thursday: early evening.

David is speaking to a woman. His deep, soft, playful tones, accompanied by bent head and slightly hunched shoulders, indicate he's seeking privacy.

He steps out onto the verandah and closes the glass door, so we can't overhear the conversation. I see the disappointment in Marli's face before she has time to assume a nonchalant facade. I cram down my own regret and continue to inventory the people who had been at the luncheon.

Euon Jellicott, solicitor, late 40s, early 50s? Grandson of Grace, Arthur's sister, unmarried. No comment on Jack, but liked Edna.

Mark Gordon, Ferna's son - first marriage? Mid 50s? Also unmarried. Don't know how he felt about either victim.

Peter Robinson, architect, 40 something, son of John, Arthur's brother. Another unmarried. *These men aren't very successful with women–or are they all gay?*

Jason Hardgreaves, doctor, 30-ish, engaged to Libby, Edna's grand-daughter. Who are Libby's parents? Beatrice

Eams, the director of the hospital is the second wife of Libby's father. The first wife is dead. *Lots of deaths in this family.*

George Murphy, developer, forty maybe, cousin. Connie's son. Married. He loathed Jack, a sliver of gossip I picked up at the luncheon.

The cricketers, Ferna's brothers. Both unmarried, but can't remember their names, so will ask Daniella if they prove important to the investigation. They thought Jack's sexual antics admirable.

Every last one of them needs to be investigated. Here's hoping David's troops are dealing with that. Now what about Sir Arthur? Hm ... a bit old for the current murders, but the right age for the original–happening. John was too young at the time. None of the women in the family are tall enough to be the killer of Edna, but were they involved? Maybe.

David returns indoors, folding his mobile into its pouch, as I finish the list

'I suppose you're going out again now?' pouts Marli, earning a startled glance from her father.

'Why would you assume that?'

'Well, you got a phone call and that means you're leaving for work,' she snarls, but before he can reply, she storms off down the hall and slams into her bedroom.

'What brought that on?' David is shocked by her vehemence.

'She's used to having me dash out at all hours to attend crime scenes, so she expects you to do the same,' I answer dryly.

He eyes me, warily. 'I know you're longing to know who phoned. Right? It was a friend.' *Yeah, right.*

'Your love-life is none of my business, David. I am

only concerned by your relationship with Marli and right now, this case.'

He takes time to digest my statement. 'What do you mean, 'this case'? It's my case, Susan. You're on leave, remember? All I want you to do is list who was at lunch today. I'll talk to Marli when she cools down.'

I measure up the distance between my hands and his throat, wondering how I can get away with killing him. *Susan, control yourself, don't blow it.* Doesn't he realise how much Marli wants him to be here for her? And how much I need to get back into harness?

His well-developed male instinct for survival kicks in. Of course this is programmed into male DNA. 'I'm sorry. I didn't mean to imply your help isn't invaluable. You're the only one of us who knows the Robinsons on a social basis, so let's look at your list and you can give me your 'take' on each one. Please?' He moves a chair over next to me and puts his hand on my shoulder. His warm, male aroma and lemon-based aftershave waft up my nostrils. My skin burns under his hand. Deep inside me, vibrations of lust drum a cicada's song.

'You need to go and talk to Marli,' I insist. Head-banging music blares out from our daughter's room. Heaven help her rats, though I suppose they're used to it.

David closes the door to the hallway and sits beside me. 'I told you, I'll talk to her later. So what do you make of this bunch?' He's clearly trying to appease me, but I'm determined to find this killer before he does.

'So how many have you checked out so far?'

He squints at the paper, sighs and takes a pair of spectacles out of his shirt pocket. Unfortunately, he looks better in them than any middle-aged man has a right to.

'Okay. I agree. It's a family thing. We've got alibis for–'

He ticks off the names as he enumerates the Robinson male contingent, finishing up with the future bridegroom, Jason Hardgreaves who is dismissed, being on duty with witnesses when both murders occurred. Some of the other males in the family are also accounted for. However, 'Slimeball' has no alibi for Edna's demise, and was actually at the showgrounds when Jack was knocked off.

'Beatrice Eams was on duty when Harlow was killed and at a dinner party when Edna died. So that lets her out. Libby doesn't have an alibi for either times, but neither of these women are tall enough. You didn't include Daniella Winslow and her daughter here,' he says, doodling on the paper, 'Adam Winslow's tall enough and where's Daniella's husband?'

'He was killed in an accident years ago at the same place John Glenwood had his accident.'

'Okay, that lets him out.' PC Winslow's name is added to the bottom of the list and his father is crossed off.

'I hadn't gotten around the lot of them yet. I think we can discount the women although they could be accessories. The twins, Grace and Connie were at the luncheon, they're Arthur's sisters and almost as old as he is. There's the Royal Couple of course and Ferna's son, Mark.'

My tone alerts him to something interesting, because he subjects me to a curious stare. 'You have a thought about him?'

'Er, no. He's invited me out to dinner tomorrow night. I'm counting on you to babysit.'

He stares at me, astonished. Light gleams along the rims of his spectacles, turning his eyes into satanic slits. *What? Don't you think anyone would want to take me out?*

'He's a suspect in this case, Susan. You can't fraternise with him.' His words are laced with chilli.

'Ah, but it's your case. You just reminded me, didn't you? I'm a private citizen right now and not bound by ethics in this instance.' I fix him with a narrow-eyed glare. '*You* are though!' *Put that in your pipe and smoke it, mate!*

'But *I'm* not dating anyone connected with the case, Susan,' he points out, reasonably enough.

My glance falls on his mobile phone. His expression is inscrutable, then a flush starts under his chin and travels up to his cheeks. *Gotcha!*

'Leanne has nothing to do with this case. I've only been seeing her since I moved to Ipswich. Now can we get on with this? We haven't had dinner yet and I'm starving.'

'And you still have to talk to Marli.'

It is 6.30pm by the time we've listed everyone who could be even remotely connected to the case. I make copious notes and phone Briony Feldman to organise a date for coffee tomorrow morning. Her grateful response betrays her loneliness.

I'm determined to take the mutilated photo to show to Ms Feldman. David will consider it his duty to take it to the station to add to the evidence and then quiz the Robinson rellies. No way. David isn't going to get his hands on it, until I've discovered who 'pin-hole' man is. 'If you take this photo to the station and ask the rellies before I've discovered who he is, they can lie and we'll never know the name.'

He concedes I am right, and heads down the

hallway to talk to Marli. I go to the kitchen, take a large container of casserole out of the fridge and put it in the microwave. Then I quietly open the cupboard door under the sink and peer inside. The tiny mouse nest heaves with transparent, pink life. Mrs Mouse peers up at me and abandons ship to hide behind the mop. I partially close the door and look around to see an empty cardboard container waiting to be binned. A creative minute with a pair of scissors and my mouse has a mansion, complete with front and back entrances.

David almost catches me, as I pop it over the top of the nest, a protective shell for the little family. They will be safe until I can decide which outside shed to place them in.

'What're you doing?' he asks, glancing around the kitchen.

'Nothing. Has Marli calmed down?' I ask, standing in front of the cupboard, hoping David won't take it into his head to investigate.

'Yes, we've had a chat. She's getting washed up for dinner. What's that?' His eyes light up. 'Casserole?'

'Yep. Beef Stroganoff. You can set the table.' I thrust cutlery into his hands and go on a sour cream hunt through the refrigerator. A few minutes later, Marli comes into the kitchen, gives me a kiss and takes the pup into the laundry to feed him.

As we hoe into the succulent casserole, Marli and David share a significant glance.

'What is it?' I ask.

David nods to Marli.

'Mum, when Dad took me to tea the other night, we got talking and we realised something about Da–Harry.' She stalls and casts a pleading glance at David.

He stops eating, his face grim. 'Susan, you need to know something ...'

As I listen to their theory I don't know whether to cry or explode with anger. Harry, aided by his secretary, would have found it very easy to separate the girls from their father by blocking letters and gifts, because I wasn't home to beat them to the mailbox.

'For the last few years I haven't sent anything, Susan. I gave up.'

'Mum, how could dad–Harry–do that? It's so *mean!*' Marli is getting her father's mixed up.

'I'm sorry I blamed you,' I say contritely to David, who accepts my apology with a gracious nod and continues eating his meal.

In the ensuing silence, my mind flips back to Harry's greatest betrayal. A year or two after we were married, I told Harry I wanted another baby and he confessed to knowing he was infertile before we were married. 'Just how long have you been aware of this?' I'd screamed.

'Since I was seventeen, when I had mumps.'

'Why didn't you tell me *before* we were married?' I wanted to kill him.

"Well, I didn't because you wouldn't have wanted me. I loved you–love you,' he hastily corrected himself.

'But that was unfair and deceitful, Harry! I had a right to know.'

'Well, get over it, all right?'

He refused to consider adoption. 'I don't believe in it,' was his explanation. But what then did he consider his appropriation of my children? Adoption, surely. Why hadn't I walked out when he admitted his monstrous deception? My love for Harry was severely rocked by his revelation, but I wouldn't–couldn't–allow myself to acknowledge I might have made a mistake. For the girl's sake, I told myself to paper over the cracks and move on. 'You couldn't face up to starting over again, could you? 'And Susan,' a little voice inside said. You were only too happy to accept Harry's protection, weren't you? *And then use it to your advantage to pursue your career.'*

And then there were my mother's words inside my head, repeating the old cliché. 'You've made your bed so you'll have to lie in it.' What right did I have to condemn Harry, when I was hardly blameless? So we stayed together and jogged along well enough, and ten years passed before I faced the fact that my second marriage had gone the way of my first, but still I hung on, to no avail. Three years later, we are separated and going for a divorce.

The dogs start barking, alerting us to someone approaching the house. David leaps to his feet and charges out the back door. As his footsteps fade, the front door opens and slams shut. High-heels tap down the parquet hallway. Marli and I exchange a "what now?' glance.

'I've been driving for hours. I thought I'd never find this fucking place!' announces Brittany, as she marches through the kitchen door, slings her backpack off her shoulder onto the floor, where we can all trip over it. 'I had to come and see what you're up to, Marli. You can't be trusted with anything, no more than you can, mother.'

'Brit–'

'Shut up, Marli. You listen to me. You insisted on staying with the emotional loser, so I've had to come back to take you to live with us. You won't get anywhere staying with her!' She shoots me a withering glare. 'She's run off two husbands so far and she managed to get her subordinate shot. What does that say about her? Stress leave, my arse. She's *crazy!'* Brittany's voice rises with each syllable.

A volcano is gathering momentum deep within me, but my voice is steady. 'Brittany, mind your mouth. I was completely cleared of negligence and I am not crazy. And Marli has a right to make her own choices without your interference. I won't tolerate you poking your nose into her life. You've made your own choice–'

Brit shouts over the top of me, enunciating each word as though she's biting pieces off my body. 'No, mother. You *influenced* Marli to come with you, playing the *sympathy* card sooooo well. '

'She did not!' shrieks Marli, tears welling.

Brit doesn't miss a beat. 'I know how you work. You're like, beyond sad,' she shouts, with practised contempt.

David comes into back into the kitchen, his face like granite.

Brit turns on him, incandescent with rage. '*You!* We were perfectly happy with dad, until he couldn't put up with her any longer!' she screams, advancing toward her father, fists clenched.

Marli listens open-mouthed and I, with interest. Her sister pulls no punches; we are all 'mentioned in despatches.' Her condemnation is evenly distributed between Marli and me, but David gets the lion's share. He is accused of everything with the possible exception of murder, and she would include that if she can drum one up for the occasion.

David lets her hang herself with words before responding. *'Sit down and be quiet!'*

Brit's mouth opens, but before she can say anything, he cuts her off. 'You heard me,' his voice is soft, his tone deadly. 'Don't you ever–*ever*–let me hear you speak to your mother and sister like that again.'

He yanks a chair forward and gestures her to sit. White-faced with shock, lips folded into a hen's-bum moue, she moves to the table and he shoves it under her bottom.

She settles gingerly onto the seat.

He pushes her up to her place with one sweep of his arm.

The silence is electric.

Marli's eyes swivel between the combatants like a metronome.

'Susan, get Brittany something to eat, please. No, I'll decide when you can speak,' he adds with narrow-eyed fury, as she opens her mouth for another tirade. He sits down and picks up his utensils, nodding to Marli to continue her meal.

I dish up a liberal serving of casserole for Brit and pop it into the microwave to heat. I'm trying to hide a smile, as I take out utensils and a serviette. At last I have some support in my on-going battle with her. It seems my wayward, volatile, but much-loved daughter has finally run into a brick wall.

CHAPTER 26

Cuckoo Cuckoo

Brittany

Thursday: after midnight.

Anger boiled inside, a writhing thing, erupting into scorching heat. It was a wonder her sheets didn't catch on fire. Humiliated and unable to take control of Marli and her mother, Brittany tossed and turned for what seemed like hours, before she slipped into the recurrent dream which pleased her most. This time the ending had changed.

She pushed past her, striving to reach the house before her twin. 'Brit, wait for me!' Marli screamed. If Brittany got to their father first, she'd be the one he would pick up and swing around. Oh no, her mother was there as well. She tried to veer away from her, but her legs refused to change direction. Then Marli got there first, and dad picked her up and swung her around.

Brittany pushed her mother's arms aside and kept running ... running ... straight into the arms of–him. Maguire. She struggled as he picked her up and swung her high into the air, higher and higher until she flew over the countryside, trying to land but totally unable to. Then Harry was beside her– 'You're not worthy, Brit,' he said, 'no one likes a smart arse. Behave yourself or we won't love you anymore.'

Brittany kicked wildly, until she got free of the sheets. Breathless and trembling, she sat up, covered in perspiration, her cheeks wet with tears. The impenetrable black and silence of the night disoriented her. A wild dog howled on the mountain, sending shivers through her. She glared at her sister, asleep in the other bed. 'I look like a fat toad next to Marli,' she thought bitterly. 'Dad doesn't like me because I'm fat.' Her lack of confidence didn't allow for them being identical twins and therefore exactly the same size. Self-pity was too enjoyable to acknowledge facts, and the interloper, Maguire, was not the pushover she'd expected. The prospect of regrouping seemed insurmountable.

She contemplated climbing into bed with Marli, but rejected the idea. She had to go to the loo, but didn't want to fumble her way along the hall to the bathroom. Couldn't the stupid Kirkbridges have put in an en suite? She supposed it was a sad environmental thing. She reached over to the bedside table and fumbled around for her watch. The tiny lighted dial said 1.30am. At least four hours before she could leave. The treatment that man had meted out to her at dinner was unbelievable. There must be someone she could report him to. The pol–he *is* the police, she reminded herself. Child Protection would do–no, that was for young kids.

It transpired that David Maguire was leading the investigation into a couple of boring murders, and her mother, who couldn't keep her nose out of anything, was helping him. What a laugh! 'Mum's a flake. Everybody knows that,' she muttered, trying to get comfortable. As for Marli, where did she get off with the attitude?

Brittany threw her pillow onto the floor and turned the second one over so it was cool under her neck.

She had treated *that man's* caution not to roam around outside at night, with the contempt it deserved, but when her mother displayed marks on her neck and told her about the attack, Brittany had hidden her shock, sneering, 'I don't give a "monkey's".'

The dog howled again, nearer this time. The family dogs, whom she had missed more than she cared to admit, answered from their yard. Marli stirred and rolled over, but didn't wake. The pet rats chased each other around as they trashed their cage, occasionally pausing to look at Brittany with disdainful shoe-button eyes.

Another sudden yearning for comfort almost sent her scurrying into Marli's bed, but she rejected the idea. Showing any sign of weakness might get her sucked into the crap going on here. She sat up, slipped her coat over her pj's and swung her legs over the side of the bed. She crept to the door and quietly opened it. The nightlight above the skiring board sent a soft glow down the hallway.

'I'll bet *he's* with mother,' she thought savagely. 'They're *disgusting.*' The ticking of the pendulum in the grandfather clock followed her to the kitchen. After she turned on the light, the dogs began running up and down outside, under the window. Footsteps sounded outside in the hall, followed by the door opening. Maguire came in, dressed in jeans, boots and a thick sweater.

'Can't sleep?' he asked quietly.

Acid dripped from her lips. 'Give the man a medal! However did you guess?'

Maguire's mouth tightened. He brushed past her, opened the back door and disappeared without replying. A moment later, the back yard became bathed in brilliant light. Brittany looked through the window at the dogs standing to attention, noses pointed toward the mountain. Her mother came into the kitchen, yawning, as she tied the belt of her robe.

'Can't sleep, Brit? Want a hot Milo?' she asked, mildly.

'What is this? The night of the cliché?'

'No, a courteous question,' her mother replied, brushed past her and went out to the back steps.

'Ooooh, my bad!' countered Brittany. She marched out of the kitchen and charged down the hallway to the bathroom. When she'd finished, she went back to the bedroom where she turned on the bedside lamp and rooted around for her clothes. 'I'm not staying here, I'm starting back now,' she muttered, jamming her belongings into the backpack. 'Marli, wake up!' she hissed, as she zipped up her jeans.

Her sister rolled over, blinking in the light. 'What're you doing?'

'I'm getting out of here and you're coming with me,' Brittany snapped.

Marli sat up and knuckled her eyes. 'No. I'm not coming and if you go back, Brit, you can stay there. I don't want to have anything more to do with you. You're blaming everyone but Harry for what's happened. I want to be with mum and dad. I'm not leaving, especially with what's happening with the murders and everything. You're being selfish, spiteful and childish.'

Her sister loomed over the bed. 'You listen and you listen good, Mar. Dad'll be back in Brisbane soon and I'm going to move in with them.'

Silence ensued, as her sister lay back staring at the

ceiling, not deigning to reply. Titch yawned and snuggled closer to Marli.

'What's she like?' Marli asked, folding her arms behind her head.

'Who?'

'Sharon? She's all right. She's got two little kids, and he's very happy,' replied Brittany, remembering her father's pleasure in playing with them. But he was often just a little too happy. Those were the times she pinched and slapped the kids when no one was looking.

'Well, bully for him!' snapped Marli.

Brittany frowned. 'Harry?'

'You know nothing about what happened, Brit, so pack it in, will you?' Marli turned onto her side and pulled the blankets tightly around her shoulders. 'Turn the light off when you go.'

Brittany, routed for the moment, placed her backpack in the corner. The dogs' barking had died down. Voices and laughter came from the kitchen where her mother and–*he*–were probably making coffee. Fury rose up and almost choked her. She turned off the light, flung herself fully clothed onto the bed and rolled into the top blanket, feeling almost safe in the warm cocoon of wool.

'Aren't you going to get back into your pjs?' Marli asked, without opening her eyes.

'No.'

'Okay. Goodnight then.'

Brittany screwed her eyes tightly shut to prevent the tears from trickling out. She'd always been the one to be the boss of the nest. The old Marli would have crawled over and climbed into bed with her, grovelling for forgiveness because she'd dared stand up to her sister. The kitchen door closed and then her mother's footsteps headed for her room, then his paused outside their door. She held her breath as it opened a little. A torch beam played over their cocooned bodies.

Maguire's voice was deep and forbidding. 'Brit, I know you're still awake. Regardless of what you think of me, don't take out your anger on your mother and Marli. They deserve better and that sort of behaviour is unworthy of you. Goodnight.'

The door closed. She let her breath out in a careful whoosh. He needed to be reminded that she was seventeen and he couldn't stop her doing what she pleased. She fell asleep, vowing to get even with all of them.

From the moment Brittany Maguire charged into the world, she needed to be first with everything. She'd wailed the loudest to be fed, so she was first to the breast and later, the bottle. She'd heard she was the first to lift her head up, to sit and roll over. Crawling had been skipped altogether. Their grandmother told her card-playing cronies: 'Brittany's my little princess. She's so advanced for her age.'

Marli didn't get a "look in" if Brittany could prevent it. She'd been the one to crawl into their father, Harry's, lap to make sure there was no room for Marli and always the first fed at table, except when her mother was home. Tantrums got her everything she wanted from Harry, for he denied her nothing. She always got to open both their birthday presents because she always tore the paper on Marli's, pretending it was a mistake. She made sure she played with new toys before her sister. When their mother supervised, things were very different. Sometimes she could hear their parents arguing about her, but that made her feel important. By the time they were five,

Marli automatically deferred to her elder sister in everything.

At school, Brittany majored in gang warfare, so her twin was safe from bullying. At home Marli kept their room clean, fed the animals and generally dogsbodied for Brit. Sometimes when she felt particularly brave, she would refer to herself as Cinders, which didn't go down well with her twin. 'Don't you tell anyone what I make you do or I'll give you a Chinese burn.'

But worms have a habit of turning.

CHAPTER 27

Doing Coffee

Susan

Friday: mid morning

Briony Feldman is wearing a bright red dress with a sort of flowing colourful cape top, the corners of which billow around her, reminiscent of curtains in front of an open window. She surges into the cafe, like a gaily painted river-barge, carefully negotiating the tables, scattered artistically al fresco.

I arrived early and selected a table in a corner of the courtyard in order to observe her as she approached. Our brief meeting at the luncheon yesterday was not conducive to discovering the secrets of the Robinson clan.

I used my waiting time to re-hash Brit's arrival last night. My mojo is reviving, but still fragile from the gale force of my eldest daughter's verbal and emotive attack on all of us. I was wounded by her diatribe, not only against her father and myself, but against her sister, who should have been exempt from her venom. David, of course, was more than capable of dealing with her fury and rudeness, but the incident didn't bode well for future father-daughter bonding.

My heart aches for my angry, unhappy child. Her low

self-esteem always manifested itself in stubborn competitiveness and outright aggression. Monstrously indulged by Harry, all her life she's been determined to beat her sister in everything. I'm amazed that my younger child is so well-balanced, and delighted that she is bonding so well with David.

We were relieved when the girls went to bed and the atmosphere settled. 'It's okay, Mum, I do love her!' Marli replied, when I'd asked her if she felt comfortable sharing her room with Brit.

Briony Feldman shakes hands with the confidence of the straightforward, 'don't-mess-with-me' career woman. We exchange pleasantries and order cappuccino, then debate whether to risk our hips with cheesecake and if so what sort. I settle for caramel, Briony, lemon. I ask how long she anticipates being in the district.

She doesn't beat about the bush. 'You mean, how long have you got to get some information out of me, Detective Senior Sergeant Prescott?'

Shock streaks through me and settles somewhere in my gut. 'I beg your pardon?'

'Mrs Prescott, I know who you are, but as far as I'm aware, the Robinsons don't yet and it's not my place to tell them.'

She spoons the froth off the top of her coffee, pops it into her mouth then licks the spoon, leaving a faint line of froth and chocolate on her top lip. Now she's more approachable.

I'm sprung, there doesn't seem to be any point in lying. 'Technically I'm on leave,' I tell her. 'Detective Inspector David Maguire asked me to see what I can find out to help with the investigation.'

Briony stares into her cup, possibly weighing where

her loyalties lie. I expound our theory of a long-ago crime, and recount the sequence of events leading up to the present. Then I show her the suspicious photograph explaining my theory as to who might have performed the mutilation. Briony nods and continues to eat, as she absorbs the information.

'Nasty. Someone didn't like him, that's for sure.' She leans down and picks up her briefcase. I sweep our empty plates aside and signal for more coffee. Briony pulls a large black folder out and thumbs through it, stopping from time to time to catch loose leaves as they flutter out of the pages.

'As it happens, I have a list of all the relatives already. I only started this contract about ten days ago, and if I can find the list of hatch, matches and despatches for that year–' she shuffles through more papers– 'it might give you a lead. Yes, here you are.' She hands me a foolscap sheet. Excitement skips around my stomach, as I read the list of who was born, married and died in 1947.

There were three births in March and June, also a wedding in September, and two deaths that year, both males. One fell into a grain silo and one was killed by a bull.

'Could one of those deaths be a murder?'

'I have no idea, but a farm accident would be fairly easy to arrange,' I reply.

'The next year there were two more deaths in the family. Here on the next page, one a tractor rollover and the other died in his bed, aged 90. Unless the cliché jealous husband smothered him, the 90 year-old is a waste of time investigating!'

'Do we have their names?' I ask, laughing as I take out my notebook.

'Yep, Warren Caldwell, the grain silo, a cousin. Bob Jellicott, Arthur's brother-in-law, the bull and Steven Murphy, the tractor accident. He was Kathleen's son, George's father. Arthur and John's father is Bertram, the 90 year-old. By all accounts, he was a dirty old thing, only bathed as a treat for Rose, his wife, so I don't think husbands would have had any reason to be jealous of *him!*'

She waits until I finish writing and then puts the folder away in her briefcase. 'Are you going to the funerals, Mrs Prescott?'

'Yes, and please call me Susan.'

'I'm Briony. Okay, but it doesn't look like any of those are murders, does it?' She looks somewhat disappointed. *Have I found a fellow-sleuth?*

'We'll investigate all of them. Of course, it could be that the murder was committed long before, or after 1947.'

'How do you get on with Lady Ferna?' I seek to turn the conversation to the rest of the family.

Briony rolls her eyes. 'Oh my God, I could strangle that woman!' She blushes, realising what she's said, but I assure her I would help, if given half a chance.

'I'm getting on quite well with Sir Arthur. Too well, actually. He doesn't know the meaning of sexual harassment. Well, maybe, he does and thinks he's going to get away with it. Trouble is, I'm free lancing and this is a contract which I can't afford to collapse. If I keep him at a distance, he's okay. As long as he's stroking Genevieve, his hands are busy.'

I try to stifle my laughter in a paper serviette. This sets Briony off and we become unglued. It's so long since I laughed, that I feel as though I'm drawing attention to myself. When we've calmed down, I wonder if I can push her further. 'So, have you interviewed any of the younger members of the clan?'

Her eyes narrow shrewdly. 'Are you asking me to spy for you?'

'Yep. Who better to ask than yourself?'

'I guess there's no one outside of the family who you could ask openly,' she concedes. 'What do you want to know?'

'Well, for starters, how about Euon Jellicott?'

'Well ...' she launches into Jellicott's résumé with little enthusiasm. 'He's not much chop as far as I'm concerned. Well educated, Scot's College no less, has everything money can buy. Ambitious, almost to the point of recklessness. All the morals of a rooster.' She cites a daring takeover bid which he apparently masterminded the year before, and which I've not heard about. 'Of course, he's a bastard in court as well as socially.'

'Ruthless enough to kill, would you say?'

She looks thoughtful. 'Enough to squash everything in his path, but to commit two murders? Hm. Doubt it. He's got his eye on becoming a barrister and word is his ultimate goal is political office, so he needs to keep his nose clean. If there is something nasty in the family archives, especially if the perpetrator is still alive and can be tried for the crime, it could be the death of his career. Or at the very least, a major embarrassment.'

'What about George Murphy?'

'I don't know much about George, except his nickname, which tells you a lot!' She laughs. 'But when all's said and done, being a much-maligned developer it's pretty much par for the course, wouldn't you say?' *But is there anything else he wants which could be ruined by familial association with a killer?*

'I tend to agree with you. After all, he's not running for public office–yet. Mind you, he's married to a trophy wife, Daphne the Dill.' We make eye contact and burst out laughing. When we've recovered, I ask about Peter Robinson.

'Much the same scenario as Euon Jellicott. Ambitious, reaching for the stars stuff. Pete punched a fellow solicitor a few years ago over a woman, but that was a hush-up job.'

'What? Okay, when was that?'

She gives me the year. 'Okay. What about Mark Gordon? The vicar?' I feel warmth in my nether regions. He really is *very* attractive, but then so is David. I thrust licentious thoughts into the background of my over-active, sex-starved mind.

'I don't know anything about him yet, apart from the fact that he's very highly thought of, and single. He's headed for a bishopric one day. Great fundraiser apparently, doesn't suffer fools gladly, as they say. I expect a killer in the family wouldn't be something he'd want known about either.'

'Why aren't these candidates married? Are they all gay?' I am hoping the Archdeacon isn't. *Down girl.*

'I haven't heard that any of them are gay. Peter Robinson frolics across the social pages with models and socialites, but that might be a cover. The Archdeacon I don't know about. One interesting point, he only came to the priesthood after he sold a technology business in the 1990s. Don't know what caused his conversion to religious life. I certainly haven't delved into his "personals" yet! And before you ask, I haven't found out much about the cricketing fanatics either, except they think with their dicks.'

We roll our eyes in unison. I make a note to ask David if his team has investigated the brothers.

'I have to tell you I feel some disloyalty to Sir Arthur by talking to you,' Briony says, anxiously.

'Nothing is sacred in a police investigation, Briony. But if it's not relevant to the case, I'll forget it.'

'Okay. Well, Sir Arthur's first wife, Lily, ran off with Ferna's first husband, Gerard, father of Mark, in 1980. Arthur and Ferna married in 1984. Gerard died in a car accident two years later. Lily was 50 when they scarpered. She lives in Brisbane in a flat in Hamilton. I think she's a couple more husbands down the track, though I haven't had time to sort that out yet.'

Is Lily knocking off husbands? Is she a prospect for these murders? But in 1947 she was only 16. Something lurks in the deep recess of my mind, and then slithers away. 'I see. Interesting ... we'll probably have to interview her, but your name won't come into it. After all, it's knowledge which any investigator would uncover. Everything you've given me is.' I smile and she looks relieved.

'Well, I've got to go, Susan. This has been interesting!' She starts to gather her belongings.

'Can I ask you to let me know if you come across anything useful?'

'Yes, but I don't want the family to find out I'm talking to you about their affairs. My contract–'

'I understand, Briony. I'll be discreet.'

She nods, says goodbye and leaves the cafe in a flutter of colour. Perhaps David has more information I can access. I glance at my watch; they'll be interviewing Penelope Harlow again about now. *We've got to get this creep before anyone else gets hurt.* I am about to leave the cafe when my mobile rings. Harry's voice echoes in my ear. Without any greeting or waiting for me to reply, he launches into the reason for the call.

'Susan? Has Brittany arrived yet? Because if she has, for chrissakes keep her there. We don't want her back; she's causing too much trouble.'

CHAPTER 28

The Ovine Monster Mash

The Detectives

Friday: early morning.

David Maguire pulled into the backyard of the Emsburg police station, out of sight of any lurking journalist, and squeezed his car under the shade tree beside that of Senior Sergeant Harris.

His ex-wife's presence stirred unwelcome sexual feelings which he couldn't dismiss. He tried to focus on his new lover, but he was getting uncomfortable insight into the truth of the old adage, 'out of sight out of mind.' He hadn't experienced such mixed emotions since his first marriage ended and to cap it off, the investigation was in danger of getting out of his control. Two murders and three attempts, one of them on his ex-wife, and two police officers near death were a subject which his Superintendant had already discussed with him, at length.

'Where's the bastard going to strike next?' Maguire wondered, as he stalked into the Incident Room to glare at the white board, then fill and plug in the electric kettle.

'Ah, Dave.' Pete Hansen followed him into the room, swinging a folded newspaper. 'Front page news again. And the boss's been on the phone,' he added, referring to the Superintendant, 'He's coming out tomorrow with the Chief Super. Bill's gone to chase up newspaper archives on the computer and Don's off interviewing more friends of Edna's.' He rolled his eyes; bigwigs putting their stamp on a major investigation were routine, but infuriating.

'Well, there's been a bit more excitement since yesterday, Pete.' Maguire proceeded to bring his partner up to date. Hansen's eyes widened as he listened to the part concerning the pinholes in the eyes of one of the photographic subjects.

'So do you reckon we've got a murder in 1947? Where is the photo?' Hansen asked eagerly.

'Susan took the photo to a meeting with Sir Arthur's biographer this morning to see if Ms Feldman recognises the subject.'

'You're letting Senior Sergeant Prescott help out? You sure that's wise? Can she–er–handle this right now?' asked Hansen, cautiously. 'Shouldn't we be taking the photo to Penelope Harlow?'

'*You* try and stop her!' Maguire moved to the kettle and started pouring coffee. 'She's coming along and this'll be good for her to get her confidence again.' He narrowed his eyes at his partner. 'I'd trust Susan with my career anytime, Pete. And I don't want anyone else to see the photo yet. If anyone in the family knows who the bloke is and what's going on, they'd cover their tracks and we wouldn't know the difference.'

'Right on,' replied Hansen. He took the steaming cup of coffee which Maguire held out. 'They got onto the hospital.' He jerked a thumb toward the front office. 'Glenwood and Smenton are still unconscious. No worse, but no better either.'

The sound of a commotion at the front office wafted

down the passageway to the room at the back of the station. Maguire rolled his eyes; the press were getting restless.

'The front desk'll take care of that lot. Right, how about we go and reinterview Penelope Harlow again? She might be more forthcoming about Jack, now a few days have passed. Then we'll have another talk with Daniella Winslow. Has Nora Glenwood come up with anything new?'

'Not that I know of. Harris will let us know if she thinks of anything.'

They tried to tiptoe the short distance to the back steps into the car park and scuttled to their unmarked car, where Hansen dived behind the wheel. Grinning conspiratorially, they drove through the side gate and set a round-about course for Harlow's farm. At the station, the press continued to bellow at the front desk, thwarted somewhat irritably, by Constables Winslow and Loy.

Maguire's phone rang before they reached the town limits. His heart sank. It was his previous girlfriend in Cairns, announcing her arrival in the nearby city, eager to bounce into his bed and make up for the time lost when he'd transferred south and slunk out of the city. It was all he could do to curb her exuberance; Hansen listened unashamedly.

'David, I got some leave! When can I see you, you sexy beast?' she shouted, 'I can't wait to get you naked! Do you miss me?'

Oh, God... 'I told you we were over before I left Cairns, Donna.' Heat started to rise from somewhere below his navel. He glanced out of the corner of his eye at his partner, who grinned from ear to ear.

'I'm in Ipswich at Jenny's flat!' she squealed, naming

a rambunctious girlfriend. 'I can't wait for you to get here, so I can rip your gear off!' How could he put her off without causing a major ruckus? *Shit.* What part of "no" didn't the woman understand? And what about Leanne?

He panicked. 'I won't be back tonight. I'm on a job out of town. We'll talk when the case is over.'

'What do you mean, when the case is over? You get time off, don't you?' she whined.

'Yes, but–'

'Don't worry, it'll all work out! I know you're out in Emsberg and I've just had an idea,' she cooed. The phone went dead.

'We're out of range,' said Maguire, snapping the cover shut, as they stopped at the main gates to the farm. Penelope Harlow had been interviewed at her sister's house previously, so they hadn't encountered the security set-up at the farm. Frowning, he got out and went to the speaker on the gate to identify them. Moments later, the left gate opened. *What did the Harlow's have to hide?* It was only a sheep farm, after all.

They drove along the bitumen driveway to the house, where they looked around curiously, as they stepped out of the car. The grass needed mowing; a light breeze ruffled the tail feathers of the chooks pecking in the back yard. At the end of the house-paddock, a few sheep lifted their heads, looked at them scornfully and continued with the busy business of filling their portly stomachs. At the back of the property, amongst a copse of trees, a collection of massive sheds was surrounded by more sheep yards and paddocks meticulously divided by white-washed fences covered in mesh.

A voice hailed them as they were about to knock on the back door. Penelope Harlow was a woman of somewhat splendid proportions. Tall, with tangled, naturally-fair hair hanging over her shoulders, she presented a stalwart and competent figure, as she came toward them through the fruit trees near the house. The ten or so dogs scattered around her, barked as they raced toward the detectives. But for Maguire's restraining hand, Hansen would have dived back into the car.

'They're fine, Pete, just curious.'

'Bloody wolves,' his partner muttered, but stood his ground, as the dogs sniffed around his cringing ankles and inspected his crotch. Maguire, who was used to dogs, patted them and skilfully avoided the exuberant overtures.

'Well, I thought you might want to talk to me again, Inspector,' Penelope boomed, as she came up to them. 'Won't you come in? It's about coffee time,' she invited, and then emitted a whistle so ear-splitting that their brains reeled around their skulls. 'Sorry,' she said, smiling slightly, as she shucked her boots off. 'I should have warned you about that!' The dogs retired to the shade of the trees and the detectives followed her into the kitchen.

'Sit down. Tea or coffee?'

'Tea, for me, thanks, Mrs Harlow,' Maguire said, 'I'm all "coffee'd" out.'

Hansen agreed and Penelope filled the electric kettle and plugged it in. She whipped cups, bread and butter plates and cake forks out of the cupboard, a cake tin from the kitchen dresser and flicked open a drawer, from which she took a knife. The aroma of freshly baked sponge wafted into their nostrils. 'Coffee cake?' she asked, smiling from one to the other. She placed large wedges of light-as-air, heavily frosted cake onto their plates, then poured tea, and waved her hand over the milk jug and sugar bowl, inviting them to help themselves.

'The weather's going to change by tomorrow,' she announced. 'Not a good day to be buried, I'm afraid.'

They almost choked. She remained unfazed. 'Well, that's what you've come to talk about, isn't it? Jack and Edna's murders?'

They agreed, through mouthfuls of cake, that it was indeed what they'd come for. Black-edged cards, promising the arrival of friends and colleagues for the interment, covered the sideboard. 'Well, ask away, gentlemen,' their hostess invited airily, before meeting their astonished glances. She sighed. 'Surely, after all the things you've learned about Jack, you can't imagine I'm grief-stricken? Because if you do, then don't. Of course, I got a shock when he was killed. He didn't deserve to be shot, only flayed with a stockwhip. I've stayed with him all these years because of the animals. They're our children. The farm is–has been–our life's work.'

Just then, Maguire's phone rang. With an apologetic word, he stepped out the back door.

'Listen, lover, I'm coming out to Emsberg now! If the mountain won't come, etc' trilled Donna, 'I'll book into the motel and be waiting for you tonight. You'll be walking bow-legged in the morning!' she promised, coquettishly.

'I can't be there. I'm on a case, remember?' he parried desperately, but she'd rung off. 'And how the hell am I going to tell her where I'm staying, without her making a scene?' he muttered, his mind zizzing like a trapped ferret.

'Now you've had time to think about it, have you come up with any reason why someone would want to kill your husband?' Hansen was asking Penelope, as

Maguire sat down again.

'Look, as I said the last time I talked to you, Jack was a lecher. He didn't care if whatever woman he chased was someone else's wife. And before you ask, I didn't care either. At least it kept him away from me. So, if it turns out a husband or boyfriend did the deed, then I won't be surprised.' She folded her lips, frowning.

'I'm sorry; I do have to ask this. Would Jack chase young girls?' Pete tried to be diplomatic.

Penelope stayed silent for a long moment. 'Do you mean little girls, or young women?'

'Both,' said Hansen.

'Not little girls, Senior Sergeant. I believe even Jack drew the line there. Young women, certainly. He was quite good-looking for a man of fifty, but not any great shakes in bed. Mind you, older women loved him. Perhaps he had hidden talents which I've been unaware of.'

The two detectives glanced at each other, taken aback by her candour, but then Penelope smiled comfortably and offered them more tea and cake, which they couldn't resist.

'You were at Sir Arthur and Lady Ferna's anniversary party last month. Were you also at the family meeting? The one where Jack and Edna stormed out?' Maguire chimed in.

'I was at the party, but not invited to the meeting. It was strictly family only. Blood family, that is.'

Maguire ran his eye down his list. 'Did Jack tell you why he was so annoyed?'

'He clammed up. It was a family trait to be secretive. I asked Edna as well, but she fixed me with one of her glares. She could be pretty intimidating, you know.'

Penelope frowned into her tea cup.

'So, you wouldn't know about a crime committed possibly in the late '40s and which might have taken place on the family farm?'

Penelope looked at him, thoughtfully. 'Of course, we had accidents on the farm, Inspector. Well ... Jack had a nightmare after the meeting, shrieking that 'he' was dead, killed, and the cops'd be out for sure. Then he said something about it was all the fault of that prick. I thought he meant Arthur, but next morning, he reckoned he hadn't dreamed.' She paused, staring at nothing as she examined her mind's eye.

'I was born and raised in this district, Inspector. I think something did happen years ago at the Robinson farm. Talk would stop when we kids came into the room and the aunts made comments like, 'Little pitchers have big ears. Funny, I'd forgotten all about that.'

'So it was more what they *didn't* say which gave you that impression?' asked Hansen.

'Yes, and Jack wouldn't tell me anything. We didn't sleep together and he wasn't in the habit of wandering into my room. I had to go into *his* room to see what he was screaming about that night.'

'Can you think of anyone in the family who might be prepared to talk about it? Anyone who was at the meeting?'

Penelope stood up, and began clearing the empty plates off the table. 'No, Inspector. I'm sure you won't get anyone to discuss what was said there. Robinson mouths are tight as fish's arses. You'll get nothing from them. The Historical Society commissioned Arthur's biography, so I assumed the meeting was about that. No one has said otherwise.'

Maguire and Hansen got to their feet to help her move the last of the crockery to the sink. Hansen surreptitiously ran his finger through some coffee frosting left on his plate, and licked it before he put it on the draining board. As they headed out the back door, followed by the cloud of dogs who appeared to think something exciting might be about to happen, Maguire asked Penelope how many sheep she had.

'Oh, about fifteen hundred altogether, Inspector.'

'That doesn't seem enough to make a living out of, Mrs Harlow,' he commented curiously.

'They're very special sheep, Inspector. Let me show you.'

They followed her down to the nearest huge complex and watched, puzzled, as she opened the door. She stood aside, and smiled as they gaped at what appeared to be hundreds of pens filled with designer-clad sheep. The half-light in the building made the light-coloured coats look like a jumble of moving tombstones. The low sound of munching, as the animals ate, added to the surreal atmosphere.

The dogs followed Penelope into the shed, where she began talking to the sheep in the nearest pen. 'Bubba, come here darling ... that's right. Lucy ... here's a treat from Mum...' she crooned, and digging into her pockets, began to dispense treats to greedy mouths. As they got closer, Maguire and Hansen saw that the coats were patterned with flowers.

'Holy cow, it's like something out of the Rocky Horror Show. Are they going to a fancy dress ball? asked Maguire, dazed.

Penelope laughed. 'This is a huge enterprise, Inspector! These sheep grow superfine 18 Micron wool for the Japanese, Chinese and European markets. They live in these sheds to keep the sun from burning the wool, so they have to wear coats when they get outside. Jimmy?' she bellowed.

'Yes, Mrs Harlow!' a voice called back, as two men bobbed up amid the sea of greyish-white blobs at the far end of the shed.

'Everything okay?' she called.

'Yes, no problems. We'll be finished here very soon.'

Penelope turned to the detectives. 'They're just checking all their dressing-gowns are on and then this flock will be let out for fresh air. We sell the wool for $16,000 and more per bale, so you see, every care is taken to make sure our babies are well cared for.' She smiled. 'These animals are priceless. Last year, we made over a million dollars after tax. And that is why we have security at the gate. We also have dog fences around the place.'

Maguire looked at her thoughtfully. *Worth killing for to get the farm?* Maybe. *Perhaps Jack was killed for control of this ... but what about Edna?*

'Tell me something, Mrs Harlow. I meant to ask you the other day why they had such a huge audience at the dog trials on Saturday? To most people, sheepdog trials are like the old cliché, as exciting as watching paint dry.'

She laughed. 'Well, for one thing, it was the championship trial and we always get more people there, but also our committee finally got their finger out and did some advertising on TV and radio, really hyped it up, hired rides, a mouse circus for the kids and sold family tickets, kids under ten free. If they hadn't done that, only the competitors' families and members of the Association would have attended. Jack was very pleased there were so many ...' her voice wobbled and trailed off.

'She's more upset than she'd like us to believe,' Maguire realised. 'Well, Mrs Harlow, we won't trouble you further if we can help it, but if you think of anything, please ring me.' He handed her another of his cards which she slipped into her pocket.

'Right. Good-bye Inspector,' she said vaguely as, surrounded by her swarm of border collies, she headed toward her staff. Shrugging, Maguire and Hansen left the shed, carefully closing the door behind them.

'Waddya reckon, Dave?'

'I don't think she had anything to do with it, but I do think she knows a lot more than she's prepared to tell us, and–'

His phone rang again.

'Hi, dearling, I've taken a room at the motel, got some champagne and I'll wait for you there–naked!' Donna screeched, lustfully. A spurt of anger shot through him. Dearling? The expression of affection, once cute, made him feel as though his balls were being rubbed with sandpaper.

'Donna, I told you I can't see you. Look, I'm staying at the fa–'

'Byeee!' she trilled, and was gone.

'She hung up.'

Pete laughed outright. 'I wouldn't want to be in your shoes, mate!'

'Jesus wept. Bloody women. Susan and the girls are expecting me to stay at the farm and I can't leave them on their own, not with this bastard around. *And* I want to spend time with my daughters.'

'Surely Donna will understand, Dave?' asked Hansen, tongue in cheek.

'Not bloody likely. She'll kill me,' Maguire said, as

Hansen turned the car onto the main road and set course for the police station. Just then his mobile rang again. At first he was disinclined to answer it, but then snapped it open without checking the incoming number and roared. 'Donna, for fuck's sake, I told you I couldn't see you–oh, it's you, George.'

Hansen struggled to contain his laughter, as Maguire listened to Senior Sergeant Harrison and turned a glittering glance on Hansen.

'John Glenwood's regained consciousness.'

CHAPTER 29

An Inconvenient Child

Susan

Friday: morning.

My fragile calm wavers, reminding me that my resurgence in emotional strength is only twenty-four hours old. The sound of my husband's voice shocks me as does the reason for his call.

'She arrived last night. What do you mean?' I sink back into the chair and rest my elbows on the table. The last thing I need is an argument with him, especially in such a public venue as a coffee shop. 'In what respect was she making trouble, Harry?'

'At first she was fine, she and Sharon and the kids got on well, but it didn't take long before she was sniping at Sharon and bossing the kids around, especially Juney. They always seemed to be crying. Then I caught her pinching and slapping them!'

'You took her with you, Harry, without my permission and you know she's very possessive of you.'

'Susan, she's over sixteen–'

Ear-splitting screams rip through my head and the sound of smashing glass sends me whipping around in shock. I expect to see, at the very least a hold-up at the cash register, but all eyes are riveted to the floor beside my table.

A girl of about five is throwing a full-blown tantrum. A few short months ago, I would have coped admirably with the noise, but now white-hot rage flares, not only with Harry's cavalier attitude, but by being unable to hear what he's saying.

'Please, shush, darling,' pleads the child's mother. 'You can't have more ice cream because we need to go and meet daddy. *Please,* Jada, darling, be a good girl for mummy.'

The child rolls across the floor, legs kicking and arms flailing. Her shrieks are deafening. My fellow customers cringe. The proprietors appear at the counter, obviously wondering just how far they can legally intervene. The strap of my handbag is hooked by one flailing, grubby paw and the bag is hurled across the tiles, scattering my belongings through the pool of liquid and shards of glass.

'Harry, stay on the bloody phone or I'll send Brittany back to you on the next plane!'

I leap to my feet and loom over the wretched child, who has settled into her Academy Award performance with practised ease. The mother is wringing her hands and bleating.

'Shut up!' I roar at the top of my lungs. Everybody freezes. The brat gapes at me, tonsils on display. I address the mother in my iciest voice, combined with my favourite death stare. 'Madam, you will control your child. If you're going to give in and give her another ice cream, which is what I suspect is your normal way of rewarding her for this type of behaviour, then go ahead. Failing that, *get out.* We do not need to listen to this *appalling racket!* Any more of this and I will have you arrested for disturbing the peace.'

She is so shocked that she doesn't think to question my authority. In the ensuing silence, I stalk through the glass, scoop up my sticky belongings and stuff them into the soaked handbag. I dump it on my table and snatch a handful of serviettes from the dispenser and wipe it, focusing all the while on the pair, like a hawk on a clutch of chickens. A rustle of something which could be approval goes around the room. I can hear Harry's voice squawking from my mobile.

The child's red-faced mother gathers up her things and drags her sour-faced daughter off the premises, watching me out of the corner of her eyes like a fear-crazed horse. I glance around at the relieved faces in the cafe, nod acknowledgement, pick up my mobile and sit down. For once, I will be happy if this roomful of witnesses says they've 'seen nothing.'

'You were saying, Harry?'

'What was all that yelling?' he asks, momentarily diverted from the matter at hand.

'A child having a tantrum in the cafe. Now, what am I supposed to tell Brittany? Don't you care that you're going to hurt her a great deal?'

'Hurt *her?* You must be joking!' he scoffs. 'That's impossible! No, you keep her there, Susan. If you won't co-operate, I can make sure our final financial settlement is delayed.'

This is the man I loved enough to marry? The fun-loving hunk who clapped onto me at a pub fourteen years ago and wouldn't be shaken off because he said he couldn't live without me? I can't give any quarter in this fight. Although Brit's revving up for revenge on David and me, I can't bear to see my child's pain and disillusionment when she finds out about Harry's rejection of her.

'Just try it. Your behaviour is outrageous, Harry. You and Mary Jello have a lot to answer for. I've discovered how you two have been intercepting David's letters and gifts for the girls. You *stole* his children. I'll bet you would have prevented me receiving his maintenance as well if it had been possible!'

'Not bloody likely, Susan. At least I didn't pay for their music and ballet lessons and those endless school camps. Maguire did!' he crows. If I could lay my hands on a knife or a gun and Harry was standing in front of me, I'd take him down right now. Two months ago this man almost caused me an emotional collapse. All right, Danny Grey's death played the major part, but crying over Harry as well? Oh my God, what was I thinking?

'Why should I be the one who has to tell her you don't want her anymore? It's your decision, not mine.' *I'll be dealing with the aftermath.*

Then Harry, true to form, laid it on the line. 'They're your girls, Susan, and if it wasn't for Mary, those girls wouldn't have had nor done half of what they've experienced.'

Harry was only too happy to enjoy the benefits my salary brought to our family over the years. 'Harry, stop the guilt trip. I've always tried to take them to sport and parties and shopping, not to mention appointments, whenever I could. And it's not as though I joined the police force *after* I met you!'

He is silent for a moment, while he gathers his arguments into one tight, nasty jibe. 'If I'd known what I was getting into with you, Susan, I'd have found someone else with children. I used to think David was a fool to leave you, but now I understand why. You're too much.' With that, he hangs up.

I close my mobile and stare into space, exhaustion creeping over me like a fog. Now Brittany is superfluous to his requirements. David and I need to tackle this together. I fear the fallout from Harry's rejection of my daughter is not only going to break her heart, but destroy her credibility. She'll think she's lost face with the three of us. I wonder if Marli can help with this. All around me, the lunch time crowd is arriving. I decide to go to the station and see if David is there.

Gorgeous Adam Winslow greets me at the front counter. 'Mrs Prescott, how are you? Mum was going to ring you today. I think she wanted to ask if you are going to the funerals with her tomorrow.' *A social occasion?*

'I've been out all morning, Adam. I'll ring her later. Is Da–DI Maguire in?'

'I'll find out, ma'am, if you'd like to take a seat?'

The reception area is bare, apart from the usual rogues gallery of 'missing and wanted', notices about licensing. A teenage girl is preparing to have her photo taken for what is obviously her first driver's licence. She runs her fingers through her spiked hair, gives me a 'What?' look, grins and puts her cosmetic pouch into her shoulder bag.

Adam Winslow lifts the counter flap for me to go into the office. 'He's down the hall, last room on the right, Mrs Prescott,' he says, and turns back to the girl at the counter, who eyes him like a python sizing up a succulent mouse. Her tongue flickers over her gleaming lips. Adam's shoulders straighten as he moves behind the camera.

David pops out to greet me. My heart gives a giddy jolt; sexual energy sends delicious shards of excitement into my erogenous zones. My breasts tingle, warmth spreads in my nether regions. I can feel the blush starting around my waist. A sharp memory of his beautiful, tanned hands moving over my naked body causes me to almost forget why I'm here, but his brilliant blue eyes show no more than calm pleasure in my company. The teasing, laughing companion drinking cocoa in the kitchen at one o'clock this morning has vanished like Scotch mist.

He ushers me into the Incident Room, gives me a chair and offers me a drink, which I decline. He then tells me that Senior Constable John Glenwood is conscious, but unable to say who caused his accident. 'He hasn't remembered who he was going to see that night, but the doctors seem confident he'll regain his memory soon. He's not speaking properly, but he did manage to get across to us something about a green light.' He looks puzzled.

There is something I should –'Could he be talking about a laser beam? The perp had to make him swerve somehow.'

David's eyes widen. 'You know, that could well be it. You're a genius, love!' David has always given credit where it's due. He leaps at the whiteboard; the pen squeaks as he writes the word beside John Glenwood's name on the timeline and circles it. 'We're not letting it out that he's out of the coma. We need to wait until he remembers something. If he does then we might set a trap. Whoever this bastard is, knows if Glenwood talks, he's toast. The doctors believe he'll remember faster if he's not pushed. Young Smenton is showing signs of coming back to us as well, but he's not awake yet. Did you get anything useful from Briony Feldman?'

As I recount my conversation with her, David takes notes and then pulls another whiteboard out from behind the current one. 'Well, that may confirm the 1947 connection,' he says, as he writes the date at the top of the board, then starts adding the players.

After we have had a run-through of the information on the white boards, he launches into their second interview with Penelope Harlow, finishing with an enthusiastic account of their visit to the sheep sheds. 'You should have seen those sheep dressed in pjs, Susan. When this is all over I must arrange to take you and the girls out to the farm to see the operation. It's really something!'

Could the perpetrators Edna was trying to tell me about still be alive? If so, it would certainly cause a scandal. The media would love it. Again something tugs in the recesses of my mind and then vanishes. I'm suddenly aware that David has pinned the note onto the board and is staring at me. I've been 'wool-gathering. My tummy gurgles, breaking the silence.

'Come on, I'll take you to lunch! Where shall we go?' He finds a piece of paper and writes something on it. 'I'm leaving a note for Pete.' He flings the pen down, grabs his leather jacket and picks up my bag.

'Oh, Cafe 21 will do,' I answer. This will be my opportunity to tell him about Harry's call.

The young constables are agog as we walk through the station. David advises them of where we are going, then tucks my arm into his and marches me across the road to the cafe. We pause at the counter and order a salmon salad each, his with chips, and cold drinks. He opts for a table at the back of the room against the far wall where the down lights are few and far between. He glances around warily as we settle in our chairs. What's he up to and who is he avoiding? Am I camouflage for something or someone? 'Now tell me what's bothering you, Susan? Something else has happened, so what is it?'

'Harry rang this morning. It seems Brit has become an inconvenience.'

'Just what did the prick say?'

As I recounted my argument with Harry, David's expression darkened. 'You mean he had the hide to demand you keep Brit here after dragging her away with him in the first place?'

'That's right,' I replied, 'and she's going to be heartbroken now.'

'Yeah, poor little devil and she'll take it out on us.'

'Well, she's taking her angst out on us anyway, so what's new?'

'You know what he's doing, don't you, Susan? He's a cuckoo in someone else's nest again. I've a good mind to find out who the woman's ex-husband is and warn him. When they get back here to Queensland, we'll find out what's going on. We must make sure Brit knows we want her and it's no hardship to keep her with us,' he promises, not altogether honestly. Our lunch arrives and we tuck in, discussing the case amicably, but not reaching any conclusion. We've finished eating, when a shadow falls over the table.

'Well, isn't this cosy, dearling? You knew I was going to the motel to wait for you. Are you going to introduce me?' The tone of her voice could slice rocks in half.

Dearling? Good grief! She's all blonde hair and cheekbones, intimidatingly beautiful and obviously furious. If looks could kill, I'd be splattered across the wall. Hurt and anger rip through me, but I've only myself to blame for allowing myself to be sucked back into David's sexy charm.

'No need, I'm leaving now.' I get to my feet with what I hope is dignity and stalk out. Let him explain why he has committed himself to spending nights with his ex-wife and daughters.

CHAPTER 30

Being No-one

Senior Constable Glenwood

Friday: mid-morning.

A blob of grey mist grew into a patch of light, where the sun shone through the window and struck the wall. His gaze wandered across the navy curtains, paused at the red flowers marching along the hems, following the uppermost line of the chairs and trolley to the bed. Puzzled, he examined the contours of his body, solid under the coverlet. Where was he and why would he be in bed during the day? He glanced at the doorway, but no one was available to enlighten him. Something slid into his mind, but vanished before he could identify it.

A mighty wallop of pain hit, sucking him into a black vortex from which there was no escape. He moaned through clenched teeth, stiffened his legs and pressed his arms down hard onto the mattress. It was some time before his mind managed to focus again. The pain eased into dull throbbing.

'Maybe I have the flu? It wouldn't be surprising with this bloody headache.' His head might fall off any second. He lifted his hand to the constriction above his eyes. A bandage. He fingered its rough contours, tracing the outline of his head, hesitating when he reached the bulge at the back, which extended over his right ear.

An accident? Had to be. *How?*

He closed his eyes and willed the pain to recede. He became aware of a regular electronic beeping coming from beside the bed. He opened his eyes again and tried to turn his head, but the pain screamed back. He must have made a sound, because a dark-haired woman bent over him. She leaned so closely, he could smell the chocolate she had been eating and see where her lipstick bled into the cracks of her mouth. Her floral perfume made him want to sneeze and sent his stomach roiling.

'John! You're awake!'

How observant. Full marks. Who the hell are you? And who's John?

His limbs felt heavy and he needed to pee. He tried to hold it, becoming distressed when he realised he couldn't. Humiliated, he waited for the warm, wet to pour over his bare legs. When nothing happened, he panicked and reached for his penis, but the movement caused a sharp jab to the back of his hand.

He moved his head gingerly to the side. Tubes ran from under the heavy bandage which turned his hand into a giant boxing glove, welded his palm to a board and led to a bottle on a stand above. Further down, another thick tube snaked from under the bedclothes and disappeared over the side of the bed.

Sensation crawled back into his body. *I've got a catheter plugged into my dick and an IV in my arm.* He couldn't decide whether to cry tears of relief or pain. People flooded around his bed, a lad came and shone a light into his eyes.

'How are you feeling?' asked the nurses, as they poked

and prodded his bandaged head. The dark-haired woman had disappeared.

Someone pressed a tube against his ear for a second, stood back and made a notation on a clipboard. The wide sleeve of the white cotton gown he wore was pushed back, and his arm threatened to explode, as a blood pressure cuff enthusiastically crushed his bicep in a python-grip. It held for endless seconds then eased, far too slowly.

'How's your head, John? Want something for it?' asked a high school lad wearing a stethoscope around his neck.

'Hm ... who ... are you?'

The ten year-old doctor frowned and leaned close enough for John to smell mint on his breath. 'Jason Hardgreaves. You've known me since I was a kid. In fact, you booted me home when I played truant on several occasions. You can't remember though, can you, John? Look straight ahead, that's right.'

The light bobbed around in front of him hurting his eyes.

'Who am I?' he croaked, unable to remember Jason what's-his-name, never mind his own identity.

'You're Senior Constable John Glenwood. You had an accident in your four-wheel drive and got a knock on your head.'

I'm a cop? Why can't I remember? What happened for chrissakes? My car?

The doctor took the clipboard from the nurse, scribbled something and lowered his voice to a murmur. She nodded and walked swiftly away. He laid his hand on John's arm. 'You mustn't worry. Everything will come back, especially if you don't force yourself to remember. We'll give you a dose for the pain and you can rest.' He smiled and left the room.

'*We'll?* What's this 'we'? How many nurses does it take to give an injection? How many antelopes to change a light globe?' John thought hazily. He must have heard that one somewhere.

His eyelids closed, only to flutter open when a voice screeched in his ear.

'John? *John?* I was so worried!' *I don't remember being John. I'm no-one.*

The dark-haired woman leant over him again, pawing at his hands. He closed his eyes against the onslaught of her emotion. Someone asked her to leave him be, he needed to rest. A thought edged into his brain. He grasped it for a moment, but it slipped away again.

He opened his eye and saw a green kidney-shaped dish on the side cabinet next to his pillow. He followed the efficient, gloved hands, as they fiddled with the tube running from an IV bag high above to the back of his hand, and injected liquid into the line.

'Thank God,' he muttered, closing his eyes. Shut out the world, you need to remember ... blessed darkness descended.

When he awoke, the patch of sunlight had darkened to a bruised thumbprint on the wall. He frowned and winced, as the pain returned. His stomach growled. Agitated movement alerted him to the dark-haired woman, ensconced in the chair nearby, knitting. *Who's for the guillotine?*

He watched, terrified, as she thrust her work into a basket down by her chair, leapt to her feet and bustled over to him. 'Darling! You're awake. Oh John, I thought we'd lost you!' she cried, her voice sliced through his head like a sabre. He tried to 'shush' her with a wave of his hand. She grasped it, crushing the IV line probe. He squeaked but, oblivious to his distress, her grip tightened.

A hoarse shout came from somewhere–himself. A uniformed police officer rushed into the room, looked wildly around, thrust his head into the bathroom and whirled back to face the bed, where a flood of medical staff gathered, checking drip lines and inspecting the catheter. John struggled to free his hand from the woman's rapacious grasp, but her grip only got tighter. Tears flowed down his cheeks and he felt himself void. Finally he managed to gasp, 'Let go, for fuck's sake, let go! You're hurting me, damn it!'

Everyone stopped still and looked at him. The woman dropped his hand and burst into tears.

'John, I'm so sorry,' she sobbed, and collapsed into the arms of a nurse, who led her out of the room. John could hear her wailing outside, begging to be let back in. No, no ... The doctor picked up his hand and gently unwound the bloodied bandage. The cannula had pierced the wall of his vein and deeply penetrated his flesh. He needed to call on every ounce of self-control he possessed not to scream. Amid a chorus of comforting words, they extracted the IV line, dressed his hand and administered more sedation and pain-killers.

'Thirsty,' he heard his voice croak piteously. *Green light.* The words popped into his mind. He didn't realise he'd spoken aloud.

'A green light? Have you remembered something?' Hardgreaves' face lit up. 'We'll let them know! Someone'll bring some tea, John, just a sip and then you'll sleep again.'

The doctor raced out of the room and spoke urgently to the young police constable who returned to the room.

'Senior, have you remembered something?' he asked eagerly.

'I don't know.' John's headache throbbed menacingly, but he knew this was important. 'I think ... it just popped into my head. Green light.'

'Okay, I'll phone it in.'

The young constable shot out the door and the nurses came back. Within seconds, John's head was gently lifted and a plastic spout placed in his mouth. The beaker tilted and warm, sweet tea dribbled onto his parched tongue.

'Thank God someone had some common sense,' he thought, sucking hard on the spout. Tea poured into his mouth, overflowing onto his chin. 'No, John, don't try to drink too fast, mate,' you'll drown!' A cloth dabbed it up and the beaker was withdrawn.

The notion came into his mind that although he didn't know anything about himself, a cup of tea was a great comfort. Who was the dark-haired woman? Was she his wife? He knew he was in hospital, *but where?*

***

Friday: late afternoon.

John appreciated the attention which they lavished on him and tried to reciprocate, but the one thing they wanted of him, he couldn't give: answers to the questions they asked. Especially those of the man called Maguire. He answered as best he could, but the Detective Inspector was disappointed. Officialise came out of his own mouth, each carefully worded phrase sounding as though he was addressing court. *Where had that come from?* 'Perhaps I really am a copper.'

The eager light in their eyes showed him how much his memory mattered, but for the life of him, John couldn't remember the events leading to his accident. They'd told him he'd run off the road on the way to Ipswich to see someone and it had not been an accident.

'Can you remember leaving home?'

'Try to visualise the road, the bends in the road. Just close your eyes and let your mind flow.'

When it became apparent he was distressed by their persistence, the exhortations changed.

'Relax. It'll come to you.' But they couldn't disguise the anxiety in their eyes. Instinctively, he knew something terrible had happened. He realised he was under guard, or being protected, but didn't dare ask which.

A uniformed police officer, a Senior Sergeant, walked into the room. 'How're you feeling?' he asked. John acknowledged he'd been better. 'You had an accident in your Land Rover, Monday night on the Ipswich Road, at Cord Creek.'

'They told me,' John muttered irritably.

'You came off the road, and someone hit you with a tyre lever.' Being protected then.

Green light. The words flickered into his mind again and then vanished. Tears of frustration pooled in his eyes. Senior Sergeant Harris twitched a handful of tissues out of the box on the side-table and pushed them gently into his senior constable's hand. John raised the wad and awkwardly wiped his eyes.

'I'm sorry, I know you want the answers, George, but I can't think ... this head ...' George? Where had that come from? He couldn't remember his own name for more than a few seconds unless someone told him. He shuffled his feet carefully, wincing as his ankle throbbed.

Something constricted it. A bandage? *Why?* Oh, the accident.

'Don't worry, mate. Just take it easy and get some rest.'

'How much rest do they think I need?' He muttered 'thanks' politely, and waited for–George–to follow up with more questions, but the Senior Sergeant left after assuring him they'd protect him and work it out.

Work what out? Protect him. Niglets of fear squirled in his gut. What did he have to be afraid of? Or who? Again something stirred deep in his mind, then vanished.

The dark-haired woman was blessedly absent. She'd hovered over his bed, getting in the way of the nursing staff, until they threatened to send her home. After that, she retired to a corner of the room and glared at everyone. John tried not to meet her pleading eyes.

He'd finally heard someone call her 'Nola,' and refer to her as his wife. His wife? That old woman? He glanced down at his hands. Callused, tough fingers, broad hands, one encumbered by a needle and tube strapped into it. He raised his free arm, examining the corded muscles, tanned and faintly freckled.

'How old am I?' he wondered. He plucked the neck of the white hospital gown back, tucked his chin down and peered inside. *Grey chest hairs?*

'Well, black and grey. Perhaps Nola is old enough to be my wife ... or me her husband ... '

He closed his eyes, the better to shut out the world, information overload, un-remembered wives, green lights, coppers ...

And he slept again.

CHAPTER 31

Back To the Drawing Board

The Killer

Friday: noon.

The information filtered slowly into his hysterical mind, that now conscious, John Glenwood would talk. Fear squeezed his chest. Was he having a heart attack?

He took deep breaths to calm down and respond coherently to the informant, an ex-girlfriend who worked at the hospital. Impatience surged through him as she waffled on about other matters, unaware of being used.

After speaking with her, he went to the china cabinet, took out an exquisite crystal glass and poured a generous belt of whisky. He switched on the stereo and selected Mozart's Clarinet Concerto, inserted the CD, pressed the play button and settled himself into an armchair to think.

Spare time during the day was a rare treat and he planned to make the most of the time. A sick relative necessitated Gloria's absence for at least 24 hours, an unexpected bonus. 'But no more smashing things ... you've got to get a grip.' *She's not completely stupid.*

Three things to cope with, Susan Prescott who remained a nuisance, and something which occurred to him minutes ago and caused him to fear he might be losing his focus. Connie said that Edna had kept a diary all her life. 'I need to get to the cottage before Daniella and Libby clear it out. They'll be preparing for the wake this afternoon, I'll slip over there then."

Satisfied, he turned his thoughts to the urgent problem of John Glenwood. Terror wreathed through his mind, constricted his throat and nestled in his stomach. He had to save himself by finding a way to avert disaster. Another attempt on the senior constable would be difficult, but not impossible, even with security doubled. How had the man managed to survive the massive dose of insulin? Someone must have worked out what it was and taken the appropriate action. 'All that trouble for nothing,' the killer muttered resentfully, thinking of the effort taken to start the diversion and get into the hospital without being seen.

He couldn't go back to the hospital. One glimpse of him might be enough to remind Glenwood of their appointment the night he was run off the road. The tyre lever, scrubbed, bleached, boiled in water and stowed in the safest place of all–the boot of the killer's car. He remained confident that not a speck of blood or hair remained to be discovered by a forensic team.

He searched his mind to come up with a new plan, but an hour passed before a sure-fire way of killing the senior constable occurred. How to implement the idea? His plan needed to be put into effect immediately, before Glenwood regained his memory. The first part was simple. Drive to the next suburb after dark, step over a low front fence and cut a small branch off a tree which grew just inside an elderly couple's yard. They were deaf and had no dog to alert them to an intruder.

The second part involved a packet which a previous girlfriend left in his office after she'd run screaming with rage during the fight a year ago, which he'd manipulated in order to end their relationship. She wouldn't come back for the box now, but if she did, it could easily have been discarded. *So sorry.*

The third action was the hard one. How to put the plan into operation? The locks on the outside entrances to the hospital would have been changed after the attack on the two police officers. Entering through the boardroom was no longer an option, so how to do it? And the man was being guarded around the clock.

Think. Keep calm.

He changed the CD and leaned back in his chair, allowing more glorious music of Mozart to cleanse his mind of all but solving the problem at hand.

Minutes later he thought of the perfect solution.

CHAPTER 32

The Stalker

Daniella Winslow

Friday: mid afternoon.

'Daniella! We haven't got enough chairs. You'll have to borrow some from the Cultural Centre. No wait, they'll charge us for them. Get yourself over to Edna's and count how many she has in the shed. You can call the carrying company to pick them up.'

By tomorrow? Daniella sighed. Ferna was doing what she did best–bullying. All the lounge room furniture was moved onto the back verandah. 'We don't want anyone sitting down, they must circulate!' she'd announced. Then she changed her mind and they had to move some pieces back in. 'Her Majesty has realised there's no throne for her to sit on,' someone hissed, as they struggled with a particularly massive armchair.

Her formerly willing helpers, members of the regional Country Women's Association, were wilting and looking for places to hide. Not easy with Ferna patrolling the house and grounds for shirkers. In one aspect Ferna and the CWA ladies were united: the Australian flag should be draped over Edna's casket. Arthur announced they were talking a lot of rot and suggested they use the white lace bedspread from one of the guest suites. This was greeted with such scorn that he retired to consider his position.

Daniella sighed again. 'Best to get this over with,' she muttered. On the way to her car, she caught sight of Genevieve peering out of an upstairs window. Even from below, Daniella could see the cat's mouth opening and closing with piteous yowls. 'I know just how you feel, old girl,' she muttered, hoping she wouldn't be around for the drama when Arthur discovered his cat relegated to the attic.

Edna Robinson's cottage already wore the abandoned air of an unloved home. Libby pronounced the building unfit for human habitation–the colours were all wrong–and refused to move in until it was completely refurbished. If it wasn't, she'd sell. However, on being advised that her inheritance was conditional on her keeping the property, she'd begun a tantrum, which was abandoned when, out of the corner of her eye, she'd spotted a doubtful look in the eye of her fiancé. Daniella reckoned Libby ought to be damned lucky she'd been given the place, because the little cow never saved a cent.

The shed where the chairs were stored stood a short distance from the house. Daniella put her shoulder to the door. It creaked open and stuff stacked against it fell over, sending dust motes dancing in the golden glow of the afternoon sun. A large quantity of harness, caked with dust and stiff from disuse, dangled from hooks on the walls, alongside some implements of agriculture–hoes, rakes, mattocks and a rather vicious-looking axe.

A mouse streaked down a pair of blackened hames and dived into the straw, which poked out of an ancient draughthorse collar. She shuddered, making a mental note to ring the historical museum committee and invite them to come and take what they thought they might be able to restore.

An old spring cart stood in one corner, shafts tied up to keep level the load of pumpkins, harvested for winter stock food. Daniella thought she would ask Penelope Harlow if she wanted the vegetables for her cattle and sheep. Not for the first time, Daniella felt that being the executor of Edna's Estate had knobs on it. There seemed to be a thousand-and-one things to do, but she cheered up considerably when she remembered the provision of a $5000 fee for the Executor.

She advanced into the building, holding a handkerchief over the lower half of her face to prevent the dust penetrating her nostrils. An ancient Austin car was crammed beside the spring cart. Curious, she went close and peered inside. A huge carpet snake slept coiled on the tattered back seat. Panting with fright, she stumbled away from the vehicle, pressing a hand to her pounding heart. She knew the snake wouldn't hurt her, but she cast nervous glances over her shoulder as she scuttled across the shed to where the light aluminium chairs were stacked.

It was getting late. Sighing with frustration, she took out her mobile and rang the local carriers to ask them to collect and transport the chairs to Arthur's stronghold. The Estate would pay. After a short but triumphant scuffle with the manager, he agreed the truck would arrive shortly. She didn't want to know his definition of 'shortly,' but when she advised him the chairs were for Edna's wake, he assured her the truck was practically on its way. *Scared of Ferna, I expect,* she thought, with vicious pleasure.

She was about to leave, when she noticed something square, covered by a tarpaulin. She edged nearer, hoping the carpet python's partner hadn't chosen to roost under the cover, took a deep breath and pulled up the corner. Neatly stacked underneath were four ammunition boxes.

Daniella couldn't remember seeing them before, but their squat military appearance, with connotations of war and death, made her uncomfortable.

She unclipped the catch on the top one and slowly lifted the lid. Her heart sank. Exercise books crammed the box. About to close it, curiosity overcame her indifference. She picked one off the top and opened it.

The writing had the appearance of the forerunner of the beautiful Gothic script which Edna had used as long as Daniella knew her. The margins were decorated with painted flowers.

> 16 March 1939
>
> Today Mummy took us to town to get ribbons for our school hats. I was bored and tried to sneak away to buy sweeties, but Grace told on me, so I missed out and have to make do with the old ribbons. I'll get her for that!

She snapped the book shut and threw it back into the top of the box, muttering, 'Oh stuff, I don't want to read the meanderings of a child.'

What on earth would she do with them? She couldn't bring herself to trawl through the pile, but deep down, understood this was because she feared answers to the questions she dared not ask. Flashes of brilliance were not part of Daniella's mental makeup, but an idea seeped through. Briony Feldman! *She* could wade through them and then get rid of them. Daniella didn't have a clue what Edna had written and didn't care.

She closed the shed door and marched briskly to her car, leaned on the side and punched Briony Feldman's phone number into her mobile. 'Ms Feldman? It's Daniella Winslow here. How are you?' Convention completed to the satisfaction of both parties, Daniella launched into the reason for the call. 'So you see, Ms Feldman, you might find a lot of information for Arthur's biography in the diaries,' she finished, pleased with herself. The carrier's could take the ammunition boxes when they collected the chairs.

Having neatly disposed of the problem, she had nothing to do but wait for the carrier's truck. Daniella glanced impatiently at her watch and settled herself into the one remaining chair on the verandah of the cottage. She would have been astonished if she'd realised an excited Briony Feldman could hardly wait to show the diaries to Susan Prescott.

Daniella had been shocked by the murders for she was fond of Edna. She hadn't associated with Jack since the early 1980s when, looking for Dutch courage to overcome the paralysing shyness with which she was afflicted, she'd drunk too much. This was why, in spite of the earlier episode with him at the family wedding, at fifteen, he'd managed to lure her into a horse float in the far corner of the racecourse during the local Cup. Fortunately, what happened then was almost clouded in alcohol.

Pain, embarrassment and Jack's threats dictated she could never tell. Twenty-one years later, his words occasionally echoed in her mind like poisoned knives. 'If you ever tell anyone what happened, Danni, I'll make sure your parents know you weren't a virgin. That you were tonguing for it.'

'That's not true!' she'd screamed.

'But who are they going to believe? I only need to whisper in a few ears about how 'talented' you are in certain areas, and bingo! Everyone will believe it then, not just your parents!'

When Jack married Penelope, Daniella tried to warn the girl she'd be taking on a lifetime of infidelity and betrayal, but Penelope either didn't understand or chose not to. When the vicar asked if there was any reason why the wedding shouldn't take place, Daniella pressed her bottom down on her hands so hard they stayed numb for the rest of the service.

Over the years, she'd been tempted to tell many times, but having carved a sophisticated, respected reputation for herself as a leading member of the community, she couldn't bring herself to face the resultant scandal. Daniella knew that, in spite of Jack's acknowledged recreational pursuits, she would be lumped in with his "women" and disgrace would automatically follow. Eventually she had managed to bury the incident. Even her late husband hadn't known. Tears came to her eyes, as his dear face swum out of her memory, for they loved each other right to the day his car blew a tyre and rolled on the way to town on the sharp turn at the Cord, many years previously.

'And now John Glenwood's come off the road at the same place,' she thought, dabbing her eyes with a tissue. 'But one thing's for sure, I'd pin a medal on the person who shot that reptile, Jack.' But Edna was a different 'kettle of fish.' If she knew who killed Edna ... Daniella's fists clenched at her sides. She had to face it; someone she knew was a murderer.

She stretched her legs out, admiring her new Gucci boots, regrettably dusty. At least she'd thought to wear thick, dark cord slacks, but wished she'd brought a cardigan. There was no sign of the carrier's truck. *Come on, hurry up, I'm cold and it's getting late.*

So far, the family, apart from Euon Jellicott, the presiding solicitor, had taken no interest in the contents of the cottage, which Edna's will stipulated were to go to anyone who wanted them. Ferna was heard to snort something about 'stinking animals.' Daniella arranged for a neighbour to keep an eye on the animals, which she would need to deal with once the funeral was over. She sighed again. Perhaps Penelope might help out with that too. At least Fat Albert scored a good home.

Jack's "send-off" would be a right spectacle, if what she'd heard about the honour guard of dogs was true. The only reason why Daniella would attend Jack's funeral was to make sure the bugger was well and truly planted. She'd tried to find out from Adam what line the police were taking in the investigation and got her head snapped off.

'Mum, I can't talk about it because I'm a male in this family, therefore a suspect and a police officer as well. Okay?'

'So they think it's one of the men in the family?'

He rolled his eyes and stormed off to his room. The door slamming shook the whole house and caused one of her Royal Copenhagen vases to rock on its pedestal.

She didn't get any further with Carissa, who looked up from her Nintendo with barely concealed impatience. 'Mum, its boooooring. They'll find out who did it!'

'But I'm sure it's someone in the family!' Daniella wailed.

'Who said? Adam's like, stringing you along, Mum. Get real and just leave it, okay?' Carissa smirked. 'Unless *you* did it of course!'

'Carissa!' Daniella scolded, feeling guilty because she wanted to dance on Jack's grave.

A slight breeze rustled the trees around the silent house, sending shivers up her bare arms. A twig snapped somewhere close by.

She froze.

Goose bumps popped out on her arms.

Another twig snapped.

Was someone sneaking up to the house? A stalker? She glanced wildly around, clutching the arms of the chair in a death grip. Standing up and peering around the side of the building was not an option. Perspiration prickled in her armpits; her heart thudded against her breastbone.

I've got to get to the car. Hurry, hurry!

She stood abruptly, but just as she was about to run to the vehicle, the delivery van from the carrying company trundled into view at the front gate. She bolted down the steps into the garden, risking a glance over her shoulder. A row of dark-eyed beauties returned her scrutiny with great conviviality.

Edna's goats!

'How stupid could you be? Fancy getting het up over a few goats!'

Daniella giggled with heady relief, tripped over a small stone statue in the garden and pretty much wet herself in the effort to remain upright. *What if she'd fallen over and the carrier's had seen*–she'd never live it down. It didn't occur to her to check if the house was still locked. If she had, she would have found the back door of the cottage open, just a little.

The watcher inside smiled grimly as he paused in the search for Edna's diaries. He stood behind the curtains, watching the carrier's van back into the shed, but couldn't really see what they were loading in there. He thought it might have been boxes and for a moment, wondered if Edna's diaries were in them, but then one of the men dropped a chair. *Seats for the funeral and probably linen.*

The dairies had to be somewhere in the house. He knew where all the photos were gone, and made sure they were taken care of. Maybe Edna put the diaries in the roof. He looked around for a chair to stand on to reach the manhole, reflecting that it was just as well for Daniella she hadn't come into the house.

It might have been the last thing she'd ever done.

CHAPTER 33

Pass the Parcel

Susan

Friday: afternoon.

I drive home from town after the aborted lunch with David, my mind in turmoil. I have no idea how to tackle the subject of Harry's rejection without deeply wounding Brittany. Her car is nowhere to be seen. Has she left and persuaded Marli to go with her? A cold lump settles in my stomach. I can't hear any head-banging music or voices to indicate the girls are home. Has the intruder been back?

I go into their room, push the door open and peer inside. Clothes are strewn all over the place, their make-up scattered on the dressing table. I am even glad to see powder spilt on the carpet. At first I don't see the note half-hidden under the fruit bowl on the kitchen table.

We've gone to a party in Brisbane. Staying at Althea Barbour's place. You can get us on my mobile. Be back in the morning. Luv ya, Marli. xxxx

P.S Took Titch. Fed the rats.

I burst into tears of relief. The dogs gather around, thrusting their silky heads into my lap. I don't know how long I sit there, but eventually I pull myself together and go to take a steaming, hot shower. Clean, powdered and exhausted, I give in and go to bed.

It's no good. As soon as I close my eyes, my mind conjures up my attack, the hands wrapped around my throat. My breath comes in short spurts, perspiration prickles my flesh. I'd been alone then too. I tell myself to get a grip, there's no one out there. Fifteen minutes pass before I give up, hop out of bed and scurry to the back door, passing a huge lump of ginger fur crouched outside my door. Albert is awaiting his chance to join me. The dogs surge inside, amid a flurry of waving tails and hot panting breath on my knees. I dive back into bed, only beaten to the sheets by Albert. The dogs arrange themselves on the floor and the bottom of the bed.

The notion of being strangled under a sea of animals is ridiculous.

***

I'm sitting in the lounge, making notes and a time-line of the events leading up to this moment, when David arrives home at five o'clock. I slept until three, then drank a cup of soup, fed my wee assistant under the sink–I still don't know what to do about her–and lit a fire in the lounge. The weather report after the news this morning warned we were in for a cold snap and they were not wrong. Tomorrow's forecast is for rain, strong winds and a sharp drop in temperature. Not a good day to be standing in a cemetery.

David tells me John Glenwood has regained

consciousness. 'But he can't remember who he is or his wife, and George Harris tells me they're coming up for their twenty-seventh anniversary. The doctors tend to think it is temporary, but I wouldn't hold my breath. He's still under guard. God only knows what this bastard's going to do when it gets out he's still alive. The insulin was bad enough, but now he'll be getting desperate. Carlson wants us to keep the guard low-key and use Glenwood as bait. We–Harris and I–aren't happy. It's been too close already and if it all goes pear-shaped again, heads will roll.'

My ex-husband looks frustrated and tired. He jingles loose change in his pocket, and stares out into the garden, obviously thinking the first head to get lopped off will be his own.

'I don't see what else you can do, David. Perhaps move Glenwood to the city?'

'Can't. It'd be easier for the bastard to get to him there.'

I don't agree, but David is a "hands-on" cop. 'Does Glenwood know about the attempts on his life? Or about Edna and Jack's murders?'

'No. The shrink warned us not to overload him with information. We had to tell John about the attack on the road because of the head wound, but the medicos thought it best to keep quiet about the murders. They've decided to keep the news about the insulin and the fire until he's stronger.' David sits down, stretches his long legs out to toward the fire and rubs his hand over his eyes.

'His wife's been causing a fracas, but they've sent her home and threatened not to let her in to see him again until she calms down. They're concerned about how Glenwood will react if she spills the beans, of course. He's not out of the woods yet in respect of the head wound. Apparently his brain's still swollen.'

I feel sorry for Mrs Glenwood. After umpteen years of marriage, to be helpless and forgotten would be horrendous, no matter what the situation. No wonder she isn't coping very well. David asks where the girls are and looks somewhat relieved when he hears they've gone away for the night. He is still angered by Harry's latest edict.

'I think we need to discuss how we're going to handle this one before we talk to Brit, don't you?' he says, going to stand in front of the fire to warm his hands. True to male form, he then stands right in front of it with his back to the flames, effectively blocking the warmth.

'My sentiments exactly, but you won't be alive to talk to anybody if you keep the heat away from me, David!' I announce, not entirely joking.

He moves aside and leans on the mantelpiece, to stare into the flames. I recognise that stance. He's avoiding my eye. 'I'm sorry you got chased away at lunch today, Susan.'

And I'll kill you if you do it to me again! 'Oh I don't mind,' I respond airily. 'After all, I've got a dinner date myself tonight! In fact, I should start getting ready. Mark Gordon's picking me up at a quarter past six.' I am excited, and it shows.

Will David head straight back into town as soon as I'm gone? I tell myself it doesn't matter. *Who are you kidding?* I spray my favourite, Tabu, around my breasts, reminding myself the Archdeacon is just a man. A sound from the doorway almost sends me into orbit. David is staring at me sitting there in my bra, knickers and lacy slip. My heart pounds in a distinctly unseemly manner. I snatch my robe around me and turn to face him. He apologises and launches into all the things I need to ask Mark tonight, reminding me to be careful not to let him pump me for information.

Is it beyond all the bounds of possibility that a man fancies me? And what does he think I've been doing for a living the past twenty years? Flushed with anger and disappointed by his business-like attitude–*did you expect him to pounce on you?*–I fling off the robe, fully exposing my lacy-slip clad body, and slowly pull my dress over my head. As I come up for air and pull the folds down, I run my hands over my hips and thighs, smoothing it into a neat fall of soft green. I glance at him and another kind of flush rushes through me. We make eye contact and suddenly I don't want to go out with anyone.

'I always liked you in that colour, Susan.' he says, his voice husky. 'Any buttons at the back?'

'Only a zip,' I whisper, watching him come toward me. I turn my back and force myself not to show any reaction, as his hands press against the bottom of my spine, hold the fabric closed and pull the zipper up slowly. As it reaches the top, I open my eyes and look at the two of us in the mirror. Our eyes meet, his darken, mine widen and I feel his warm breath skate over my skin, in a tiny sigh. Oh my God.

The dogs break into hysterical barks, completely crashing the moment.

David drops his hands. 'I'll get it,' he says and leaves the room. My legs feel like cotton wool. I sink onto the chair. God help me, I still care about him and want him in my bed; desperately. But he has Blondie, apparently aka Donna, in town and is probably just waiting for me to leave so he can pole-vault in there. I try not to allow pain and jealousy to overcome common sense. Don't be so stupid, you nitwit. He's a man. *He can switch his feelings on and off like a light switch.*

The sound of male voices filters through from the lounge room. With a final glance at my reflection and a tweak of my dress, I pick up my coat and bag. My mobile phone rings as I head for the door. The number in the screen is unknown, but the voice on the other end of the line is vaguely familiar.

'Mrs Prescott? Susan? It's Euon Jellicott here. Sir Arthur's nephew, John's son.'

'Uh ... oh ... yes, I remember you. We met at Sir Arthur and Lady Ferna's luncheon yesterday.' *What the hell does he want?*

'Look, I'm aware I was a bit abrupt with you when we were walking in the garden and I'd like to show you I'm not at all like that. Please let me take you out tomorrow night?' *What? After the funerals?*

'It's not necessary to do that, Euon. Really. I didn't mind.' *Didn't I just, you little turd.*

'I'd like to talk to you, Susan. Won't you please forgive me and let me take you to dinner?'

Euon's got to have an ulterior motive; I'm hardly attractive enough to warrant such enthusiasm. Has he worked out I'm a police officer and needs to find out what I know? I don't want to go out with him and am about to frame a regretful reply, when I remember he's an Olympic-standard archer and change my mind. Perhaps he will let information about the family slip in conversation. He will have to collect me from the house where I will make sure he is well aware that David knows where I am and who with.

'All right, thank you. That would be very nice.'

'Great! Shall I pick you up at six thirty?' I can hear

the smile in his voice.

We exchange goodnights and he hangs up. Quelling my anxious feelings, I go to greet my date for this evening. The men are ensconced in front of the fire engrossed in male bonding. David is full of good fellowship and graciousness about handing me over to the Archdeacon. The word "mate" is bandied about a good deal. I want to smack him out; it feels as though he can't wait to get me off his hands.

Our breath turns to puffs of steam in the brisk night air. I beam joyfully at Mark, snuggling into his protective arm as he guides me down the steps. He hands me into the car and I feel his lips brush my cheek in the merest of butterfly kisses.

I'm smugly gratified to see David's thunderous expression.

***

It's been years since a man other than Harry has kissed me 'with intent.' Mark Gordon is an attractive, sexy and interesting companion. I haven't dined in such style for years, certainly not on a police officer's salary. We ate exquisitely grilled lobster, mushroom, banana and macadamia nuts in white wine sauce, with tiny potato balls rolled in garlic; to follow, crème caramel topped with brandy cream.

Our conversation roves from travel, to the arts, music – his job, but not my job, I haven't lost my head completely. I announce my intention to look into the history of the district and the Robinsons in particular. 'After all, they are such an interesting family,' I flutter. *Oh silly, giddy me.*

'You're going to stay down here for awhile, then?' he asks. 'Where are you going to start your investigation?'

I become aware that I'm within a skerrick of blowing my cover. I back-pedal hastily. 'Oh, I might not be here long enough to bother. I'll think about it.'

We arrive back at the farm just after eleven o'clock. I am not prepared for him to stop the car a little way down the track from the house. Before I can speak, he swoops across the front seat of the car and sweeps me into his arms. His mouth presses insistently on mine, his tongue flickering around my lips, seeking an opening. His left arm is holding me tightly against his side, his right hand slips inside the neck of my dress and under my bra to cup my breast. *And this is a vicar?*

My mind is in free-fall. My nipples leap to attention. He squeezes and strokes, before his hand slides onto my stomach and is working its way further down when the front verandah light goes on and in lieu of my father, David appears. We spring apart. Mark starts the engine and we drive slowly to the house while I re-arrange my clothing.

'Would you like to come in for a nightcap?' I ask, in defiance of my ex-husband's ferocious scowl. Perhaps my date decides discretion is the better part of valour, because he declines gracefully, helps me out of the car and escorts me to the bottom of the steps. With a gentle push, I'm passed back to 'the man of the house.' Then, with a cheery wave, my date drives off.

'Did you have a good time?' David growls, closing the front door behind us with unnecessary force.

'Of course I did. Good food and good company!' I throw my coat and handbag onto the lounge. Fat Albert blinks at me from the armchair nearest the fire, where

David has organised a comfortable nest. A bottle of port and a book are on the coffee table. *He didn't go into town to see Donna.*

I'm tired and sexually frustrated; celibacy is no fun. I am also cranky about being passed from man to man like a parcel. He wants to know why I have a mouse family residing under my kitchen sink. I'm not inclined to give a lengthy explanation, but he is so insistent I finally tell him about the rodent's part in the investigation. When I finish, he snorts with laughter.

'You should be thankful they're little scavengers,' I snap. 'There'd have been nothing left of the photos if my mouse hadn't dragged them into her nest.'

'I'm sorry, Susan. You're right of course. Did the Archdeacon try to get information out of you?'

I've experienced a hell of a time trying to prevent the man finding out I'm a police officer and I'm not in the mood for verbal skirmishes. 'No. He was a perfect gentleman.'

'That's not the impression I got from where I was standing on the verandah,' he says waspishly. 'Anyway, I want to talk to you about Brit.' He ignores my yawns, prepared to debate the matter here and now.

'It's after midnight. We'll talk about it in the morning. The girls won't be back until later in the morning. *Goodnight,* David.'

I scoop up my coat and handbag and head for my room, leaving him taken aback by my abrupt departure. Good. I am about to close the door when Fat Albert slips inside and camps on the bed. It's comforting to have at least one male wanting to sleep with me.

The warm, furry body is snugly tucked into my back, but I am unable to sleep. My mind scuds over the events of the day– the session with Briony, Harry's call, the tantruming child, the heat between David and myself. Am I imagining it? Perhaps it's all in my fevered, sex-starved little mind. I forgot to tell him about my date with Euon Jellicott.

I hear the firescreens clang as he parks them across the front of the grate and his footsteps as he checks security, the way he used to do years ago. His mobile rings as he walks along the hallway to his room. I hear him say the name, "Leanne" and then laugh just before he goes inside.

Shit shit shit shit shit. How many more females has he got hanging around? My pathetic little victory with the Archdeacon has back-fired.

I bury my face in Albert's fur and cry myself to sleep.

CHAPTER 34

Bon Voyage

Senior Constable Glenwood

Saturday: mid-morning.

He opened his eyes and checked the wall. He couldn't tell what time of day it was, but before he could ask, a nurse loomed over him. 'Good morning, John! It's almost 10 o'clock. You didn't have a very good night, did you, luv? So we let you sleep a while longer.' She whipped the bedclothes off him. He cringed, as her professional eye swept over his naked body, now minus the catheter. The IV line had been removed from the back of his hand.

'We're going to give you a bed-bath,' she chirped. His eyes widened, but before he could protest, another nurse, who he was sure couldn't have been more than fifteen, swayed into the room. Snapping her fingers to a hidden beat, she pulled the curtains around his bed and beamed at him.

'No, no. I don't want ... a bath ...' he croaked, making a pathetic attempt to claw the sheet back. The girls laughed and tugged it out of his hand.

'Don't be embarrassed, John, we've seen it all!' they trilled happily, setting up a basin and towels. The teenager took a container of talcum powder out of his locker.

Where did that come from? The woman they said was his wife?

Knowing it was futile to argue, he resigned himself to their ministrations. If he closed his eyes, perhaps he wouldn't see them eyeing his 'equipment.' *Who am I kidding?* Well, at least it's presentable, he comforted himself. 'They called me 'Donk' in the soccer locker ...' Where did that come from? His eyes flew open and he looked straight into the girl's face. 'I remember–'

'What, John? You *remembered* something?' she squeaked.

He blushed all over. He could tell this fresh-faced child what actually surfaced. 'Just a personal thing,' he muttered.

'I'm sure that yummy Inspector will be happy to know you've remembered something!' she said eagerly, running a sponge gently around his genitals. He could feel them shrivel and discarded the equine memory for the time being.

He couldn't get used to the undeniable fact of his profession. The cops, his colleagues. 'I still can't remember anything important. I suppose they'll be back to bully me today. 'He knew he was being unfair to Harris and the city Inspector. That set up another train of fear in his mind. He couldn't even remember the DI's name after one night. Would this be the pattern of his future?

The nurses rolled him gently from side to side as they wiped him over with warm, wet face flannels and sprinkled powder into his armpits and groin. They skilfully manoeuvred him into a clean hospital gown and cheerfully informed him breakfast would be soon. 'We told the kitchen to save it for you. Doctor's coming to do your dressings after that. If you're well enough, they might even move you out of ICU.' *Is that where I am?*

They emptied the basin in his bathroom and put fresh towels behind his locker, then with cheery calls of, 'Bye, mate!' left the room. John felt abandoned. He looked around and spotted a newspaper on the chair by his bed, just out of reach. 'If I can just–' he leaned across and tried to snag the corner with his fingers.

'John! You shouldn't be doing that!'

Brisk feminine fingers whipped the paper out of his hand. The top half of his body lurched over the side of the bed. He slung his arm around the woman and clutched her backside to keep from falling out of bed.

'John! What *are* you doing?' she shouted, trying to spring away, but effectively trapped by his grasp.

'Sorry, sorry ...' he gasped, using her as leverage to heave himself back into bed. The headache, which had blessedly receded until that moment, returned full force. Sweat broke out all over his newly washed body; the cotton gown clung to his heaving chest. He lay back, panting, trying to calm himself.

Nola, for of course it was she, stared down at him, perplexed. 'What were you trying to do? You can't read anyway, it's not good for you,' She thrust the newspaper into a nearby wastepaper basket.

'I want to read it!' John snapped. He didn't know why he would have married this woman in the first place and didn't want to be tied to her now.

Nola, trying to keep the news of the murders and second attempt on him secret, as advised by the medical profession, was furious because someone left the paper where he could get it. She wondered if the husband she knew might return and whether he would be 'normal.' Unable to put her fears into words, she took refuge in a carefree, practical attitude. 'It's old. We'll get you tomorrow's when it comes in. Here, you've got a lovely lot of cards!' She laid a pile of mail on the top of his table-trolley. 'Do you want to open them yourself, or shall I do it for you?'

'I'm not entirely helpless. I'll do them myself,' he growled, fighting to keep the pain in his head at bay. Being a woman who had always found it hard to keep quiet, Nola 'bit her tongue,' picked up the remote attached to the bed mechanism and pressed 'up.' Slowly his torso travelled upward, until he attained a sitting position.

'That better?' she asked, warily.

Curtly, he nodded his thanks, aware he was being a bastard, but unable to help himself. What he felt could be his normal persona remained hidden under a mass of fears and pain. He looked at the pile of cards and reached for the top one, a cream-embossed envelope with his name printed on the front. Carefully, he brought his bandaged hand up to hold it, while he awkwardly tore the flap open. Nola reached over and tried to help, but a hard glance from her husband sent her into retreat.

He drew out the card, examined the pansy–a real one–stuck inside the card. Purple, almost black, it glistened in the light from the top of his bed. He squinted at the computer generated letters. "ALL THE BEST ON YOUR NEXT TRIP BON VOYAGE."

He couldn't breathe.

All the oxygen had left the room.

His chest heaved. His hands flew to his throat; the card fell to the floor.

'John!'

Piercing screams filled his head. His nails raked over

his mouth; great gasping wheezes forced air past what little space remained in his throat. The inside of his nasal and throat passages swelled. He coughed, but only succeeded in losing the minute amount of air left in his labouring lungs. His heart felt as though it would leap out of his chest. As he dropped into full blown anaphylactic shock, his last sight before he lost consciousness, was of people all around, filling the room with energy.

He was unaware of the oxygen mask placed over his face, or 0.5 mg adrenalin and hydrocortisone injected directly into his bloodstream.

'Tracheotomy,' snapped Hardgreaves, snatching the scalpel, as nurses took the pillows from under John's head and tilted it to expose his throat. Within seconds, a tube was inserted in the hole in his windpipe and an oxygen line attached.

No one saw the weeping Nola pick the card and envelope off the floor, tuck them into her bag and stagger out into the passageway. The young constable on guard, ashen with fear, put his arm around her and eased her into the chair on which he'd been sitting. 'Mrs Glenwood, what happened? Is John all right?'

'I don't know, Ron.' She wiped her eyes with the back of her hand. 'He collapsed. He couldn't breathe. He was reading his cards–he'd only just opened the first card!' She closed her eyes and leaned back into the chair. Her handbag dropped onto the floor.

The constable glanced down. The card and envelope were poking out of the open zip section. The card had fallen open, exposing the black pansy. Curious, he reached over and picked it up. 'Nothing strange about this,' he thought, puzzled. 'Funny inscription, no signature.' He turned the card over to see if anything was written on the back. A flash of red caught his eye. He turned it back, but could see nothing, turned it again, then realised there was something stuck in the card. He looked closer. Whoever sent it had put a false cover on ... he gently prised the two pieces of paper apart ... a poinsettia flower!

Understanding dawned.

He grasped the paper by the edge, picked up the envelope by one corner and rushed into ICU. 'Latex poisoning!' he shouted above the hubbub. 'It was in the card!' He waved the offending items in the air.

'Let me see that!' Hardgreaves, who was watching the monitor beside the patient, reached to take the card and envelope from him, but the officer backed away.

'I have to keep these for forensics, but you can see it. Look!' He held out the card, revealing a glimpse of red petals to the shocked medical staff. They all knew of John Glenwood's acute latex allergy; only rubber gloves were used in his care. Everyone in the room realised the significance of the card's intended purpose.

The young constable hurried out of ICU, placed the card and envelope carefully on a trolley in the corridor and called Senior Sergeant Harris on his mobile phone. His voice rose with agitation, as he advised his superior officer of another attempt on Senior Constable Glenwood's life.

Nola watched him dully, too shocked to react

CHAPTER 35

Déjà Vu

Susan

Saturday: mid- morning.

I'd never imagined sitting drinking coffee with my ex-husband, but I am and moreover, enjoying his company. We're not talking, just gazing at the mountains, half-shrouded in mist. His face is inscrutable, but I am well aware he's plotting his day. He could well be thinking about the woman who phoned last night, but I refuse to allow thoughts of her to mar my equilibrium.

Eloise's hens sail by like little red-feathered yachts in the cold, stiffening breeze. The dogs are lying in heaps on the lawn in front of us and the cows are standing by the fence, waiting for someone to bring them bread treats. In front of us, the huge granite rocks on the mountain glisten with moisture from overnight rain. In the distance, the escarpment wall is deep grey-blue against the green, brown and yellow paddocks of crops. Rain is gathering in the west again. How can this splendid landscape form a backdrop to the ugliness of murder?

Who was it said, 'Most folks are happy as they make up their mind to be?' I don't know, but if I follow the advice, *forgive yourself,* I shall recover. No more agonising over what I deem my part in Danny Grey's death. I need to accept, as even his widow has, that the shooting was the fault of the criminal. And there are other things to focus on now, like the funeral of Edna Robinson later today.

David is still worrying about John Glenwood and what he might know. 'He can't remember his wife, anything about his life.' His voice rings with frustration. 'I think you're right about the laser. Glenwood was a very experienced driver, it would be hard to force him off the road, but if he'd been blinded, then it'd be another story. But anyone could have forced him off the road. It could have been a simple road-rage incident, but someone followed him down to the wreckage and hit him with something like a tyre lever ...' David scrubbed his designer-stubbled jaw with the back of his hand. 'We've established that he wasn't attacked in his car by a passenger, by the way the blow landed.'

We mull this over in silence for some time, gazing at the mountains. Then I become aware his focus has changed.

'You look great this morning!' David is eyeing me with appreciation. A little squiggle of happiness trills through me.

'Thank you. I feel good.'

'What time do you leave for the funeral?' he asked.

'Half-past one, the service starts at two,' I reply, glancing at my watch. It's seven now. David is dressed in a smart T-shirt, the inevitable black jeans, boots and a blue cable sweater which matches his eyes. He's gorgeous, damn him. I'm still married to Harry and will be for over another twelve months at least, but David has Miss Blondie, whether he wants her or not, it seems. A very possessive madam from what I saw at lunch yesterday. After last night's self-induced disappointment, I tell myself to forget my ex-husband. Susan, *who are you kidding?* I quell my libido ruthlessly.

'The girls will be home soon. What are we going to say to Brit about Harry?' David asks, after draining the last of his coffee.

'I think the best way is to tell the truth.'

He gapes at me, horrified, and I understand where he's coming from. Our daughter is a monster when upset. I know this from years of experience, David from one night in her company. 'Can't we simply tell her we want her to stay with us? Beg her to, if necessary. Not even mention Harry?'

My heart leaps. He doesn't seem to realise he's coupled us and I am not about to comment on what may be a casual remark with no substance. The thought of him setting up campsite with yesterday's blonde, is appalling. *Do you really need to get entangled with another man, especially this one, after only two months of freedom?*

Yes. Shit, no. Yes. I sigh, and try to apply my mind to the matter in hand. 'I don't think there's any other way than to tell her the truth, David, because sooner or later she's going to find out we lied.' I pick up my empty coffee cup and march inside. I need to get my head around the coming funeral and wake and the people I'm going to meet there. Arthur's ex-wife, Lily for sure, Daniella says, not to mention the unspeakable Jack Harlow's send-off.

David comes into the kitchen behind me, and starts washing up the breakfast dishes. Without thinking, I grab a tea towel and get ready to dry. Suddenly he looks into my eyes, smiling, and I know a memory of when we were first married springs into both our minds. David always liked to plunge his strong, brown hands into the suds and methodically wash each dish, then flick suds down the front of my shirt, laughing as I jumped back.

I flush, remembering the next part of the game, where those gorgeous, strong hands open the buttons, dive after it, followed very quickly by his mouth. Heat rises from my breasts, melts the skin of my throat, skitters along my jaw line and floods my cheeks.

'We had a lot of fun, didn't we?' he says softly, watching my face, 'Before. I wish it had turned out differently, Susan.' His expression lapses into regret.'

Tears well into my eyes, spill over and trickle down my face. An exclamation and David gently wipes them from my cheeks, and then crushes me against his broad chest. His heart thuds against my ear. Inhaling the warm, male smell of him, I press closer, seeking comfort and affection. His arms tighten, he rests his cheek on the top of my head, and one hand trails down my back and cups my bum. I feel definite evidence of his state of mind. *Damn it, I was married to him, I can–*

David sighs, sending shivers of lust through me. Old memories surface; need for him ignites a furnace inside. The way he used to hold me, the feel of his powerful, well-honed body pressed against mine, the hard ridge of his erection and his warm male aroma is driving me insane.

No matter the consequences, I want him.

Now.

I disengage myself from his shirt to look into his face and meet his mouth descending. His tongue skims my mouth, searching for a way inside. I part my lips; he dives in. I can hardly breathe. My heart is pounding. My hands find their way inside his shirt, smoothing over his hot skin, pressing the powerful muscles. We can't get enough of each other. He steps back, grabs my woollen sweater, rips it over my head and pulls at the front of my shirt, sending buttons flying. My bra slips up. Miraculously, his hands find their expert way underneath. My breasts ambush his hands, responding to the excitement of his eager fingers.

Somehow we are in the hall, working our way to the bedroom, kicking our shoes off as we go. My hands are in the front of his jeans–my God he's gone commando! *No, I've bypassed his underdaks*–something bounces off my head and thuds into the wall.

'You again! How dare you. Let go of him!'

Oh shit.

The voice is strident and coming closer with each footstep. David lurches away from me, we're leaning against the wall, staring at the blonde virago confronting us, hands on hips. Her face tells the tale; she wants to kill me. *You and whose army, dearling?* Hysterical giggles work their way up my throat. She is standing lopsided, with one shoe on. The other connected with my head, but the throes of lust ensured I barely felt it. For a very long moment, we gape at each other, a triad of shock.

I am the first to break the impasse. I pull my shirt across my breasts and stalk into my bedroom, leaving David to 'fight zee bull'–in this case, *cow*. I'm shaking all over; I wonder if I'm coming down with something. Well, I almost came down with David. A battle is raging out in the hallway. I slink over to the door to listen, not sure who is winning. The sounds of conflict are drawing closer.

A body rams up against the other side of the door. She is screeching like a steam-kettle, something about he broke up with her when he left Cairns, then he'd broken up with her again last night. But he was laughing with her. I heard him. Perhaps they'd argued later in the conversation? Or was it someone else phoning him? Just how many women has he got on a string?

One thing is clear from the dialogue outside the door; he hasn't slept with this one since he came back from up north and isn't pleased about her being in Emsberg. He's furious with her for coming into the house. She replies that the door was open, so why shouldn't she? They move away, still arguing. I change my shirt, put on another sweater and follow their voices to the lounge.

'You! You. You–' Incoherent with rage, her eyes bore into mine like the spikes on a corn cob holder.

'Yes?' I am now in my Senior Sergeant Prescott persona.

'What are you doing with my boyfriend?' she demands, in stereophonic surround sound.

'I might ask you what you're doing with the father of my children? And from what I heard,' I jerk my head toward the bedroom, 'he is no longer your concern.'

Out of the corner of my eye, I see a tiny smile quirk the corner of David's mouth, as he acknowledges my prevarication. I want to thump him. 'And *what* are you doing in my house? As a police officer, I could have you for assault, unlawful entry and possibly intent to commit a crime. I'm sure I can think of a few other charges as well.'

Her mouth opens for another torrent of abuse, but she obviously thinks better of it. She picks up her shoe and backs away, shooting venomous glances at David, who appears sheepish, as well he might. The dogs barking out the front of the house herald the arrival of another car. I catch a glimpse of red as she reaches the door and fires a parting shot.

'You were never much chop in bed anyway, David. She's welcome to you!'

The sound of her high heels clacking down the stone steps is followed by a yelp from one of the dogs. David curses and races for the front door, followed closely by myself. The old spaniel is limping. The harridan's car scatters gravel as she charges down the driveway, forcing Brit's red car off the track. The vehicle slews across the lawn in an effort to dodge, straightens and lurches to the bottom of the steps.

'Who the hell was that? She kicked Henry!' snaps Marli, as she climbs out, pup clutched protectively in her arms. Brit stands by the car door, staring narrow-eyed at David and me. Is my bra hanging out of my pants? I reach behind my back and surreptitiously feel around. Henry, expecting sympathy, which of course he will get, throws himself on his back, legs in the air. I examine his paw, but find nothing obviously wrong with it. I pick him up, stagger up the steps and plonk him on the verandah.

'Only someone we know,' David offers smoothly. I'm careful not to look at him as he goes to the car and starts to unload their bags. I go back to help, while Brit storms toward the house and Marli hovers uncertainly.

'Brittany!' roars her father. She stops, shocked and then surges forward again.

'Get back here now.'

It's the Detective Inspector's turn. Brit turns and stares at him. His face is grim and uncompromising; hardened criminals have not been able to withstand it. For a moment, I think his daughter could be the exception, leading me to wonder how far her depths are hidden, but she stamps sullenly back, snatches the lightest bag she can find and marches back to the house. David frowns; I shrug. It's a victory of sorts.

Once we've settled the girls back in their room, fed the puppy and made morning coffee, it is time to tell Brit about Harry's phone call. Wishing I didn't need to disturb the rare moments of peace, I sit beside Brit and take a deep breath.

'Darling, I've got something to tell you–'

'Don't tell me, you're going to marry *him* again!' she screeches, jumping up, sending the cat racing up the shelves and setting the dogs barking on the side verandah.

'No, actually.' I daren't look at David who looks shell-shocked. 'The fact is ...'

Quietly, I tell her about Harry's edict, ending with the wish that she will move in with Marli and me.

'What about him?' she snaps, stone-faced.

David stares impassively at her. Marli wraps her arms around herself and leans possessively against her father. Wisely, he makes no move to hold her.

'That's not an issue,' I state firmly. *Yet.*

'You all hate me. I know when I'm not wanted! Even my dad doesn't want me! I thought Sharon liked me, but she was just pretending! Like you all are,' cries Brit, trying to hide her pain. Throwing caution to the winds, I wrap my arms around her and rock her gently. She stiffens and tries to push me away, then as her sobbing gets out of control, snuffles into my shirt, shoulders heaving. Another pair of arms surrounds us–Marli–and then David encircles the three of us.

'I do, Brit. I want you,' he murmurs into her hair, and means it. We've a lot of fence-mending to be done, but it will take time.

Brit and Marli have gone to bed, apparently having been up partying all of last night. I am settling at the computer, when the Skype phone rings. Eloise is calling from the UK, this time with momentous news. She and James are staying on; the Wiltshire estate has been left to James by his brother. They are going to sell the property in Emsberg, complete with livestock, but she's concerned about transporting the elderly spaniel to the UK. Of course, 'big-mouth' me offers to keep him. She is delighted and offers me first "dibs" on the property.

I tell her I will think about it and that I'm attending Edna's funeral and the family wake later. After promising to give her condolences to the family and a hug for Daniella, I say goodbye.

David is ready to leave for his appointment with the upper echelons of the police force in the city, when his mobile rings.

'Maguire. Yes. *What?* What's going on? You mean he got to Glenwood again? Oh, for chrissakes, how? His face sets into grim lines, the expression in his eyes is arctic. He snaps the phone shut and tells me about the latest attempt on Senior Constable Glenwood's life.

CHAPTER 36

A Flag-raising Occasion

Susan

Saturday: afternoon.

In spite of my good resolution to not allow heartbreaking memories of Danny Grey's death to upset me, I need to summon all my courage to attend Edna's funeral. White roses and lilies fill the cavernous reaches of the church, distributing a heady cloud of perfume over the congregation.

They are a sombre crowd, composed of diverse groups. The local gardening club I recognise because I met their president at Ferna's luncheon. The Lion's Club are in matching blazers with emblems on the pockets; a cluster of red and purple identifies the Red Hat Club. Edna's Country Women's Association–the CWA–proudly wearing their badges, troop in and occupy a prominent position on one side of the church, leaving just enough space in front of them for the immediate family.

The next wave consists of locals with whom I'm not acquainted, but some of whom I've seen in the street. I move into a short, empty pew behind the lesser members of the family who are roosting opposite the Robinson heavyweights. Euon Jellicott leans around the cricketing twins and their down-trodden girls, and winks at me. I nod coolly, wondering how I can get out of going to dinner this evening.

I glance around, pinpointing the chief players. The family occupy the front row. Lady Ferna, heavily disguised as the Queen, and Sir Arthur are flanked by the twins, Grace and Constance. Next to them is a scruffy old man I think is Arthur's brother, John. On the other side of him is Kathleen, whom I've not met, mother of Daniella. Edna's granddaughter, Libby, and young doctor Hardgreaves are plastered together by the wall under a picture of a somewhat distressed looking Saint

Edna's coffin, covered by the Australian flag, rests at the front of the church. Masses of colourful tulips, dahlias and camellias counter the profusion of white roses throughout the church, bringing a sense of warmth to this cold, sad day.

Briony Feldman, resplendent in deep mauve, sits next to me and jogs my elbow. 'There's Lily, Sir Arthur's first wife,' she hisses, jerking her head in the general direction of the opposite front pew.

'Dark blue, Melbourne Cup hat,' Briony has mastered the useful art of speaking without moving her lips.

Lily is a small, elegant woman, at least seventy-five and groomed to perfection. Her face is suspiciously unlined and there are plenty of diamonds on display. She has done well for herself and it shows. 'How many husbands has she outlived so far?'

'She's had four, all rich, three dead and Sir Arthur. None of them had kids, so guess who got the loot every time?' Lily strikes me as a rather practical lady.

'By the way,' Briony continues, 'Edna filled four exercise books in 1947, but nothing untoward so far in the one I'm reading now. The other three are here for you to go through.' Briony taps her cavernous black shoulder bag.

'Okay. I'll get them from you when it's over and look at them after the wake.' I can hardly wait to get my hands on them.

Penelope Harlow stands beside Daniella, with Carissa on the other side of her mother. They're all wearing black, which goes well with Penelope's blond hair, but turns mother and daughter into extras in the Adam's Family. In the distance I hear dogs barking, the guard of honour for the next event. I'm tempted to attend for the pleasure of seeing Lady Ferna spontaneously combust.

Mark Gordon, immaculate and suave, the officiator of both funerals, is attired in the majestic robes of priesthood. He hovers by the vestry door, watching the remainder of the mourners file into the back of the church. I'm barely able to equate this stately Archdeacon with the man who took me to dinner, charmed, then kissed and groped me last night.

I hear the entrance door to the church close, and a few moments later, he glides down the aisle to his place at the front of the congregation. Across from him, is the star of the show, Edna, who could reasonably have expected a few more years. Anger cuts through me at the thought of her terrifying final moments, smothered by someone she might have known and trusted.

Bastard.

A gang of local businessmen and a person I recognise as the regional Member of Parliament, bustle importantly into the pew across the aisle from me, out-grandstanding each other. I can't be bothered watching them and pass the time reviewing my action-packed previous night and aborted sexcapade this morning.

David had roared off to the hospital, vowing to tear John Glenwood's attacker apart with his bare hands. He admitted a personal interest in the senior constable's survival; his ability as an investigator is being challenged. A short time later, he called me to explain how the attempt was carried out. 'He pasted a poinsettia flower inside the front of a Get Well card, and then glued another page over the top, so the petals were sandwiched between the two pieces of card paper. Then he poked pin holes through it so the latex would ooze out. As soon as Glenwood opened it, he got a full blast of the stuff. He's lucky to be alive'

'I guess most of the Robinson family are aware of his allergy?'

'The whole bloody town knows! Glenwood was born here, so the city fathers chopped all the poinsettia trees down when he was a kid. He came back to work at the station ten years ago, so they did another chop around.'

'What if Mrs G had opened the card?'

'It wouldn't matter, because Glenwood's allergy is so bad he can't even be in the same room as latex. This arsehole knew that sooner or later he'd read it. As a way of getting to the poor bastard, it was ingenious.' David's disgust and frustration came through loud and clear.

After his reminders to be careful and of what to observe at the funeral and the wake, after he left I settled down to research newspaper archives on the net, looking for reports into the deaths of the three members of the Robinson family in 1947. Call it a combination of woman's intuition, combined with the photograph with the pin holes, but I feel the answer will be found during that year. According to Edna, one of the so-called farm accidents was murder, but which?

I finished locating, downloading and printing the articles relating to the agricultural tragedies for that year by about midday. Warren Caldwall, checking the depth of the wheat in a silo on his own, leaned in too far, lost his balance, fell into the grain and suffocated. His wife went looking for him when he didn't come home for tea, heard his dog barking and found the animal tied onto the back of Caldwell's truck. No sign of Caldwall.

The neighbours, summoned by the hysterical woman, found the top access cover to the storage tower lying open. The silo needed to be emptied before the body could be retrieved from deep in the grain. I shuddered, imagining the dreadful death. Farm accidents are a way of life and farmers can be notoriously careless, but Caldwell *must* have known how dangerous it would be to check the level of the wheat on his own. During my research, I read that at that time, silos didn't have an outside gauge to check the level of the contents. But did he have help falling into it?

The next report wasn't any better. Bob Jellicott, for reasons best known to himself, entered a small yard containing a wild, aggressive, scrub bull. He was found hours later by his mother-in-law, Agatha Rose Robinson, who'd summoned help. The bull was subsequently shot and eaten. Why on earth would Jellicott put himself into a position where he could be cornered by a dangerous animal? I'd like to see the scene where he died. Perhaps he dropped something into the yard and foolishly climbed in to retrieve it? Did he try to go over the top of the rails? Maybe the bull was too fast or perhaps another party locked him in with the animal. Butchering and eating the unfortunate murderer would be an excellent way to hide incriminating evidence.

The two incidents raised questions: why were both men doing such dangerous things on their own? And the most important question of all–if both or either of these men was murdered, then *why?* I still need to check out the tractor accident, but concede it would be harder to organise a deliberate rollover. My eyes wander back to Lily, Arthur's first wife, the unknown quantity. 'What do you know about Lily? Will she talk to us if we ask nicely?' I murmur to Briony, under cover of the chatter around us.

'She'll probably hit the sauce at the wake. We can corner her there.'

So, Lily is a 'tippler.'

The service is beginning. The congregation stands and focuses on the lavishly decorated back of Mark Gordon who stands at the head of the coffin facing the altar. 'I am the resurrection and the life,' says the Lord. 'Those who believe in me, even though they die, will live, and everyone who lives and believes in me will never die.' And the service is underway.

From time to time in my career, I've been blessed with strong feelings of intuition and I've learned not to ignore them. Now I'm feeling my stomach muscles tighten. A presentiment of evil and tension surrounds me. I gently stroke my throat. The bruises are less obvious today, but I'm still wearing a high-necked blouse and pearl choker to hide any signs of attack. Only the murderer, David, his colleagues and our daughters are aware it took place.

We listen obediently to several attention-seeking eulogies. George 'Slimeball' Murphy, extols Edna's virtues as a good Aussie pioneer-type woman. Briony snorts softly into her handkerchief. We make eye contact and stifle smiles. Her gaze flickers in the direction of the family, sitting motionless, like a line of black crows on a fence, not a fidget to be seen, as Murphy rolls on and on.

A shaft of sunlight shoots through a stained-glass window, sending bright flashes of colour over the casket. A chill wind sweeps through the church. Has someone opened a door? A movement catches my eye. The Australian flag quivers as though alive and slowly lifts. Someone sniggers. *Oh dear Lord, what next?*

The congregation gasps, as the flag hovers above the coffin. Murphy stands, open-mouthed, and blessedly speechless.

An ear-shattering scream rends the air, followed by a commotion as Lily leaps to her feet, fighting for air and bolts down the aisle toward the front door of the church, heels clacking on the stone paving like rifle shots. As she runs, her toe catches on an uneven flagstone and she almost hurtles into the person on one end of a pew. A hand comes out to steady her. She pushes it aside and keeps going. The usher in the last row darts forward and flings open the door, allowing her to escape.

The assembled company erupts into excited speculation. I switch my attention to the Robinson family. Lady Ferna is snarling like a wolf at Daniella and Carissa. The twins, Grace and Constance, are trying to calm them down. John Robinson is trumpeting into a huge white handkerchief. Euon Jellicott, laughing outright, catches my eye, realises I'm watching and true to form, winks.

'Please be seated,' bellows the Archdeacon, attempting to bring everyone to their senses and remind us of the seriousness of the occasion.

'What in God's name happened to Lily?' Briony muses, as we struggle to obey. The muttering ceases, the flag has settled over the coffin again. Ashen-faced and tight-lipped, Mark Gordon resumes the service.

'Do you think we should go and see if she's all right?' whispers Briony, under cover of the rustling of hymn books.

'Can you get out over there?' I flash a glance at a solid wooden side door a metre or so away. She nods and quietly slips along the pew. The door creaks mightily as she opens it. Everyone in the immediate vicinity cranes their necks. Briony's flushed face is momentarily visible as she turns to close the door.

'All things bright and beautiful, all creatures great and small, all things wise and wonderful, the Lord God made them all,' we chirp resolutely. *God wasn't looking out for Edna.* The organist, a CWA stalwart, fumbles, almost loses her place and then scrambles to catch up as we forge ahead, like the good Christian soldiers some of us might be.

Refocusing my attention on the Order of Service pamphlet complete with hymns, I realise someone is watching me. I try to keep my eyes resolutely on the page, but to no avail. My gaze wanders to Sir Arthur and I catch my breath. Gone is the bumbling, genial, elderly knight and cat-loving eccentric, in his place is a ruthless man of steel. He's exchanging complicit stares with someone, but because people are now sitting and preparing to kneel for prayers, it's impossible to figure out whom.

A cold lump settles in my stomach. This case has to be solved. Fast. *God, please give me a clue.* What is it that someone doesn't want known? And why would a long-ago incident make these killings necessary? My thoughts scurry back to the mutilated photograph. Lily and Arthur's sisters would no doubt know who he was. My mind races around the notion of those elderly ladies in 1947. Did either Warren Caldwell or Robert Jellicott serve in the armed forces? A notion is stirring in my brain. If I'm right, one or both of these men remained on the farm during World War 2, with the women and girls of the family...

I've been lost in the past and the service has ended. I get up quickly, trying not to allow Euon Jellicott to make eye contact, but he leans across, eyes sparkling. Edna's funeral has obviously provided him with much entertainment. 'Pick you up at six o'clock, Susan. Looking forward to it!' Before I can cancel the date, he's stepped through the side door and vanished. After gathering my purse and watching the family file out of the church, I follow, anxious to pounce on Lily.

I hope Briony has managed to corner the much refurbished old trout before she escapes.

CHAPTER 37

All About Control

The Killer

Saturday: afternoon.

The nightmare of the first funeral was almost over. He braced himself for the second. The only difference in the congregation at Harlow's would be exchange of the CWA and gardening club for the sheepdog fraternity. He'd be obliged to look at and talk to pretty much the same people, not only at both services but during the wake as well.

Lily bolting out of the church unnerved him, but he was more than equal to shutting her up. Unreliable, drunken Lily might spill the beans or clam up completely. Lily, who knew the whole story, who'd been there when it all happened, but who also understood what would happen to her if she talked.

He quite liked her but felt no compunction in leaving a carefully-wiped bottle of whisky, laced with rat poison, on the floor under the dashboard of her car before he entered the church. He knew the sight of it would negate all her struggles to remain sober and her fingerprints would be all over the bottle. She might take a day or two to die, maybe a week or two if he got lucky. Vomiting blood was also a symptom of an ulcer burst through alcoholism.

Of course, the police would find out she'd been murdered, but not until the autopsy. 'Pity it has to be this way but it's so easy to buy rat poison 'off the shelf.' Terror was a great incentive. Catching her eye while that idiot Murphy was pontificating had been a masterstroke. A draught lifting the flag was a bonus.

But John Glenwood remained the greatest threat. The latexed card should have done the trick, but at least Glenwood hadn't recovered his memory. According to Cecily, his source in the hospital, the man still didn't remember anything, even his wife. Getting information from his inside source, an ex-girlfriend had a limited life, even though she'd not showed any curiosity over his interest in John Glenwood's welfare. After all, he was known to be a good friend of John's and his position in the community made his enquiry unremarkable.

And then there was Susan Prescott, who had watched Lily running out of the church, and looked very thoughtful afterwards. Was she beginning to get ideas? He feared so. His stomach erupted with rage. It sounded as though there were burbling pipes in his gut. He sighed and pressed his hand to his abdomen, trying to suppress the commotion. Things were getting out of hand. If it hadn't been for Arthur's biography and the family meeting to caution those 'in the know,' not to even hint about the family secret. He had to get to Arthur.

' ... all creatures great and small. All things wise and wonderful, the Lord God made them all.'

'They always pick that bloody hymn when some fucking animal lover dies.' His anger churned deep inside, a vast ball of ectoplasm threatening to blow him apart. The dogs barked outside, waiting to form a guard of honour for Jack Harlow, rapist and suspected molester of young girls, including, he suspected Carissa. Why Jack couldn't have stuck to his wife and let well alone, he couldn't imagine. His breath was coming in short gasps and he stopped pretending to sing.

He'd eyed Penelope's nicely rounded bum, as she turned to look at the congregation. He wouldn't have minded a piece of it, but eyeing the rest of her–too fat. He admitted to himself that a well-rounded, normal woman made him feel inadequate. They needed to be like a boy, or he couldn't get it up. What does Penelope know?

The service was coming to an end. He coughed, forcing himself to breath slowly and regularly. *Calm now, calm.*

'...kindle our hope, and let our grief give way to joy; through Jesus Christ our Lord. Amen.'

Control was everything.

And control was something he was losing.

Rapidly.

CHAPTER 38

A Right Good Send-off

Susan

Saturday: afternoon.

The cold wind bites through my light suit coat. I struggle into my warm fleece-lined jacket. There is no immediate sign of Briony and Lily, so I trot around the side of the building, trying not to let my shoes crunch on the gravel. The shrubbery near the vestry door impedes my progress and I stop to find a way through. The voices of Euon Jellicott and Sir Arthur come through the foliage.

'You need to get to Lily, pretty damn quick,' Sir Arthur says, coldly. 'We can't afford to have her blabbing at the wake. Of all the things to happen, that flag was the last straw. See to it.'

'Right. I'll find out what's happened to her,' replies Euon. They're silent for a moment, and then Sir Arthur says, 'You know what to do.'

Sir Arthur and Euon Jellicott? And what is Euon going to do? What is between them? Perhaps I will find out tonight, but now I have to get to Lily. Tiptoeing silently back along the pathway to the forecourt is not easy. The congregation is letting off steam, gathering their strength for the next service. A hip flask or two flashes as the sun peeps through.

The CWA ladies depart, presumably to Sir Arthur's property to put the finishing touches on the afternoon tea, as the agricultural mourners arrive en masse for Jack Harlow's service. The guard of honour, tied under a nearby truck, bark expectantly as the hearse bringing Harlow to the church backs up to the side door.

I dodge Daniella, to catch up with Briony and Lily, who are perched on the edge of a concrete seat between the rectory wall and the church. Lily snuffles into a handful of tissues; Briony is coaxing her to explain why she ran out of the service.

As I arrive in front of them, Lily snatches at her handbag, preparatory to escape. Her large blue eyes are the one remaining natural feature in her perfect face, below which is a raddled old-woman's neck. She passes an age-mottled, shaking claw over her cheeks to wipe her tears away, as Briony speaks soothingly. 'Lily, there's no need to be afraid. Just tell us what happened. Did you see something? Was it the flag lifting? Because it was only a draught from outside that picked it up. It wasn't Edna's ghost.'

'I don't know anything, I tell you!' she quavers. *You old liar, you know it all. And I'm going to shake it out of you, believe me.* 'Lily, I'm Susan Prescott, a friend of Briony's. How about we take you for a cup of coffee in town, unless you want to go to *Jack's* funeral?'

I couldn't have received a more outraged reaction if I'd poked a crocodile with a stick. 'Jack's funeral? I'd no more go to his funeral than I'd fly to the moon! That rotten bugger! I'd have shot him myself if I had a rifle!' she screeches.

Briony glances around nervously, but the mourners are out of earshot. I sit and take one of Lily's hands. 'Lily, what are you so frightened of? We'll protect you, there's nothing to fear. No one can get near you, so you can talk to us quite safely.'

She looks undecided. I feel we could be getting somewhere when she focuses on someone over Briony's shoulder. I stare hard at the group of people talking in the forecourt. Euon Jellicott, the twins, their girls and George Murphy all stand with members of the family, but their backs are turned to us. Sir Arthur's head is bobbing around on the other side of the group, next to Ferna. Mark Gordon is standing on the steps of the church watching the undertakers open the doors of the hearse. I can't imagine who's struck such terror into Lily.

She snatches her hand away and stands, shaking visibly. 'I can't. You don't know what he's capable of. I need a drink! Besides, I don't know anything!' she finishes triumphantly. The crafty glint in her eyes reminds me of Marli's pet rats when they're stashing food. Before we can ask who "he" is, Lily pushes past and scuttles back toward the crowd. I'd like to wring the old bag's neck.

'Shit, what do we do now?' Briony frowns in exasperation.

'We go to town and have coffee. Then we go to the wake and see what we can find out there. Sooner or later someone's going to let something slip.' *And I can watch Euon Jellicott.* Right now, he is talking to someone in the crowd.

Briony fossicks in her bag and hands over the three exercise books. 'You'd better take these now, so I don't forget to give them to you later.'

'There's no way I'd forget them! I just hope the old

dear wrote something useful.'

'Well, there's nothing in the first one which she started when she was ten. Altogether there are about twenty books. I can't think why Daniella didn't read them before she gave them to me.'

'I don't think reading is one of her strong points. One thing's for sure, if she is involved in the murders, she'll have kept the relevant ones back. Are they sequential?' This will make my investigation easier.

'Yes, as far as I can tell, but the actual entries are all over the place. These were all written in 1947.'

Excitement spurts through me. 'Okay, good. Still want to do Arthur's biography?'

Briony grimaces. 'I honestly haven't got any yen to write it. I liked him when I first met him, but now ... and I'm sorry Lady Ferna wasn't the first murder victim. Of them all, I'm beginning to think Genevieve's the only one worth knowing!'

'The family isn't much chop if that cat has all the integrity,' I reply dryly, as we ease our way through the remaining crowd.

Two minds with a single thought, Briony asks, 'Do you think Lily'll turn up at the wake?'

'Yes. I don't think she would dare stay away.' I tell Briony about the encounter between Arthur and Euon. 'So it could be anything from murdering Lily to keeping an eye on her drinking.'

A movement attracts our attention. Lily is weaving between the parked cars, obviously intent on leaving. With a complicit glance, we dart in the direction of Lily's car and see her fumbling under the dashboard. When she tips her head back and takes a swig from a bottle, Briony pounces and rips open the door. 'Lily! Give me that!'

Before the woman can protest, Briony grabs the bottle and tips it upside down. Lily screeches in protest, as the rich amber liquid gurgles into the gravel at our feet. I must say I'm with Lily; what a waste of good liquor.

'You don't need this! And you can't drink and drive anyway!' Briony trumpets.

'Leave me alone! I don't know anything and if I did I wouldn't tell you anyway! It's none of your business!' Lily screams.

'We just wanted to make sure you're all right. Are you going to the wake?'

The old woman wipes a raddled hand across her mouth, nodding miserably. 'I can't tell you anything. Please, you don't know. Leave me alone. Please.'

My mind twirls through available options. As a serving police officer–albeit on leave–I can legally take Lily in for an interview with David, but this could be counter-productive. Instinct tells me to bide my time; I'll get more information by backing off. Briony picks up my thoughts with ease and seeks to reassure her.

'Lily, we don't want to harass you, just make sure you're okay. We're willing to listen if you want to talk. We'll see you at the wake, okay?'

Lily jerks her head in sketchy agreement and then starts the motor. We watch her drive away, sitting bolt upright, peering through the steering wheel.

'Do you think she'll go to the wake or take off?' asks Briony.

I shrug. 'God only knows. We've nothing to hold her on, but I'll keep an eye on her.' I glance at the bottle which Briony's still holding and grin.

'I should book you for public littering or something over that!'

'Waste of good whisky.' A litter bin is discreetly hidden tucked into the corner of the small parking lot. Briony walks briskly across and pitches the empty bottle in.

As she returns, a thought occurs to me. 'Are you going to make writing biographies your life's work?'

'I hope not. I went to university and did a degree in English Lit with a view to becoming a teacher. Then I went on to try a Graduate Dip Ed, but I hated teaching. I sort of fell into this by accident when I was asked to write a politician's biography. My God, what a shit-stirring, arsehole ferret he was! But I suppose it's a living.'

'Why don't you apply for the police force?'

'I'm twenty-eight. Aren't I too old?'

'You're exactly the right age, you already have a degree and you're very astute. Briony, you're an ideal candidate.'

'I'm too fat!' she says, anxiously, but I can see interest dawning. She's got a large frame which could lose a few kilos, but physical training would soon fix that.

'You'll trim down with some jogging and sensible eating,' I assure her, as we walk toward our cars. 'Let's talk about it over coffee and then we'll take ourselves off to this shindig. Mustn't let the CWA ladies' baking go to waste! Besides, diets always start on Monday morning and it's only Saturday!'

***

Sir Arthur and Lady Ferna's homestead roars with well-dressed, over-excited mourners. This is a monumental 'send-off' for the departed. We hang our coats over the verandah railing, drinks are thrust into our hands as we are swept into the scrum surrounding the white-clothed, trestle tables. Every delicacy known to woman is laid out in colourful splendour. Lamingtons and scones, jam and cream are displayed alongside dainty sandwiches, savouries and cream cakes. Briony takes a plate and gleefully helps herself. 'As you said, dieting begins on Monday,' she grins.

'Too damn right. Let's split up and start circulating. Keep an eye out for Lily if you can and I will too.' I scavenge a few sandwiches and a slice of caramel tart, for which I have a weakness.

Traditionally, mourners shift around, screaming happily into each other's ears until the main event, the Family Brawl, erupts. There seems to be a strange pattern to the distribution of this crowd. People keep disappearing and re-appearing from the depths of the house, as though summoned. Of Sir Arthur there is no sign. Is he holding court in a back room?

I spend time with Daniella and Carissa then ease my way around, pursued by a sense of unease. Each time I try to head toward the elderly twins, Grace and Constance, a Robinson relative diverts me with conversation. The cricketing twins waylay me with questions about buying a few of Eloise and James's cattle. As the owners of a Brahmin stud, their interest in Scottish Highlands is unconvincing.

When I finally escape them, Peter Robinson pops up beside me. 'Susan, have a drink.' He whips my empty glass away and thrusts a full one into my hand as he steers me toward the corner, where he plies me with questions about my "government" work. I manage to evade the truth about my job and his conversation shifts imperceptibly to Edna's belongings. I realise he's trying, not very subtly, to discover if Edna has left a diary.

'I wouldn't know *what* Edna left,' I reply, a little tartly, thinking of the three exercise books nestling in the boot of my car. I can't wait to get to them, but I need to stick it out here for a little longer. 'You must talk to Daniella. She's the executor of Edna's Will. Excuse me a moment, I've seen someone I'd like to talk to.'

I back away, throwing him a flirtatious glance, so as not to alienate a prospective source of information. Penelope Harlow's blonde plait peekaboos between the members of the agricultural community swarming around the verandah.

I ease my way between them, almost tripping over a dog. Nearby, Mark Gordon is enchanting a couple of elderly ladies. He catches my eye and winks conspiratorially, reminding me of our lustful moment in the car after dinner. Perhaps he's hoping for seconds. The CWA ladies spring through the double doors into the hallway, carrying trays laden with more food, obscuring him from my view. Lily is sitting at the end of the verandah, scoffing cream cakes and boozing to her heart's content, with Euon Jellicott whispering in her ear. *As per Arthur's instructions?* I catch Briony's eye and jerk my head toward the pair. She nods and starts to move in Lily's direction.

I sidle through the crowd and arrive beside Penelope. 'Mrs Harlow?' She turns, with a smiling enquiry. I introduce myself and we fall into conversation about nothing in particular. I'm about to ask some leading questions about Jack, when she administers a shock. 'Has Daniella found Edna's diaries?'

A jolt of excitement hits me. 'What do you know about them, Mrs Harlow?' I ask, forgetting my role as the innocuous sister-in-law of Eloise.

She blinks and stares at me, astonished. 'Er ... I know

she kept one. Has done for years. But why do you ask me? You're friends with Daniella, so if she hasn't told you anything then perhaps I shouldn't either.'

I slip my hand inside her elbow to whisk her into a quiet corner, but suddenly we're surrounded by the clan males. Euon Jellicott is by my side, teeth flashing like a timber wolf. Sir Arthur stands beside Penelope and the cricketing twins magically appear. I feel Penelope's pulse rate quicken; we need a diversion. 'Mrs Harlow was just about to show me to the ladies toilet,' I announce firmly, snatching Penelope's hand. The men blink in unison. This is thinking outside of their square. I steer Penelope briskly between the cricketers and propel her through the crowd. It's like wading through treacle.

We are within sight of the loo when George "Slimeball" Murphy lands in our path, accompanied by his trophy-wife, who is obviously much given to the wearing of bangles. 'Mrs Prescott–and Penelope! I didn't realise you knew each other,' he trumpets.

'We don't!' snaps Penelope. Slimeball glances at our entwined hands and smirks. His wife is admiring her reflection in a nearby mirror. Her bangles clink like horse harness as she plucks at her hair.

'Oh, for heaven's sake!' Penelope snatches her hand out of mine, but I am nothing if not persistent. I grab her wrist, propel her to the door of the loo and drag her behind a screen, artistically placed to hide the entrance to the toilet.

'I need to speak to you!' I whisper. Seeing she's about to raise the alarm, I whip my ID card out of my bag. Her eyes widen.

'What are you–oh my God, you're a cop!'

'Sssh. Make no mistake about it! Now for goodness sake, shut up and talk!'

She snorts. 'Shut up and talk?'

We look at each other. She's trying to keep a straight face.

'Oh ... yes ... you're right.' I grin acknowledgement. 'Well, I'm on leave, but I'm still a serving police officer and entitled to ask you questions if I think they're warranted.' I deliberately soften my approach. 'Please, Penelope, would you talk to me?'

'Detective Inspector Maguire and his mate came to the farm yesterday morning and I told them everything I know.'

'Tell *me* now,' I command.

Quickly she tells me the little she knows about Jack's involvement in the family secret. A movement nearby attracts my attention. I step over and stick my head around the screen. Someone's aura lingers; we've been overheard and my anxiety becomes full-blown fear. 'Have you got somewhere you can go or a friend you can ask to stay with you?' I pitch my voice low, so Penelope is compelled to follow suit.

Penelope stares at me, white-faced.

'Just a feeling I have. Make sure you're not alone under any circumstances. Go and stay with someone from your own family in town. Now. I can't stress this too strongly, Penelope.'

'But Mrs Prescott–Senior Sergeant–'

'It's Susan and don't tell anyone I'm a policewoman. *Promise me?'* I whisper. I hope she's taking me seriously. I don't think she knows any more than she's told me, but the eavesdropper can't know that. Penelope's horrified gaze focuses on my throat and I discover the two top buttons of my blouse have opened. How many people have seen the remains of my bruises?

'Edna tried to tell me something at the hospital before she had her heart attack and I believe the murderer overheard. He attacked me at the farm on Wednesday night, but no one knows about it, except the police, my daughter and now yourself. It's confidential. I can't impress this on you enough. Ring someone you can trust in your family and sort out some security for yourself. But before you do, what do you know about Euon Jellicott?'

'He's a relative of Jack's, but nothing bad. Why?'

'He's asked me out to dinner tonight, that's all.'

Her face breaks into a smile. 'He's very much the gentleman. Not like Jack,' she adds sourly.

'I'm sorry, Penelope. It can't have been easy for you.'

'Daniella tried to warn me when I got engaged to him, but I wouldn't listen. My sheep and dogs are my babies.' She looks at her watch. 'Good grief, it's almost four thirty. I've got to get home to do the evening chores, anyway.' She waves her mobile at me. 'I promise I'll call a friend now and have her come over.'

I say goodbye to Lady Ferna who is all warmth and light. 'Thank you for coming, Mrs Prescott. You will say goodbye before you leave the district, won't you?'

Well, if that isn't a hint, I don't know what is. Briony inclines her head in acknowledgement of my signalled intention to leave and turns back to Lily, who hasn't stirred from her position close to the makeshift bar. It's odds-on whether she could if she wanted to. I collect my coat and trot down the front steps. *Thank God that's over.*

My mobile rings as I open my car door. 'You won't forget I'm picking you up at 6 o'clock, will you Susan?'

Euon Jellicott. I look back at the house and see him standing at the top of the steps.

'Of course not, Euon. I'll be ready.' Behind him the crowd parts and slightly to the right, I can see the silhouette of a man looking out of a window at the far end of the house.

I know he's watching *me.*

CHAPTER 39

A Family Scuffle

David, Marli & Brittany

Saturday: evening.

Maguire drove back to the farm, growling with frustration and hunger. No progress on the case, the Chief Super in a snit, Glenwood still hadn't remembered anything, and Susan was going out to dinner with another suspect. Exhaustion threatened to swamp him, as he stowed his car around the side of the house and climbed out. As he went to lock it, a scream tore through the air.

He ran for the house, drawing his gun as he pelted up the side steps. Shrill squeals came from the kitchen; girlish insults were exchanged. Crockery smashed. Marli and Brittany were having a fight. The dogs huddled together on the verandah, looked at him, tails waving. The old spaniel whimpered and pawed at his leg. *'Bloody hell!'* He stowed his gun away, let the dogs into the house and followed them to the kitchen doorway, ear-drums ringing with angry shrieks. The sink was piled high with dirty dishes, broken crockery lay on the floor and the garbage can kicked over. It was a disaster.

Marli shouted 'Sod off, Brit!' as she tried to scoop up

broken egg on the floor in front of the refrigerator. The dogs jostled each other to scoff it up. Brittany slapped Marli with a wet tea towel. 'You stinking little pig! You *sneak!*'

'Ow, stop that.' Marli grabbed the side of her head.

'What's going on here?' Maguire roared, slamming his briefcase on the table. Dirty dishes bounced. Fuming, he grabbed the dogs by their collars, dragged them to the laundry door and shoved them through, shutting it firmly behind them.

'Dad! She said–' Marli scrambled up and launched herself at him, but he wrested her out of his left armpit.

'And don't come the Little Princess act with me, Marli. It won't wash.'

'I told you, you're a sneak!' screamed her sister.

'I'm not. You weren't–'

'Quiet!'

They froze, open-mouthed. 'I want this place cleaned up right now. If you don't get it done within twenty minutes, you can get to bed, both of you. You want to behave like babies, then that's the way you'll be treated.'

'But we haven't had any dinner!' wailed Marli, glinting at Brittany, who narrowed her eyes and scowled viciously at her father.

'Make some!' he snapped.

'Why should we? Mum always does the cooking, or Har–dad,' sneered Brittany. She snatched her cigarettes off the table and stuck one in her mouth.

'I don't tolerate rudeness, nor do I put up with smoking, Brittany.' Maguire snatched the cigarette out of her mouth and threw it into the bin. 'And take that sanctimonious look off your face, Marli. I don't accept bad language, which I've heard you using more than once in the last few days. When you two have cleaned up here, you can get cracking with dinner. I don't care what you cook–bacon and eggs, spaghetti on toast–whatever. After that we're going to get a few things straightened out.' He turned to leave, but swung back. 'Where's your mother?'

The girls looked at each other, silently deciding who would answer. 'She's gone out with a man,' snapped Brittany, 'all done up.' Her eyes glittered, as she gauged her father's reaction to the news. Surprised by a fierce spurt of jealousy, Maguire struggled to keep his expression neutral.

'How long ago did she leave?' he asked, glancing at his watch.

'An hour. He got here at six o'clock.'

'Right. I'm going to have a shower. I want this lot sorted by the time I finish. And clear that up!' He gestured to the broken saucer, then, without another word, walked out of the room. The girls heard the bathroom door slam a few minutes later.

'I'm not doing this! You can if you want, but he's not the boss of me!'

'Brit, don't be stupid. You can't win so you may as well do what he says.' Marli put the plug in the sink and turned the water on full, sending splashes all over her clothes. Hastily, she turned it down. While the sink filled, she swept up the shards and put them in the bin.

Brittany picked up a tea towel and fired the only salvo she could think of. 'You rotten, shitty little bitch! Daddy's little *girl!*' The worm had turned; something had to be done to get her back into line.

As Marli was about to retaliate, the dogs set up a racket in the laundry. Someone had arrived. Brittany threw the tea towel down and stalked to the front door, to be confronted by a uniformed cop, so good-looking she was struck dumb.

'Hi, Adam!' chirped Marli from behind her, delighted that for once she had the drop on her domineering sister. Adam Winslow glanced at them in confusion and then, with the ease of far too much practice, diplomatically divided his smile between them.

'I've got some information for your dad. Is he here?'

'In the shower; come on in.'

Needing no encouragement, Adam went inside, escorted by a triumphant Marli. 'Want a drink?' she asked, making sure she remained the focus of Adam's attention.

'No thanks, I just want to speak to the DI.'

'Oh, come on, at least have a Coke.' Greatly daring, she grabbed his hand, pulling him toward the kitchen, where she proceeded to pour drinks all round. Brittany seethed. Marli got the drop on *her?* Well, she'd soon make sure his focus switched to herself.

Adam took a sip of cola and looked speculatively at Brittany. 'No need to tell me this is your sister.'

Marli pouted. 'This is Brittany. She's just come up from Sydney.' Brittany smirked, but was interrupted before she could answer.

'Adam?'

Maguire stood in the doorway, wrapped in a bathrobe. Adam hastily put down his drink.

'I've got some information for you, Sir,' he said, casting a cautious glance at the girls.

'We can talk out here,' said Maguire, well aware of why Adam had come out to the farm instead of phoning. They moved onto the back verandah. 'What have you got for me?'

'We've traced the card used in the attempt on Senior Constable Glenwood to a gift-box batch which was on the market three years ago. It was only sold in Australia, and the series of stock from which this came was distributed in Ipswich.' He named the outlet, a small gift store.

'Where is it?' asked Maguire.

'Limestone Street, sir. Of course they have no records available of who bought them.'

'It figures ... okay, what else have you got?' Maguire ran an impatient hand through his hair. They never got a break when they needed one.

'This might have nothing to do with the case, but I was talking to a mate in Ipswich uniform and he mentioned a call out they received late Friday night. An elderly couple reported an intruder in their garden cutting small branches off their poinsettia tree. He'd gone by the time the patrol car arrived, but some of the cut branches were on the ground.'

Excitement surged through Maguire. 'Did they get a description?'

'Yes, Sir. They described the perp as a very tall, thin hoodie, almost certainly male. They didn't get a look at his face, but the householder said the way he moved reminded him of someone. Of course he couldn't remember who.'

Maguire narrowed his eyes, sifting the suspects through his mind. Euon Jellicott, tall and slim–nothing would give him greater pleasure than to lock the bastard up. Peter Robinson–too stocky. Either of the "cricketing twins," as Susan called them, would fit the bill, especially in the dark. Mark Gordon, the archdeacon ... not likely ... but the right size. Adam Winslow ... he looked at the constable thoughtfully. No one would describe him as skinny. He was well-built and had the shoulders of a front-row forward.

Giggles caused them to swing around. Brittany and Marli were standing in the doorway behind them. Adam Winslow's face turned red, not because the girls were drooling over him, but because their father was home. 'Have you two cleaned up the kitchen?' Maguire snapped, surprised by how protective he felt.

They laughed in unison. 'Yes, David!' trilled Brittany, without taking her eyes off her quarry. 'We're making omelette for tea. Would you like some, Ad-aam?' she sing-songed his name, which made the young constable squirm.

'No thank you, er–er–mum's got dinner waiting.' Obviously desperate to leave, he flung a glance at the DI, who nodded his dismissal. It was time to have a serious talk with the girls.

Sighing and wishing Susan were home, he herded his daughters back into the kitchen and fed Fat Albert, while the girls argued over making a rather watery omelette. Two eggs dropped on the floor, to the delight of the elderly spaniel, allowed into the kitchen as a treat, some crying from onion fumes and finally dinner was on the table.

'Before we discuss anything, I don't want you girls hanging around Adam Winslow. Do I make myself clear?'

'Why ever not? Adam's okay,' said Marli, petulantly.

'He's too experienced and he can run rings around you two. He's a member of the Robinson family, which puts him off limits anyway.'

'So what? Mum and Mrs Winslow are friends and Carissa's my friend,' she countered.

Maguire drew his lips back in a wolfish smile. 'Mrs

Winslow and Carissa are not suspects.'

Wide-eyed silence greeted this remark, as the girls digested the information, and then Brittany fired the next shot in the battle. 'How long are you going to stay here?' she asked David, as she scraped up the last of her food.

He sensed Marli's anxiety, as he got up to fossick in the refrigerator for something to drink. 'As long as the case takes to clear up. Might be awhile yet.' He reefed out a box of Chateau Cardboard and took three glasses out of the cupboard.

'Why don't you go back to the motel then?'

Marli gasped. 'Brit, don't be so rude! Mum needs protecting, remember? And so do we.'

'Like hell! We can look after mum. *He* doesn't have to stay here!' Brittany jumped to her feet and hurled her empty plate into the sink, where it bounced. A piece flew out, ricocheted off the refrigerator door and hit the wall.

'Brittany!' roared David. 'You're a guest in this house. In fact you're not even an invited guest. Marli and your mother are, you and I are hangers-on! And you will pay to replace that bowl.'

'Yeah, right. Like, if I'm not invited, what was that all about last night? You changed your mind now? Or was that all, like, fake?' Brittany faced her father off, hands on hips.

'No, it wasn't fake. You're my daughter and I love you. However I do not love your behaviour and nor does anyone else.' He finished pouring the wine and dumped a glass in front of each of his daughters. 'Sit down. Now.'

She sat, sulky and silent. Marli took a sip of wine and looked up at her father. Brittany picked at the tablecloth.

'Rest assured the Adam Winslow's of this world wouldn't have a bar of you, Brit, if they could see you now. You're seriously in need of a change of attitude. No one–employers, the law, anyone you come into contact with–likes a smart-arse, cheeky and down-right nasty young woman, so it's a choice to behave well or badly. I'm told you want to be a doctor. Well, you won't last five minutes in medical school behaving like a spoilt brat.'

He took Brittany's hand. 'You don't have to fight the world. No one's out to get you, but if you keep on going like this, they will be. Your problem is, you're afraid to let people get close in case they won't like you, so you push them away before they get the chance. You're beautiful and clever. The whole world is waiting for you to burst into it. Don't sabotage yourself.'

Brittany's stuck her bottom lip out and jerked her hand away. 'Don't patronise me! You're as bad as Mum. She says things like that and I know she doesn't mean them, anymore than you do! I know what you want. You want Mum back, but she's married to *my father!*'

David sighed inwardly. Brittany took a gulp of wine, watching her father with narrowed, mean eyes.

'I know she's still married to Harry. But remember it was Harry who left and went to live with another woman. What do you expect your mother to do about that?'

He sat down wearily and picked up his glass. Marli pushed her plate aside and reached for a banana, watching her sister closely. David realised she was gaining confidence. He was determined to be support for them. 'And Susan,' he thought, 'but would Susan want me around?'

He couldn't get the passionate encounter, aborted by his ex, Donna, out of his mind. Continued association with their daughters would ensure he could be with Susan regularly, but it wouldn't be enough. An exciting notion flashed into his mind. He would use the time until her divorce was finalised to ... court her. Warmth curled in his gut, as the unexpected, old-fashioned word sprang to mind.

Two months of her legal separation from Harry had already passed. Hopefully not more than about fifteen months would pass before she was single again. Plenty of time to see if they could make a "go" of it. Where they would live, what Susan would do career-wise, he didn't care. Those details could be worked out any time. Donna had stormed back north, and breaking off with Leanne in Ipswich was next on his agenda. Then, he would launch a full-out assault on Susan's heart and mind. He leaned forward to put his elbows on the table, the better to hide the evidence of his desire.

'If *you* weren't here, she might go back to him,' said Brittany, with devastating lack of logic.

Marli weighed in. 'Oh, get real! Like, she's going to do *that?* Like, he's going to dump "rabbit-face" and those kids?'

Brittany glared at her sister. 'What would you know about it? You haven't even had a steady boyfriend!' she retorted, kicking the leg of the kitchen table so hard, everything on top jerked.

'Stop that!' David caught her glass before it hit the floor.

'Of course I have! Simon was my boyfriend, until *you* grabbed him!' shrieked Marli, referring to a former "crush."

It was time to intervene. 'Be quiet, both of you.' He looked at their mutinous faces and wondered if he was biting off more than he could chew. 'Whatever your mother does, it's none of your business. She can do what she likes and you'd do well to remember that she's virtually a single woman.' *And I plan to make sure she doesn't stay that way.*

'I think it's time we got this cleaned up and you girls can watch some TV then if you want.' Perhaps they'd calm down watching a film or something. He went to the sink and started scraping the frying pan out, preparatory to washing up. The twins stood up, exchanging sulky glares and started clearing the table. 'We have a dishwasher,' said Marli, petulantly.

'It'll do you good to do it by hand for once,' replied David, as he filled the sink with hot, soapy water and stacked dishes. At the periphery of his vision, the girls flicked each other viciously with the tea towels, but he didn't have the energy to get into another brawl. Once he finished reading reports, he wanted to sit in front of the fire, brooding over Susan's return home from her date. The image of Mark Gordon kissing her seethed in his memory. If Jellicott did the same, Maguire planned to spoil the moment by swooping out front. He made a note to turn the front security light on. That would halt any moves Jellicott might make.

In their bedroom, Brittany opened her rucksack and took out a small box.

'Look at this! I got it from Sandy. You know, that blond boy we met at the party last night?'

Marli leaned close, frowning. 'What is it?'

'Sandy works for a private investigator and he gave me this.'

'Why? What are you going to do with it?' Marli's eyes narrowed in suspicion. 'You'll be in deep shit if anyone sees it.'

Brittany giggled. 'Nah. No one will know what it is, if

you don't tell them.' She flung a hard look at her sister.

'But I don't know what it is,' answered Marli, reasonably enough.

'Then you can't get into trouble!'

CHAPTER 40

Contents of a Diary

Susan

Sunday: late morning.

The phone rings at ten o'clock. A woman says she has information I'm looking for and to meet her in town. The utmost secrecy is essential. David has gone into Ipswich for a meeting with the big-wigs. I try to call him, but his mobile is switched off or out of range. I resolve to try again on the way to town. The girls are playing on their laptops surrounded by dogs. I am satisfied they are safe. It's raining, cold and not a day to be driving, but I have to go. This might lead to nothing, as did my date last night.

Euon Jellicott had arrived punctually at six o'clock, heavily disguised as a gentleman. Harry would have loved his navy blue, XJ40 Jaguar. Inadvertently rising to the occasion, I'd worn a sapphire pantsuit, pearl choker at my throat, high heels and black jacket.

The girls watched us leave with narrow-eyed scrutiny. I felt as though two rifles were aimed in the middle of my back and Euon Jellicott's ears blushed. They didn't approve of me going out with anyone other than Harry, but after Brit's moment of weakness, when we'd told her about Harry's rejection of her, it was "venom as normal."

Euon set himself out to be charming, plying me with exquisite food, outstanding wine and humorous stories. In spite of my reservations, I enjoyed myself, until we got back to the farm. The moment I said 'Goodnight,' and took off the seatbelt, he crushed me against him with his left arm, while his right hand snaked between us to enclose my breast. *Not very creative.*

I started to berate him, but he thrust his tongue into my mouth, let my breast go and whipped his hand into my crotch. Just as well I had slacks on. I grabbed him by his 'bunch in front,'–which had increased in size and made a good target–tightened my hand around it and jerked my head away.

'Let me go now,' I hissed, 'or you'll be singing castrati.'

His hands instantly returned to the steering wheel and I let go.

'Thank you for spoiling what was, until now, a very pleasant evening, Euon.' I picked my handbag up, opened the door and scrambled out. The wind caught the door and slammed it behind me.

'Dickhead!' I snarled, glaring at him over my shoulder as I marched to the steps. The security light came on, momentarily blinding me. I turned back to look at Jellicott. Stony-faced, he started the motor, yanked the gear stick back and lurched into reverse. Gravel flew as he roared away, no doubt uttering curses like the Black Fairy at the christening.

'You look pretty pissed off. Wasn't he a gentleman after all?' smirked David, from his position in the shadowed side of a bay window.

'Until just now he was, the bastard.' I headed for the kitchen, seething.

'Want me to go after him? I can shoot him for you if you like.'

'I'm perfectly capable of shooting him myself, thank you. It was nothing I couldn't handle. Want a cup of coffee?' I turned the kettle on and took two cups out of the cupboard.

'Wouldn't you rather have a scotch?' he invited, waving a full glass under my nose. *What a grand idea!* I took a piece of broken biscuit out of a tin and went to the cupboard under the sink, surprising my wee mouse mum in the act of carrying something into her nest. She stopped and looked up at me, before dashing for cover.

'I really don't know what I'm going to do about them,' I sighed, squatting to place the treat carefully outside their makeshift home. I checked the egg cup beside her house was full of water. 'On the one hand, I can't have mice all over the house, but on the other, I owe her! And she's only a fieldmouse.'

He laughed. 'I'm sure you'll think of something. Did you have an opportunity to look at the diaries before you went out?'

'No, they're in my bedroom. I'll get them and we can go through them now. Have the girls gone to bed?'

'Yes, thank God.' He ran his fingers through his hair and proceeded to tell me about the fight he'd interrupted upon his return to the farm and the ensuing battle at dinner. 'Believe me, Susan, it was awful.'

I sighed. 'Girl's fights are always like that, David. You'll have to get used to it if you're going to hang around.' We stared at each other for a long moment, shades of our aborted sexual adventure filling the space between us. After a moment, I broke eye contact and scuttled for the lounge room.

We settled into easy chairs with our drinks and some cheese biscuits. The walls of the room glowed in the light from the fire. A Brahms symphony played on the stereo, Fat Albert forced his more than ample person into my chair and the old spaniel flopped his head on David's feet. Outside, the wind raged. *Bliss.*

David took one of Edna's diaries, I bagged the others, but it wasn't until I got half-way through the second, that I discovered the Robinson's secret. Edna's entries in this book, written in an almost printed style, started in January, 1947 when she was sixteen. Mostly her ramblings were about boys and church doings, but suddenly I'm riveted.

There it is. All laid out clearly and pretty much as I suspected.

'David, listen to this.'

July 15.

They found out about Bob today. We were bottling apricots and Kath started crying and Mum and Auntie Ethel thought she was joking when she said she's going to have a baby. Mum shouted, you're only fifteen then we all started crying and she made her tell. Alice cried and cried. They wanted to know why and she told. He did IT to her too when she slept over at our house. Mum went sort of white and she and Auntie Ethel went into the bedroom. We tried to hear what they said but couldn't. Then Mum called dad and

> Arthur in from the paddock. I didn't know Bob was doing it with all of us. I thought it was only me, but Connie and Kath said he pushed their beds together and got in with both of them at once. He used to come to my room sometimes, but not as much as Kath and them. It hurts but he said they'll belt me if I tell. And no one would believe me because he's Grace's husband and he'd say I'm lying to cover up doing it with someone else. I'm so scared. They might tell the police and then everyone will know about me. How could he do it? Grace's baby is due soon.

'Bob, the one who got killed by the bull. Coincidence, do you think?'

'How come the parents didn't hear this bastard creeping around?'

'I think I can answer that! At lunch the other day, someone said that the original homestead had bedrooms opening onto the garden. The side verandah was added in the early 1950s.'

'Ah, this is probably why they added it. What else is there?' he asked, eagerly.

'Not much here just stuff about everyday things...' I flipped the page. 'Ah, here we go again ...'

> Mum, Auntie Ethel, Dad and Arthur spoke in the kitchen after we

went to bed. We had to answer lots of things, like when did he do it, how often and since when. Dad got really angry when we said it started while he was away in the Army Reserve and Arthur was in New Guinea. Dad said Bob only managed to stay home to run the farm because he has heart trouble. I don't think he has heart trouble. Arthur said after the Japs, it wouldn't worry him none to do Bob.'

They were really angry and shouted at us why didn't we tell mum what Bob did? We said we were scared no one would believe us. I told them what Bob said and mum said to dad, if he yelled at them like he was now, it was no wonder they didn't tell. Dad said Aggy he's going to pay for this. I don't care that he's Grace's husband. They're going to tell Alice's mum and dad too. Johnnie cried because Dad scared him, yelling at us. Mum took Kath to the doctor.

Nothing else of note was recorded that week, apart from comings and goings between people, presumably relatives and neighbours. Alice, it transpired, was the daughter of a neighbour.

The shocking details went on.

The women finished bottling the fruit. Between blaming her sisters for leading Bob on, Grace had screaming fits and spent a lot of time crying. Edna didn't say how Kath felt about it. According to Edna, Grace and Bob lived on a cottage on the farm.

I fast-forwarded the entries, looking for the vital pages which might disclose what eventually happened. Nothing for a couple of weeks, apart from Bob being ordered to the house and Edna and the girls sent to their rooms while he was there. There was a lot of shouting and Edna, who'd sneaked out and listened, wrote that her dad told Bob he'd a good mind to 'fix him up.' Grace moved back in the main house with their parents, and spent most of the time hiding in her room, as far as I could make out.

There were arguments over whether they should get Kath an 'operation.' The mother, Agnes, is terrified Kath might die if they do that. The father insists the disgrace of Kathleen having a baby out of wedlock will be too much for the family. My heart twists for them in their dilemma. Abortions in those days frequently ended in death. Poor Kathleen, I thought remembering the staid, well-dressed matron at Edna's funeral that afternoon. I wondered what happened to the baby.

Frustrated, I began to comb the book from the back, and it was there amongst the last pages that we discovered the price Jellicott paid for his predatory behaviour.

July 30

Grace screaming outside woke me up. Arthur and Alice's father were unloading a bull from Tomlinson's truck and shut it in the side yard they use for killing steers. Then dad and Arthur and Alice's brothers marched Bob out of the shed. Grace was hanging on to Bob. Mum and Mrs Tomlinson ran down the paddock and grabbed Grace by the arms and brought her back to the house. She was shouting no no no.

Then Mum came in and said we weren't to go out, no matter what. She pulled the blind down and we came away from the windows. Connie and Kath went out to the kitchen with mum, but I looked around the edge of the blind and out the window. There was lots of dust flying and I couldn't see anything, then they dragged Bob around the side of the shed. He looked all limp and his head kept hitting the ground, like he was dead and I couldn't see anymore. The bull was roaring and charging around the yard. Mum and dad made us swear on the family bible that we'll never tell anyone about this morning. No matter who asks. Not the police, not even God.

There was a gap here of several pages, before the diary started again on the 3rd of August.

> We went to Bob's funeral. The coffin was shut. I'm so scared. I keep having nightmares about what happened. It's all mixed up with Grace crying and things. Kath is going to stay with Aunty Maureen in Sydney and Mum said, again, that we're never ever ever to tell what's happened or what Bob did to us. Ever!

The last 'ever' was underlined many times and so thickly, that the pen had gone through the paper. We went through the diaries we had, but as far as we could tell, Edna never told anyone outside the family about that terrible event, until the day I'd visited her in the local hospital. The day someone thought she'd revealed the family secret and may have killed her for it.

'Would the police have investigated it then?' I asked David.

'Yes, but forensics weren't as technical as they are now. From what Edna says in the diary, they beat him up first, so he was too groggy to get away from the bull, which they probably tormented into attacking. Technically, it could be first degree murder because they clearly knew Bob would be killed, but they could argue that they only wanted to teach him a lesson which would be second-degree murder. It was obviously passed off as an accident caused by his carelessness. The cops at the time may have had their suspicions, but murder would be very hard to prove unless they could get the girls to talk. The cops probably didn't even question them. They'd take the adults word for what happened. And now a defence counsel would argue that their recollections are well over sixty years old and unreliable due to their present age.

I stop to try and call David again, but no ring tone at all. I am in one of the "dead spots" in the road. I fling the mobile onto the seat and keep going. The windscreen wipers are not much help against the driving rain.

I shudder, as the whole terrible scenario runs through my mind again, like an old time newsreel, never ending. Rough justice, murder certainly, but Arthur had just come back from fighting the Japanese in New Guinea. Would a jury blame him? I doubted it. And how much did John, the youngest child remember of that time?

I'm saddened by the thought of the pain the girls carried throughout their lives – Arthur and their father to all intents and purposes, murderers, Grace, a young wife whose husband had been proved a rapist. Kathleen, Connie, Edna and Alice Tomlinson living through the horror and shame of his abuse, probably never to tell they weren't virgins when they wed. Those days it was very important to remain pure, or be seen to remain so. Did their husbands know their wives had been raped? Maybe they'd used the "horse riding' excuse, if their virginity was questioned.

As for Kathleen, no one could ever appreciate the agony she must have endured. Grace is not Jellicott anymore, so she married again somewhere along the way. Euon, of course is the grandson of the child she carried when the abuse was discovered and undoubtedly knew the story. I could well imagine the joy with which the media would greet such juicy news attached to such a prominent family. It would almost certainly tarnish the professional careers of the younger men and women.

It wouldn't do much for the Tomlinson family either. I wondered how many of the older members of the valley community knew about the murder. *Probably all of them.*

The wind buffets my car, sleet pings on the bonnet. I turn the heater and demisters up. Traffic is starting to build up around me. I turn down Athertons Street. Meter after meter is taken up and I'm thinking I'll have to go around the block again, I suddenly see one just near the address I'm seeking and pull in. Is there time to ring David's mobile again? No, I'll check this out first.

Dreading getting out into the cold, I reach into the back seat, grab my heavy coat and drag it into the front. I gather up my shoulder bag and swing open the door. Iced rain pelts into the car, turning the legs of my jeans sodden and sending my French braid swinging around my head. I force myself into the wind and sling the coat around my shoulders. Pedestrians bowl past, hunched into their umbrellas like colourful mushrooms. I turn and start up the pathway, hurrying to get into the warmth of the building.

A young woman opens the door and rushes me inside before I can introduce myself. 'I'm Gloria,' she announces, takes my coat and leads me through the hallway into a study, complete with roaring fire. Before I can ask her anything, she disappears. The walls are lined with books; chocolates nestle on the desk amongst stacks of papers. Perhaps Gloria is the secretary.

A movement outside the window startles me; something red has flashed by. I put my coat and handbag down and walk toward the window to look out, but as I skirt the desk I notice the drawer is slightly open. Something metallic picks up the light.

A cold lump forms in my stomach and spreads rapidly

throughout my body. It's a laser. The type teenagers aim at aircraft – or at a vehicle being driven along a country road after dark.

A swirl of movement behind me, but before I can turn, a hand wraps around the base of my braid. The knuckles bite into my flesh. 'I'm sorry you saw that, Susan.' Before I can react, he swings me around and punches me in the stomach, then twists my plait around his fist, tight against my head and throws me to the floor. My scalp feels as though it is on fire. My face is being mashed into the carpet; I can't breathe.

He yanks me to my knees and propels me across the room toward the fire. No, no – I grab for his genitals. Somewhere, sometime, he's learned to street fight. He jerks out of my reach and pushes my head back down onto the carpet. Out of the corner of my eye I see him reach for the poker.

I twist my body sideways and manage to hook my foot back around his leg. We fall to the floor. His grip on my hair doesn't loosen for a second. The fire screen tips half-way into the fire, spraying sparks onto my skin. I can hear myself grunting. *Save your breath.* He scrambles to his feet and heads for the door, towing me along the floor by my hair. The pain from my scalp is so bad I can't concentrate.

I cling onto the bottom of the door jamb as we pass through, but he chops his hand down on my wrist. As he hauls me along the hall, I try desperately to get a grip on his jeans to slow him down, but he turns back and kicks me viciously in the ribs. My face bumps painfully on the polished floorboards; my clothes don't protect me from skid rash. Suddenly, he pauses. The pressure on my scalp is momentarily released but he doesn't let my hair go. I lash out with my feet, almost unbalancing him again, but beyond a curse, he shows no sign of discomfort.

Then he starts towing me again, while I try to clutch whatever I can. Glass is breaking somewhere. He steps through a doorway, swings me across the floor. My head crashes into the bottom of a cupboard. Before I can regroup, he throws himself onto me. Someone is screaming – is it me?

No. His hands are fighting for my throat. I tuck my chin into my chest, dig my fingernails into his face and jerk sideways. We roll over and over, his hot breath blasting me, eyes popping with hate. I catch momentary glimpses of the young woman who let me in. Her mouth is wide open.

Stop screaming and get help.

CHAPTER 41

In the Nick of Time

Marli & Brittany

Sunday: late morning.

'You can't do that!' shouted Marli, as her sister pulled on a red anorak and grabbed her bag, preparing to follow their mother's car. 'Mum said we had to go straight to Mrs Winslow's and she'd ring us there. I'll tell!' she finished childishly.

'Well, go on, ring *Da-vid!* Be a sneak,' snapped Brittany. Marli, frantically punching her father's mobile number into her phone, didn't reply. Brittany ran down the hallway, knee-deep in dogs and fell over the puppy, who let out a series of pitiful yelps. Marli rushed out of their room. 'You didn't have to do that!' she screeched angrily.

'I didn't mean to!' The wind snatched Brittany's voice away as she pelted down the steps. Marli one-handedly thrust all the dogs into the kitchen, almost screaming with frustration as the metallic voice announced her father's phone was switched off or out of range. She raced for the side verandah, in time to see Brittany backing her car out of the shed.

'She'll recognise your car, you idiot!' she yelled to her sister.

'Oh shit.' Brittany was nonplussed, before she remembered their cousin, Ally's car, which was started regularly to keep the battery charged. She turned off the motor, grabbed her bag, leapt out and ran back into the shed, glancing over her shoulder. Their mother's car had turned onto the main road, heading for Ipswich. She scrabbled for the keys which were kept under the driver's seat. She had just backed out and turned around when Marli came running out of the house again, dragging on a windcheater, dilly bag hanging off her arm.

'I'm coming too,' she screamed, wrenching the passenger-side door open to hurl herself in.

'Pooh, you smell of wet dog!' Brittany put her foot on the accelerator. A steady electronic peeping distracted Marli, who dived into Brittany's bag and took out her mobile phone.

'What's this doing?'

'Gimme–' Brittany reached over, took it out of Marli's hand, pressed some buttons and handed it back. Marli's eyes widened, as she looked at the road map displayed on the screen. A small red dot travelled along the road to town.

'That's Mum's car!' announced Brittany, peering through the windscreen into the driving sleet which deflected off the wipers. 'Tell me if she turns off.'

Fascinated in spite of her disapproval, Marli watched the red dot move up the screen. 'Is this legal?' she asked nervously.,

'Sandy uses one!'

'Sandy has a *license* to use one and look out for speed cameras,' Marli replied.

The sisters maintained a cranky silence until they reached the city and began to negotiate the traffic, when

Marli flipped her phone open again and began to text.

'Who are you texting?' Brittany snapped, exasperated by the slowness of the traffic.

'Dad. I have a nasty feeling about that phone call mum got. She's already been attacked and he needs to know. He's in town this morning, so he won't be far away!'

Brittany's smirk, worn for the duration of the trip, vanished immediately. Their father had told Marli where he was going, but didn't think she had a right to know? Jealousy flared. 'Mum's not really in danger. Like, it's broad daylight? Come on, Marls, get real!' she growled, but a slight tremor in her voice betrayed her uncertainty.

The red dot stopped in front of what appeared to be a park, thirty metres ahead.

'She wouldn't meet someone here! Like, it's freezing outside?' Brittany peered through the sleet. Their mother's Renault was three cars away, but there was no sign of her. They moaned in unison, thinking they'd have to drive endlessly around the block, but suddenly a car pulled out in front of them. Ignoring the horns blasting behind them, Brittany swooped into the parking space.

'Mum's gone into that building.' Marli pointed to the back of the park. 'I can't see what it is though ...someone's let her in.'

'You stay here.' Brittany pushed the car door against the wind, wrestled briefly and stepped out, hunched against the cold.

Marli tried their father's number again; to her utmost relief, he answered. 'Dad! A woman rang mum and said for her to come into town because she had something to tell her about the murders. Mum's just gone into a house at the back of the garden. The woman let her in.'

'Where are you?' he asked, urgently. Marli heard the sounds of traffic in the background.

'On Athertons Street, just before the mall. We're parked beside a garden. She's gone into a place like an old house in the back corner amongst a lot of oleander bushes. Can't see what it is from here!' She went on to describe the building.

'Bloody hell! Stay out of there! We're on our way to–' The signal broke up. Marli shook the phone impatiently. Her father's voice came back, loud and clear. 'What are you doing?'

Marli made herself keep her voice level. If she sounded reasonable, her father mightn't actually kill them for spying on their mother. 'Brit has a thing some bloke gave her at the party the other night. A GSP tracking device,' she explained, reading the caption on the leaflet which Brittany had tucked into her phone cover. 'She put the tracker under Mum's car and we've been following it on Brit's mobile. I'm scared something's wrong. Wouldn't the woman tell the Ipswich police if she was ... genuine? And how did she know who mum is?'

'Stay where you are. *Don't* follow your mother into the building. It's dangerous! We've just discovered–' his voice vanished again. Marli could have screamed with frustration. *'Dad!'*

'–murderer, so stay away where you are, Marli!'

The call dropped out before she could tell him Brit was already pushing into the shrubbery near one of the windows. Marli snapped her phone shut and leaned forward to keep her sister's red windcheater in sight. She forced her door open and lurched around the front of the car, cannoning into the parking meter.

'Oh God, we haven't put the money in!' she cried,

holding her breastbone where she'd smacked against the metal. Fighting tears, she scrabbled in her pocket for change, slammed money in and ran across the garden, straining to see her sister. As she reached the clump of bushes, Brittany appeared with a brick in her hand, swung her arm back and threw the brick through the window. When the glass stopped falling into the room beyond, she whipped her coat off, threw it over the sill, grabbed the ledge and hauled herself through, head first.

As her sister's legs disappeared, Marli hoisted herself up to the windowsill and looked inside. It was a study, with papers blowing all over the place. Her sister scrambled to her feet and waved her arms urgently.

'He's got mum! Ring dad!' She cast around desperately, then ran to the fireplace, snatched up the poker and ran from the room.

Marli called their father again. 'Dad, a man's got Mum! Brit smashed a window and she's gone after them!'

'For chrissakes, I told you to stay where you are. We're almost there, stay put!'

She could hear sirens in the distance, and nearby someone was emitting hear-splitting shrieks. Mum? She scrambled over the ledge and fell head first into the room. Sounds of a struggle came from somewhere in the depths of the building. Casting around her for a weapon she spotted the doorstop.

She blundered into the hallway, staggering under the heavy iron weight, past a large empty room with stacked chairs along one wall. The sound of crockery smashing and screaming got louder. She reached the kitchen, gasping for breath.

A big man was rolling over and over on the floor, trying to strangle her mother. Her mum's head was tucked into the man's chest, her hands gripping his ears. His face was contorted into a hideous, wide-mouthed scream. His eyes bulged. Her sister was whacking his back with the fire tongs. A strange young woman was backed against the sink, screaming.

Marli darted into the room, skirted around the bodies on the floor and smashed the doorstop down on the back of the man's head.

CHAPTER 42

Delivered from Evil

Susan

Sunday: mid morning.

A familiar face looms over me. What's David doing here?

Then–Marli's voice?

'Mum, mum!'

'Wha–?'

'Mum, it's us!'

My eyes refuse to focus at first, but then I zero in on their shocked, ashen faces. Blue uniformed legs are all around me. A ring of faces stare down, reminding me incongruously, of Jack Harlow lying dead in the middle of the showground.

The faces give way to paramedics, who crouch over me, bringing out their tools of trade.

'Are you in pain?' *What do you think? I've been scalped!*

'No, I'm fine.'

Behind them, David appears, face twisted with anxiety. Brittany and Marli are sheltering under his armpits. I watch him unpeel them from his person and pass them over to a policewoman, before kneeling beside me. His hands shake as he touches my face. I am not badly hurt, but detachment holds me in a dreamlike state. 'Susan, thank God. If it wasn't for the girls, we couldn't have gotten to you in time.' He glances at the medics and asks if I can get up.

'In a moment. We haven't finished examining her,' they say firmly, poking my ribs and running their fingers across my scalp. Strands of my hair are stuck to a medic's fingers. My head aches and rivulets of fire are searing my scalp. Once they pronounce themselves satisfied I'm alive, David takes my hands and assists me to stand. My legs buckle, but he swoops me off my feet and carries me out of the house to a bench beside the front door.

'You know what I have to do. Constable–would you take my wi–Detective Senior Sergeant Prescott and her –our–daughters back to the station?' The policewoman by the door looks at me solicitously. 'Ma'am, I'll have a car brought around.' She calls for a patrol car and the girls and I are handed into the back seat as though we are princesses. Marli wails about Ally's car being on a meter. I don't give a damn about mine; let the parking inspectors do their worst. A uniformed officer asks for our car keys and details. 'My handbag's back in there–somewhere–' I say, vaguely. 'Study, I think. Coat too.'

'I left mine in the car,' says Brit.

'I locked it,' Marli contributes, 'but I lost my bag.'

Having been assured my colleagues would sort everything, we huddle together in the back of the squad car all the way to the station.

***

Sunday: early afternoon, at the police station

'Mum, did you know *he* was the murderer?' asks

Marli, as we sit in the client's lounge, sipping hot chocolate. I'm finding it hard to drink and talk, my stomach and ribs ache and my scalp is raw. Brit is in a trance, not able to do anything, much less abuse anyone.

'No, I have to admit I didn't, but I have an idea why.' I sift through my theories. The girls watch me, round-eyed.

'Well, why?' asked Brittany, taking a sip of her hot drink.

'I suspect that all his life he's been driven by ambition and just when his goal is within his grasp, an old family scandal threatens his future career.'

Deep, burning hatred, waiting to come out, like acid DNA.

'Briony Feldman, Sir Arthur's biographer, is digging into the family archives so he couldn't have it come out. None of them could. Trouble is, deep down the perpetrator is unstable and probably a psychopath, unfortunately for his victims.'

Marli screws up her face. 'Who is he then? I've never seen him before.'

'His name is–'

David walks into the canteen, accompanied by his partner, Senior Sergeant Peter Hensen. They are smiling and looking very pleased with themselves.

Marli jumps to her feet, looking distraught. 'Is he dead? Did I kill him?'

'No. But he's going to have a terrible headache!' David beams, as they sit with us. 'Brit, you saved your mother's life by swinging a brick through the window. You forced him to drag her away from his study and that slowed him down. And Marli, if you hadn't stopped him when you did–'

He shakes his head. 'John Glenwood remembered who he was going to see when he was attacked and run off the road and Pete discovered that the–' words appear to fail him. 'He was a sharp-shooter in the forces in 1960s in the UK, Queens Medal no less. No problem for him to pick off Harlow, in spite of his age. Just *that* warranted bringing him in. We interviewed Lily earlier this morning and discovered he's Kathleen's son, the one she had to Bob Jellicott. He's a lot older than he looks–63. Ferna and her first husband brought him up as theirs. He's actually Daniella's half-brother. He had a lot to lose if the authorities discovered he had an uncle and a grandfather who were murderers, so he had a two-fold purpose in shooting Jack, but I'll tell you about that later.' His eyes flick to the girls.

'Well, it explains his desperation,' I say, wearily.

'I don't know how he could do that to Edna, though, poor old girl. Jack Harlow I might be able to understand,' David finishes grimly.

'But, dad, who is he?' insists Marli. Even Brittany is curious.

'Oh, it's–'

The door swings open. 'Detective Inspector Maguire!'

The Chief Superintendent has arrived to pay his respects.

CHAPTER 43

Unfinished Business

Susan

Sunday: evening.

Endless dark, tumbling over and over, staring face, maniacal eyes. Hands and arms are crushing me, can't hold him back. A knife flashing and Danny's–killing me. Someone's screaming but he's tied my legs–

'Susan! Susan! It's all right. You're safe!'

My eyes fly open, blinking in the light from the bedside lamp. David's face comes into focus. My legs are tangled in the blankets; I'm sure my heart rate can be measured in thousands. My nightie is wet with perspiration, my mouth swollen, my stomach muscles twang like guitar strings and meat ants are taking chunks out of my scalp.

David is still dressed in the clothes he wore today, or was it yesterday? One of the lounge chairs is in the corner of my bedroom with a blanket thrown aside, where he's been camping while I sleep. He helps me to sit up and holds a glass of water for me to sip. The cold liquid feels good going down my throat.

'You've had a nightmare. Not surprising under the circumstances,' he says.

'How are the girls?'

'They're sleeping in my bed covered in dogs. You were the only one having a bad night.'

'What time is it?' Now my throat is lubricated, my voice is almost back to normal.

'Nearly midnight'

'It's not every day I almost get murdered. Twice in one week is over-doing things.'

'You can say that again.' David pulls the blanket up around my shoulders then takes the one off the lounge chair. He adjusts the spare pillows, stretches out beside me and flips the blanket over himself.

When we came back from the city earlier this afternoon, exhaustion claimed me for its own. David had gone back to sort out the aftermath of the attack on me and a middle-aged constable had stayed with us until he returned in the early evening. I had showered, climbed into bed and slept until dinner when I had crawled out of bed, drunk some soup and gone straight back to sleep. 'What's been happening?' I asked, wide-awake and interested.

'The phone's been running hot. Daniella Winslow gave me a message for you. She was very surprised when she found out what you do for a living, but sends her love and wants you to lunch with her next week.'

'Oh? I'm surprised she still wants to be friends.'

'Why wouldn't she? It's not your fault Jack and Edna were murdered. Your mother rang. 'He rolls his eyes, so I can imagine how convivial that conversation was. 'She heard about the attack on you and the arrest on the six o'clock news. And Melanie, Evan Taylor, everyone from your team, the Chief Super from Brisbane and-oh, I've got a list here of your friends for you. They all phoned.

You can read it in the morning.' He smiles. 'So you've got plenty to look forward to, especially lunch with Daniella.'

'I'm not sure if I'm going to be here next week.' *Don't be stupid, Susan, you have nowhere else to go. The house is Brisbane is being sold, remember?*

'Aren't you?' he asks, surprised. 'You've only just arrived.'

'I still have lots of leave, but so far my house-sitting hasn't been what I expected.'

He laughs. 'You can say that again. Oh, and Briony Feldman rang to invite the girls on an expedition to Toowoomba in the morning. I told them to go, because the quicker they're back to normal, the better and it will get them away from the media. They're delighted. Something about the quality of the op shops up on the range.'

I'm grateful to Briony for giving them a treat.

'All in all, you've had rough day,' he said, quietly.

We were checked over by a police doctor to make sure we were all in one piece before we left town. The girls were, thank goodness, unharmed. I was sore and battered and my lips swelled within a few minutes of being punched, giving me a spectacular trout-mouth. The girls dictated their statements to a young, patient constable, whose ears turned red whenever he made eye contact with them. 'But why would he go mad and, like, kill everybody?' Brittany asked, amazed. 'He's supposed to believe in God. But he killed people!' She shuddered.

'Brit, it's a long story which I'll tell you soon, but not right now. The media will be a howling mob, so you'd better brace yourself for lots of publicity.'

Marli pulled a face. 'Will they come out to the farm?' she asked.

'I think your father will make sure they don't get to the house,' I replied wearily. For once, Brit didn't sneer and correct me.

We were a subdued group as David drove us back to Emsberg. Our cars were in the police holding yard to be collected later. The girls were exhausted and in shock, wrapped around each other like two koalas. My mouth was too sore to talk. David reached out and took my hand as he drove.

Mark Gordon's face re-appeared in my mind. The lips I'd kissed were drawn back in a ferocious snarl and the stench of madness permeated my nostrils. As soon as he'd pounced on me in his study, I realised he was my attacker of four nights ago. He felt the same. He had been unconscious when taken to hospital, but when he'd revived, raved and screamed his motives.

After a takeaway dinner which no one felt like eating, David had taken me out of earshot of the girls and told me what they had uncovered.

'Mark Gordon is the illegitimate son of Kathleen Robinson by Bob Jellicott. Ferna and her first husband knew the family well and because she couldn't have children, they adopted him. When he was fourteen, kids in the family about the same age teased him about who he really was. Guess the little shits must have been eavesdropping on adults somewhere along the line. It must have been a terrible shock for him. From then on, he set himself to become a force to be reckoned with. And I guess he hated his dead father with a vengeance, because as far as we can make out, he transferred his feelings to Jack Harlow, who had a penchant for young women and teenage girls. Apparently, Jack sexually assaulted Daniella when she was a teen and Mark found out she was-is- his half-sister. Kathleen married and her husband was killed in an accident when Daniella was two. She never married again.'

The memory of the fleeting, haunted expression in her eyes when I first met Daniella, came to mind. David continued. 'So Mark felt justified in shooting Jack, thereby keeping the family secret as well as revenge for his sister. I don't think Daniella knew that Mark was her half-brother. She will now.'

Oh dear, such heart-ache for everyone concerned. If Mark hadn't overheard Edna talking to me the day I visited her in hospital, she might well be alive.

'Would you like a hot drink?'

'No thanks, David. Just tell me rest.'

'He reached the top echelons of the corporate world relatively young, thirty-five, but then he met a priest, who impressed him,' says David. 'But whether he went through an epiphany, or saw a faster path to power, is not clear. He couldn't go any further career-wise in the corporate sector, so maybe he thought he needed a change. I suspect the cricketing twins may have been the ones who told him about Bob raping his mother and aunts, but we'll probably never know. Brisbane CIB tried to get some sense out of Lily, but the old girl was sick and rambling when they tried to talk to her.' David took a sip of my water. 'Funny, her doctor said they suspected she'd ingested a small amount of rat poison, but they're puzzled as to how she came by it.'

For some reason the memory of Lily sipping from the bottle of Scotch in her car comes to mind. Someone left that on the floor under the dashboard, knowing she couldn't resist it. Mark? I tell David about our session with Lily outside the church.

'Have you still got the bottle?' he asks, eagerly.

'Unfortunately, no. Briony threw it in the rubbish bin.'

'Never mind. I'm told she'll recover. And we've got him on the murders. We'll be interviewing Gordon's former employers and of course, his current colleagues. Apparently, he was expecting to be given a Bishopric, but of course, if the circumstances of the murder of Jellicott came out ... the church is very traditional. The resultant publicity would have hurt him and there's not much doubt that his promotion would have been discreetly withdrawn.'

David shakes his head, smiling coldly. 'The Historical Society hiring Briony Feldman tipped him over the edge. In my opinion he's insane, and I doubt he'll stand trial. We'll need to talk to Daniella at some stage, but don't worry, we'll go gently.'

'Did he ever marry?'

'No, he batted for both sides, but I'm sure his boyfriend, if he has one, will melt into the woodwork. Gloria, his so-called secretary, told us everything. He terrified her, but she is addicted to him. He had a contact at the hospital, which of course was how he heard that John Glenwood had come out of his coma, hence the toxic card.'

His face settles into grim lines. 'We're questioning Sir Arthur about Jellicott's murder, though I doubt we'll be able to get enough evidence, despite Edna's diaries. We'll speak to the sisters, including Kathleen, though I doubt they'll confirm what happened. Alice Tomlinson is still alive, but their generation understands how to keep a secret."

He took a deep breath, and squeezed my hand. 'The

circumstances of Mark Gordon's birth were not his fault. Many people get hard starts in life, but they don't murder people on the strength of it.' He turned to face me. 'What are you going to do, Susan? You are going back to work when your leave's up?'

'I don't know what to do. I love being a police officer. I've enjoyed my career and worked hard for it, but David,' I looked at him, willing him to understand,' I can't forgive myself for letting Danny Grey down.' Tears welled in my eyes.

He remained silent for awhile, then reached over, gently pushed a lock of hair away from my face and stroked my cheek. 'You let Danny Grey go into that warehouse, didn't you? In fact, you told him to?'

'Er, no. But I should have stopped him.'

'How? The inquiry found that you expressly ordered him not to go to the warehouse and he disobeyed you. People heard what you said to him. So how is it your fault? What more could you have done? You were too far away to stop him and didn't even know he'd gone in until he called.'

'I should have realised that he would go,' I cried.' I knew he was a hot-headed kid. If we'd have taken him with us that night, he wouldn't have gone after Crimmons on his own and he would still be alive.'

'Susan, listen to me. You issued an order and it was deliberately disobeyed. Grey knew he should not have gone in without backup. You have to move on or this will destroy you.'

I nodded. There were other considerations as well. 'I do need to spend more time with the girls, even though they're seventeen and finished school. Harry was right. I put too much time and effort into my career, to their detriment,' I said slowly, trying not to cause my mouth any more angst. 'But I don't want to go private or become a security consultant.'

Here come the tears. I grope under the pillow for a wad of tissues and proceed to blow my nose in the robust style for which I am famous throughout the CIB.

'You could transfer down to my team,' David says, with a beguiling smile. 'We worked well all those years ago and we could again. I have a slot on my team for a Senior Sergeant. Pete's transferring to Toowoomba. His wife has a teaching job up there.'

'I don't know if that's a good idea.' Senior Sergeant sleeping with the DI?

'I've got my own team back in Brisbane and I don't want to leave them.'

'You've still got four months leave, so there's plenty of time to think about it. You need to get some rest and have some fun.' That sounds good to me.

'I've made new friends down here. Briony, Daniella and maybe even Penelope, if she will forgive me for harassing her at the wake. I want to see those incredible, up-market sheep, which David described in awed tones. I'd like to meet Senior Constable John Glenwood too, poor man.

David clicks his fingers. 'Oh yes, Lady Ferna gave Sir Arthur's cat to Daniella with strict instructions to 'get rid of her.' Daniella said she can't keep it, but she wondered if perhaps you ...'

'What am I? A repository for unwanted cats?'

'I suppose because of him,' replies David, jerking his head in the direction of Fat Albert, who is eavesdropping from a vantage point on the dressing table.

'I'll think about it.' An image of the huge, bad-tempered Genevieve slides into my mind. Perfect; a soul mate for Brit.

'And then there's us.'

I look at him doubtfully. Much as I want him, I need to make certain of his situation. 'What about Donna? And Leanne? And whoever else you've got hovering around you?'

He actually blushes. 'I promise you, Donna is history. Believe me Susan, I broke that relationship off before I came back down here. All that nonsense,' he looks even more sheepish, 'was desperation on her part. And in the morning I'll phone Leanne and end things with her. She won't be too upset. We only met two weeks ago.' He turned to face me. 'I'm so sorry I was such an idiot all those years ago. I didn't give us a chance, because I didn't want to understand what you were going through after you had the babies. But we've got everything going for us now and I want you for a lot more than just sex.'

I can't think straight. The thought of us starting a serious relationship again takes my breath away, but the sex will do very well to begin with. Marriage is definitely not an option at this stage. 'We could date and see if we have much in common anymore.' Harry's defection has left me with an alarming lack of confidence.

'We have two daughters together, that's an excellent start,' reasons David. But how does he envisage our geographical logistics?

I try him out. 'I love this area and this house. And in spite of all the trouble, I've become attached to it. And what about the girls? How will they accept our, er, dating?'

He's full of confidence. 'I think after today, they'll be far more receptive to the idea,' *Hm.* He's got quite a shock coming if he thinks Brittany has had a miracle sweetness cure overnight.

My subconscious has been harbouring a decision since my sister-in-law's phone call. 'Eloise and James want to be in the UK near their daughter, Ally. Their first grandchild is on the way, so they're offering me first option buying this house and I'd like to accept.'

'Want to go halves?'

What I see in his eyes sends heat storming through my body, consigning my aches and pains to oblivion.

'And we have unfinished business,' he adds, dropping gentle kisses on my shoulder, up my neck and across to my face...

THE END

GLOSSARY OF TERMS

Aussie words in order of appearance in the novel.

Mob – crowd

Wanker – idiot, fool.

Underdaks – underpants

Copper – police officer

Yabby – freshwater crayfish found in Australian creeks and dams.

"Had all their marbles" – mentally competent.

Fit the bill – measured up, were right.

Twigs – understands

Cicada – locust.

Don't give a monkeys – don't scare

Chateau Cardboard – wine in a box, a delightful Australian invention.

Big wigs – the higher ups.

DISCLAIMER

Emsberg is a typical Australian town, no doubt inspired to a certain extent by the lovely valley in which I actually live. Those who wish to tar and feather me, please use only the very best of plumage, preferably those of a frizzle hen. The characters in this novel are products of my fevered imagination. If you think you recognise yourself in there, you would be well advised to keep it secret.

Sample chapter of
Diana Hockley's next
Susan Prescott Novel,
After Ariel

AFTER ARIEL

CHAPTER 1

The Pickup.

Friday 5pm.

He shouldn't have squeezed the baby. He had known that for twenty years, a six year old's recollection. His mother's voice returned, like a fragment from a radio play–'You must always be gentle, my darling heart.'– words imprinted on his mind to surface when he least expected, bearing no relationship to any of the tangled events which coursed through his REM sleep.

He jerked into wakefulness, momentarily disoriented until he got his bearings. The movement of the train reminded him of his destination and his reason for going before his sleep-befuddled mind cleared. He winced, as piercing ring tones flared from the seat opposite. His brow crinkled in annoyance, but when the mobile phone was answered, he forgave the intrusion.

The clear bell-like sound of her voice took him back to the Australian bush where he had spent his childhood. He closed his eyes and allowed her words to wash over him, before his attention focused on her face. She was small, dainty and dark-haired, with the Bailey's Irish Cream liquor complexion and velvety skin enjoyed by many English girls which he always longed to touch, but didn't dare. He wasn't too charmed by the ring in her nose, but the multi-coloured jewellery shimmering in her ears fascinated. He wanted to skim his fingertips over the mirrored shards, to glide across her milky skin.

'I'm on the train ... yes, on my way home ... no, I'm having a night in on my own, because mam and dad want me to be there to look after the house and answer the phone, but thanks lots. I'll see you tomorrow. Do you–'

The elderly woman sitting next to him by the window gave what sounded like a hiss of disapproval and muttered to herself, drowning out some of the girl's the words, but he'd caught the most important part. She would be home alone. He glanced at his fellow travellers, each pretending not to have overheard the girl's conversation, though her clear enunciation made a mockery of their pretensions.

She snapped off her mobile and thrust the plug of her iPod past the dangling trinkets into her ear, where it spouted incongruously, like black fishing line and pulled a somewhat lurid paperack out of her tote bag. Then she stuck her little pink tongue out and moistened the tip of a forefinger, with which she flicked the pages until she found her place in the novel. He watched through half-closed eyes as she became engrossed in the story, her foot tapping in time to a rhythm which danced in her head. The facing seats were so close that her knee occasionally brushed his.

I wonder if she'd like to go to the movies tonight ... but would she want to meet me?

Had he spoken his thoughts aloud? He flushed and risked a glance at the travellers sitting in the collection of four seats. No one appeared to have reacted. The long-legged, blond woman in the window seat diagonally opposite was trying to avoid contact with the bulging shopping bag invading her personal space as it spilled off the lap of the old woman sitting beside him. The geriatric's elbow bumped his ribs as she wriggled, trying to get comfortable. He edged toward the aisle, trying not to obviously avoid her plump arm and generous hip.

The eyes of the blond met his, commiseration in her twinkling gaze. Confused, he stared blankly at her for a moment before responding but he was too late. She had returned to the book in her lap, a music score. "Mozart" was typed in big letters on the top of the page, but he couldn't read the title of the piece. There was something familiar about her face.

Before he could recall where he might have seen her, his attention snapped back to the dark-haired girl who had taken her iPod out of her ear and was speaking on her mobile again.

'Hi, it's me, Ariel. Doing anything tonight?' Her face scrunched as she listened. 'Oh, well it's like, I can't go out. Have to be home on my own ... yeah, it sucks.' She listened for a moment or two more, then trilled, 'Okay, by-ee.'

As she snapped her mobile shut, their eyes met. A thrill shot through him. Heat spread throughout his body, sending pulses of fear and longing flooding along his limbs, chasing prickles of perspiration out to the tips of his fingers and toes. He clenched and unclenched his huge hands, overcome with shyness, averted his gaze and shifted in his seat, unable to decide if she intended to send him a message.

Did she want him to say something? To introduce himself? Sometimes he wasn't sure if girls liked him or not. 'Don't be so ready to assume, love. Not *everyone* wants to play.' The stricture floated into his mind and was angrily dismissed. *Get away from me, mum.*

He stole a look at the blond woman who appeared to have abandoned her study and was watching the houses and factories pass as their train crawled through the outer suburbs of Cardiff. Automatically, he began to count the houses as they flashed past. *No, stop. You know what the doctor said.*

He forced his mind back to the woman. Was she a musician? He liked classical music. The final performance in the Australian flautist, Pamela Miller's tour was on in the concert hall the following night. Would the blond woman be attending as well? As though picking up his thought processes, she looked straight at him. They assessed each other for a moment, after which she blinked slowly, a feminine acknowledgement of his attention. Embarrassed by being caught staring, he glanced down at his hands. When he got the courage to peep at her again, she had laid her head against the padded backrest and closed her eyes.

He realised he was holding his breath, exhaled slowly and allowed his gaze to wander nonchalantly back to Ariel. She was watching him again! 'Don't get excited, love. You're too impetuous!' *Shut up, mum.*

He became aware that the train was pulling into Cardiff Central. Ariel stood and stretched to the luggage rack, but the rack was too high for her to reach the faded denim zip bag crushed into the meagre space. He leaped to his feet, stumbling over those of the blond. The older woman hastily swung her knees to the side to avoid clashing with his long legs as he stepped across and dragged the bag off the parcel shelf.

Ariel's hazel eyes, framed by long lashes met his.

'Thanks. It's like, too high for me,' she said, grinning appreciation of his help. He heaved the heavy bag onto the seat and nodded.

'I'll help you get it out' His voice came out in a squeak.

'Thanks millions.' She threw him a laughing glance as she stuffed her iPod and the paperback into her tote bag, picked it up and prepared to race ahead toward the doors of the carriage. The train slid to a stop. People on the platform peered in the windows, hunting for friends and rellies. He picked up the zip bag, hastily gathered his backpack and turned to follow Ariel down the aisle.

The blond had pulled her case down from the rack and waited patiently for him to move off. Startled by her extreme height, he hesitated, about to step aside, but she gestured for him to proceed. Behind her, the old girl scowled and pushed forward with her shopping bag. Ariel, a good way along the carriage, turned to see where he was. He hefted her bag above the seats and surged forward.

The blond had vanished from his mind before he reached the end of the carriage.

The girl introduced herself as Ariel Maxwell and announced that she lived a few miles away. She kept up a steady stream of chatter as they found their way out of the station. He hefted her case into a taxi, confessing that he needed to find somewhere to stay, a pub perhaps.

'That's all right, there's one just near us, The Fox and Duck,' she chirped. The jewellery in her ears caught the light as it jingled. 'We'll share a cab.'

'How about dinner later, then?' he asked, greatly daring. 'Is the food any good at that place? Or we could go somewhere else if you like.' Suddenly, he appeared shy, his gaze skittered away from hers and then almost reluctantly it seemed, back to her.

'Maybe.'

He leaned forward: 'I go on to the pub after this, thanks,' he told the cabbie.

Ariel didn't want to appear too eager, but she couldn't help regarding him with keen interest and growing excitement. His skin had a bronzed tinge which set off his handsome features. She wondered how much time he spent on the beach. Perhaps he worked outdoors. His dark brown eyes and longish, glossy dark hair gave him a rakish, gypsy appearance. She wondered what it would be like to run her fingers through the silken strands and smirked inwardly. What would Deanna say, when she heard what a prize she, Ariel, had discovered on the train? A gorgeous, tall, broad-shouldered Australian no less! And well spoken, not an "ocker."

From having to suffer her own company this weekend – her younger brother had got himself stranded with his motorcycle, so her parents drove to Calne in Wiltshire to rescue him–things were looking up. She could do worse, she thought, as he handed her out of the taxi and dragged her bag out onto the footpath.

'This home?' He eyed up the neat house planted in the pretty garden. *Fourteen fence posts along the front, five rose bushes, ten–*

'Yeah.' She took the money out and paid the driver, who grunted, stuffed the note into his cash bag and coughed impatiently as he waited for his other passenger to get back into the cab.

He forced his mind back to the girl, not about to let her go without obtaining a commitment. 'Shall I come back for you, about seven?'

She smiled. Tonight dinner and who knew what would be next? Caught up in the excitement of her unexpected date, her parents request to stay in that night had flown from her mind.

'No, I'll come down there. Seven in the lounge bar.'

He gestured to the bag. 'Do you want me to carry this in for you?'

She thought quickly. What if they ended up back there? The house would be a tip; she had two hours to get it sorted. 'No thanks, I'm good.'

She watched as the cab turned the corner. A little thrill shivered down her spine. Australians, everyone said, were great fun but not to be taken seriously. And they'd be in a pub, surrounded by the Friday night crowd.

What could possibly go wrong?

Author's Bio

Diana Hockley lives in a southeast Queensland country town, surrounded by her husband, Andrew, two cats and six pet rats. She is a dedicated reader, community volunteer, and presenter of a weekly classical program on community radio. She and her husband once owned and operated the famous Mouse Circus which travelled and performed throughout Queensland and northern New South Wales for ten years. They also bred Scottish Highland cattle. She has three adult children and three grandchildren.

She has had articles and short stories accepted and published in a variety of magazines, among them, *Mezzo Magazine* USA, *Honestly Woman* (Australia) *The Highlander, Austin Times* and *Austin UK, Australian Women's Weekly, It's A Rats World, Solaris UK, Literary Journal of University of Michigan* USA, Foliate Oak, children's website Billabong, *King's River Life,* USA. In 2006, she was awarded Scenic Rim Art Festival prizes for poetry and fiction.

The Naked Room was launched in November 2010. Her next crime novel, *After Ariel,* will be published before Christmas, 2011.

www.ingramcontent.com/pod-product-compliance
Lightning Source LLC
LaVergne TN
LVHW050921080826
845145LV00001B/161

* 9 7 8 0 9 8 7 0 6 1 2 9 4 *